The Literature of Vermont: A Sampler

**The University Press
of New England**

Sponsoring Institutions:
Brandeis University
Clark University
Dartmouth College
The University of New Hampshire
The University of Rhode Island
The University of Vermont

The
Literature of
Vermont:
A Sampler

Arthur W. Biddle and

Paul A. Eschholz, Editors

Published for

The University of Vermont by

The University Press of New England

Hanover, New Hampshire 1973

Stone walls, fences, rivers, apple trees—
These speak of a slow country,
Of white-spired villages between two hills
And the loves and hates and passions between two hills.
These talk of abandoned farms and abandoned lives
And of men who ask no questions of the earth,
Knowing earth will not answer.
Stone walls, rivers, fences, apple trees—
These are the language of a slow country,
The curious speech of a rock-bitten,
Inarticulate heart.

—Frances Frost, "Language"

Acknowledgments

This anthology of Vermont literature has been compiled with the cooperation of many people to whom we owe a debt of gratitude. For their encouragement and support, we are obliged to our colleagues at the University of Vermont—T. Alan Broughton, Margaret Edwards, and Leonidas Jones of the English department, Edward Miles of Geography, Edward Feidner of Communication and Theater, and Dean William H. Macmillan of the Graduate College—and to Johnson State College's John Duffy, formerly of the Vermont Historical Society. At UVM's Guy W. Bailey Library, Claire Buckley, reference librarian, T. D. S. Bassett, archivist, and John Buechler, Elizabeth Lovell, and David Blow, Special Collections, have all provided invaluable assistance in researching this book. For their helpful suggestions concerning Vermont authors and their writings, we are grateful to Eugene Novogrodsky of Union 32 High School, Esther Urie of South Burlington High School, N. Wendell Weeks of Rutland High School, and to the executive committee of the Vermont Council of Teachers of English and two of its presidents, Laurel Reed and Edward Darling. For her help in the preparation of the manuscript, we thank Evelyn C. Kyle.

Betty Bandel's love for her adopted state and its history has served as an inspiration to us as it has to a generation of students at the University of Vermont. Special thanks go to Alfred F. Rosa of UVM's English department for his editing of the introduction and to David Horne of the University Press of New England for his help in the preparation of this book. Finally, the patient support of our wives and children has not gone unrecognized—God bless them.

Burlington   A . W . B .
February 15, 1973   P . A . E .

Contents

2. Potash, Morgan Horses, and Merino Sheep

3. A Time for Reflection

4. Vistas Old and New

Introduction

Conceived in the controversy of the land grants and reared in the rebellion of the American Revolution, Vermont established, early on, a tradition which it has handed down and maintained into the twentieth century. Visitors need not be in the state for long to sense its distinctive heritage. When it comes to defining the quality that sets Vermont apart, however, most are at a loss. During the Revolutionary War, General Burgoyne was impressed by the settlers of the Wilderness. For him, the New Hampshire Grants, that territory disputed by New Hampshire and New York, abounded with "the most active and rebellious race of the Continent." A century later another outsider, Prince Bismarck, a student of political history, saw Vermont as the ideal republic. When asked to defend his selection, he replied, "Vermont is small in area, of slow growth, has a larger percentage of school attendance than any other state, is not devoted to manufactures nor so much to farming as to make its interests political, owes nothing to the general government for Civil War expenses, and aims primarily and purely at the educational and religious evolution of the individual."[1] More recently, Burges Johnson has described Vermont as "just a lot of lovable but pig-headed individuals divided up into townships widely scattered on mountainsides and in valleys who will not let even their chosen officials command them or their chosen leaders lead them."[2] Today, some people point to the rustic farmer, the local craftsman, the annual town meetings, or maple-sugar-on-snow socials and call these Vermont. Others turn for evidence to Vermont's acclaimed natural endowments—her

1. Cited by Robert D. Benedict, "Bismarck on Vermont," in *Vermont Prose: A Miscellany* (Brattleboro, Vt.: Stephen Daye Press, 1932), p. 115.
2. Burges Johnson, "Vermont the Nonconformed," *Saturday Review* (24 October 1953), p. 28.

friendly wilderness, her crystal lakes, rivers, and streams, her fertile valleys, and her rugged, unchanging hills. Yet the sum of all these qualities fails to capture the spirit of Vermont, the essence of the Vermont tradition. "The basic, primary concern of the Vermont tradition," as Vermont's first lady of letters Dorothy Canfield Fisher saw it, "is with the conduct of human life;" it is a code "based on overcoming obstacles rather than in contriving a way of life without difficulties." [3] In short, Vermont is a philosophy as well as a place.

Literature has always played a role in Vermont. The early settlers were learned men, not in terms of formal education, but in being widely read and experienced. They valued books, no small expense in colonial times, and supported the cause of public education. Many of these settlers kept diaries or journals in which they recorded their reactions to the pioneer experience. Others wrote extensive, detailed letters to friends and relatives in the colonies of Connecticut and Massachusetts. To communicate their political ideas and to unite the settlers of the Grants, Ethan and Ira Allen published a number of pamphlets; others like Thomas Rowley used the broadside for the same purpose. First-hand accounts of history-making events and records of local lore and legend were compiled and later published. Some frontiersmen even tried their hands at poetry. Despite its meager population, Vermont engaged in a surprising amount of literary activity before printing presses were established in the Grants by the first Green Mountain printers—Judah Paddock Spooner, Alden Spooner, and Timothy Green—a dozen years before statehood. The introduction of the printing press stimulated literary efforts; soon newspapers and magazines made their appearance, and by the turn of the century one hundred and thirty-five books and pamphlets had been published. Although it is difficult to measure literary activity in a rural state like Ver-

3. Dorothy Canfield Fisher, *Vermont Tradition: The Biography of an Outlook on Life* (Boston: Little Brown, 1953), p. 8; and D. C. Fisher, "Introduction," *Green Mountain Verse,* ed. Enid Crawford Pierce and Helen Hartness Flanders (New York: Farrar and Rinehart, 1943), p. xxii.

mont, some indication of the remarkable output is afforded by Abby Maria Hemenway's anthology *Poets and Poetry of Vermont,* published in 1858; the volume contains the work of 111 Vermont poets. By 1900, according to G. G. Benedict, there were "no less than 3,489 distinctively Vermont imprints—that is titles of books and pamphlets printed and published in Vermont—while the titles of books and pamphlets by Vermont authors, printed and published outside of Vermont . . . swell the total to upwards of seven thousand titles." [4] Since the turn of the century, Vermonters have witnessed the steady growth of the literary arts in Vermont: the publication of the popular magazine *The Vermonter* and its successor *Vermont Life;* the appearance of the poetry journals *Driftwind, Hill Trails,* and *The Mountain Troubador;* and the establishment of The Poetry Society of Vermont, The League of Vermont Writers, Penwomen, the Vermont Council on the Arts, and the Vermont Academy of Arts and Sciences.

"Vermont," as the advertising slogan has it, "is an undiscovered country." The literary heritage of the Green Mountain State, likewise, is largely undiscovered territory. Much of the literature that is a part of this tradition is not easily available to the modern reader. Books have gone out of print, sketches and poems are buried in old newspapers, manuscripts lie neglected in local archives. *The Literature of Vermont: A Sampler* presents a collection of representative Vermont writing from the days of early settlement to the present. As American society in the twentieth century has become increasingly homogeneous, more and more Americans have begun to seek their identity in that which is distinctive and local, an impulse that has been nourished by the nostalgic yearnings for a simpler past. This *Sampler* presents the richness that is Vermont's literary tradition. In this tradition the reader will discover the heart of Vermont.

Anyone who looks into Vermont's literary heritage is immedi-

4. G. G. Benedict, "Early Vermont Bibliography: Vermont Books, Pamphlets and Printers of the Eighteenth Century," *The Vermonter,* 5 (May 1900), 171.

ately impressed by the enormous wealth of material. Although Vermont has produced few writers of the first magnitude, it has fostered much good writing. Since it would be impossible to provide a sample of every author's writing, we, in assembling this collection, sought those writers who have had a long and close relationship with Vermont and have achieved renown or who, although relatively unknown beyond the boundaries of the state, have produced work of exceptional quality and interest. There are but two exceptions to this criterion, Cornelius A. Logan and Alton H. Blackington. Although not Vermonters, their work has strong connections with the state, Logan's through the subjects and themes of his dramas and Blackington's through his study and use of Vermont folklore. Since we wanted to limit excerpts from longer pieces, we have necessarily slighted some of the state's novels and narrative poetry. In the selection of specific works, their quality as literature was of primary concern. Secondly, we stressed readability and human interest, especially when there was an emphasis on the Vermont way of life. Lastly, we sought to give the anthology balance, attempting to achieve thematic variety as well as distribution by genre. The works have been arranged chronologically to suggest the development of Vermont letters and to give the reader an historical perspective.

I

Having successfully waged a war for independence, Americans turned to the tasks of building a nation and shaping its destiny. Philip Freneau and Royall Tyler, among others, urged authors to forsake the models of the mother country, to expunge that which smacked of British accents and origins. Instead, they called for a national literature to be created from the unlimited possibilities of the American scene. What the early nationists envisioned was a distinctive and unmistakably American idiom, which would exhibit, as Longfellow phrased it, "those distinguishing features which literature receives from the spirit of a nation—from its scenery and climate, its historic recollections, its government, its various institutions . . . and, in a word, from the thousand external circumstances, which . . . give it a marked and individual character." [5] It soon became evident, however, that there was no single national voice; the shared past, the sense of traditions, and the homogeneity of manners, attitudes, and topography so necessary for a distinctive national literature were not present. As Hawthorne so rightly perceived, the United States had "no limits and no oneness; and when you try to make it a matter of the heart, everything falls away except one's native State." [6] Writers therefore followed the regionalist impulse and looked to their own locale for their materials.

Vermont literature, predominantly regional or local, is the direct outgrowth of the quest for literary nationalism. Regional writers sought to provide vivid and authentic pictures of everyday life as they experienced it. Many Vermont authors were driven by a need to preserve a vanishing past. As Rowland E. Robinson states in the preface to *Danvis Folks* (1894), many authors wrote

> with less purpose of telling any story than of recording the manners, customs, and speech in vogue fifty or sixty years ago in certain parts of New England. Manners have changed, many customs have become obsolete, and though the dialect is yet spoken by some in almost its original quaintness, abounding in odd similes and figures of speech, it is passing away; so that one may look forward to the time when a Yankee may not be known by his speech, unless perhaps he shall speak a little better English than some of his neighbors. In truth he uses no worse now, nor did he ever, though he is accused of it.

By consciously exploiting the distinctive habits of the people and the characteristic scenery of the area, writers realistically portrayed

5. Henry Wadsworth Longfellow, "Defence of Poetry," *North American Review*, 34 (January 1832), 69–70.

6. *Complete Works*, Riverside Edition (Boston: Houghton Mifflin, 1888), x, 456.

life around them. Though some of Robinson's predictions have, indeed, come true, Vermont has come into the modern period largely unscathed by the encroachment of an increasingly homogeneous national culture. In refusing to bend to the pressures of modern America, Vermonters have maintained their simple, autonomous ways. While most of us do not know a person who talks like Gran'ther Hill or Sam Lovel, we can readily identify with their experiences. In reminiscing about Ethan Allen's heroics at Fort Ticonderoga, Gran'ther Hill says, in *Sam Lovel's Boy:*

> By the Lord Harry! it allers tickled me for tu hear tell what Ethan said when he met the cap'n. He writ a book a-tellin' on't, haow he demanded the fort "In the name o' the Gre't Jehover an' the Continental Congress!" . . . When he came tu the cap'n's quarters he says, says he, "Come aout o' yer hole, you damned ol' skunk, or by the Gre't Jehover I'll let daylight through ye!"

Gran'ther Hill is a veteran of the Revolutionary War; his speech has much in common with that of Royall Tyler's Brother Jonathan, who is of the same generation. In another story, Robinson's Sam Lovel explores his secret passion for the forest, a love that the modern Vermonter shares.

> It comes nat'ral fer me tu run in the woods. 'F I du git more tu show for it 'n some does, I get suthin besides 't I can't show. The air o' the woods tastes good tu me, fer't hain't ben breathed by nuthin but wild creeturs. I luffter breathe it 'fore common folks has. The smell o' the woods smells good tu me, dead leaves 'n' spruce boughs 'n' rotten wood, 'n' it don't hurt none if it's spiced up a leetle bit wi' skunk an' mink an' weasel an' fox p'fum'ry. An' I luffter see trees 'at's older'n any men, an' graound 't wan't never plaouwed ner hoed, a-growin' nat'ral crops. 'N I luffter hear the stillness o' the woods, fer 'tis still there. Wind a-sythin', leaves a-rustlin', brooks a-runnin', birds a-singin', even a blue jay a-squallin'

hain't noises. It takes folks an' waggins an' cattle an' pigs an' sech to make a noise. I git lots o' things a-huntin' 't I can't show ye ner tell ye 'baout, an' a feller 't don't don't git the best o' huntin', 'cordin' tu my idee.

Each of these passages is an historical record of manners, customs, and speech, and preserves a vanished past as Robinson wished. More importantly, however, once the dialect differences are mastered, we are charmed by Gran'ther Hill's delight in his wryly humorous anecdote about one of Vermont's heroes and share Sam Lovel's rude sensitivity to his environment.

In this century, Vermont's regionalists have developed in several directions. Some fiction and verse, like that of Marguerite Wolf, Robert Duffus, Frances Millet Hoyt, and Daniel Cady, maintain the tradition of the nineteenth century, a tradition that emphasizes setting and local color through use of humor and anecdote. This kind of writing at its best is often characterized by nostalgia, at its worst, sentimentality. Other authors, most notably Frederic Van de Water and Ralph Nading Hill, have discovered a usable past in the history of the state and from this raw material have created a literature of contemporary interest. Finally, Frank Howard Mosher, Zephine Humphrey Fahnestock, Frances Frost, Dorothy Canfield Fisher, and Robert Frost, in treating the local and specific consciously seek out those aspects of the human condition that seem applicable to men in all ages and places. The best of this writing rises above the limitations of regionalism in its universality.

Interest in matters historical has always flourished in Vermont. Probably as a result of their early history, their ambiguous position in the land-grant controversy and their frustrating attempts to gain statehood, Vermonters have had an acute awareness of self, have had what might be termed an "historic sense." They have valued their past heritage and have perceived the bearing of present events on the future. The strong regional impulse in literature to record the native idiom, to capture the still unravaged rural place, and to delineate local customs, manners, and dress before they disappeared is akin to the historian's desire to chronicle the events of a people. Ira Allen, Samuel Williams, and Zadock Thompson, Vermont's first generation of historians, established a foundation upon which future historians and writers could build. Thompson's comprehensive *History of Vermont, Natural, Civil, and Statistical* (1842) is still valuable as a primary source for the early history of the state. The most industrious and resourceful historical project undertaken, however, was one proposed and carried out by Abby Maria Hemenway. First conceived as a quarterly journal to which Vermonters could contribute articles and notes on local historical matters, the project resulted in the five substantial volumes entitled *The Vermont Gazetteer*. Finally, two important books which seek to correct the exaggerated and sentimental pictures of early Vermont life are Walter H. Crockett's *Vermont, The Green Mountain State* and Charles Miner Thompson's *Independent Vermont*.

The desire to anthologize the state's literature reflects the same interest in the historical; numerous editors have worked to assure the renewal of past values and the preservation of present achievements in the literary arts. The first major collection was Hemenway's four-hundred page *Poets and Poetry of Vermont*. Miss Hemenway's work was updated in 1872 by Sanborn in *Green Mountain Poets*.

The most valuable work for the modern reader has been the Green Mountain Series, "undertaken as the first major project of the Committee on Traditions and Ideals, organized in 1929, under the Vermont Commission on Country Life." The historical function was clearly in the mind of the general editor, Arthur Wallace Peach, when he wrote in the foreword to the series:

> It is the hope of the editors that the four books in the Series may serve as interesting byways from Vermont's past into Vermont's present and also may tend to throw some definite light, as reflected from verse, prose, and the lives of notable Vermont men and women, on the attitudes of mind and heart, faiths, beliefs, and loyalties that woven together through the

years have formed those traditional characteristics so generally associated with the state and its people.

The four volumes in the Series are *Vermont Verse: An Anthology; Vermont Prose: A Miscellany; Vermonters: A Book of Biographies;* and *Vermont Folk Songs and Ballads.* The editors of the individual volumes were among the best-known men and women of letters in the state.

The instinct that spawned these state histories and literary collections can also be found in the writer's use of historical materials as sources for his imaginative work. Writers of fiction have appropriated setting, character, and plot from the past for the purposes of telling a good story. Daniel Pierce Thompson's historical romances *The Green Mountain Boys* and *The Rangers,* for example, are two novels that portray the swashbuckling adventures of Ethan Allen and his men. And his *Locke Amsden; or, The Schoolmaster* presents an accurate portrayal of Vermont pioneer life as well as the author's own theories on education. Often Thompson's tales and sketches have for their focus a particular historical event; "The Indian's Revenge" and "Ethan Allen and the Lost Children" are two cases in point. Much in the same vein as Harriet Beecher Stowe's *Uncle Tom's Cabin,* John Townsend Trowbridge's antislavery novel *Neighbor Jackwood* draws upon Vermont's long-standing abolitionist sentiments. The novel was successfully dramatized by the author and produced throughout the North prior to the Civil War.

History permeates Rowland E. Robinson's stories and sketches. In them one finds a microcosm of Vermont as it was during the nineteenth century. His "An Old Time March Meeting," "Shooting Pickerel," "In Sugar Camp," "Recollections of a Quaker Boy," and "The School Meeting in District 13" are vivid vignettes of specific segments of rural life. In *Along Three Rivers,* a history of the development of the town of Ferrisburg, Vermont, Robinson "beautifies the history with description and humanizes it with gossipy reminiscences." Much of the drama in his stories in *Out of Bondage* grows out of the author's experiences helping his family operate a station on the underground railroad. The stories provide insight into a neglected aspect of Vermont's role in events leading up to the Civil War. Historical elements are also unmistakable in stories and sketches by Elizabeth Allen, William H. Murray, Charles M. Thompson, and Marguerite Grow.

More recently, Robert Duffus based his *Williamstown Branch* on recollections of his own boyhood, and Frederic Van de Water's sequence—*Reluctant Rebel, Catch a Falling Star, Wings of the Morning,* and *Day of Battle*—explores in fictionalized form the early history of the state. In *The Voyages of Brian Seaworthy,* Ralph Nading Hill vividly brings to life again the era of steamboating on Lake Champlain that he had chronicled in *Sidewheeler Saga.* Justin Morgan, schoolmaster, hymnist, and horse breeder, and Justin S. Morrill, statesman, legislator, and author of the Morrill Land Grant Act, are the subjects for Betty Bandel's *Amanda; or, The World of Justin Morgan* and *The Merits of the Case.*

Green Mountain poets, too, have made extensive use of the past. During the nineteenth and early twentieth centuries, national and local holidays and historic anniversaries were marked in Vermont, as elsewhere, by the composition of occasional poems. Independence Day has a reputation for being the excuse for long speeches by local politicians; it was also the occasion for poetic commemorations. Twenty years after the signing of the Declaration of Independence, Royall Tyler wrote his "Ode Composed for the Fourth of July," nostalgically recalling earlier celebrations of the day. Tyler's Ode was but one of many such traditional pieces. A more ephemeral sort was the Fourth of July toast, spoken at political rallies in the days when party factionalism ran strong. These toasts were invariably recorded verbatim in the state's newspapers. The Burlington *Mercury* reported this one in 1796: "The Congress of the United States: May the virtuous part thereof be the delight of the people, and those who intentionally swerve from true republican principles meet with the greatest disgrace a freeman can suffer—the contempt of his countrymen." And this one to "The State of Vermont": "In her laws, her councils and determinations, may the vigour of youth be properly intermixed with the prudence of old age."

In addition to marking annual holidays, Vermont poets have traditionally composed verses for public commemorations of special events. Best known is the work of Daniel Cady, whose busy pen produced dozens of such pieces, many now long forgotten. Two still remembered, however, are "Champlain and Lake Champlain," which Cady read at the Champlain Tercentenary Celebration of 1909, and "The Hill of Bennington," written for the one-hundred-fiftieth anniversary of the Battle of Bennington.

Occasional poetry is not always limited to recalling past glories. Frequently, it is written in response to a contemporaneous event. Thomas Rowley's "When Caesar Reigned King at Rome" is an angry reaction to the high-handed activities of the New York courts that tried Ethan Allen and other popular leaders *in absentia,* found them guilty of felonies, and sentenced them to death without benefit of clergy. The election ode, for many years a popular part of the installation of the new governor, called the attention of the people to the achievements of the present and the hopes for the future. Although the practice declined in the nineteenth century, it was revived in grand fashion in 1961, when John F. Kennedy called upon the poet laureate of Vermont to commemorate his inauguration as President of the United States. Robert Frost responded with a touching and memorable reading from the windy steps of the Capitol, examining the nation's past and its effects on the present and hailing the prospects for the future.

This is the finest use to which Vermonters have put their sense of history. Not in attempting to escape a trying present or a doubtful future by a return to some golden yesterday, but in seeking to find strength and wisdom in a past that is always present.

II

The visitor to Vermont usually arrives with a preconceived picture of the typical Vermonter—big boned and sinewy, leaning on a fence post in faded bib overalls with a chaw of tobacco bulging his cheek—a man of few joys and even fewer words. Calvin Coolidge, "Silent Cal," was to many Americans the embodiment of this stereotype, hardworking and virtuous but without passion or mirth. Yet throughout the Vermont tradition humor of a special variety has sunk its roots. It is a native variety of humor that derives not so much from older cultures as from the folk wisdom of the people themselves. And like any native American humor, it is clearly stamped by its place of origin.

Ethan Allen possessed that special sense of humor, displaying it even in the most trying of times. During the land-ownership controversy in the 1770's between the colonial government of New York and the settlers of the New Hampshire Grants, Allen and his fellow citizens terrorized any Yorker who tried to evict the farmers or survey the territory. Finally the legislature at Albany, outraged by the antics of these freedom-loving "outlaws," offered a reward for the capture of Allen and several others. Not to be outdone, Allen and his friends circulated their own advertisement, mocking the proprietors and their lawyers:

TWENTY FIVE POUNDS REWARD
Whereas James Duane and John Kemp of New York have by Their Menaces and threats greatly disturbed the Publick Peace and repose of the honest peasants of Bennington and the Settlements to the northward which peasants are now and ever have been in the peace of God and the King and are Patriotic and liege Subjects of George the Third—Any person that will apprehend these common disturbers, viz James Duane and John Kemp and bring them to landlord Fay's at Bennington shall have fifteen Pounds Reward for James Duane and ten pounds for John Kemp paid by,

Ethan Allen
Remember Baker
Robert Coughran

Perhaps as amusing as Allen's impudence toward the New York authorities is the irony of this agnostic living "in the peace of God" as "a Patriotic and liege Subject" of George the Third, for within four years he rebelled against the king and captured Fort Ticonderoga in the name of "the great Jehovah and the Continental Congress."

Impudence, even irreverence, is often the mark of the frontiersman's view of established institutions. Indeed, such an attitude is possible only for a free man, one who is beholden to no manor lord or bank or interfering government. And the men of the Green Mountains have always fought to maintain their freedom. Of course, the target of that irreverence need not always be a momentous one. Thomas Rowley, a contemporary of the Allens and a veteran of Ticonderoga, voices the complaint of many a long-suffering church-goer:

> "Watch and pray," says the text;
> "Go to sleep," says the sermon.

The somberness and pomposity of the Massachusetts Bay divines were perhaps lacking in most of Vermont's first citizens or, if they did appear, must have been quickly ridiculed by Rowley or someone like him who could view his life and times with detachment and even occasionally a bit of frivolity.

With this native brand of humor and the distinctive rural New England character as raw materials, Royall Tyler created a fictional personality, Brother Jonathan. In the spring of 1787 Tyler, a Bostonian by birth and a Vermonter by choice, was in New York City on a diplomatic mission when he saw performances of Sheridan's *The School for Scandal* and several other popular English comedies of manners. Amused and intrigued, he immediately began writing a play of his own and in less than three weeks had created the first American comedy to be performed in this country. Unlike the plays that Tyler saw, the *Contrast* is set not in a London drawing room or at an English country estate but in New York City, and the hero is an American, Colonel Manly. The drama concerns the efforts of Manly to win the girl of his heart from a Europeanized dandy who toys with her affections. The subplot revolves around Jonathan, the rustic Yankee servant, and his counterpart, the foppish Jessamy. Thus the "contrast" is between native, homespun virtues and artificial imported manners which American society of the time prized so highly. In his creation of Brother Jonathan, a prototype of Uncle Sam, Tyler draws upon the best and the worst in the Yankee character. Naive yet shrewd, Jonathan's basic good nature and lack of pretension endear him to the audience and show up the witty, but shallow, foreigners. The situation of the provincial Yankee visiting the city and exposing not only his own ignorance, but, inadvertently, the foolishness of city people and their manners was so effective that it became a stock plotting device during the nineteenth century. Colonel Manly, in his moment of triumph at the end of the play, echoes the author's own feelings: "I have learned that probity, virtue, honour, though they should not have received the polish of Europe, will secure to an honest American the good graces of his fair countrywomen, and I hope, the applause of the Public." In *The Contrast* Tyler created a genuine American folk character, urged his countrymen to be true to themselves, and pointed the way to a new and native American literature for the generation of writers that followed.

Daniel P. Thompson was one of those writers who made use of Tyler's pioneering efforts. "A Vermonter in a Fix, or a New Way to Collect an Old Debt" is the story of John Hobson, "a plain, hardy, shrewd Vermont farmer" who buys cattle on credit and drives them to the market in Montreal, hoping to make a financial killing. In his greedy attempt to get the very best price, he is swindled by a city slicker. It is in the nature of the Vermont sense of justice that whenever a man gets a little too greedy or begins to act better than his neighbors, he gets his comeuppance. It is not exactly the Greek concept of *hubris* or pride; though the retribution is swift, it is seldom tragic and sometimes even comic. Perhaps it is just the unwillingness of Vermonters to be bossed or to accept a position of servility, an independence that came to the Green Mountains with the earliest settlers and still flourishes there. Properly terrified at the thought of returning home without cattle or money, Hobson outwits the swindler and leaves Montreal, a richer and wiser "Jonathan."

Cornelius Logan offers an outsider's view of this Yankee type in his 1840 farce, *The Vermont Wool Dealer*. Baltimore-born, Logan capitalizes on the Jonathan character through the exaggerated use of comic dialect and other elements of folk humor without adopting the sympathetic stance that both Tyler and Thompson take toward the figure. This play also incorporates the same tension, hinted at by Tyler and Thompson, between the countryman's attraction to the city's wonders and his distrust of its ways. Deuteronomy Dutiful, the Vermont wool dealer, has come down the Hudson River to New York City on business. He and Captain Oakley, a punctilious military man, vie for the same girl—and for the same reason, her money. When Dutiful's shrewdness backfires, he is challenged to a duel; it requires a rather forced wrenching of the plot to get him out of his predicament. Although his life is spared, the girl is lost and he goes back to Vermont, wiser to the ways of the city and of love.

The light-hearted treatment of the battle of the sexes became a major element in Vermont writing throughout the nineteenth and into the twentieth century. Thomas Fessenden's early satire of a rural beauty is downright uncharitable. Of the village belle he wrote:

> Miss Tabitha Towzer is sleek,
> When dress'd in her pretty new tucker,
> Like an otter that paddles the creek,
> In quest of a mud-pout or sucker.

This early attempt at dialect humor must also be seen as a satire of the starry-eyed lover, he whose rural metaphors reveal a knowledge of country things if not of feminine beauty. In the same tradition is Charles Saxe's poem "The Explanation," in which the gallant male, after observing that women play such negligible roles in world affairs, feels compelled to explain

> Such a paragon is woman,
> That, you see, it *must* be true
> She is always vastly better
> Than the best that she can do!

The folk song "John Grumlie" has a man and his wife arguing over who works harder. To settle the point they agree to change jobs, and after a wearying and bumbling day of milking the cows, feeding the pigs and the hen, and overlooking the rest of the woman's chores, he grudgingly admits that "she could do more work in one day / Than he could do in three." Then there is Walter Hard's poem about Charlie Barney and his wife: "Between Charlie and his wife / There was an armed truce." One wash day Charlie was turning the wringer as she fed through the clothes. When the cranking became difficult, he turned harder until he realized that her arm was caught in the wringer, "half way up to the elbow." The next day when a friend asked, "Didn't your wife make an outcry?" Charlie's measured reply was, "O yes. She hollered. But Lord —she's always hollerin'."

By and large, Vermonters are not given to bragging, which is regarded as unseemly. Boasting, on those rare occasions when it does surface, is likely to be within the value system of the state. Thus the claim of an earlier day that "Vermont has more cows than people" is announced with the knowledge that according to the values of the outsider it makes the state appear backward and "unprogressive." And that is fine with the Vermonter. The one exception to this reluctance to boast is the figure of Ethan Allen. As in the case of his southern counterpart, Davy Crockett, the legend of Allen has its roots in actual exploits romanticized and exaggerated. Allen's *Narrative* was certainly instrumental in the birth of a myth which has continued to grow in both the oral and the literary traditions. Vermonters like Robinson's Gran'ther Hill have always chuckled as they recount Allen's bravado. By the time the hero of Ticonderoga appears as a character in Thompson's *The Green Mountain Boys* and Herman Melville's *Israel Potter,* he has achieved mythic proportions. But the case of Ethan Allen is the exception and not the rule in the state's literature, for to Vermonters exaggeration is uneconomical. Its effect depends on the piling of detail upon detail in a mountain of words. Vermonters are subtracters, not adders.

The alternative to exaggeration is understatement, which Vermonters employ with more than usual zest. The distaste for exuberant display of emotion is an attitude that affects all aspects of human relations and is clearly reflected in works such as Fisher's *Tourists Accommodated* and Duffus' *Williamstown Branch*. Robert Frost's appreciation "On Being Chosen Poet of Vermont" is quietly tailored to both the occasion and the audience:

> Breathes there a bard who isn't moved
> When he finds his verse is understood
> And not entirely disapproved
> By his country and his neighborhood?

This characteristic restraint, which is the tone of most of Frost's poetry, humorous or serious, also informs the verse of twentieth-century poets like Genevieve Taggard, Frances Frost, and James Hayford. Sometimes irony is the vehicle as in Sarah Cleghorn's famous quatrain:

> The golf links lie so near the mill
> That almost every day
> The laboring children can look out
> and see the men at play.

Vermont satire is nearly always smiling and gentle, lacking the bitterness and anger of a "Modest Proposal."

In the early decades of the state's development, satires were usually of a political nature, like Thomas Rowley's "When Caesar Reigned King at Rome," Thomas Fessenden's "Eulogy on the Times" or, later, Leonard Marsh's delightful burlesque *A Bake-Pan for Dough-Faces,* and the influence of foreign literary styles and techniques was strong. But as the Enlightenment and Neoclassical spirits waned, Vermont authors began to focus on the daily rounds of life, and the influence of Pope and Sheridan gradually gave way to the richness of native humor. What the tourist failed to notice about the overalled farmer was the twinkle in his eye.

III

As Royall Tyler conceived him, Brother Jonathan embodied the characteristics of frontier New England—openness, independence, naiveté, common sense, and shrewdness. But as outsiders began to appropriate this figure, they tended to exaggerate the comic aspects at the expense of a sympathetic treatment of a rounded character, resulting in a stereotype that was perpetuated throughout the nineteenth century. Those who lived in Vermont and knew better, however, looked to their models, the people of the state, and there discovered a variety of highly individualized human beings. They also discovered that, with the passing of the frontier, the nature of the state was undergoing a slow transformation as institutions were generated and more regular patterns of existence were established. As Dorothy Canfield Fisher has since observed, Vermonters, "by the act of living together in accordance with local tradition, have made for each other an unvaryingly safe and orderly social framework for widely varying individual lives." [7] They have intuitively recognized that to preserve personal freedom and liberty it is necessary to accept certain self-imposed rules of conduct.

These unwritten rules, so often misunderstood by outsiders, mean to a Vermonter: Do not intrude on the privacy of others, accept the differences and eccentricities of a neighbor, be slow of judgment, resist the encroachment of government, and, above all, be alert to threats to justice and freedom. For as Genevieve Taggard recalls in her recent tribute "To Ethan Allen":

> . . . many customs sweet
> Prolong an enduring impulse this citizen took
> To be his passion: to be Freedom's servant rude.
>
> .   .   .
>
> . . . Those who remember you
> Wish never to outgrow such servitude.

The adaptations necessitated in a developing society did not substantially change many of the basic qualities of individual character. The deep and abiding closeness to the land that Tyler expressed in his "Lines on Brattleboro" is reiterated by Rowland Robinson's Sam Lovel fifty years later, and again in the twentieth century in Walter Hard's "Youth of the Mountain." In the latter, Rob, the

7. *Vermont Tradition*, p. 390.

eighty-two-year-old narrator, leaves town and returns to his mountain farm house:

> —They say I'm too old to stay up here.
> Old?
> Mebbe I am old down thar in th' valley
> With all the rushin' and new fangled idees
> Clutt'rin things up with what they call civ'lization.
> But up here . . .
>   .   .   .
>
> —Up here,
> I ain't nothin' but a yearlin'.

Whereas Rob is psychologically rejuvenated by his contact with the land, the narrator of Robert Frost's lyric "The Onset" finds spiritual truth in nature. Momentarily startled by the onset of a winter storm, he likens it to the coming of death. Nature provides solace in the remembrance that "winter death has never tried / The earth but it has failed." Oftentimes nature's solace has been the only kind available to this stoic people. Open expression of love or of any emotion is not in character, perhaps because of the belief that anything easily and freely given must be of little value, and that which matters most is too important for words. In a "Tide of Lilac" Frances Frost sensitively portrays this attitude. The tide

> . . . invades the marrow
> of reticent strong bones.
>
> And careful housewives shiver,
> and cautious men bite lips,
> when they, with no one looking,
> touch blue with their fingertips.

Such an existence starves the soul that requires love and may drive a wedge between people, as in Robert Frost's "Home Burial." The farmwife still mourns the loss of her child, a loss that she does not realize her husband shares. In his inarticulateness he is unable to reach her grief with his, and the two live out their lives alone.

The existence of a farm woman, living back in the hills, cut off from neighbors and town most of the winter, is a deadening fate seldom portrayed in Vermont writing. Ann Batchelder, a woman who experienced some of that narrow life, reflects:

I would fare away on the world's broad highways
I would hear the alien winds singing through the sails;
Here must I stay and roam the dusty byways,
Looking for berries to fill my berry pails.

The decades following the Civil War witnessed the tide of emigration flowing toward the activity and excitement of urban areas. The hard, stony soil of the hill farms proved unyielding in its seeming determination to deny those farmers the rewards of their toil, and as year by year their farms declined, so did their fortunes and health. Many were unable to scratch a living from the hillsides and left for the richer flat lands of the Midwest or the promise of a job in the city.

Some stuck it out, though, either consoling themselves by reflecting on an earlier era or turning inward in a peculiar silence of acceptance. Zephine Humphrey Fahnestock felt a peculiar reward in remaining on the land and submitting to its will. "Life seems to me mostly a matter of discipline, stern, inexorable. Character cannot be forged except with straight blows, at white heat."

Despite, or perhaps because of, the hardships of rural life, Vermonters have retained a fierce loyalty to their state. During the peak years of emigration at the end of the nineteenth century and into the early decades of the twentieth, expatriates across the nation joined together in Vermont clubs to maintain old ties and to reaffirm their heritage. Wendell Phillips Stafford's "Song of Vermont" was set to music and sung at such meetings in Michigan, Illinois, and California.

No queen has had for followers
A bolder train of men;
And when again the need is hers
They shall be hers again!

While Vermonters have freely boasted of their birthright, they remain characteristically modest about personal achievement. Robert Frost's humble acknowledgment on being chosen poet of Vermont is in this tradition of accepting recognition with something bordering on embarrassment. Perhaps Julia Dorr's couplet, "The joy is in the singing / Whether heard or no," best explains the attitude.

In weighing liberty against an ordered society, or the comforts of town life against rural independence, Vermonters are acutely conscious of debit and credit. In their own way they have discovered the wisdom of Henry David Thoreau's observation on economy: "the cost of a thing is the amount of what I will call life which is required to be exchanged for it, immediately or in the long run." While Vermonters may seem to resist "progress," it is not really that simple. Perhaps they are merely unwilling to be stampeded into a decision without first considering the implications, the "cost," for themselves, their children, and their way of life. As early as 1864, George Perkins Marsh warned in *Man and Nature* that the price of careless development of natural resources might be the ultimate destruction of the resources. Dollars are not necessarily the issue for, as Dorothy Canfield Fisher has observed, "Vermont esteems highly certain human qualities even though they do not conduce to the making of large incomes." This truth is illuminated in "The Wisconsin Emigrant's Song." Trying to convince his wife to leave Vermont, the struggling farmer in this folk song argues for the comfort and wealth they could find on the fertile land of the Midwest. When her objections to the difficulty of clearing the new land fail to sway him, she voices her fear of marauding Indians who might destroy the farm and murder her and the children. This appeal to human values succeeds, and he agrees to remain in the land of their birth.

The process of weighing cost against worth in an environment that cannot satisfy every desire has led to the development of a system of values and a way of life that have at times seemed out of the mainstream of American life. Neither boastful nor apologetic, Vermonters have accepted the consequences of their choices as stoically as they made them, believing in the wisdom of Thoreau's aphorism, "If a man does not keep pace with his companions, perhaps it is because he hears a different drummer."

> VERMONTERS
> These are the people living in this land:
> proud and narrow, with their eyes on the hills.
> They ask no favors. Their lips defend
> with speech close-rationed their hoarded souls.
>
> You cannot love them or know them at all
> unless you know how a hardwood tree
> can pour blond sugar in a pegged-up pail
> in the grudging thaw of a February day.[8]
>
> —Dilys Bennett Laing

IV

In good measure Vermont's distinctive literary voice is attributable to Vermont's relatively isolated development. After the period of initial settlement the state experienced only minor and infrequent waves of new immigrants; thus the population's essential homogeneity was preserved. The only New England state not bordering on the Atlantic Ocean, Vermont has lacked the flow of ideas and commerce that an international seaport so often provides. Further, the predominantly rural character of the state, reflecting the desire for small farms and homesteads, precluded the development of a major urban center which might have fostered and focused the cultural activities of the area. With the exception of Tyler and his circle, Vermont authors have not fully experienced the influences of literary trends and fashions. This self-containment has been conducive to the development and the preservation of a common culture. With rare exceptions, the state's writers have chosen to ex-

8. Reprinted from *Another England* (New York: Duell, Sloan and Pierce, 1941), by permission of Alexander Laing.

plore the local and familiar as subject matter rather than the exotic or sensational. For themes they have looked to the comforts of hearth and home, the uncertainties of rural life, and their relationship to the environment. Sometimes nostalgic toward the past, usually sympathetic toward the limitations of the present, these authors have sought to maintain a perspective of themselves and their place in the scheme of things through a recognition of the ironies of existence. A dominant element in the literature is a sense of proportion: seriousness is tempered by a wry humor, idealism balanced by stubborn realism.

One of the greatest values of Vermont literature is the record, social and historical, that it preserves of this common culture. Indeed, Marius Péladeau's assessment of early colonial literature is applicable to much of the writing of the last two centuries in the state, writing which "must be studied from a social, rather than a critical, point of view. It should be judged as an expression of the thought, feeling, and emotions of the times . . ." [9] Several of these writers, however, are capable of withstanding critical scrutiny and have received national notice for their skill, artistry, and ability to entertain. Royall Tyler, Rowland E. Robinson, Frances Frost, Dorothy Canfield Fisher, and Robert Frost stand out as representatives of the best of the Vermont literary tradition.

Had Royall Tyler written nothing more than *The Contrast,* he would be assured of a place in the literary histories of the United States along with his contemporaries Joel Barlow and Philip Freneau. In writing the first native American comedy and creating the prototype of the stage Yankee, Tyler influenced later generations of authors. Often considered a one-play dramatist, this successful lawyer and jurist also wrote two lost satires, a farce based on *Don Quixote,* and three sacred dramas. But his claim to distinction rests on an even broader base. His picaresque work *The Algerine Captive* (1797), which satirizes education, the medical profession, and slavery in this country, and the life of a captive abroad, was one of the first American novels to be reprinted in

9. Marius B. Péladeau, ed., *The Verse of Royall Tyler* (Charlottesville, Va.: The University Press of Virginia, 1968), pp. xxxvii–xxxviii.

England. His other assay into fiction, a series of letters ostensibly from an American resident of England, *The Yankey in London,* became immensely popular.

Tyler's poetic contributions have remained, until recently at least, largely overlooked. In 1794 he and a New Hampshire friend, Joseph Dennie, formed the literary team of "Colon and Spondee," regularly contributing columns to *The Farmer's Weekly Museum* and other newspapers. Under the pseudonym of Spondee, Tyler wrote most of the verse to appear in the column and rapidly achieved a wide following throughout New England. Even his early work shows a remarkable variety of subjects and treatments. "The Origin of Evil: An Elegy," a lusty and sensuous account of the Fall, is in sharp contrast to the reverent "Christmas Hymn." The broad humor and rustic setting of his tribute to New England's favorite drink in "Anacreontic to Flip" differs markedly from the work of the popular Della Cruscan school, which was flamboyant and highly artificial. Tyler singled out these poets and their American imitators for harsh treatment in several satires and parodies. His strong sense of national pride, reflected in his early call for an American literature and culture, gave impetus to a number of patriotic odes and is further demonstrated in his devotion to the affairs of government, both in his roles as citizen and lawyer as well as in his many political satires. Despite his urban upbringing and genteel breeding, his writing expresses a faith in the common man and the redeeming virtues of his labors on the land.

With advancing years, however, illness and financial hardships took their toll, and the quantity of his output declined. If these later poems lack some of the zest of his youthful work, they make up for it in greater reflection and depth of feeling. In "Stanzas to ****" the speaker pleads with a former lover, perhaps life itself, not to stir youth's desires in him:

> Touch not again—touch not again thy lyre!
>   Forbear that hallow'd strain!
> Again forbear to wake my bosom's fire,
>   O wound it not again!

> For he whose spring-like years are o'er
> Can listen to its strains no more.

Although the theme of death always intrigued Tyler, he turned to it more and more frequently in such late poems as "November," "On the Death of a Little Child," and "Evening." The most ambitious poetic work of his later years was "The Chestnut Tree." Written in 1824, it forecasts the effects of the coming industrial age on the rural and village life that he had learned to love so well.

Rowland Evans Robinson was a product of the age of dialect and local color fiction, an age that fostered such writers as Sarah Orne Jewett and Mary Wilkins Freeman in New England, Joel Chandler Harris in the South, and Bret Harte and Mark Twain in the West. Unlike other practitioners of local color writing, Robinson is unpretentious; his stories and sketches are relatively plotless and unsensational. This does not mean, however, that they are colorless and uneventful. Robinson's writings depict the daily lives of people who lived in Vermont during the nineteenth century. As Fred Lewis Pattee has observed, "All Vermont is in his books—its uncouth diction, its Puritan inflexibility, its Yankee prejudices and superstitions, its dry and noiseless humor, its fundamental kindliness. To read the books through is like boarding for a month in a Green Mountain farmhouse in sight of Otter Creek or Vergennes." [10] Above all, Robinson was a master of dialects. His stories contain accurate phonetic transcriptions of the peculiarities of Vermont speech. He savored the curious idioms, unique figures of speech, and strange syntactic structures that his neighbors used. He employs dialect not to enhance exotic or strange effects, but rather to capture the individuality of his characters. In addition to the speech of the proverbial Yankee, one finds other examples of dialect: from the New England Indian, the runaway black slave, and the southern slave owner. Among his more fascinating characters is Antoine Bassette, a French Canadian. When in *Uncle Lisha's Shop* the pompous Solon Briggs reproves Antoine

10. Pattee, "Foreword," in Rowland E. Robinson, *Uncle Lisha's Shop and A Danvis Pioneer* (Rutland, Vt.: Tuttle, 1937), pp. 8–9.

for making a motion at a school meeting when he was not a natu-
ralized citizen, Antoine humorously replies,

> Wal, Ah don' care 'f Ah don' nat'ral lie, so much you do,
> Ah'll show you jes' many chillun for go school anyboddee,
> bah gosh! More of it all a tam, evree year, evree year. Ah
> guess Ahm's more norder you was, M'sieur Brigg. You be
> marree more as Ah was, an' don' have it on'y one chillun,
> bah gosh.

Although remembered primarily as an accomplished illustrator
and a writer of local color fiction, Robinson was also an historian
of Vermont. At the invitation of Horace E. Scudder, editor of
Houghton Mifflin's American Commonwealths Series, Robinson
wrote *Vermont: A Study of Independence.* To this work he brought
the talents of a man of letters; he was no slave to facts and dates.
The subtitle sounds the keynote of the volume, which is a concise,
eminently readable account of what the state has stood for from
the time Champlain first laid eyes on it in July 1609. Of special
interest is the chapter devoted to "Old-Time Customs and Indus-
tries," the product of Robinson's life-long investigations of the
manners, customs, and occupations of Vermont's people. In *A
Danvis Pioneer* Robinson tells the story of Seth Beeman and his
struggles in settling the Grants. Seth's son Nathan achieved fame
when he guided Ethan Allen into Fort Ticonderoga in May 1775.
Robinson recounts Nathan's story in *A Hero of Ticonderoga.*

During his own lifetime, especially during the decades of the
1880's and 1890's, Robinson achieved national prominence. His
sketches were read by subscribers to *Atlantic Monthly, Youth's
Companion,* and *Forest and Stream.* Many readers who wrote Robinson to tell of their delight with his work added that they particularly enjoyed hearing his stories read aloud by someone who had
mastered the dialects. In this way his works came alive. After his
death in 1900, Robinson's reputation outside of Vermont faded
rapidly. His dialects, unlike Twain's, are difficult on the eye; they
do not reflect a judicious selection of dialect markers. Perhaps Robinson, in trying to capture nineteenth-century Vermont, was too accurate.

Frances Frost, a St. Albans native related to Robert Frost only in the kinship of poetry, achieved early and widespread recognition for her sensitive treatment of the New England scene. A reviewer for the *New York Times* dubbed her the "Passionate Pilgrim," suggesting the paradox inherent in her work. Nourished by the Vermont tradition to which she belonged, she also found herself constrained by its limits. She discovered her early themes in the same north country where Robert Frost found his. Nature, the land, the human life of her native state—these are the subjects of her first books, *Hemlock Wall* and *Blue Harvest*. Frequently her method was to let the smaller moments of life and landscape stand for larger truths; thus the prickly problem of getting through a barbed-wire fence yields the recognition:

> But he who trespasses must heed his soul,
> Find his own devilish and delightful knack
> For crossing fences—and for getting back.

In "The Inarticulate" as she presses forehead to rock, she hears the voiceless earth speak through her stone heart. Fascinated, almost obsessed, by the limits that the "Vermont-self" imposed on the "passionate-self," she frequently dwells on signs of thoughts and feelings that are otherwise unexpressed. In "Language" she explains: "Apple trees on a slope say what a man cannot say / And ask questions a man cannot ask." Apple trees, a grindstone, old wagons, and a scythe "are the stunted speech of a country / Slow to live and equally slow to die."

Despite her great early productivity—five books of verse in five years—her range tended to be narrow, broadening only slightly in her third book, *These Acres,* to an exploration of the relationships of men and women and woman and earth. These relationships were still treated, however, in terms of the world of nature. There are the thin-lipped, repressed women "in whom the chill green stem, unwakened, / Lifts no flower into furious air." Sometimes there is a momentary release of passions, as in "Year of Earth":

Man and woman, on the driven earth,
Gathered to the reeling night, we bear
Love and wind like tides within the blood.

During these years from 1929 to 1932 her rise to national prominence was astonishing. If reviews of *Hemlock Wall* and *Blue
Harvest* were warm, the acclaim accorded *These Acres* was enthu-
siastic: "She is one of the most importantly gifted lyrists writing
today." [11] Her fifth book, *Woman of This Earth,* was an extension
of the themes of *These Acres;* a long sequence of related poems in
six books, it represents the six ages of woman in an effort to define
twentieth-century womanhood in terms of the earth. Although her
imagery sometimes presents the sensuous, it also evokes the barren
and sterile:

The cedars are bronze beyond the naked orchard,
the sky is scooped flint in the cold, the crows are starved
in frozen stubble: there were no stars last night.

Writing of this sequence in the *New York Times,* Percy Hutchinson asserted boldly: "American poetry . . . has received no single contribution more distinguished than this by Frances Frost.
'Woman of This Earth' rises to major heights." [12] But other critics
were disappointed: her vision had not broadened beyond the Vermont earth, her scenes were "provincial," her treatment "subjec-
tive." Noted author and critic Alexander Laing regretted her pro-
lificacy, wishing instead that she had worked more slowly and
permitted her poems to mature in mind before committing them
to print. Themes, even turns of phrase, were repeated without true
further development. [13]

The approach of World War II, however, deeply affected her
sensibilities and brought with it a greater sense of the large am-

11. "The Poetry of a Passionate Puritan," *New York Times Book Review* (10 July 1932), p. 9.

12. "Frances Frost's Poem: *Woman of This Earth,"* *New York Times
Book Review* (15 April 1934), p. 19.

13. Laing, "Finality and False Starts," *Saturday Review of Literature*
(27 October 1934), p. 240.

biguities of modern existence. Published in 1946, *Mid-Century* is a collection of the verse she wrote during that conflict. Here, for perhaps the first time, she confronts the tensions between peace and war, country and city, love and hate.

> What shall we save in cities ruinous
> of precious crucibles, of fiddles crying,
> when mortal meteors made luminous
> scream down the fiery plummet of their dying?

Although her poetic world now encompassed the foxholes and beachheads, the perspective from which she viewed that world remained the pasture and the hillside. The New England rural scene provided the standard of sanity against which the madness of modern life could be measured: "Here I am mending fence today / who shall be wounding men tomorrow."

Although Miss Frost wrote several novels and upwards of a dozen children's books, it is for her poetry that she is best known. Her last book of verse, published in 1954, shows a melding of earlier themes in an easy style. Never fully reconciled to the paradoxes of her life and times, to "the death of the russet vixen" or "the breath turned fire in the airman's lungs," she preferred instead the invasion of spires of lilac, "clustered to plague New England souls."

Dorothy Canfield Fisher's ten novels, eleven volumes of short stories, twenty volumes of nonfiction, and scores of magazine articles attest to her position among writers of the twentieth century. Her knowledge of the world both outside and inside Vermont has put her in a unique position as a literary artist. She is, in a way, Vermont's literary ambassador to the world. Sensitive to dangerous trends in American society at the beginning of the century, Mrs. Fisher spoke out against materialism and the dehumanizing aspects of industrialization, as well as war and those ideologies which threaten basic human rights.

In Vermont, Mrs. Fisher found a pre-industrial society that retained the close ties of village life based on nonmaterial values. What most impressed her was Vermont's tradition of protecting human rights, and as movements in modern society began to erode man's image of himself, she found strength in that tradition. Even though her Vermont stories present a somewhat romantic and optimistic view of the state and its people, they are valuable for their criticism of the ills plaguing modern cities. Mrs. Fisher has the uncanny ability to draw meaningful lessons from her dramatizations of the little incidents of daily life. In *Hillsboro People,* her first collection of Vermont stories, she ardently defends village life against the attacks of city-dwellers who have criticized it for being sterile and debilitating. As Lois McCallister perceives it, "Vermont was Mrs. Fisher's most instructive metaphor." [14] The theme of village versus city is treated again in *The Brimming Cup,* when the outsider Vincent Marsh tries unsuccessfully to convince Marise Crittenden that she is wasting herself by living in Vermont. *Bonfire* and *Seasoned Timber* provided lower-keyed, more subtle arguments in favor of village life.

Mrs. Fisher was greatly disturbed by war. While in France with her husband during World War I, she witnessed the carnage and the waste of human life. When war threatened to break out again less than two decades later, Mrs. Fisher responded with *Seasoned Timber,* a parable on antisemitism. The story centers upon Professor Timothy Hulme and his financially stricken school, Clifford Academy. Just as matters seem their bleakest, Hulme receives word that the school has been bequeathed one million dollars with the stipulation that no Jews be admitted. Since so few Jews apply to Clifford in the first place, the request did not seem that important. Hulme comes to view the stipulation as an infringement upon human rights, however, and in the end, he campaigns for his own kind of financial support.

Throughout her life, Fisher was interested in child development and public education. As a leader in the so-called "permissive" movement, her books *Mothers and Children* and *Fables for Parents* speak out against tyranny in the home and encourage parents to develop integrity and responsibility in their children. An advocate of

14. "Dorothy Canfield Fisher: A Critical Study," dissertation, Case Western Reserve University, (1969), p. 94.

progressive, innovative education, she popularized the ideas of John Dewey and Maria Montessori in *The Montessori Mother* and *Montessori Manual for Parents and Teachers.*

Although Mrs. Fisher had employed Vermont as an instructive example in her fiction, it was not until 1953, when she produced *Vermont Tradition: A Biography of an Outlook on Life,* that she fully articulated her feelings about the state. Perhaps she needed a lifetime of experience and writing in order to produce the book, which displays her great powers of synthesis. Seen in the light of *Vermont Tradition,* her earlier fiction takes on added significance. Although she will never gain the critical recognition and stature of her contemporaries—Willa Cather, Edith Wharton, and Ellen Glasgow—her fiction stands in the mainstream of humanitarian writing in this century. So vividly has she interpreted the meaning of life in Vermont that the public finds her name and that of her beloved state inseparable.

Robert Frost's New England homes, first in New Hampshire and then, for the last forty years of his life, in Vermont, left an indelible mark on his thinking and his language. Like his north country neighbors, he clothed intensity of feeling with understatement and restraint. His few words are as carefully weighed and frugally spent as those of a hill farmer. Characteristic of the manner in which he offers his readers small events and concentrated emotions in lean lines of deceptively simple language is his discovery of faith in a snowstorm or love in a tuft of flowers. "I might be called a Synecdochist," he admitted, "for I prefer the synecdoche in poetry—that figure of speech in which we use a part for the whole." Turning to the people and places north of Boston, he discovered in them a pastoral myth of the rural world ideally suited to his poetry and temperament. A modernist in his need to develop in his poems "a momentary stay against confusion," he remained a traditionalist in most other respects, rejecting the solipcism, the deliberate obscurity, and the involuted myth-making of his contemporaries.

His pastoral world was not a sunny garden of unmixed blessedness, however. Like the outside world, it too harbored a principle of entropy and perverseness, like the "dimpled spider, fat and white" that he discovers in "Design" or the mocking laughter of the demiurge hiding behind him. Whether it be the principle of death or evil or disorder, Frost accepts it as an inescapable fact of the universe, hoping merely to arrange a tentative truce. Just as winter cold is necessary to the growth of an apple tree, so is a dynamic tension between the forces of life and death essential to the equilibrium of this poet. Within his country world he does not seek perfection, only equipoise. He, like most of his fellow Vermonters, will gratefully settle for a winter Eden "as near a paradise as it can be / and not melt snow or start a dormant tree."

Chronology

1787	Royall Tyler's *The Contrast* is performed in New York
1791	Vermont becomes the fourteenth state The University of Vermont is chartered Justin Morgan brings his soon-to-be famous horse to the state
1795	First issue of *Rural Magazine,* the state's first periodical
1798	Ira Allen publishes *The Natural and Political History of the State of Vermont*
1800	Middlebury College is chartered
1802	Publication of *Selections and Miscellaneous Works of Thomas Rowley*
1808	The *S.S. Vermont,* the second commercial steamer in the world, begins Lake Champlain runs
1810	Merino sheep are introduced and launch an economic boom
1811	Flourishing potash industry is destroyed by German discovery of a cheap substitute
1816	Eighteen-hundred-and-froze-to-death, the year without a summer
1819	Norwich University is chartered
1825	General Lafayette tours Vermont
1840	The Vermont Historical Society is founded
1842	*History of Vermont, Natural, Civil, and Statistical* is published by Zadock Thompson
1848	The Central Vermont, first railroad, begins operations
1858	Abby Maria Hemenway's collection *Poets and Poetry of Vermont* is published
1859	Miss Hemenway publishes the first of five volumes of the *Historical Gazetteer of Vermont*

John Dewey, world-famous philosopher and educator, is born in Burlington

1861 Vermont offers men and money to the Union as the Civil War begins

1864 *Man and Nature* is published by George Perkins Marsh

1881 Fairfield's Chester A. Arthur becomes the twenty-first president

1895 *The Vermonter, the State Magazine,* begins publication

1920 First session of the Bread Loaf School of English

1921 Walter Hill Crockett publishes the first of five volumes of his *History of Vermont*

1923 Calvin Coolidge is sworn in as President at Plymouth Notch

1926 *Driftwind,* poetry magazine, founded by Walter John Coates

1932 The Green Mountain Series—four volumes of Vermont poetry, prose, folk songs, and biography—is published

1936 *Hill Trails,* literary magazine, begins publication

1946 *Vermont Life* magazine begins publication

1947 The Shelburne Museum is established

1956 *The Mountain Troubadour* is founded by the Poetry Society of Vermont

1959 The Champlain Shakespeare Festival begins its first summer season on the UVM campus

1973 The Royall Tyler Theatre opens at the University of Vermont

1

Settlement, Revolution, and Early Statehood

Continuing our course in this lake on the west side I saw, as I was observing the country, some very high mountains on the east side, with snow on the top of them. I inquired of the savages if these places were inhabited. They told me that they were—by the Iroquois—and that in these places there were beautiful valleys and open stretches fertile in grain, such as I had eaten in this country, with a great many other fruits; and that the lake went near some mountains, which were perhaps, as it seemed to me, about fifteen leagues from us.

—Samuel de Champlain,
The Voyages and Explorations of Samuel de Champlain, Narrated by Himself

Lake Memphremagog, Owl's Head Artist Unknown, courtesy of Shelburne
Museum, Inc., Shelburne, Vermont

Ira Allen (1751-1814)

Coming to the Grants

I contemplated the extent of the New Hampshire Grants, and probable advantages that might arise by being contiguous to lake Champlain, and determined to interest myself in that country; as soon as able to ride. I set out to purchase some lands in the towns contiguous to Onion river, that were owned in Connecticut. At Bennington I met with my brother, Ethan, who exerted himself to discourage me; yet I proceeded to Salisbury, and informed Heman of my intentions. He also advised against it, observing that I had not property to make payment, or commence settlement. I proposed obtaining credit for the lands I purchased, and to undertake some job of surveying to defray the expense of exploring the country. At length Heman gave me a letter of credit for two hundred pounds and I proceeded and purchased 52 rights of land and got bonds for six rights more on payment. I also contracted with the proprietors of Mansfield to run the outlines of the town, lay a division of 50 acres to each right and build six possession Houses for ninety pounds to be paid on the return the survey, plan, etc. late in the fall. I then returned to my brother and gave him up my recommendation, as I had done this business on my own credit. I saw my brother appeared pleased with my enterprise, and asked how I expected to procure stores, etc. to make the survey. I observed that I should contrive some way for it; although I had little more money than to carry me back. In the morning, as I was taking my leave, Heman handed me 32 dollars, observing that I might remit it, when convenient, (this and the letter of credit was without any solicitation). I then proceeded with good courage. At Arlington I took Capt. Remember Baker into partnership with me for the survey of Mansfield on condition of his advancing all the stores and hiring the men for assistance taking his pay when made by the proprietors; setting his advances against any enterprise expenses, etc., in making the contract. I then showed him the money advanced by my brother, observing in the case of necessity it might be of use to me. A day was assigned to meet at Skeensborough. Baker was to bring on the men and stores, and I to go to Crown Point to purchase a boat and meet him. I then went to Hubbardton and continued my surveys till it was time to go to Crown Point. I then set out through the woods, though again afflicted with boils. I procured a batteau and Waywood, a discharged British soldier, to assist me to Skeensborough where we arrived about one hour before Baker. I then looked for some salts I had purchased to purge my blood on account of the boils, which I had been advised to by a physician, but I had left it. Baker arriving we set out for Onion river. A few hours after I was taken with a dysentery that was severe for three days and nights and reduced me to be very weak. Baker advised me to steep white oak bark in water, and take it to check its operation. But I declined, considering that my constitution was throwing off the effects of the measles, boils, etc. as was intended by Doctr. Fay which I really effected, and I never enjoyed better health in my life. We proceeded to Shelburn and stopped at Acres Point, being wind-bound, when Baker and I. Vanornom set out through the woods to see the lands and find New Huntington corner, which Baker had seen when in pursuit of Cockburn; and to see if they could discover any signs of N. York surveyors in the woods. We were to meet at the falls of Onion river as soon as the wind would admit. The other men with me went on with the boat to said falls. On landing, I found a camp with some provision, etc. that induced me to suppose that a New York surveyor was in the woods. I carefully left the camp, leaving no signs of our having been there, and went down the river about two miles to a large intervale, and there formed a camp. I left a sentinel to look out for Baker at the falls, and so see who might come to the camp. My sentinels not being old soldiers, were inattentive, and Baker passed them; and, not finding me, or any signs of my being there, was very hungry and ate some of said stores. After we met, we continued a sentinel and waited some days for the party to come in. When they arrived, Capt. Stevens the Surveyor discovered that somebody had been there, and before we could attack the camp, and made his escape with most of his party, leaving two men in the camp, which we made prisoners of. Not being able to learn certainly where Stevens was gone, we waited till near dark; when we took Stevens' boat, stores, and prisoners, and set out for our camp. In the twilight two boats were discovered coming towards us, who turned and made off faster than we could pursue; nor could we discover their number, etc. We hurried them by our stores, etc. which we had taken the precaution in some measure to secrete. It was then agreed to remain there for the night and keep a lookout. In the morning before sunrise we discovered two boats coming up the river towards us, which proved to be two bark canoes, four of his men and ten Indians, all well armed with guns, etc. and our whole party was seven men. Capt. Baker had a cutlass, I. Vanormon a gun and I a case of pistols. These were all the arms we had; nevertheless, we determined to defend the ground. I prepared our men with axes, clubs, etc. and arranged ourselves on the bank about two rods from the water, tying our prisoners to a pole behind. Stevens was the first man out of the canoes, and while the rest were getting out, he came up the bank with a hatchet in his hand, with large pistols pocket, and made towards Baker, brandishing his hatchet. Baker opened his brest [sic], inviting to strike, if he dared. Stevens demanded why his men were tied. Baker answered it was his pleasure. Stevens drew a scalping knife from his bosom, and turned towards them, (not daring to attempt to strike Baker, as Vanornam's gun was pointed on him). When about 30 feet of me, I presented a pistol at him, with a solemn word that death was his portion instantly if he stepped one step farther, or attempted to touch the pistols in his pocket. At this, he stopped with a pale countenance, & by this time his party appeared prepared to come up the bank; when I spoke to Vanornam, who had been a prisoner with the Indians to tell the redmen in their own language, that they and we were brothers, that they were welcome to hunt, etc. on our lands when they pleased, that this was a land quarrel, that did not concern them. Vanornam spoke to them in their own language to that effect, and they instantly leaped to their canoes, leaving Stevens and his men prisoners. Stevens then asked me whether I should have fired if he had not stopped. I told him I should for I (had) no notion of being a prisoner & tryed by the Supreme Court of New York by the acts of outlawry etc. Then pointing the same pistol to a small mark, less than a dollar, in a pole, about the same distance as Stevens was from me, observing that I would suppose that pole to be his body and the mark his heart, I fired. The ball (by chance) struck the pole about half an inch under the mark. There being a truce between Govr. Tryon and the people of the district of the New Hampshire Grants, we thought it would not be polite to inflict corporial punishment on Stevens. He and his men were dismissed, on pain of death never to come within the district of the New Hampshire Grants again. Their boat, stores, etc. were also returned to them and we parted.

While waiting for the surveying party to come out of the woods I explored the intervales below the falls of said Onion river, and pitched my tent by a large pitch pine tree nearly opposite to an island, about one and a half miles below the falls, where I had observed large intervales on both sides of the river, when I first went up, and landed for the first time I ever set my foot on the fertile soil of Onion river, at the lower end of the meadow now known by the name of the old fields, where I discovered from my boat an opening like cleared lands. In consequence I directed my men to refresh themselves with spirits and water, while I went to view the lands. I went up the open meadow where the blue joint grass etc. was thick till in sight of a large and lonely elm. Computing the open field about fifty acres, I was much pleased with this excursion, promising myself one day to be the owner of that beautiful meadow. I observed that the intervale continued on both sides of the river to the pine aforesaid, which was the reason of my coming from the falls down to said pine to wait the return of Baker and Vanornam, as also the surveying party, as before described. After Baker joined me I took some men with me and laid

out lots No. 1 and 2, including the ground we were encamped on,
and began a small improvement, declaring to the party that I
would make a farm for myself there—I, then crossed the river and
laid out lots No. 1 and 2, promising them to Isaac Vanornam.
(Afterwards the Onion river company gave one of said lots to
Vanornam, and sold him the other for fifteen pounds.) While
making the first corner of said lots, John Whiston by accident
struck an axe into his shin up and down to lay the bone bare for
two inches. This appeared to me as a great misfortune considering
that we had to get our stores near 20 miles up the river over falls,
etc. and then go six miles back from the river to survey Mansfield.
Whiston was carried in canoes, except hobling as well as he could
past falls, to the mouth of the brook on which Capt. Holembeck
has since erected mills, which by Capt. Hubel's survey was within
Bolton. There we erected a tent. Whiston's leg was swollen and
red, and painful. We applied several poltices made of the bark of
bass wood roots, male elm, spikenar and old beech leaves which,
in the course of one night, abated the swelling, pain, etc. Baker
then found some balsam of fir, which, on lint, we applied to the
bottom of the wound, and by repeated dressings, in the course of
six days, he was able to walk to Mansfield and pursue business.
Baker and the party made themselves some sport at my laying out
said lots for Vanornam and myself so far in a wilderness, and in
which town I did not own one foot of lands.

Thomas Rowley (1721-1796)

Addressed to a Clergyman

By our pastor perplext,
      How shall we determine?
"Watch and pray," says the text;
      "Go to sleep," says the sermon.

When Caesar Reigned King at Rome

When Cæsar reigned King at Rome
St. Paul was sent to hear his doom;
But Roman laws in a criminal case
Must have the accuser face to face,
Or Cæsar gives a flat denial.
But here's a law, made now of late,
Which destines men to awful fate,
And hangs and damns without a trial;—
Which makes me view all nature through
To find a law, where men were tied
By legal act, which doth exact
Men's lives before they're tried:
Then down I took the sacred book,
And turned the pages o'er,
But could not find one of this kind,
By God or man before.

The Rutland Song

"An Invitation to the poor Tenants that live under the Pateroons in the province of New York, to come and settle on our good lands, under the New Hampshire Grants: Composed at the time when the Land Jobbers of New York served their writs of ejectment on a number of our settlers, the execution of which we opposed by force, until we could have the matter fairly laid before the King and Board of Trade and Plantations, for their direction."

1

Come all ye laboring hands
   That toil below,
Amid the rocks and sands
   That plow and sow,
Come quit your hired lands,
   Let out by cruel hands,
'Twill free you from your bands—
   To Rutland go.

2

Your pateroons forsake,
   Whose greatest care
Is slaves of you to make,
   While you live there;
Come quit their barren lands
And leave them on their hands,
'Twill make you great amends;—
   To Rutland go.

3

For who would be a slave,
   That may be free?
Here you good land may have,

But come and see.
The soil is deep and good,
Here in this pleasant wood,
Where you may raise your food
    And happy be.

4

West of the Mountain Green
    Lies Rutland fair,
The best that e'er was seen
    For soil and air.
Kind zephyr's pleasant breeze
Whispers among the trees,
Where men may live at ease,
    With prudent care.

5

Here cows give milk to eat,
    By nature fed;
Our fields afford good wheat,
    And corn for bread.
Here sugar trees they stand
Which sweeten all our land,
We have them at our hand,
    Be not afraid.

6

Here stands the lofty pine
    And makes a show;
As strait as Gunter's line
    Their bodies grow.
Their lofty heads they rear
Amid the atmosphere
Where the wing'd tribes repair,
    And sweetly sing.

7

The butternut and beach,
   And the elm tree,
They strive their heads to reach
   As high as they;
And falling much below,
They make an even show,—
The pines more lofty grow
   And crown the woods.

8

Here glides a pleasant stream,
   Which doth not fail
To spread as rich as cream
   O'er the intervale;
As rich as Eden's soil,
Before that sin did spoil,
Or man was doom'd to toil
   To get his bread.

9

Here little salmon glide,
   So neat and fine,
Where you may be supplied
   With hook and line;
They are so fine a fish
To cook a dainty dish,
As good as one could wish
   To feed upon.

10

Here's roots of every kind,
   The healing anodyne
And rich costives:

The balsam of the tree
Supplies our surgery;
No safer can we be
    In any land.

11

We value not New York
    With all their powers,
For here we'll stay and work,
    The land is our's.
And as for great Duane
With all his wicked train;
They may eject again;
    We'll not resign.

12

This is that noble land
    By conquest won,
Took from a savage band
    With sword and gun;
We drove them to the west,
They could not stand the test;
And from the Gallic pest
    The land is free.

Ethan Allen (1738-1789)

The Capture of Fort Ticonderoga

Ever since I arrived to a state of manhood, and acquainted myself with the general history of mankind, I have felt a sincere passion for liberty. The history of nations doomed to perpetual slavery, in consequence of yielding up to tyrants their natural born liberties, I read with a sort of philosophical horror; so that the first systematical and bloody attempt at Lexington, to enslave America, thoroughly electrified my mind, and fully determined me to take part with my country: And while I was wishing for an opportunity to signalize myself in its behalf, directions were privately sent to me from the then colony (now state) of Connecticut, to raise the Green Mountain Boys; (and if possible) with them to surprise and take the fortress Ticonderoga. This enterprise I cheerfully undertook; and, after first guarding all the several passes that led thither, to cut off all intelligence between the garrison and the country, made a forced march from Bennington, and arrived at the lake opposite to Ticonderoga, on the evening of the ninth day of May, 1775, with two hundred and thirty valiant Green Mountain Boys; and it was with the utmost difficulty that I procured boats to cross the lake: However, I landed eighty-three men near the garrison, and sent the boats back for the rear guard commanded by col. Seth Warner; but the day began to dawn, and I found myself under a necessity to attack the fort, before the rear could cross the lake; and, as it was viewed hazardous, I harangued the officers and soldiers in the manner following; "Friends and fellow soldiers, you have, for a number of years past, been a scourge and terror to arbitrary power. Your valour has been famed abroad, and acknowledged, as appears by the advice and orders to me (from the general assembly of Connecticut) to surprise and take the garrison now before us. I now propose to advance before you, and in person conduct you through the wicket-gate; for we must this morning either quit our pretensions to valour, or possess ourselves of this fortress in a few minutes; and, in as much as it is a desperate attempt, (which none but the bravest of men dare undertake) I do not urge it on any contrary to his will. You that will undertake voluntarily, poise your fire-locks."

The men being (at this time) drawn up in three ranks, each poised his firelock. I ordered them to face to the right; and, at the head of the centre-file, marched them immediately to the wicket-gate aforesaid, where I found a centry posted, who instantly snapped his fusee at me; I ran immediately toward him, and he retreated through the covered way into the parade within the garrison, gave a halloo, and ran under a bomb-proof. My party who followed me into the fort, I formed on the parade in such a manner as to face the two barracks which faced each other. The garrison being asleep, (except the centries) we gave three huzzas which greatly surprised them. One of the centries made a pass at one of my officers with a charged bayonet, and slightly wounded him: My first thought was to kill him with my sword; but, in an instant, altered the design and fury of the blow to a slight cut on the side of the head; upon which he dropped his gun, and asked quarter, which I readily granted him, and demanded of him the place where the commanding officer kept; he shewed me a pair of stairs in the front of a barrack, on the west part of the garrison, which led up to a second story in said barrack, to which I immediately repaired, and ordered the commander (capt. Delaplace) to come forth instantly, or I would sacrifice the whole garrison; at which the capt. came immediately to the door with his breeches in his hand, when I ordered him to deliver to me the fort instantly, who asked me by what authority I demanded it; I answered, "In the name of the great Jehovah, and the Continental Congress." (The authority of the Congress being very little known at that time) he began to speak again; but I interrupted him, and with my drawn sword over his head, again demanded an immediate surrender of the garrison; to which he then complied, and ordered his men to be forthwith paraded without arms, as he had given up the garrison; in the mean time some of my officers had given orders, and in consequence thereof, sundry of the barrack doors were beat down, and about one third of the garrison imprisoned, which consisted of the said commander, a lieut. Feltham, a conductor of artillery, a gunner, two serjeants, and forty four rank and file; about one hundred pieces of cannon, one 13 inch mortar, and a number of swivels. This surprise was carried into execution in the gray of the morning of the 10th day of May, 1775. The sun seemed to rise that morning with a superior lustre; and Ticonderoga and its dependencies smiled on its conquerors, who tossed about the flowing bowl, and wished success to Congress, and the liberty and freedom of America. Happy it was for me (at that time) that the then future pages of the book of fate, which afterwards unfolded a miserable scene of two years and eight months imprisonment, was hid from my view: But to return to my narration; col. Warner, with the rear guard crossed the lake, and joined me early in the morning, whom I sent off, without loss of time, with about one hundred men, to take possession of Crown Point, which was garrisoned with a serjeant and twelve men; which he took possession of the same day, as also upwards of one hundred pieces of cannon.

Royall Tyler (1757-1826)

The Death Song of Alknomook

I

The sun sets in night, and the stars shun the day;
But glory remains when their lights fade away!
Begin, ye tormentors! your threats are in vain,
For the son of Alknomook shall never complain.

II

Remember the arrows he shot from his bow;
Remember your chiefs by his hatchet laid low:
Why so slow?—do you wait till I shrink from the pain?
No—the son of Alknomook will never complain.

III

Remember the wood where in ambush we lay;
And the scalps which we bore from your nation away:
Now the flame rises fast, you exult in my pain;
But the son of Alknomook can never complain.

IV

I go to the land where my father is gone;
His ghost shall rejoice in the fame of his son:
Death comes like a friend, he relieves me from pain;
And thy son, Oh Alknomook! has scorn'd to complain.

Anacreontic to Flip

Stingo! to thy bar-room skip,
Make a foaming mug of Flip;
Make it our country's staple,
Rum New England, Sugar Maple,
Beer, that's brewed from hops and Pumpkin,
Grateful to the thirsty Bumkin.
Hark! I hear thy poker fizzle,
And o'er the mug the liquor drizzle;
All against the earthen mug,
I hear the horn-spoon's cheerful dub;
I see thee, STINGO, take the Flip,
And sling thy cud from under lip,
Then pour more rum, and, bottle stopping,
Stir it again, and swear 'tis topping.
   Come quickly bring the humming liquor,
Richer than ale of British vicar;
Better than usquebaugh Hibernian,
Or than Flaccus' famed Falernian;
More potent, healthy, racy, frisky,
Than Holland's gin, or Georgia whisky.
Come, make a ring around the fire,
And hand the mug unto the Squire;
Here, Deacon, take the elbow chair,
And Ensign, Holiday, sit there:
You take the dye-tub, you the churn,
And I'll the double corner turn.
   See the mantling liquor rise!
And burn their cheeks, and close their eyes,
See the sideling mug incline—
Hear them curse their dull divine,
Who, on Sunday, dared to rail,
At *Brewster's* flip, or *Downer's* ale.
—Quick, Stingo, fly and bring another,
The Deacon here shall pay for t'other,

Ensign and I the third will share,
It's due on swop, for pie-bald mare.

Ode Composed for the Fourth of July

Calculated for the meridian of some
country towns in Massachusetts, and Rye
in Newhampshire

Squeak the fife, and beat the drum,
INDEPENDENCE DAY has come!!
Let the roasting pig be bled.
Quick twist off the cockerel's head,
Quickly rub the pewter platter,
Heap the nutcakes fried in butter.
Set the cups and beaker glass,
The pumpkin and the apple sauce,
Send the keg to shop for brandy;
Maple sugar we have handy,
Independent, staggering Dick,
A noggin mix of *swinging thick,*
Sal, put on your ruffel skirt,
Jotham, get your *boughten* shirt,
To day we dance to tiddle diddle.
—Here comes Sambo with his fiddle;
Sambo, take a dram of whiskey,
And play up Yankee Doodle frisky.
Moll, come leave your witched tricks,
And let us have a reel of six.
Father and Mother shall make two,
Sal, Moll and I stand all a row,
Sambo, play and dance with quality;
This is the day of blest Equality.
Father and *Mother* are but men,
And Sambo—is a Citizen,

Come foot it, Sal—Moll, figure in,
And, mother, you dance up to him;
Now saw as fast as e'er you can do,
And Father, you cross o'er to Sambo.
—Thus we dance, and thus we play,
On glorious *Independent Day*—
Rub more rosin on your bow,
And let us have another go.
Zounds, as sure as eggs and bacon,
Here's ensign Sneak and uncle Deacon,
Aunt Thiah, and their Bets behind her
On blundering mare, than beetle blinder.
And there's the 'Squire too with his lady—
Sal, hold the beast, I'll take the baby.
Moll, bring the 'Squire our great arm chair,
Good folks, we're glad to see you here.
Jotham, get the great case bottle,
Your teeth can pull its corn cob stopple.
Ensign,—Deacon never mind;
'Squire, drink until your blind;
Come, here's the French—and Guillotine,
And here is good 'Squire Gallatin,
And here's each noisy Jacobin.
Here's friend Madison so hearty,
And here's confusion to the treaty.
Come, one more swig to southern Demos
Who represent our brother negroes.
Thus we drink and dance away,
This glorious INDEPENDENT DAY!

Lines on Brattleboro

There is a wild sweet valley, hid among the mountains blue,
And fairer, brighter vales methinks are "far between and few."

'Tis cradled in the granite arms, and 'neath the Sky serene
Of all New England's lovely spots, the loveliest, I ween.

When morning looks with dewy gaze from o'er Monadnock's crest
On foliage, flowers, and fields beneath, and hills pil'd in the west,
And gleams on Whetstone's silver brook, now lost, now seen again,
Soft murmuring as it winds adown this wild green Mountain glen,

Or when Eve's stellar lamps burn bright in heaven's star-flowered
   field
O'er Hill and Tree and River dark at the base of Chesterfield,
Oh! then is wrapt in beauty rare, the sylvan mountain scene
The spot of all the Pilgrims' land, where Beauty's home hath been.

Oh! if fond nature ever wakes the spirit's thrill of bliss,
And stirs within the heart, a thought of gushing happiness,
'Tis when she groups with wayward hand the woodland hill and
   dale
A scene so true, yet romance like, as Brattleboro Vale.

Old Simon

A SONG

Tune—in a Mouldering Cave

In his crazy arm chair, on the downhill of life,
   Old Simon, sat calm and resign'd;
He had outliv'd his friends, he had buried his wife,
   Old Simon was lame, deaf and blind.

But the Being of Love! who still tempers the blast
   With devotion had sweet'ned his mind;
Her gay smiles, o'er his wrinkles, contentment had cast,
   And cheer'd him tho' lame, deaf and blind.

His misfortunes, his woes, could you hear him relate;
   Insisting, they all were design'd

To reclaim him from ill, *or some bliss* to create,
   You'd long to be lame, deaf and blind.

When I learn, says Old Simon, that topics of State,
   Inflame each political chief;
That they back-bite, snarl, slander, in noisy debate;
   Old Simon's content to be deaf.

When Fashion, that tempter, than the serpent more sly,
   To folly, Eve's daughters inclin'd;
When with scarce a fig-leaf, they obtrude on the eye;
   Old Simon's content to be blind.

When battles' fell trumpets so frequently sound
   And blood marks our annals with shame,
When *abroad,* war and murder, are raging around;
   At *home,* I'm content to be lame.

Thus, this worthy old man, by contentment and pray'r,
   To the ills of his life was resign'd;
And in death, he exclaim'd, as he sunk in his chair,
   What bliss, to the lame, deaf and blind.

With chaplets of joy in regions above,
   His temples the angles entwin'd,
Old Simon *there* blesses the Being of Love,
   Who *here* made him lame, deaf and blind.

Ode to the Hummingbird

Thou insect bird! thou plumed bee!
The muse attunes her lay to thee,
Of all that spread the tiny wing,
And float upon the gales of spring,
None boast so fine a form as thine,
No flower has hues that can out-shine
The crimson down thy neck that rings,

The verdant gold that tints thy wings;
To leave the leaf by zephyr borne,
And rove the roscid meads at morn,
Or down the garden's alleys wing,
And seem the fairy power of spring,
That views her buds with anxious care
And fans them with her softest air.
Such is the life decreed to thee,
So blissful do thy moments flee;
And when thy darling flowers at last
Fade and die by winter's blast,
Thou fliest where happy instinct leads,
And sport'st with spring on other meads.

November

Come old November, since again
We meet upon a withered plain,
Give me thy hand—I'll not repine,
Perhaps thy influence is divine.

Yet such thy rude and wild career,
Such are thy ruins of the year:
I'd almost stoop and bless the hour,
To see the[e] robbed of so much power.

A few days past the fields were green,
And every beauty might be seen;
The flower and vine ambitious vied,
In charms of youth and summer's pride:
The woods and fields were gaily dressed,
And musick soothed the mind to rest.

But now, alas! the scene is changed,
And nature almost seems deranged.
In throwing round thy frosty spear,

The vine and leaves, the grass and ear;
The woods, and plains, and village green,
Reflect a dull and blighted sheen.

Thus early summer's blossoms fade—
Thus the bower, and thus the shade—
The songsters of the woods are still,
No longer echo to the rill—
And such is man—his prime today,
To-morrow sees him swept away.

Stanzas To ****

Touch not again—touch not again thy lyre!
        Forbear that melting strain!
It will awake to life my bosom's fire,
        My heart will feel again;—
    That heart which once, with gentle flow,
    Felt all the joys that love could know.

Enchanting thought, and joy and love were there,
        And Hope's delightful dreams:
But Hope was false—and cankering despair
        Dissolv'd each pleasing theme;
    What then my tortur'd breast befel,
    Forbear, O MEMORY, to tell.

Touch not again thy lyre—my heart's to passion dead,
        Nor fires my lukewarm mind;
Its tort'ring pangs, its pleasures long have fled,
        And left a dream behind;
    Alike reliev'd from joy and pain,
    Reason again resumes her reign.

Touch not again—touch not again thy lyre!
        Forbear that hallow'd strain!

Again forbear to wake my bosom's fire,
    O wound it not again!
  For he, whose spring-like years are o'er
  Can listen to its strains no more.

The Contrast

The Contrast *is concerned with the comparison between native American honesty and good sense and the affected foreign manners so fashionable in society after the Revolutionary War. Engaged to marry the foppish Billy Dimple, Maria Van Rough realizes that she really loves the noble Colonel Manly. Meanwhile Dimple secretly courts two of Maria's friends. The subplot revolves around Manly's servant Jonathan, a Yankee rustic of little sophistication but much shrewdness, and Jessamy, who is, like his master, witty and devious. Jessamy hopes to win the affections of the maid Jenny. In the scene that follows, Jessamy deliberately gives Jonathan bad advice on how to court the girl, hoping that the Yankee will make a fool of himself.*

ACT II, SCENE II. *The Mall*

Enter Jessamy

Jessamy. Positively this Mall is a very pretty place. I hope the cits won't ruin it by repairs. To be sure, it won't do to speak of in the same day with Ranelegh or Vauxhall; however, it's a fine place for a young fellow to display his person to advantage. Indeed, nothing is lost here; the girls have taste, and I am very happy to find they have adopted the elegant London fashion of looking back, after a genteel fellow like me has passed them.—Ah! who comes here? This, by his awkwardness, must be the Yankee colonel's servant. I'll accost him.

Enter Jonathan

Votre très-humble serviteur, Monsieur. I understand Colonel Manly, the Yankee officer, has the honour of your services.

Jonathan. Sir!——

Jessamy. I say, Sir, I understand that Colonel Manly has the honour of having you for a servant.

Jonathan. Servant! Sir, do you take me for a neger,—I am Colonel Manly's waiter.

Jessamy. A true Yankee distinction, egad, without a difference. Why, Sir, do you not perform all the offices of a servant? do you not even blacken his boots?

Jonathan. Yes; I do grease them a bit sometimes; but I am a true blue son of liberty, for all that. Father said I should come as Colonel Manly's waiter, to see the world, and all that; but no man shall master me. My father has as good a farm as the colonel.

Jessamy. Well, Sir, we will not quarrel about terms upon the eve of an acquaintance from which I promise myself so much satisfaction;—therefore, sans ceremonie——

Jonathan. What?——

Jessamy. I say I am extremely happy to see Colonel Manly's waiter.

Jonathan. Well, and I vow, too, I am pretty considerably glad to see; but what the dogs need of all this outlandish lingo? Who may you be, Sir, if I may be so bold?

Jessamy. I have the honour to be Mr. Dimple's servant, or, if you please, waiter. We lodge under the same roof, and should be glad of the honour of your acquaintance.

Jonathan. You a waiter! by the living jingo, you look so topping, I took you for one of the agents to Congress.

Jessamy. The brute has discernment, notwithstanding his appearance.—Give me leave to say I wonder then at your familiarity.

Jonathan. Why, as to the matter of that, Mr. ——; pray, what's your name?

Jessamy. Jessamy, at your service.

Jonathan. Why, I swear we don't make any great matter of distinction in our state between quality and other folks.

Jessamy. This is, indeed, a levelling principle.—I hope, Mr. Jonathan, you have not taken part with the insurgents.

Jonathan. Why, since General Shays has sneaked off and given us the bag to hold, I don't care to give my opinion; but you'll promise not to tell—put your ear this way—you won't tell?—I vow I did think the sturgeons were right.

Jessamy. I thought, Mr. Jonathan, you Massachusetts men always argued with a gun in your hand. Why didn't you join them?

Jonathan. Why, the colonel is one of those folks called the Shin —Shin—dang it all, I can't speak them lignum vitæ words—you know who I mean—there is a company of them—they wear a china goose at their button-hole—a kind of gilt thing.—Now the colonel told father and brother,—you must know there are, let me see—there is Elnathan, Silas, and Barnabas, Tabitha—no, no, she's a she—tarnation, now I have it—there's Elnathan, Silas, Barnabas, Jonathan, that's I—seven of us, six went into the wars, and I staid at home to take care of mother. Colonel said that it was a burning shame for the true blue Bunker Hill sons of liberty, who had fought Governor Hutchinson, Lord North, and the Devil, to have any hand in kicking up a cursed dust against a government which we had, every mother's son of us, a hand in making.

Jessamy. Bravo!—Well, have you been abroad in the city since your arrival? What have you seen that is curious and entertaining?

Jonathan. Oh! I have seen a power of fine sights. I went to see two marble-stone men and a leaden horse that stands out in doors in all weathers; and when I came where they was, one had got no head, and t'other wern't there. They said as how the leaden man was a damn'd tory, and that he took wit in his anger and rode off in the time of the troubles.

Jessamy. But this was not the end of your excursion?

Jonathan. Oh, no; I went to a place they call Holy Ground. Now I counted this was a place where folks go to meeting; so I put my hymn-book in my pocket, and walked softly and grave as a minister; and when I came there, the dogs a bit of a meeting-house could I see. At last I spied a young gentle-woman standing by one of the seats which they have here at the doors. I took her

to be the deacon's daughter, and she looked so kind, and so oblig-
ing, that I thought I would go and ask her the way to lecture, and
—would you think it?—she called me dear, and sweeting, and
honey, just as if we were married: by the living jingo, I had a
month's mind to buss her.

Jessamy. Well, but how did it end?

Jonathan. Why, as I was standing talking with her, a parcel of
sailor men and boys got round me, the snarl-headed curs fell
a-kicking and cursing of me at such a tarnal rate, that I vow I was
glad to take to my heels and split home, right off, tail on end, like
a stream of chalk.

Jessamy. Why, my dear friend, you are not acquainted with the
city; that girl you saw was a———

[*Whispers.*]

Jonathan. Mercy on my soul! was that young woman a harlot!
—Well! if this is New-York Holy Ground, what must the Holy-
day Ground be!

Jessamy. Well, you should not judge of the city too rashly. We
have a number of elegant, fine girls here that make a man's leisure
hours pass very agreeably. I would esteem it an honour to announce you to some of them.—Gad! that announce is a select
word; I wonder where I picked it up.

Jonathan. I don't want to know them.

Jessamy. Come, come, my dear friend, I see that I must assume
the honour of being the director of your amusements. Nature has
given us passions, and youth and opportunity stimulate to gratify
them. It is no shame, my dear Blueskin, for a man to amuse himself with a little gallantry.

Jonathan. Girl huntry! I don't altogether understand. I never
played at that game. I know how to play hunt the squirrel, but I
can't play anything with the girls; I am as good as married.

Jessamy. Vulgar, horrid brute! Married, and above a hundred
miles from his wife, and thinks that an objection to his making
love to every woman he meets! He never can have read, no, he
never can have been in a room with a volume of the divine Chesterfield.—So you are married?

Jonathan. No, I don't say so; I said I was as good as married, a kind of promise.

Jessamy. As good as married!——

Jonathan. Why, yes; there's Tabitha Wymen, the deacon's daughter, at home; she and I have been courting a great while, and folks say as how we are to be married; and so I broke a piece of money with her when we parted, and she promised not to spark it with Solomon Dyer while I am gone. You wou'dn't have me false to my true-love, would you?

Jessamy. May be you have another reason for constancy; possibly the young lady has a fortune? Ha! Mr. Jonathan, the solid charms: the chains of love are never so binding as when the links are made of gold.

Jonathan. Why, as to fortune, I must needs say her father is pretty dumb rich; he went representative for our town last year. He will give her—let me see—four times seven is—seven times four,—nought and carry one,—he will give her twenty acres of land—somewhat rocky though—a Bible, and a cow.

Jessamy. Twenty acres of rock, a Bible, and a cow! Why, my dear Mr. Jonathan, we have servant-maids, or, as you would more elegantly express it, waitresses, in this city, who collect more in one year from their mistresses' cast clothes.

Jonathan. You don't say so!——

Jessamy. Yes, and I'll introduce you to one of them. There is a little lump of flesh and delicacy that lives at next door, waitress to Miss Maria; we often see her on the stoop.

Jonathan. But are you sure she would be courted by me?

Jessamy. Never doubt it; remember a faint heart never—blisters on my tongue—I was going to be guilty of a vile proverb; flat against the authority of Chesterfield. I say there can be no doubt that the brilliancy of your merit will secure you a favourable reception.

Jonathan. Well, but what must I say to her?

Jessamy. Say to her! why, my dear friend, though I admire your profound knowledge on every other subject, yet, you will pardon my saying that your want of opportunity has made the female heart escape the poignancy of your penetration. Say to her! Why,

when a man goes a-courting, and hopes for success, he must begin
with doing, and not saying.

Jonathan. Well, what must I do?

Jessamy. Why, when you are introduced you must make five or
six elegant bows.

Jonathan. Six elegant bows! I understand that; six, you say?
Well——

Jessamy. Then you must press and kiss her hand; then press and
kiss, and so on to her lips and cheeks; then talk as much as you
can about hearts, darts, flames, nectar and ambrosia—the more in-
coherent the better.

Jonathan. Well, but suppose she should be angry with I?

Jessamy. Why, if she should pretend—please to observe, Mr.
Jonathan—if she should pretend to be offended, you must ——
But I'll tell you how my master acted in such a case: He was seated
by a young lady of eighteen upon a sofa, plucking with a wanton
hand the blooming sweets of youth and beauty. When the lady
thought it necessary to check his ardour, she called up a frown
upon her lovely face, so irresistibly alluring, that it would have
warmed the frozen bosom of age; remember, said she, putting her
delicate arm upon his, remember your character and my honour.
My master instantly dropped upon his knees, with eyes swimming
with love, cheeks glowing with desire, and in the gentlest modula-
tion of voice he said: My dear Caroline, in a few months our hands
will be indissolubly united at the altar; our hearts I feel are already
so; the favours you now grant as evidence of your affection are
favours indeed; yet, when the ceremony is once past, what will
now be received with rapture will then be attributed to duty.

Jonathan. Well, and what was the consequence?

Jessamy. The consequence!—Ah! forgive me, my dear friend,
but you New England gentlemen have such a laudable curiosity of
seeing the bottom of everything;—why, to be honest, I confess
I saw the blooming cherub of a consequence smiling in its angelic
mother's arms, about ten months afterwards.

Jonathan. Well, if I follow all your plans, make them six bows,
and all that, shall I have such little cherubim consequences?

Jessamy. Undoubtedly.—What are you musing upon?

Jonathan. You say you'll certainly make me acquainted?—Why, I was thinking then how I should contrive to pass this broken piece of silver—won't it buy a sugar-dram?

Jessamy. What is that, the love-token from the deacon's daughter?—You come on bravely. But I must hasten to my master. Adieu, my dear friend.

Jonathan. Stay, Mr. Jessamy—must I buss her when I am introduced to her?

Jessamy. I told you, you must kiss her.

Jonathan. Well, but must I buss her?

Jessamy. Why kiss and buss, and buss and kiss, is all one.

Jonathan. Oh! my dear friend, though you have a profound knowledge of all, a pugnency of tribulation, you don't know everything.   [*Exit.*]

Jessamy [*alone*]. Well, certainly I improve; my master could not have insinuated himself with more address into the heart of a man he despised. Now will this blundering dog sicken Jenny with his nauseous pawings, until she flies into my arms for very ease. How sweet will the contrast be between the blundering Jonathan and the courtly and accomplished Jessamy!

Thomas Green Fessenden (1771-1837)

A New England Country Dance

How funny 't is, when pretty lads and lasses
Meet altogether, just to have a caper,
And the black fiddler plays you such a tune as
           Sets you a frisking!

High bucks and ladies, standing in a row all,
Make finer show than troops of continentals,
Balance and foot it rigadoon and chasse,
           Brimful of rapture.

Thus poets tell us how one Mister Orpheus
Led a rude forest to a country dance, and
Play'd the brisk tune of Yankee Doodle on a
           New Holland fiddle.

Spruce our gallants are, essenc'd with pomatum,
Heads powdered white as Killington-Peak snow-storm;
Ladies, how brilliant, fascinating creatures,
           All silk and muslin!

But now behold a sad reverse of fortune,
Life's brightest scenes are checkered with disaster,
Clumsy Charles Clumfoot treads on Tabby's gown, and
           Tears all the tail off!

Stop, stop the fiddler, all away this racket—
Hartshorn and water! See the ladies fainting,
Paler than primrose, fluttering about like
           Pigeons affrighted!

Not such the turmoil, when the sturdy farmer
Sees turbid whirlwinds beat his oats and rye down,

And the rude hail-stones, big as pistol-bullets,
      Dash in his windows!

Though 'twas unhappy, never seem to mind it,
Bid punch and sherry circulate the brisker;
Or, in a bumper, flowing with Madeira,
      Drown the misfortune.

Willy Wagnimble dancing with Flirtilla,
Almost as light as air-balloon inflated,
Rigadoons round her, 'till the lady's heart is
      Forc'd to surrender.

Benny Bamboozle cuts the drollest capers,
Just like a camel, or a hippopot'mus,
Jolly Jack Jumble makes as big a rout as
      Forty Dutch horses!

See Angelina lead the mazy dance down,
Never did fairy trip it so fantastick;
How my heart flutters, while my tongue pronounces,
      "Sweet little seraph."

Such are the joys that flow from country dancing,
Pure as the primal happiness of Eden,
Wine, mirth and musick kindle in accordance
      Raptures extatick.

Eulogy on the Times

Let poets scrawl satiric rhymes,
And sketch the follies of the times,
   With much caricaturing;
But I, a *bon-ton-bard,* declare
A set of slanderers they are,
   E'en past a Job's enduring.

Let crabbed cynics snarl away,
And pious parsons preach and pray

Against the vices reigning;
That mankind are so wicked grown,
Morality is scarcely known,
   And true religion waning.

Societies, who vice suppress,
May make a rumpus; ne'ertheless,
   Our's is the best of ages;
Such hum-drum folks our *fathers* were,
They could no more with *us* compare,
   Than *Hottentots* with *sages.*

It puts the poet in a pet
To think of THEM, *a vulgar set;*
   But WE, thank G—d, are QUALITY!
For we have found this eighteenth century
What ne'er was known before, I'll venture ye,
   Religion's no reality!

Tom Paine, and Godwin, both can tell
That there is no such thing as hell!
   A doctrine mighty pleasant;
Your old-wives tales of a *hereafter*
Are things for ridicule and laughter,
   While we enjoy the *present.*

We've nought to do, but frisk about,
At midnight ball, and Sunday rout,
   And Bacchanalian revel;
To gamble, drink, and live at ease,
Our great and noble selves to please,
   Nor care for man, nor devil.

In these *good times,* with little pains,
And scarce a penny-worth of brains,
   A man with great propriety,
With some small risk of being hung,
May cut a pretty dash among
   The foremost in society.

Good reader, I'll suppose, for once,
Thou art no better than a dunce,
 But wishest to be famous;
I'll tell thee how, with decent luck,
Thou may'st become as great a buck
 As any one could name us.

When first in high life you commence,
To virtue, reason, common sense,
 You'll please to bid adieu, sir;
And, lest some brother rake be higher,
Drink, till your blood be all on fire,
 And face of crimson hue, sir.

Thus you'll be dubb'd a *dashing blade,*
And, by the genteel world be said,
 To be a *man of spirit;*
For *stylish folks* despise the chaps,
Who think that they may rise, perhaps,
 By industry and merit.

With lubric arts, and wily tongue,
Debauch some maiden, fair and young,
 For that will be genteel;
Be not too scrupulous; win the fair;
Then leave the frail one to despair:
 A rake should never feel.

When wine has made your courage stout,
In midnight revel sally out,
 Insulting all you meet;
Play pretty pranks about the town,
Break windows, knock the watchmen down,
 Your frolic to complete!

Besides exhibiting your parts,
You're sure to win the ladies' hearts
 By dint of dissipation;
Since "every woman is a rake,"

A fool may know what steps to take
  To gain her approbation.

By practising these famous rules,
You'll gain from *wicked* men and *fools*
  A world of admiration:
And, as we know from good authority,
Such folks compose a clear majority,
  There needs no hesitation.

Tabitha Towzer

Miss Tabitha Towzer is fair,
  No guinea-pig ever was neater,
Like a hakmatak slender and spare.
  And sweet as a musk-squash, or sweeter.

Miss Tabitha Towzer is sleek,
  When dress'd in her pretty new tucker,
Like an otter that paddles the creek,
  In quest of a mud-pout, or sucker.

Her forehead is smooth as a tray,
  Ah! smoother than that, on my soul,
And turn'd, as a body may say,
  Like a delicate neat wooden-bowl.

To what shall I liken her hair,
  As straight as a carpenter's line,
For similes sure must be rare,
  When we speak of a nymph so divine.

Not the head of Nazarite seer,
  That never was shaven or shorn,
Nought equals the locks of my dear
  But the silk of an ear of green corn.

My dear has a beautiful nose,
  With a sled-runner crook in the middle,
Which one would be led to suppose
  Was meant for the head of a fiddle.

Miss Tabby has two pretty eyes,
  Glass buttons shone never so bright,
Their love-lighted lustre outvies
  The lightning-bug's twinkle by night.

And oft with a magical glance,
  She makes in my bosom a pother,
When leering politely askance,
  She shuts one, and winks with the other.

The lips of my charmer are sweet,
  As a hogshead of maple molasses,
And the ruby red tint of her cheek,
  The gill of a salmon surpasses.

No teeth like hers ever were seen,
  Nor ever described in a novel,
Of a beautiful kind of pea-green,
  And shaped like a wooden-shod-shovel.

Her fine little ears, you would judge,
  Were wings of a bat in perfection;
A dollar I never should grudge
  To put them in Peale's grand collection.

Description must fail in her chin,
  At least till our language is richer,
Much fairer than ladle of tin,
  Or beautiful brown earthen pitcher.

So pretty a neck, I'll be bound,
  Never join'd head and body together,
Like nice crook'd neck'd squash on the ground,
  Long whiten'd by winter-like weather.

Should I set forth the rest of her charms,
    I might by some phrase that's improper,
Give modesty's bosom alarms,
    Which I would n't do for a copper.

Should I mention her gait or her air,
    You might think I intended to banter;
She moves with more grace, you would swear,
    Than a founder'd horse forced to a canter.

She sang with a beautiful voice,
    Which ravish'd you out of your senses;
A pig will make just such a noise
    When his hind-leg stuck fast in the fence is.

2

Potash, Morgan Horses, and Merino Sheep

Vermont, thy sons are more than blest,
In wealth increasing, public rest;
Thy rulers from the people's choice,
Obedient to the public voice,
Possess the pow'r, the goodness, will,
A nation's interests to fulfill.

    —"Election Ode: 1801"

Clearing the Stumps Rowland E. Robinson, courtesy of Rowland E. Robinson
Memorial Association

Zadock Thompson (1796-1856)

The Character of the Settlers and
Their Modes of Punishment

The settlers on the New Hampshire grants were a brave, hardy, but uncultivated race of men. They knew little of the etiquette of refined society, were blessed with few of the advantages of education, and were destitute of the elegancies, and in most cases of the common conveniences of life. They were sensible that they must rely upon the labor of their own hands for their daily subsistence, and for the accumulation of property. They possessed minds which were naturally strong and active, and they were aroused to the exercise of their highest energies by the difficulties, which they were compelled to encounter. The controversy in which they were engaged involved their dearest rights. On its issue depended not only their titles to their possessions, but, in many cases, their personal liberty and safety. Though unskilled in the rules of logic, their reasoning was strong and conclusive, and they possessed the courage and perseverance necessary for carrying their plans and decisions into execution.

We have already observed that, at the head of the opposition to the proceedings of New York, stood Ethan Allen, a man obviously fitted by nature for the circumstances and exigencies of the times. Bold, ardent and unyielding, he possessed an unusual degree of vigor both of body and mind, and an unlimited confidence in his own abilities. With these qualifications, the then existing state of the settlement rendered him peculiarly fitted to become a prominent and successful leader. During the progress of the controversy, Allen wrote and dispersed several pamphlets, in which he exhibited, in a manner peculiar to himself, and well suited to the state of public feeling, the injustice and cruelty of the claims and proceedings of New York. And although these pamphlets are unworthy of notice as literary productions, yet, they were at the time extensively circulated, and contributed much to inform the minds, arouse the zeal, and unite the efforts of the settlers.

The bold and unpolished roughness of Allen's writings were well suited to give a just description of the views and proceedings of a band of speculating and unprincipled landjobbers. His method of writing was likewise well adapted to the condition and feelings of the settlers, and probably exerted a greater influence over their opinions and conduct, than the same sentiments would have done clothed in the chaste style of classic elegance. Nor did it differ greatly in style, or literary merit, from the pamphlets which came from New York. But although Allen wrote with asperity and freedom, there was something generous and noble in his conduct. He refrained from every thing which had the appearance of meanness, injustice, cruelty or abuse towards those who fell into his power, and protested against the same in others.

Next to Allen, Seth Warner seems to have acted the most conspicuous part among the settlers. He, like Allen, was firm and resolute, fully determined that the decisions of New York against the settlers should never be carried into execution. But while Allen was daring and sometimes rash and imprudent, Warner was always cool, calm and comparatively cautious. After Warner was proscribed as a rioter, as related in a preceding section, an officer from New York attempted to apprehend him. He, considering it an affair of open hostility, defended himself against the officer, and in turn, attacked, wounded and disarmed him; but with the spirit and generosity of a soldier, he spared his life.

After Ethan Allen and Seth Warner, no person on the New Hampshire grants, up to the close of this period, acted a more distinguished part, or was more serviceable to the settlers, than Remember Baker. He was the pioneer in many an enterprise and was always in readiness for any emergency. Being a joiner and mill-wright by trade, he built the first mills which were erected at Arlington and Pawlet, and was preparing in connection with his cousin, Ira Allen, for the erection of mills at Winooski falls, when the war of the revolution commenced.

During the protracted controversy in which these men acted so prominent a part, there had been, up to this time, frequent attempts to arrest it and bring it to an amicable settlement. Orders from the crown had likewise been often given to New York to suspend further prosecutions and make no more grants of the lands in dispute till his Majesty's further pleasure should be known respecting them. But in despite of royal orders and the remonstrances of the settlers on the grants, New York continued to assert and to endeavor to enforce her claims, and the repeated but vain attempts at reconciliation, served only to embitter the resentment of the contending parties and produce a state of hostility more decided and alarming.

The affairs of the inhabitants of the grants appear to have been managed during this period by committees appointed in the several towns, and who met in convention as occasion required, to adopt measures for the common defence and welfare. The resolutions and decrees of these conventions were regarded as the law of the land, and their infraction was always punished with exemplary severity. The punishment most frequently inflicted was the application of the *"beech seal"* to the naked back, and banishment from the grants. This mode of punishment derived its significant name from allusion to the great seal of the province of New Hampshire, which was affixed to the charters of the townships granted by the governor of that province, of which the *beech rod* well laid upon the naked backs of the *"Yorkers,"* and their adherents, was humorously considered a confirmation.

That the reader may have a just idea of the summary manner in which the convention and committees proceeded against those who violated their decrees, we will lay before them the sentence of Benjamin Hough, as a sample. It appears that Hough, who resided in the vicinity of Clarendon and who was a violent Yorker, went to New York in the winter of 1774, for the purpose of obtaining the aid of government against the Green Mountain Boys, and that on the 9th of March, the very day of the passage of the extraordinary law of which we have already spoken in the fourth section of this chapter, he accepted the appointment of justice of the peace for the county of Charlotte, under the authority of New York. On his return he proceeded to execute his new office within the grants, in defiance of the decree of the convention which forbade it. He was repeatedly warned to desist, but being found incorrigible, he was arrested and carried before a committee of safety at Sunderland. The decree of the convention and the charges against the prisoner being read in his presence, he acknowledged that he had been active in promoting the passage of the law above mentioned and in the discharge of his duties as magistrate, but pleaded the jurisdiction of New York over the Grant, in justification of his conduct. This plea having no weight with the committee, they proceeded to pronounce upon him the following sentence viz. *"That the prisoner be taken from the bar of this committee of safety and be tied to a tree, and there, on his naked back, receive two hundred stripes; his back being dressed, he should depart out of the district, and on return, without special leave of the convention, to suffer death."* This sentence was forthwith carried into execution, with unsparing severity, in the presence of a large concourse of people. Hough asked and received the following written certificate of his punishment, signed by Allen and Warner:

"Sunderland, 30th of Jan., 1775.
This may certify the inhabitants of the New Hampshire Grants, that Benjamin Hough hath this day received a full punishment for his crimes committed heretofore against this country, and our inhabitants are ordered to give him, the said Hough, a free and unmolested passport toward the city of New York, or to the westward of our Grants, he behaving himself as becometh. Given under our hands the day and date aforesaid.

Ethan Allen,
Seth Warner."

On the delivery of the paper, Allen sarcastically observed that the certificate, *together with the receipt on his back,* would no doubt be admitted as legal evidence before the supreme court and the governor and council of New York, though the king's warrant to Governor Wentworth and his excellency's sign manual with the Great Seal of the province of New Hampshire, would not.

Hough repaired immediately to the city of New York, where he gave, under oath, a minute account of the transactions above mentioned, and this matter, together with the particulars of the transactions at Westminster on the 13th of March, was made the subject of a special message to the colonial assembly by Lieut. Gov. Colden. The Assembly, after discussing these subjects on the 30th and 31st of March, finally resolved to appropriate £1000 for the maintenance of justice and the suppression of riots in the county of Cumberland, and that a reward of £50 each be offered for apprehending James Mead, Gideon Warren and Jesse Sawyer, and also a reward of £50 each, in addition to the rewards previously offered, for the apprehension of Ethan Allen, Seth Warner, Robert Cochran, and Peleg Sunderland. These resolutions constituted the last and dying efforts of the royal government of New York against the New Hampshire Grants. The assembly was soon prorogued and never met again, being superseded by the revolutionary authority of the provincial congress.

Although the application of the beech seal was the most common punishment, others were frequently resorted to. Some of these were in their nature trifling and puerile. The following may serve as a specimen. A Dutchman of Arlington became a partisan of New York and spoke in reproachful terms of the convention and of the proceedings of the Green Mountain Boys. He advised the settlers to submit to New York, and re-purchase their lands from that government. Being requested to desist, and disregarding it, he was arrested and carried to the Green Mountain tavern in Bennington. The committee, after hearing his defence, ordered him "to be tied in an armed chair, and hoisted to the sign, (*a catamount's skin, stuffed, sitting upon the sign post twenty-five feet from the ground with large teeth, grinning towards New York,*) and there to hang two hours in sight of the people, as a punishment merited by his enmity to the rights and liberties of the inhabitants of the New Hampshire Grants." This sentence was executed to the no small merriment of a large concourse of people; and when he was let down he was dismissed by the committee with the exhortation to "go and sin no more."

Anonymous

Election Ode: 1801

Written for the Inauguration of
Isaac Tichenor as Governor

Welcome the day from which our State
Computes the era of its date;
This day a government began
Essential to the rights of man;
O may its blessings ne'er expire,
'Till time's extinct, the globe on fire.

Secure upon his well-earn'd spot,
The farmer cultivates his lot;
The city's din, and tinkling sounds,
Where gladiators walk their rounds,
And pirates launching from Algiers,
Excite in him no racking fears.

Not fifty years have roll'd away,
Since savage yells spread wide dismay;
Where now rich fields of yellow corn,
The suburbs of our towns adorn;
The maple, screen for Indian darts,
Now yields the wealth of Indies' marts.

Vermont, thy sons are more than blest,
In wealth increasing, public rest;
Thy rulers from the people's choice,
Obedient to the public voice,
Possess the pow'r, the goodness, will,

A nation's interests to fulfill.
But most in him the Chief who guides
The factious waves of pop'lar tides,
Whose patriotism none impeach,
Whose virtue no vile slanders reach,
To whom the graces long have paid
The homage of a patron's aid.

Ye mountaineers, to you are giv'n
These favors by propitious heav'n;
Let gratitude employ your themes,
By day your thoughts, by night your dreams,
Then freedom, like your mountains' scene
Shall flourish in perennial green.

Charles Gamage Eastman (1813-1860)

The First Settler

I

His hair is white as the winter snow,
His years are many, as you may know,—
   Some eighty-two or three;
Yet a hale old man, still strong and stout,
And able when 'tis fair, to go out
   His friends in the street to see;
And all who see his face still pray
That for many a long and quiet day
   He may live, by the Lord's mercy.

II

He came to the State when the town was new,
When the lordly pine and the hemlock grew
   In the place where the court-house stands;
When the stunted ash and the alder black,
The slender fir and the tamarack,
   Stood thick on the meadow lands;
And the brook, that now so feebly flows,
Covered the soil where the farmer hoes
   The corn with his hardy hands.

III

He built in the town the first log hut;
And he is the man, they say, who cut
   The first old forest oak;
His axe was the first, with its echoes rude,

To startle the ear of the solitude,
　　With its steady and rapid stroke.
From his high log-heap through the trees arose,
First, on the hills, mid the winter snows,
　　The fire and the curling smoke.

IV

On the land he cleared the first hard year,
When he trapped the beaver and shot the deer,
　　Swings the sign of the great hotel;
By the path where he drove his ox to drink
The mill-dam roars and the hammers clink,
　　And the factory rings its bell.
And where the main street comes up from the south,
Was the road he "blazed" from the river's mouth,
　　As the books of the town will tell.

V

In the village, here, where the trees are seen,
Circling round the beautiful Green,
　　He planted his hills of corn;
And there, where you see that long brick row,
Swelling with silk and calico,
　　Stood the hut he built one morn;
Old Central Street was his pasture lane,
And down by the church he will put his cane
　　On the spot where his boys were born.

VI

For many an hour I have heard him tell
Of the time, he says, he remembers well,
　　When high on the rock he stood,
And nothing met his wandering eye
Above, but the clouds and the broad blue sky,
　　And below, the waving wood;

And how, at night, the wolf would howl
Round his huge log-fire, and the panther growl,
  And the black fox bark by the road.

VII

He looks with pride on the village grown
So large on the land that he used to own;
  And still as he sees the wall
Of huge blocks built, in less than the time
It took, when he was fresh in his prime,
  To gather his crops in the fall;
He thinks, with the work that, somehow, he
Is identified, and must oversee
  And superintend it all.

VIII

His hair is white as the winter snow,
And his years are many as you may know,—
  Some eighty-two or three;
Yet all who see his face will pray,
For many a long and quiet day
  By 'the Lord's good grace, that he
May be left in the land, still hale and stout,
And able still when 'tis fair, to go out
  His friends in the street to see.

The Old Pine Tree

By my father's house, this side of the hill,
As you followed the road to the cider-mill,
      Was the "swamp," as we called it then,—
A low, wet spot, where the cat-bird mewed,
The tadpole bred, and the bullfrog *spughed,*

And the muskrat built his den;
And stealing out from his hiding hole,
Through the rotten grass, came the meadow-mole
    To peep at the works of men.

In the swamp, on a knoll, in the summer dry,
But half-covered up when the springs were high,
    A magnificent Pine had grown:
Last of a race that the State shall see,
Last of his race! that glorious tree,
    Supreme on his forest throne,
Like a man of strong and wondrous rhyme,
Towering above the rest of his time,
    Stood up in the land alone!

The swamp by the road to the cider-mill,
And the old Pine-Tree, I remember still,
    And well, you will think, I may;
For there were the boys of the village seen
When the ice was strong, or the leaves were green,
    From morn till the night at play,
Skating stones, or rolling the snow
Into cities and forts and castles, you know,
    Or chasing the frogs away.

In winter time, when the snow was deep,
Through the drifts by the old slash-fence they'd leap,
    And tumble each other in;
Then all hands hold, they would "snap the snake!"—
How the old "Red Lion" his mane would shake,
    When his prey he chanced to win!
And then, with the old Pine-Tree for a *"gool,"*
They'd play "I-spy" till 'twas time for the school
    In the afternoon to begin.

In the spring when the winter had gone to the North,
And the weeds on the knoll came peeping forth,
    And the little wild flowers between,

When the buds swelled out in the April sky,
And the farmer saw that his winter rye
    Came up on the hill-side, green,
From the three-months' school and the ferule free,
With shout and laugh, at the old Pine-Tree
    Again were the boys all seen.

And there on the grass for hours they'd lie,
Making ships and things of clouds in the sky;
    While clear in the fragrant spring,
The bobolink, on the mullein stalk,
Would rattle away like a sweet girl's talk,
    And the gay yellow birds would sing
And chirp to each other with merry call,
As, poised on the top of the milk-weed tall,
    In the wind they reel and swing.

When summer came, and the weeds were thick,
And their blood grew warlike, warm, and quick,
    The train-band company,
With a brake for a plume and a shingle sword,
The gloomy wilds of the swamp explored,
    Their trowsers rolled to the knee;
With broken bricks, and hands full of stones,
At their deadly fire how the cat-tail groans,
    And the hosts of the thistle flee!

'Fore George! what a siege we had one time
With a brave old frog who lived in the slime
    Of a lordly pool at the south!
How he'd dodge out of sight, till our hail had sped,
Then poke up again his great, green head,—
    And wink in the cannon's mouth!
The bricks round his head went thud! thud! thud!
Till the captain lisped, all covered with bl-mud,
    "We can never tear down hith houth."

There many an hour Thanksgiving Day,
When the ice was glare, the girls would stay
    And share in our glorious fun:
While the shouting boys, with cap in hand,
Would chase them off from the ice to the land,
    Till the Governor's meeting was done;
Till grace was said, the turkey carved,
The mince-pie cooled and the pudding sarved,
    And the gravy too cold to run.

They are gone, ah, me! those merry boys,
All gone from the scene of their early joys;
    Alas, that it should be so!
Some have gone to the West to shake with the *ague,*
And some to the South to die with that plague-
    Y Jack, "Yellow Jack," you know;
One's made a great spec' in Missouri lead;
And one, they say, got a broken head
    At the fall of Alamo;

And one has gone where the soft winds blow
O'er the vine-clad hills of Val d'Arno,
    With his wife, and children two,
And his cheek's regained the glow it lost
In our Northern land of snow and frost;
    One's in Kalamazoo;
And one through the drifts of the Northwest snow
Tracks the prairie wolf and the buffalo,
    With a tribe of wild Sioux.

The swamp is ditched: where the leaves used to float
A Frenchman has raised some "vary fine oat,"—
    The frogs have all hopped off;
And the little green knoll, where the boys used to play
Through the spring and the fall and the winter day,
    And the cares of manhood scoff,
Is gouged by a premium Berkshire brood,

And the old Pine-Tree by the great high-road
    Is used for a watering trough.

Song

"Bring me a cup,—a brimming cup!
    Bubbling with rosy, red wine;
For, soon as the blossoms of summer shall bud,
    Sweet Alice has sworn to be mine.
           Joy! joy!
    Sweet Alice has sworn to be mine!"

"But women are gay, and light as the air,
    As faithless as faithless can be;
And their love is as fickle and as false as the
      moon,
    The wind, or the waves of the sea!
          Drink, boy!
    But Alice will never be thine!"

"Bring me a cup,—a brimming cup!
    Laughing with rosy, red wine;
For women are true as the sun,
    And Alice has sworn to be mine!
          Joy! joy!
    And Alice has sworn to be mine!"

"A gallant I saw at her feet but now,
    I swear by this goblet of wine!
And he said, as he pressed her lip to his own,
    Sweet Alice has sworn to be *mine!*
          Drink, boy!
    But Alice will never be thine!"

"Bring me a cup,—a brimming cup!
    Laughing with rosy, red wine;

For women are true, and thou liest, I know,
    For Alice has sworn to be mine!
        Joy! joy!
      For Alice has sworn to be mine!"

"Well! since, foolish boy, thou wilt never believe,—
    Nay, drain off that cup of red wine!
Then say who that bride is that comes from the
    church!
    Is it Alice who swore to be thine?
        Drink, boy!
      But Alice will never be thine!"

"Bring me a cup,—a brimming cup!
    Sparkling with rosy, red wine:
The blossoms of summer will bud, alas!
    But Alice will never be mine.
For women are gay, and light as the air,
    And faithless as faithless can be;
And their love is as fickle and false as the moon,
    As the winds, or the waves of the sea!"

The Reaper

Bending o'er his sickle,
    Mid the yellow grain,
Lo, the sturdy reaper,
    Reaping on the plain!
Singing as the sickle
    Gathers to his hand,
Rustling in its ripeness,
    The glory of his land.

Mark the grain before him
    Swaying in the wind,

See the even gavel
   Following behind!
Bound, in armful bundles,
   Standing one by one,
Yester-morning's labor
   Ripens in the sun.

Long I've stood and pondered,
   Gazing from the hill,
While the sturdy reaper
   Sung and labored still;
Bending o'er his sickle,
   Mid the yellow grain,
Happy and contented,
   Reaping on the plain;

And as upon my journey
   I leave the maple-tree,
Thinking of the difference
   Between the man and me,
I turn again to see him
   Reaping on the plain,
And almost wish *my* labor
   Were the sickle and the grain.

John G. Saxe (1816-1887)

On an Ugly Person Sitting for a Daguerreotype

Here Nature in her glass—the wanton elf—
Sits gravely making faces at herself;
And, while she scans each clumsy feature o'er,
Repeats the blunders that she made before!

A Connubial Eclogue

> *"Arcades ambo,*
> *Et cantare pares et respondere parati."*
> Virgil

HE.
Much lately have I thought, my darling wife,
Some simple rules might make our wedded life
As pleasant always as a morn in May;
I merely name it,—what does Molly say?

SHE.
Agreed, your plan I heartily approve;
Rules would be nice,—but who shall make them, love?
Nay, do not speak!—let this the bargain be,
One shall be made by you, and one by me,
Till all are done—

HE.
　　　　—Your plan is surely fair,
In such a work 't is fitting we should share;

And now—although it matters not a pin—
If you have no objection, I'll begin.

SHE.
Proceed! In making laws I'm little versed;
And as to words, I do not mind the first;
I only claim—and hold the treasure fast—
My sex's sacred privilege, the *last!*

HE.
With all my heart. Well, dearest, to begin:—
When by our cheerful hearth our friends drop in,
And I am talking in my brilliant style
(The rest with rapture listening the while)
About the war,—or anything, in short,
That you're aware is my especial *forte,*—
Pray don't get up a circle of your own,
And talk of—bonnets, in an undertone!

SHE.
That's Number One; I'll mind it well, if you
Will do as much, my dear, by Number Two:
When we attend a party or a ball,
Don't leave your Molly standing by the wall,
The helpless victim of the dreariest bore
That ever walked upon a parlor-floor,
While you—oblivious of your spouse's doom—
Flirt with the girls,—the gayest in the room!

HE.
When I (although the busiest man alive)
Have snatched an hour to take a pleasant drive,
And say, "Remember, at precisely four
You'll find the carriage ready at the door,"
Don't keep me waiting half an hour or so,
And then declare, "The clock must be too slow!"

SHE.

When you (such things have happened now and then)
Go to the Club with, "I'll be back at ten,"
And stay till two o'clock, you need n't say,
"I really was the first to come away;
'T is very strange how swift the time has passed:
I'm sure, my dear, the clock must be too *fast!*"

HE.

There—that will do; what else remains to say
We may consider at a future day;
I'm getting sleepy—and—if you have done—

SHE.

Not I!—this making rules is precious fun;
Now here's another:—When you paint to me
"That charming woman" you are sure to see,
Don't—when you praise the virtues she has got—
Name only those you think your wife has not!
And here's a rule I hope you won't forget,
The most important I have mentioned yet,—
Pray mind it well:—Whenever you incline
To bring your queer companions home to dine,
Suppose, my dear,—Good Gracious! he's asleep!
Ah! well,—'t is lucky good advice will keep;
And he shall have it, or, upon my life,
I've not the proper spirit of a wife!

The Explanation

Charles, discoursing rather freely
    Of the unimportant part
Which (he said) our clever women
    Play in Science and in Art,

"Ah!—the sex you undervalue;"
   Cried his lovely cousin Jane.
"No, indeed!" responded Charley,
   "Pray allow me to explain;
Such a paragon is woman,
   That, you see, it *must* be true
She is always vastly better
   Than the best that she can do!"

To Spring

"O ver purpurem!"—Violet-colored Spring
   Perhaps, good poet, in *your* vernal days
   The simple truth might justify the phrase;
But now, dear Virgil, there is no such thing!
Perhaps, indeed, in your Italian clime,
   Where o'er the year, if fair report be true,
   Four seasons roll, instead of barely *two,*

There still may be a verdant vernal time;
But *here,* on these our chilly northern shores,
   Where April gleams with January's snows,—
   Not e'en a violet buds; and nothing "blows,"
Save blustering Boreas,—dreariest of bores.
O ver purpureum! where the Spring discloses
Her brightest purple on our lips and noses!

The Great Magician

Once, when a lad, it was my hap
   To gain my mother's kind permission
To go and see a foreign chap
   Who called himself "The Great Magician";

I recalled his wondrous skill
   In divers mystic conjurations,
And how the fellow wrought at will
   The most prodigious transformations.

I recollect the nervous man
   Within whose hat the great deceiver
Broke eggs, as in a frying-pan,
   And took 'em, smoking, from the beaver!
I recollect the lady's shawl
   Which the magician rent asunder,
And then restored; but, best of all,
   I recollect the Ribbon-Wonder!

I mean, of course, the funny freak
   In which the wizard, at his pleasure,
Spins lots of ribbons from his cheek
   (Where he had hid 'em, at his leisure).
Yard after yard, of every hue,
   Comes blazing out, and still the fellow
Keeps spinning ribbons, red and blue,
   And black and white, and green and yellow!

I ne'er shall see another show
   To rank with the immortal "Potter's";
He's dead and buried long ago,
   And others charm our sons and daughters;
Years—years have fled—alas! how quick,
   Since I beheld the Great Magician,
And yet I've seen the Ribbon-Trick
   In many a curious repetition!

Thus, when an author I have read
   Who much amazed the world of letters
With gems his fluent pen has shed
   (All nicely pilfered from his betters),
Presto!—'t is done!—and all complete,
   As in my youth's enraptured vision,

I've seen again the Ribbon-Feat,
    And thought about the Great Magician!

So, when a sermon I have heard
    Made up of bits of borrowed learning,
Some cheap mosaic which has stirred
    The wonder of the undiscerning,
Swift as a flash has memory then
    Recalled the ancient exhibition;
I saw the Ribbon-Trick again,
    And thought about the Great Magician!

So when some flippant man-o'-jokes,
    Though in himself no dunce was duller,
Has dazzled all the simple folks
    With brilliant jests of every color,
I've whispered thus (while fast and thick
    The changes flashed across my vision) :—
"How well he plays the Ribbon-Trick!
    By Jove! he beats the Great Magician."

I ne'er shall see another show
    To rank with the immortal "Potter's";
He's dead and buried long ago,
    And others charm our sons and daughters;
Years—years have fled—alas! how quick,
    Since I beheld the Great Magician,
And yet I've seen the Ribbon-Trick
    In many a curious repetition!

Somewhere

Somewhere—somewhere a happy clime there is,
    A land that knows not unavailing woes,
Where all the clashing elements of this

Discordant scene are hushed in deep repose.
Somewhere—somewhere (ah me, that land to win!)
   Is some bright realm, beyond the farthest main,
Where trees of Knowledge bear no fruit of sin,
And buds of Pleasure blossom not in pain.
Somewhere—somewhere an end of mortal strife
   With our immortal yearnings; nevermore
The outer warring with the inner life
   Till both are wretched. Ah, that happy shore!
Where shines for aye the soul's refulgent sun,
And life is love, and love and joy are one!

Daniel Pierce Thompson (1795-1868)

A Vermonter in a Fix,
or a New Way to Collect an Old Debt

Young Hobson, not he of *choice* memory, but John Hobson, a
plain, hardy, shrewd Vermont farmer, having by dint of delving
and scrambling among the rugged rocks of his native hills, gathered a respectable share of the solid lucre, began to bethink him,
with certain other secret motives, of rising a little faster in the
world by way of a spec. For this purpose he laid out his little stock
of cash in fat cattle, and, purchasing enough more on credit to
make out a decentish kind of a drove, as he termed it, took up a
line of march with his horned regiment through the long woods
to Quebec. After undergoing his full share of fatigue and suffering from swimming rivers and worrying through the mud of ten-
mile swamps, sustained only by the meagre fare of French taverns,
which, but for the name of taverns had been hovels, which a
decent farmer in Vermont would have been somewhat ashamed
to have housed his hogs in, Hobson arrived safe and sound at the
great Northern Market. He soon had a bid that exceeded his most
sanguine expectations, and after receiving from a by-stander an
assurance of the bidder's pecuniary ability for such a purchase, he
struck off the whole lot; while the purchaser, directing him to his
lodgings, told him to call the next day and he should receive his
money. Chuckling with the thought of his great bargain, and in
fact the price was a thumping one, Hobson returned to the Inn
where he had bespoken quarters, and informed the landlord of his
lucky sale.

"To whom did you sell, friend Hobson?" said the landlord.

"Derrick, he called himself, the good looking man of the Market, there"—

"And you didn't trust him, man, did you?"

"To be sure, I did, till to-morrow, when he promises the money all on the nail—and another tall fellow told me Derrick was good for thousands."

"Bill Derrick," then said the landlord, "and Catch-Gull Luck, his everlasting surety, suppose they have made another haul. It may be as you expect, Mr. Hobson, but this much I will say, if you get your money to-morrow, or *all* of it ever, I will agree to keep Lent twelve months at least."

"But I shall though," said Hobson, "or by the hocus-pocus of my grand mother, I will soon teach him the true cost of cheating a Yankee."

The landlord shook his head, and Hobson retired for the night with his spirits wofully down towards zero; and though he still could not persuade himself but that the man would be punctual, yet he acknowledged to himself that he had been a little too fast among these city folks, in taking every thing for gold that shines, on their own word or the word of an abettor.

The next day Hobson waited on Derrick according to agree-ment, and was received with all possible politeness by the smooth tongued dealer—Mr. Hobson was very welcome, but really he had ten thousand pardons to beg, that in the great hurry he had entirely forgotten to make arrangements to meet his promise, but the man he was to receive the money from he supposed would re-quire a day's notice or so, but he would see him immediately, and by calling again to-morrow, every thing would be regulated to Mr. Hobson's wishes, he presumed. All this, however, Hobson was not quite as ready to take for gospel now as before; and in order that he might know a little better the state in which he stood with this ready promise, he diligently betook himself to making inquiries into the man's situation and character.—

From these he soon learnt that Derrick had disposed of the cattle as soon as he had purchased, and that although in reality he might be worth some property, yet his promise was considered good for nothing, for he always contrived to conceal his effects from his crediters, and, acting the bankrupt as occasion required, he always put the law at defiance.—In fine, that he was an arrant knave and had before played the same game on several unwary drovers, who in their eagerness, to close a bargain at the great price which he was ever ready to offer, had neglected the precaution of making inquiries, and sold their cattle to him on a short credit, and after being amused and dallyed by his promises a few weeks, had given up their debts as lost and gone off in despair. "So, ho! John," said our hero, soliloquizing along as he trudged back to his lodgings, with the feelings of one whose own folly had made him the dupe of a knave, and whose anger is so nearly balanced between himself for his own stupidity, and him who had taken advantage of it by an act of baseness, that he is perfectly at a loss on which he shall give vent to his laboring resentment. "So, ho! John, then it seems you're bit.—Yes, I John Hobson, who about home was thought to be up to any thing for a bargain, who out-witted old Clenchfist the shave, and Screwfast the pettifogger, I John Hobson, am bit, cursedly bit, like a great gull, as I am, by this palavering quintessence of a pack of d—d rascals, it's a good one though, by the pipers if it a'nt!

The next day Hobson renewed his visit to Derrick with no better success than before. The next, and the next, it was put off with some new and ingenious excuse, and, his hopes excited with a fresh promise of payment, till he entirely lost all faith in the fellow's promises. What must be done? He could never go back and face his neighbors in Vermont of whom he had purchased part of his drove on credit till he returned, without the money to pay them; besides, nearly all his own property was vested in the drove. Yes, said he to himself, something must be done to get me out of this dilemma—so now John Hobson for your wits, and let them be stretched to their prettiest. With this view of his case he sought the landlord.

"Is this evil genius of mine, this Derrick," said he, "at all tinctured with notions of a religious or superstitious nature?"

"No! as it regards a future reckoning he neither fears God or Devil."

"Well, then, does he wish to be tho't a man of honor and honesty with any of the big fishes of your city?"

"No, he has nothing to hope from them, nor does he care what they think of him."

"And what say you of his courage, can he face?"

"No! he is said to be a great coward and always a sneak from danger."

"Ah! that is something," said Hobson, "hold easy and say nothing."

Our hero now mused awhile and retired to bed with a brightened look, and the air of one who has got a new maggot in his head, as he probably would have himself expressed it. The next morning he was stirring as soon as it was light. Sallying out into the town he soon came across a couple of Indians lazily lounging about the street."

"Sawnies, or whatever they call ye," says he, "I want to hire you to-day."

"Me go," said the spokesman of the two, "me go for the money or de rum."

"Well, then, do you know Derrick there about the market, with a white coat and a black cane?"

"Me know him."

"Very well, I will give you a broad shiner apiece if you will dog that fellow untill bed time; don't touch him, or say one word to him, but always keep your eyes on him; if he turns a corner, you turn too; if he goes into a house, you watch till he comes out, and if he comes near you, run till he stops and then turn and watch again. Will you do it?"

"Yes! me do him," was the reply.

Hobson now returned to his lodgings and remained there till night, when he set out for Derrick's, to see if his plan of operations had produced any effect; and if so, to give it such a turn as he might think best calculated to accomplish his purpose.

Derrick was at home, and obviously, in no very cheerful mood. After framing his usual excuses for not having the money ready, he soon fell into a sort of reverie. Hobson now began to have some hopes that his scheme would succeed; and while he was endeavoring, by various questions to draw out something which would open a way for him to act his own part in the plan, Derrick observed,—

"I have noticed a rather mysterious circumstance to-day Mr. Hobson; a thing I can't exactly account for."

"What may that be," said Hobson, "if I may so bold with your honor?"

"Why there has been a couple of Indians dogging and spying me out in every spot and place I have been in since morning.—I tried to come up with them once or twice, and they vanished like apparitions, but as soon as I turned, I could see them peeping out after me from some other place; they kept at a distance, to be sure, but they looked d—n'd evil, and I don't know exactly what it all means."

"It *is* quite singular," said Hobson, "but what kind of looking fellows were they?"

Derrick described them.

"Why, sir," said Hobson, "they must be the very fellows that helped me with my cattle through the long woods; I am rather sorry that I employed them, for I begin to suspect they are desperate and bloody minded fellows, though they stuck to me as close as brothers on the way, and I should have paid them, but I told them I could not until you paid me for the cattle; then I mean to pay them well and get rid of them, for they begin to look rather askew at me, and I confess, between you and I, that I feel rather shy of the imps myself; but I believe I must be jogging; you say I may call to-morrow?"

"Yes—yes, certainly," said Derrick.

Hobson retired, and signing to the Indians, who were lurking round the house to follow him, he took them aside.

"Well my lads, you have done well—here are your wheels—go and drink, then come back to your business; he seen once or twice more to-night, and be at your post early to-morrow morning, and keep up the same game till to-morrow night; here are another pair of shiners for you—will you do it?"

"Yes! me do him," was again the laconic answer.

The next day, Hobson again waited on Derrick and found him looking extremely ill and haggard, with the appearance of one who had been sadly disturbed of his rest.

"I am glad to see you, Mr. Hobson," said he, "I am very happy at length to be able to pay you; but you must be sensible Mr. Hobson, that the sum I promised you for your cattle was a hundred dollars over the market price; I made a losing go of it, and I think that you will discount the hundred dollars at least."

"I fear that cannot be," said Hobson, "for I have already made a contract to pay away all this money, before I leave the city, except enough to pay my expenses home and pay off the bloody Indians; perhaps I could get away, however, by dodging the knaves; could I not?"

"O no," said Derrick eagerly.

"No, for heaven's sake no; pay them well, why, last night, they waylaid my house and have been seen several times this morning, though I have been so unwell that I have not been out to-day; not that I fear them Mr. Hobson, but on your own account, pay them off to the last farthing, for otherwise, depend on it they will do you some cursed mischief, I was only in jest about the discount."

With this, Derrick brought out a bag of gold, and without further ceremony counted out the full sum to the inwardly exulting Hobson, who, pocketing the guineas with great composure, bid Derrick good morning and marched off in triumph to his lodgings and recounting his good fortune to his admiring landlord, took a hearty breakfast, and departed, having good-naturedly absolved the landlord from his promise of perpetual secret, and leaving the Indians to earn their days wages to the sad discomfeiture of the nerves of poor Derrick. In two hours Hobson had crossed the great river, on his way homeward, and pronouncing his parting blessing on the walled city, "And you didn't knab John Hobson after all," said he, turning his head and spurring his pony into a round trot up the great road towords the States; "you didn't knab him so easily, ye mongrel, scurvy, rascalious crew of beef-eating John Bulls, and *parley vou francez* frigazee, frog-eating Frenchmen, so leaving this specimen of Vermont fashions in turning the tables on a rascal for your benefit, good bye says I and be hanged to you."

It was about a month after the occurrences we have described that a gay wedding party was assembled at the house of Esquire ————— at the Four corners in Slab City. The balance that had been, for more than a year, doubtfully trembling at equipoise between our young farmer and a more wealthy, but a less loved suitor of the Squire's fair daughter, had at length turned in favor of our hero, who always attributed his subsequent happiness to his lucky speculation at the walled city.

Cornelius A. Logan (1806-1853)

The Vermont Wool Dealer

CAST OF CHARACTERS
Deuteronomy Dutiful: the Vermont wool dealer
Mr. Waddle: wealthy businessman
Amanda: his attractive young daughter
Captain Oakley: Amanda's suitor, a proud young officer
Con Golumby: Irish waiter
Bob: Negro waiter
Slap: bar keep
Betty: Amanda's servant

SETTING
A hotel in New York City in the 1840's

SCENE I (*hall in the hotel*)

Enter Captain Oakley *with* Amanda *and* Betty, *carrying band boxes and portmanteau, left.*

Captain Oakley. Carry those things into the house, and provide separate apartments immediately.

Amanda. Take care of those bandboxes; don't crush them, for they are filled with perishable merchandise.

[*Exit* Betty *with bandboxes.*]

Cap. Why, yes, bonnets and bouquets, flounces and flowers, ribbons and roses—perishable, indeed. Not only do the articles perish, but the fashion which gave them birth! As variable as the price of stock on a lady's heart.

Ama. If you mean my heart, I'm sure you have no cause to complain of inconstancy, for the impression made on it by you, Captain, has defied the tests of time and space.

Cap. Time and space?

Ama. 'Tis! time—fourteen hours; space—all the distance between this and Saratoga. Did I not treat with chilling coldness all the pretty fellows who were so civil to me during the passage? Did I not almost petrify your persevering friend from Vermont, as often as he addressed me?

Cap. My friend, you are in error; he is no friend of mine. He introduced himself to me, by inquiring who you were—your name—your residence—family—present object and future intention.

Ama. I'm sure I should be grateful for the interest he so eagerly manifests in my concerns. I'm sorry I lost the opportunity of thanking him.

Cap. I fancy you may have an opportunity of doing so still, for among other important items he informed me that he intended to establish his residence at this hotel.

Ama. I am glad of it, I like his quick humor, and his indomitable perseverance.

Enter Slap *from house, right.*

Slap. An elderly gentleman is inquiring for you and the young lady, sir.

Ama. My father! Where is he?

Slap. He came in through the bar-room, ma'am.

Cap. Where is he now?

Slap. It necessarily follows that he is in the front parlor, up stairs.

Cap. Does it, then I suppose it necessarily follows that he wishes us to follow him there?

Slap. He signified his wishes to that effect!

Cap. He did? Now let me signify mine; you I take, are waiter here!

Slap. It does not necessarily follow, I am the bar-keeper.

Cap. Well then, Mr. Bar-keeper, you will be good enough to receive my instructions respecting dinner. In the first place—

Waddle. [*Within house.*] Amanda! Amanda!

Ama. Oh! Lord! there's my father; he's impatient as usual; I must attend him, Captain you'll follow me.

[*Exit* Amanda *into house.*]

Cap. Follow you? through the world my dear! She is indeed a charming girl! charming in her person, charming in her manner, and charming in her circumstances. The latter indeed are fifty thousand times more charming than the others, as I understand she has exactly that number of dollars at her own disposal, a sum that would just replenish my exchequer—for tailor's bills, tavern bills, wine bills, and billiard bills have completely stripped me of bank bills.

Slap. It necessarily follows.

Cap. And if you should make such an impertinent remark again, I know another thing that would necessarily follow.

Slap. Might I be favored with a knowledge of it?

Cap. Oh! certainly! you shall know it feelingly and feel it knowingly, 'tis simply the application of this rattan to your shoulders.

Slap. Sir, if any gentleman should so far forget himself, as to inflict manual chastisement on my person, it would necessarily follow, that independent of the personal resistance he would experience—

Cap. Personal resistance, you villain? What do you mean by that?

Slap. I'm too polite to mention it, sir!

Cap. Oh! I presume you hold some rank in the militia service. Are you a Colonel? a major? a Captain? or a shoe-black?

Slap. No sir, I'm a bar-keeper, and in that capacity it necessarily follows, that I am waiting your orders.

Cap. Oh! sir, since you descend from your personal resistance, to the duties of your station, allow me to ask you what you can give me for dinner?

Con Golumby. [*Outside right.*] Two bootjacks.

Cap. Two bootjacks, rather an indigestible dish.

Slap. 'Tis our stupid waiter, sir, answering the customers.

Enter Con Golumby *from house, right.*

Con. Now, sir, you have only to life your legs, and the divil a boot you'll have on.

[*Business with bootjack.*]

Cap. A most summary proceeding, on my honor! pray sir, who gave you authority to clap me in the stocks in this manner?

Con. Wasn't it yourself that called for bootjack?

Cap. Bootjack, you scoundrel! Release my feet, or I'll kick you.

Con. Will you? Faith then if it's kicking you're after, I've a notion your feet are safest, just where they are!

Cap. Why, you impudent Irish, bull headed—

[*Chases him round stage, till he meets* Dutiful, *entering left.*]

Enter Deuteronomy, *a trunk on his shoulder.*—Golumby *runs against him, overturning it.*

Deu. Hello! hello! What on earth's broke loose. You see that ere trunk?

Con. I do

Deu. Maybe you'd like just to mention what you put it there for?

Con. The gentleman was presenting me wid the bootjack.

Deu. That ain't no reason you orter keel over my trunk. If there's any damage happened to the inside, you shall make it straight—you shall, now—mind I tell. There's a heap o' notions in thar, and some on 'em almighty tender.

Cap. Well, Paddy, you may thank this gentleman for your safety. Now, begone, sir.

Con. I can't without my instruments.

Cap. What do you call your instruments?

Con. My jack, sir, you may want them another time.

Cap. Take them, and be gone.

[*Exit into house, right.*]

Con. [*To* Deuteronomy.] Have you anything to polish, sir?

Deu. Well, let's see if we can make a trade—what do you tax?

Con. Sixpence, sir.

Voice. [*Within, right.*] Golumby.

Con. Coming, sir.

[*Exit* Con *into house, right.*]

Deu. [*Getting on trunk.*] Lookee there, you, is your house full of lodgers? How'd you like to take me in?

Slap. Why, our house is so full that it necessarily follows—

Deu. What? oh, I see, you don't like to trust strangers—want the chinks, a week's board in advance—well, here's a dollar!

Slap. Now, 'tis obvious—

Deu. No 'taint—'tis genuine—rale spelter—aint no counterfeit about me.

Slap. But, sir we are so crowded—

Deu. Why that was pretty much the case aboard that consarned steamboat. There war'nt room enough for as many Nova Scotia herrings, packed and pickled as there was men aboard. We was piled up on the floor about four foot high, and a leetle thicker than sugar house molasses. When I first went down in the cabin I writ on one bunk with a piece of chalk "this birth is mine"—but another chap said it was hisen, and so I was choused out, and they put me into the pantry a top o' the coffee pots and gridirons. Somehow when I got asleep there was a fellow a layin' across my legs, and he snored so distressed loud that I was obliged to ram his head into a butter firkin, when the butter began to melt it kind o' greased his nose, and he snored a good deal easier afterwards.

Slap. Well, sir, we'll endeavor to make room for you.

Deu. Half a dozen feathers will do for me if beds are scarse, jest to ease those sharp pints of my body that comes in contact with the floor—you needn't put yourself out more than a rod— I'll look out for number one.

Slap. Number one is occupied, but I'll squeeze you into some corner.

[*Exit into house, right.*]

Deu. Yes, and let's have suthin' to eat, for I'm as hungry as a juvenile hippopotamus, and as dry as a squash bed in April.

Enter Captain Oakley *from house, right.*

Cap. Waiter! oh, sir! you are here. Haven't I seen that impudent face of yours somewhere else?

Deu. You haven't seen it no where but in the front of my head.

Cap. Now, sir, I would say a word to you—during our passage down the river, I observed your leering at the young lady in my company in a manner which calls forth this remark. Should I observe any more such demonstrations of your regard I shall expect you to answer it to me.

Deu. Answer it to me? Why, what do you mean by that?

Cap. Why, sir, I shall take the liberty of calling you out.

Deu. Well, suppose I don't want to go out?

Cap. Then, sir, you know the alternative. I shall you post for a coward!

Deu. Oh, I understand what you mean—to challenge me. Hum, if the gal likes me, and I do believe she does, I shall court her the worst kind. I don't want to fall with you, Captain, cause I got great respect for military men—I was pretty near being made a major on myself once—but I shall court the gal—I wouldn't fight with you on no account hardly, but I shall court the gal—and I know I shouldn't like to be posted for a coward, but I shall set up late o' night with the gal.

Cap. You will?

Deu. Roll me into pig iron, if I don't.

Cap. Then, sir, you know what will follow.

[Crosses to left.]

Deu. What will follow my courtin' the gal? Why marrying her I suppose, and you can't surmise what'll follow that.

Cap. Well, sir, you shall hear from me.

[Exit left.]

Deu. And let me, won't you? That chap will get some of his sharp pints filed down, if he don't look out. I will court the gal, by grasshopper! 'Cause she's got $55,000, I hear, and 'cause she likes me, I do opine; and furthermore, I'll give that ere chap a chance to challenge me. I writ a letter to her on board that steamboat, makin' the awfulest love to her, but I don't know how I shall get it into her hands. [*Bell*] That's for breakfast.

[Exit very hastily into house.]

SCENE II. (*an upstairs corridor, with chamber doors each side.—No. 3 over right door—No. 2 over left door.*)

Enter Bob, *left, meeting* Golumby, *right.*

Bob. I say, Golumby, why ain't you down stairs at the breakfast table?

Con. Because I've had my breakfast.

Bob. Wall, now, is dat any reason 'cause you ain't goin' to wait on de gentlemen?

Con. Faith it is, for the devil a one of them waits upon me.

Bob. Well, now, listen to what I tells you; No. 5 wants his breakfast carried up to his room—No. 2 is sick, and wants catnip gruel—No. 3 wants brandy and water—No. 10 wants a bootjack, and No. 6 wants fresh towels.

Con. Which is the number that wants the brandy and water?

Bob. No. 3.

Con. I'll attend to that first—how many glasses?

Bob. Two.

Con. I'll call for three—there's luck in odd numbers. [*Going.*] No. 2 wants three glasses.

Bob. No—no—No. 3 wants two glasses.

Con. Don't bother, you'll put me out. No. 2—three glasses of brandy! I say Bob, here—sure you're as white as the general run of Africans, you're a dacent lad, cuffee, you are, do you step down to the bar now, and get the liquor, and Bob, tell Mr. Slap to send me a wee sup.

Bob. Tink he send him.

Con. You disbelieving infidel, away with you, tell him that No. 2 wants three glasses of brandy, and I want one, tell him to charge 'em all to No. 2. Go, Bob, and we'll share the sureptious glass between us.

Bob. Mind you give me half.

[*Exit* Bob, *left.*]

Con. Bad luck to the drop you get, except you stale a mouthful as you're fetchin it up stairs, and if you're after doing that, I'll sue you for burglary.

Enter Bob *with salver containing 3 glasses of brandy, and pitcher of water, left.*

Bob. Here am dree glasses, Mr. Golumby, but massa Slap would'nt gib me one for you.

Con. It's a falsehood, you murdering Curthegenian, you, you have drank the liquor—don't I see the lavins of it on the thick lips of you. Get me another, or I'll tell the master of the robberies, you have committed, I will, you Asiatic African.

[*Exit* Bob, *left.*]

Now I'll carry these to No. 2, and hand them to the gentlemen.

[*Exit* Con Golumby *into No. 2, left.*]

Ama. [*From within.*] Leave the room, you Irish brute.

Con. [*In No. 2.*] Oh! ma'am, I beg your pardon—I thought it was for you.

Enter Con *from No. 2.*

Con. I've made a mistake; there's a young lady in there, singing "Over the water to Charley," and she told me she did'nt want any brandy with the water, she called me an Irish brute, for interrupting her in her ditty—I like a ditty myself.

[*Sings.*]

Oh, there's not in this wide world a valley so sweet,
As that vale in whose bosom the bright waters meet.

My bosom is not wide enough for water to mate in it, so by my father's son, I'll let the brandy mate the water. [*Mixes one glass.*] Och! how beautiful they amalgamate; see how the pair of them are laughing—it's a pity they should ever be drowned, och! jewels that tumbler's but a cold and hard lodging place for ye; faith I'll give ye a softer and warmer bed; my stomach come to my heart, ye blackguard.

[*Drinks.*]

Voice within. [*right*] Con Golumby.

Con. The divil Con Golumby ye! ye've sent the brandy one way, and the water another—they've taken the wrong roads, too—for the liquors gone up my nose, and the water down my throat.

Voice again. Golumby.

Con. May the divil go a hunting with you, there's not half a glass here. I'll make mine a little stronger and the gentleman's a little weaker, for surely their throats must be copper bottomed, if they can drink such stiff horns as these; so I'll just divide wid ye;

fair play's a jewel, and so is the liquor—I've put too much water in this.

[*Mixes them.*]

As Golumby *is drinking,* Deuteronomy *enters left, and walks up to him.*

Con. Are you No. 3?

Deu. No—be you?

Con. No, sir—but it is a touch of the cholera I'm having, and the doctors told me that I had a collapse, and to drink freely of the chloride of lime.

Deu. Do you belong to this house?

Con. No, sir, I am only hired.

Deu. What do you do?

Con. Sir?

Deu. What did they hire you for?

Con. Bokase I wanted a place.

Deu. Do you know where the boarders lodge?

Con. Most of them lodge in their beds, I believe, except some that slapes out all night. If you've no particular business wid me, you'll plase not to be detaining me, but pay me for my services, and let me be taking the gintlemen their liquor.

Deu. Why, you haven't done me no service.

Con. No sarvice? haven't I been talking to you till my mouth is as dry as—

Deu. Well, tell me, which room is the young lady in, who arrived this morning in the steamboat?

Con. Does she sing over the water to Charley?

Deu. Considerable likely she does.

Con. Does she call people names?

Deu. Yes, when they've got any.

Con. Did she ever call you an Irish brute? Oh! you're not Irish, but how the devil did she find it out in me? Maybe it was by the ginteelness of my deportment. Och, you should have seen the grace with which I handed her the liquor. "Ma'am," says I, "you called for three glasses of brandy, here they are—mix them to your own palate." "Get out, you Irish brute!" says she. But I must get No. 3, maybe the gentleman may be wanting the same.

[Exit right.]

Deu. See here, stop. Where's the room where the young lady is?

Con. In No. 2.

Deu. Where is No. 2?

Con. Behind ye.

Deu. Is she there now?

Con. Unless she's gone over the water to Charley. [*Going right.*]

Deu. Here, Irisher!

Con. Sir?

Deu. Can't you carry this letter to the girl that lives in that room? I'll give you sixpence.

Con. Sixpence? Will you be waiting till I carry this to No. 3?

Deu. Why, if you should meet anybody else on the road, I guess I shan't see you again to-day.

Con. Och, do you suppose I'd neglect your business, and when there's a letter to carry and sixpence t' airn? Give me the letter. [*Takes letter.*] I'll be wid you immediately.

[Exit Golumby into No. 3.]

Enter Bob, *with breakfast things, left.*

Deu. Hello, you Ethiopian, where are you goin' to take that victuals to?

Bob. Why, I take 'em to the young lady in No. 2.

Deu. Well, see her, just tell her that I want to see her on business.

Bob. I tell her.

[Exit Bob into No. 2—re-enters and exits.]

Deu. That are fellow's hide is as full of rum as a pine knot is full of gum; he ain't white, no way you can fix it, unless you turn his skin inside out, and then I reckon it would be flesh color.

Enter Golumby, *with coal-scuttle, right.*

Con. I'm a-going to take this fire-wood into No. 18 and then I'll deliver your letter.

[Exit, left.]

Enter Amanda, *from No. 2.*

Ama. A man want to speak to me? Where is he? Sir, I under-stand—

Deu. [*Nodding from corner.*] How du you du? Miss Amanda, I calculate?

Ama. Oh! Mr. Dutiful, I believe?

Deu. Deuteronomy Dutiful, ma'am. How hev you been?

Ama. Well, thank you. You wish, probably, to see my father? You'll find him below. Good morning, sir. [Amanda *is about to go.*]

Deu. Stop, look here; what's your hurry? I want to talk to you; I got suthin' petickler to say to you. Set down, won't you?

Ama. Certainly, sir. [*They sit. A pause.*] I'm all impatience for your communications, sir.

Deu. What's the price of wool?

Ama. Wool, sir? Why, really, you should know more of the article than I.

Deu. Wool! well, I do feel a little sheepish; but you see I come down to York to sell wool, and just thought you might know the price of it. You know I came down in the steamboat along with you.

Ama. Yes, sir, I remember.

Deu. That journey cost me considerable. I say, how did you sleep on board of that 'ere steamboat?

Ama. Sleep! very well, sir.

Deu. I didn't. They told me I might have the third of a bunk, but a fat man got in first—

Ama. And is this your sole business with me?

Deu. Oh! now I was only just tellin' you. [*Ruffle shirt.*] That chap that came down in your company, you know, from Saratoga —he's a captain, ain't he? I like military men. I came pretty near being made a major on once myself, but when the court of ex-amination axed me how I could effect a retreat, I answered right out that the only way I ever heard of anybody's retreating was movin' backwards. Now whenever you want to be made a ma-jor on—

Ama. [*Rising.*] Sir, as I've no pretensions to that office, I beg you'll spare me the recital of the causes of your failure.

Deu. Well, don't get into a blaze about it. I want to talk to you about the captain.

Ama. Well, sir, what about the captain?

Deu. Why, he talked suthin' about calling me out.

Ama. Calling you out, sir?

Deu. He said if ever I dared to speak another word to you, I'd hev to fight him, and so I'm resolved to hev a long talk with you to begin with.

Ama. Oh, sir! for heaven's sake, don't think of fighting.

Deu. I don't think nothin' about it, because I don't think the captain's got any notion on't. [*A pause.*] Be you engaged?

[*Business with gloves, brooch and watch.*]

Ama. Sir!

Deu. Are you engaged to be married?

Ama. Married? No, sir. Why do you ask?

Deu. 'Cause I'll marry you myself.

Enter Captain Oakley, *right.*

Cap. The devil you will, sir. I am your humble servant.

Deu. Are you?

Cap. So, madam, this is the manner in which you trifle with my feelings?

Ama. Captain Oakley will understand that I can give no reply to such remarks, and that if he will intrude himself into the presence of a lady in so abrupt and ungentlemanly a manner, he can excite no other feelings than those of contempt.

[*Exit, into No. 2.*]

Deu. I guess you feel kinder streaked—ha! ha! ha!

Cap. Villain! I demand immediate satisfaction.

Deu. No, do you?

Cap. I presume you are a gentleman?

Deu. Presume I be.

Cap. Enough, sir; I'll chastise you instantly.

Deu. Chastise!

Enter Waddle, *pulling on* Golumby, *left.*

Con. Och! if your honor plase to believe me, I'm the innocent-est man!

Wad. Don't talk to me, you scoundrel!

Con. But if your honor would listen to m—

Wad. I'll not listen to you! Which is the man? You, sir [*to* Deuteronomy], what's your name?

Deu. Umph!

Wad. [*Violently.*] What's your name, sir?

Deu. Wall, you needn't get in a fever about it. Why, you look out of your eyes like a catfish with cholic. Don't approximate your bombastical rotundity to me.

Wad. Is your name—pshaw—the divil!

Deu. No, that ain't it.

Wad. This letter sir—did you write this letter! [*Shows it.*]

Deu. Pretty good hand—that P. has got a swingin' tail.

Wad. Damn the P's tail, did you write the letter?

Deu. Why it does look considerable like my hand.

Wad. No trifling sir—how dare you address a letter to my daughter?

Deu. You got a daughter?

Wad. How dare you write a letter, and above all, such a letter to any member of my family?

Deu. You got any members to your family.

[Betty *appears at door of No. 2, business watching.*]

Wad. I demand satisfaction, sir—Captain Oakley, you will be good enough to act as my friend on this occasion and arrange pre-liminaries.

[*Exit* Waddle, *left.*]

Cap. I, sir, am the first claimant on your attention. [*Crosses left.*] So you shall hear from me instantly.

[*Exit* Captain Oakley, *left. Exit* Betty *into room, No. 2.*]

Con. They'll shoot you betweixt 'em. The last one is a desperate character; if he should miss you the old one will plug you! Have you got no one to back you?

Deu. No—but I've got two to front me.

Con. You may depend on me, 'twas me that got you into this hobble! The letter you gave me for the young lady, I put into the coal-scuttle for safe keeping, till such a time as I could deliver it, when the ould gentleman himself called for coal, and I, not thinking that the letter was amongst it, pitched it down by the side of the grate, and out flew the letter, and the ould thafe picked it up —I told him it wasn't for him, but his daughter—damn his maneness he opened and read it, then he picked up a chunk of coal, and bad luck to him, he struck me on the head wid it—the devil choke the ould murderer! och, it's laughin' ye are, wid two deaths starin' you in the face; I like you, by the hill of Hoath I like you! I'll be your bottle holder—let 'em come on, we'll whop the pair of 'em —hillo hoo! hoo!

Deu. Where's the place they go to fight?

Con. I believe they call it Hobuken.

Deu. Where's Hubuken?

Con. Over the water to Charley—I mean it's beyond there, fornenst the city.

Enter Slap, *with card, which he gives* Deuteronomy, *who reads it.*

Deu. That's as clear as flour starch; you hev'nt got a gun or nothin', hev you—I must get a shootin' iron of some sort.

Enter Betty *from No. 2.*

Bet. Massa Deuteronomy, Missus like to see you a few minutes, 'sponse you at leisure.

Deu. Tell her I'm goin' to fight a duel or two, and if I get back any way hullsome, I'll come.

Con. And I'm the second.

Bet. Missus says she want to see you tickler business immediately.

Deu. Twelve o'clock this chap says; why it only wants a quarter of that now—what an almighty hurry he's in, but the lady must be attended to first by all means; Golumby do you go over to Hubuken and tell them I'll be thar in about an hour at farthest.

Con. I can't leave the house, here's the major—maybe he'll go.

Enter Bob, *left, with a glass of brandy.*

Deu. Here blackee, I'll give you two shillins' if you'll go over to Hubuken, and tell a gentleman you'll find waitin' thar for me, I'll be thar in an hour.

Bob. Two shillings—where are dey?

Deu. But, I say, won't you take one and ten pence?

Bob. Yes massa, I'll go.

Con. Give me my cruisken!

Bob. Let me taste him first.

[*Drinks all, gives empty glass to* Golumby,

who kicks him off, left.]

Con. Bad manners to you—may the divil go wid you and a drum, and then you'll want neither company nor music.

Bet. Now you come to Missus, sir!

Enter Amanda, *from No. 2.*

Ama. Betty, what has detained you? [*Down right.*] Have you delivered my message! oh, here is the gentleman. I beg pardon for the liberty I have teken, but I perceive you are not alone?

Deu. Oh, yes, I am particularly alone, except the Irishman, you and the nigger. Golumby, carry that gold colored lump of humanity into the cellar.

Con. Faith will I.

Bet. Why, you drunken wretch, touch me, I wool you!

Ama. Let Betty remain.

Con. [*Going.*] Och, if you should find them both one too many for you, whistle, and I'll come to your assistance.

[*Exit* Golumby, *left. Exit* Betty *into No. 2.*]

Ama. I have just learnt from Betty, with alarm, that you have been challenged, both by my father and Captain Oakley, and I have sought this interview to entreat you to forego any intentions you may have entertained of answering them.

Deu. Let down, won't you? Why shouldn't I answer them?

Ama. Oh, sir, can you coolly ask me why? Will not your meeting either of them in all probability cause bloodshed?

Deu. Conglomerate the fools! What made them challenge me then?

Ama. Oh, sir, be generous—do not sacrifice to a false notion of honor—lives so dear to me! My father's life—my lover's—I mean your own, sir!

Deu. The hevens! my life! By scrumsky! she's in love with me —I know'd it all along. How could she help it? Well Miss Amanda, since I have riz the muscles of your heart!

Ama. Done what, sir?

Deu. Roused the ramifications of your rampant sensibilities, ma'am.

Ama. Upon my life, sir I am at a loss to comprehend your meaning.

Deu. Why, in plain words, then, since I've been lucky enough to rouse up your sanguine sensations—since I found out you love me as you do—

Ama. Love you, sir?

Deu. Needn't blush 'bout it—'cause I respect your feelings— chop me into live oak fence rails, if I don't.

Ama. Sir, you have strongly misconceived; I only—

Deu. Yes I know you didn't like to speak of it plain outright, at first, but you flew round and round the subject like a chicken-hawk, but you folded up your wings—pinted your bill—and darted down slap-dash on me at last! Well, Miss Mandy, since things have gone so far between us, and my life is so precious to you, why, I'll not answer the challenge, but will content myself with lickin' that old captain like smoke, for sendin' it.

Ama. Oh, no sir, do not molest him—'twill cause further danger—for my sake don't!

Deu. Well, I won't for your sake. Hokey! for your sake, I'd do anything on airth—I'd almost swear never to eat no more clam chowder! On one condition, though—that we bring our business immediately to the conclusion that it must eventually arrive at. I'm every way a match for you—my family is good, none better in Vermont. My grandfather was one of the first settlers in our part of the country—brought up pretty nighly one third of the hull country. He was sent to our State Legislature—old Michael Dutiful—you must a'heern on him—he was my grandfather.

Well, Mike, he married old Squire Holliday Harrindon's daughter, Harrietta, as like a gal as ever drove a pair of oxen, so they say that seed her when she was young and spry, but when I seed her, her face was furrowed like a new plowed cornfield. She had only one eye and two teeth, or two eyes and one tooth, I don't know which, but Harriet brought suthin' considerable to the old man when he married her; she had an all-sufficient quantity of quilts and blankets—in fine, I hearn say she warn't short of body clothes, nyther.

Ama. I haven't a doubt of the respectability of your family, sir, but to return to the subject of our conversation.

Deu. Oh, yes, certainly—return to our marriage, you mean. Well, you see, I haven't got time to make a long courtship of it, because my business is all out o' kilter, and has to go on in Vermont without me; besides, this seems to be a pretty dear tavern, and you know every dollar I spend in staying here courting you, is so much out of your pocket after I marry you, for I swan, if you don't marry me right away, I'll charge the extras to you—I will—honor bright.

Ama. Marry you, sir? You surely jest, ha, ha, ha!

Deu. Jest! you been jesting with me all this time? [*Rises.*] Then I've no more time to waste with you, for I must go and blow them ere fellows to the land of nod.

[*Going.*]

Ama. Stay, sir. [*Aside.*] How shall I prevent this duel? I have it. I'll practice a little innocent deception on my impudent friend here; it will at least gain time, and that may prevent the mischief. You are very hasty in your determination, Mr. Dutiful. Do you ever hope to obtain a wife, if you take her first refusal as decisive?

Deu. Eh! oh! Ay, ay; it's well you spoke, or I should have been off like a long-nine at the end of a port-fire. Such matches as I am are not to be 'lighted on every day. Well, now, as we have agreed the thing shall be done, let's have it done was quickly as possible; we'll run away to-night.

Ama. Oh, Mr. Dutiful! impossible, to-night. Really, it cannot be accomplished; my father is so vigilant, and the captain so suspicious, we should be detected. My father's chamber is so immediately between mine and the street, that I could never pass it unobserved. However, a plan has struck me—but I fear you will think me forward.

Deu. Never, unless you go backwards. What is your plan?

Ama. I might disguise myself in my servant maid's clothes, and so pass without suspicion.

Deu. What, put on that mulatto gal's clothes? That will do, all but the face not being the same color.

Ama. A vail thrown over it would prevent the color being seen.

Deu. Swampy! that's true. I'll have a coach at the next corner; I'll come here to escort you to it, and then, Heliogabulous! we'll drive to the parson's and get grafted.

Ama. We had better perhaps fix eight o'clock for the expedition. When the clock tolls the hour, knock at my door, softly, and on the wings of love fly with your prize.

Deu. The wings of love wouldn't carry us far, but the wheels of the coach shall roll us to the parson's. Well, rather guess I've made some marks on her heart. She's almighty rich, and she can talk like a hornet in a buckwheat patch.

[*Exit* Amanda *into No. 2.*]

Enter Con Golumby, *with a bottle—endeavors to conceal it from* Deuteronomy.

Con. Are you safe? The divil take me but I was afeard the young woman would play some trick upon you. She has the divil's own look out of her eye.

Deu. Then I shall marry the divil's tricks, her eyes and herself with them, for I'm going to marry her this night.

Con. That's cool.

Deu. I want you to help me.

Con. To marry her? I don't belong to the clargy.

Deu. No, guess I'll make out to marry her without your help—all I want of you is to help me to get her out of the house.

Con. To run away wid her. Oh, shame! I never run away wid a young woman since my father run away wid my mother.

Deu. If we get along pretty sharp in this business, I shall take her to Varmont. You see I'm a wool-dealer, and I sell notions o' all sorts by hullsale.

Con. I like wholesale stores.

Deu. I shall want a man to qualify my liquors.

Con. I'll qualify liquors, by the wholesale, with any man.

Deu. Well, I want you to keep watch till I return here with a hack at eight o'clock—it wants a few minutes of it now—and when I appear at the end of the passage, you tap at the door No. 2, and say, "All's ready;" then the young lady will come out, dressed in Betty the yellow gal's clothes; you hand her to me, and we'll drive off together like Jehu.

Con. You've the devil's own cunning. She'll be disguised in the mulatto gal's clothes?

Deu. Now I s'pose that captain chap is waitin' for me. Well, may be we'll have time enough to get over to Hubuken and put him out of his misery afore eight o'clock. No, I'll marry the gal first, and then, if he sends me a challenge, I'll squeeze him till he ain't got no more wind in him than there is in the gizzard of a snappin' turtle.

[*Exit. Darken stage gradually.*]

Con. [*Drinking and singing.*]

> Oh! the oily Irishoun
> It's down my throat is going;
> It warms the very blood of my heart;
> It's like water to a mill,
> Or to a pig its swill,
> Or grease to the wheels of a cart.

Enter Betty, *from No. 2.*

Bet. Massa Golumby, missus send me to tell you you mustn't make such a noise.

Con. My singing disturb a lady, aveneen! Out of that, you squaw papoose!   [*Sings, introducing song. Exit* Betty, *into No. 2.*]

Enter Captain Oakley *and* Waddle, *left.*

Wad. Well, sir, but having given the business into your hands, it behooved you to forward it. You undertook the conduct of the affair and therefore should have brought it to an issue.

Cap. But, sir, you will not hear me—if you reflect a moment, you must remember that I did not engage myself on your behalf; on the contrary, the same rascally Yankee had undergone my challenge before he had insulted you. The cowardly knave has deceived us both—instead of meeting me, he sent a negro to excuse him; I thought the fellow was a gentleman.

Con. [*Sings.*]
> Let the Dutchman bolt his schnapps,
> 'Till his eyelids do callapse.

Wad. Silence, fool!

Con. Faith, if you knew all, 'twould be soon seen which is the fool. If I am a fool, my folly is confined to myself, but your hallucination is shared equally by yourself and daughter.

Wad. My hallucination! and shared by my daughter, you impertinent bootjack, what do you mean?

Con. I mean that your daughter is going to run away wid a Yankee man this very night, at eight o'clock—ha! ha! ha! Now then, which of us is the fool? [*Recollects himself.*] By St. Patrick, I've let the cat out of the bag—oh! I'll be kilt.

Wad. What do you say? my daughter running away with a man? how? when? what for? what man?

Cap. A Yankee? I'll annihilate the villain—speak what are their plans?

Con. I'm bound not to tell—honor—

Wad. Here! [*Gives money to* Golumby.] How is my daughter to escape from the house?

Cap. Speak the truth, [*Gives money*] and instantly.

Con. The cherrybims could'nt concale the truth, under all the circumstances. [*Looks at money.*] Your daughter is to change her garments with the yellow gal, and pass out with the Yankee as Betty, with a vail over her face.

Wad. We'll prevent it and detect the undutiful jade in the very act of elopement—I'll then secure her under lock and key, until we leave this city, this hot bed of intrigues; at eight o'clock, you say—'tis now the time. My young friend, dispose yourself near the door, and when she appears instantly, seize her—do *you*, remain where you are—sir, I'll prevent your giving assistance to the intriguing parties.

Deu. [Re-enter.] I've got the coach at the next corner; now if that Irisher is any way spry, there won't be no trouble 'bout it— Golumby!

Con. I'm here.

Wad. Silence you villain.

Con. [*Starts to go—they stop him.*]

Cap. Hush!

Deu. Is all fixed?

Con. I'm fixed.

Enter Betty *and* Amanda, Betty *veiled.*

Ama. Betty, my cloak you say is in the parlor; go and get it.
[*Exit* Amanda *into No. 2.*]

Deu. There she is, sure enough—upwards of a few voices sounding somewhere along here.

Wad. A trick to blind any one who may be listening. She comes.
[*Business. Steals toward* Betty, *seizes her.*]

Betty *advances, right.* Waddle *and* Captain *seize her, she screams.*

Deu. Don't you holler or you'll wake up the wrong passenger.

Wad. Lights there! lights! So madam, you are caughty pretty innocent.
[*Lights up as* Slap *comes on.*]

Enter Slap, *with lighted candle, left.*

Cap. Why, this is not your daughter, sir!

Wad. Eh!

Deu. Why, it's the saffron colored nigger, you got hold on in the dark—why old man at your time of life.

Wad. Then this fellow has been telling a falsehood all the time —how dare you say my daughter was disguised as this girl?

Con. I tould the truth; that's the young lady disguised.

Deu. I swow, maybe she's soaked her face in a pitch pine gum.

Enter Bob.

Oh, no, here comes the rale white feminine specious herself. Come along, my productive aborgina! Golumby, hold on to the old man.

Slap. Hold, madam. [*Takes vail off* Bob.] What, Bob—ha!

Con. It's the nager boy!

Deu. I'm rather flummixed.

Enter Amanda, *from No. 2.*

Ama. What means all this noise?

Wad. Amanda, you have come in good time to join in the laugh against the gay seducer. How dare you presume to write letters to my daughter, and then attempt a shallow stratagem to elope with her?

Cap. A cowardly scoundrel, who accepted a challenge, not having courage to answer it.

Deu. I'll whip the hull boodle of you at once. [*Skipping.*] Make me mad, and I'll lick a thunder-storm!

Con. So can I.

Deu. Want to use fire weapons, I'll fight you with rifles loaded to the muzzles with three cornered slugs, and rammed into each other. Get my Ebenezer riz, and you'd think somebody was a blowin' rocks! I've the almightiest notion to pick up this awful nigger and knock out somebody's brains with his shin!

[*Walks the stage.*]

Con. So have I too.

Deu. Git my dander up, and you'd think it was the Cape Cod sea sarpant in convulsions.

Con. Yes, we're all in convulsions. [*Hiccups.*]

Ama. [*Advances to* Deuteronomy.] What's the price of wool, sir?

Deu. It's riz considerable—black in pertickler.

Cap. What says the lovely Amanda to my suit?

Deu. I'll sell you a woolen suit, cheap.

Ama. Captain, my father consenting, there's my hand.

Deu. You she catamount, didn't you promise to cut stick along with me?

Ama. Do what, sir? I made use of your vanity to punish his jealousy. I have no doubt you have left a score of sighing damsels —victims to their passions for you, in Vermont. Oh, you look like an American Blue Beard!

Deu. Blue Beard? So you thought you'd give me an American Black Beard? Don't you think, Miss Mandy, that you've used me a lettle damned scurvy?

Ama. Perhaps your disappointment has been a little greater than you deserve, but forgive me, sir, this time, and I give you my word never to promise to elope with you again.

Deu. I reckon I shan't come swooping round you any more. You're going to marry her, captain—to prove I can laugh at a joke, though at my own expense, I'll stand the champagne to-night, till all's blue again. I bought six baskets everlastin' cheap, and it's the shockinest nice liquor ever you masticated, and having completed my sales in wool, I shall depart from hum tomorrow, trusting that some amusement has been derived by friends from the visit to New York of the Vermont Wool Dealer.

THE END

George Perkins Marsh (1801-1882)

The Destructiveness of Man

Man has too long forgotten that the earth was given to him for usufruct alone, not for consumption, still less for profligate waste. Nature has provided against the absolute destruction of any of her elementary matter, the raw material of her works; the thunderbolt and the tornado, the most convulsive throes of even the volcano and the earthquake, being only phenomena of decomposion and recomposition. But she has left it within the power of man irreparably to derange the combinations of inorganic matter and of organic life, which through the night of æons she had been proportioning and balancing, to prepare the earth for his habitation, when, in the fulness of time, his Creator should call him forth to enter into its possession.

Apart from the hostile influence of man, the organic and the inorganic world are, as I have remarked, bound together by such mutual relations and adaptations as secure, if not the absolute permanence and equilibrium of both, a long continuance of the established conditions of each at any given time and place, or at least, a very slow and gradual succession of changes in those conditions. But man is everywhere a disturbing agent. Wherever he plants his foot, the harmonies of nature are turned to discords. The proportions and accommodations which insured the stability of existing arrangements are overthrown. Indigenous vegetable and animal species are extirpated, and supplanted by others of foreign origin, spontaneous production is forbidden or restricted, and the face of the earth is either laid bare or covered with a new and reluctant growth of vegetable forms, and with alien tribes of animal life. These intentional changes and substitutions constitute, indeed, great revolutions; but vast as is their magnitude and importance, they are, as we shall see, insignificant in comparison with the contingent and unsought results which have flowed from them.

The fact that, of all organic beings, man alone is to be regarded as essentially a destructive power, and that he wields energies to resist which, nature—that nature whom all material life and all inorganic substance obey—is wholly impotent, tends to prove that, though living in physical nature, he is not of her, that he is of more exalted parentage, and belongs to a higher order of existences than those born of her womb and submissive to her dictates.

There are, indeed, brute destroyers, beasts and birds and insects of prey—all animal life feeds upon, and, of course, destroys other life,—but this destruction is balanced by compensations. It is, in fact, the very means by which the existence of one tribe of animals or of vegetables is secured against being smothered by the encroachments of another; and the reproductive powers of species, which serve as the food of others, are always proportioned to the demand they are destined to supply. Man pursues his victims with reckless destructiveness; and, while the sacrifice of life by the lower animals is limited by the cravings of appetite, he unsparingly persecutes, even to extirpation, thousands of organic forms which he cannot consume.[1]

1. The terrible destructiveness of man is remarkably exemplified in the chase of large mammalia and birds for single products, attended with the entire waste of enormous quantities of flesh, and of other parts of the animal, which are capable of valuable uses. The wild cattle of South America are slaughtered by millions for their hides and horns; the buffalo of North America for his skin or his tongue; the elephant, the walrus, and the narwhal for their tusks; the cetacea, and some other marine animals, for their oil and whalebone; the ostrich and other large birds, for their plumage. Within a few years, sheep have been killed in New England by whole flocks, for their pelts and suet alone, the flesh being thrown away; and it is even said that the bodies of the same quadrupeds have been used in Australia as fuel for limekilns. What a vast amount of human nutriment, of bone, and of other animal products valuable in the arts, is thus recklessly squandered! In nearly all these cases, the part which constitutes the motive for this wholesale destruction, and is alone saved, is essentially of insignificant value as compared with what is thrown away. The horns

The earth was not, in its natural condition, completely adapted to the use of man, but only to the sustenance of wild animals and wild vegetation. These live, multiply their kind in just proportion, and attain their perfect measure of strength and beauty, without producing or requiring any change in the natural arrangements of surface, or in each other's spontaneous tendencies, except such mutual repression of excessive increase as may prevent the extirpation of one species by the encroachments of another. In short, without man, lower animal and spontaneous vegetable life would have been constant in type, distribution, and proportion, and the physical geography of the earth would have remained undisturbed for indefinite periods, and been subject to revolution only from possible, unknown cosmical causes, or from geological action.

---

and hide of an ox are not economically worth a tenth part as much as the entire carcass.

One of the greatest benefits to be expected from the improvements of civilization is, that increased facilities of communication will render it possible to transport to places of consumption much valuable material that is now wasted because the price at the nearest market will not pay freight. The cattle slaughtered in South America, for their hides would feed millions of the starving population of the Old World, if their flesh could be economically preserved and transported across the ocean.

We are beginning to learn a better economy in dealing with the inorganic world. The utilization—or, as the Germans more happily call it, the Verwerthung, the *beworthing*—of waste from metallurgical, chemical, and manufacturing establishments, is among the most important results of the application of science to industrial purposes. The incidental products from the laboratories of manufacturing chemists often become more valuable than those for the preparation of which they were erected. The slags from silver refineries, and even from smelting houses of the coarser metals, have not unfrequently yielded to a second operator a better return than the first had derived from dealing with the natural ore; and the saving of lead carried off in the smoke of furnaces has, of itself, given a large profit on the capital invested in the works. A few years ago, an officer of an American mint was charged with embezzling gold committed to him for coinage. He insisted, in his defence, that much of the metal was volatilized and lost in refining and melting, and upon scraping the chimneys of the melting furnaces and the roofs of the adjacent houses, gold enough was found in the soot to account for no small part of the deficiency.

But man, the domestic animals that serve him, the field and garden plants the products of which supply him with food and clothing, cannot subsist and rise to the full development of their higher properties, unless brute and unconscious nature be effectually combated, and, in a great degree, vanquished by human art. Hence, a certain measure of transformation of terrestrial surface, of suppression of natural, and stimulation of artificially modified productivity becomes necessary. This measure man has unfortunately exceeded. He has felled the forests whose network of fibrous roots bound the mould to the rocky skeleton of the earth; but had he allowed here and there a belt of woodland to reproduce itself by spontaneous propagation, most of the mischiefs which his reckless destruction of the natural protection of the soil has occasioned would have been averted. He has broken up the mountain reservoirs, the percolation of whose waters through unseen channels supplied the fountains that refreshed his cattle and fertilized his fields; but he has neglected to maintain the cisterns and the canals of irrigation which a wise antiquity had constructed to neutralize the consequences of its own imprudence. While he has torn the thin glebe which confined the light earth of extensive plains, and has destroyed the fringe of semi-aquatic plants which skirted the coast and checked the drifting of the sea sand, he has failed to prevent the spreading of the dunes by clothing them with artificially propagated vegetation. He has ruthlessly warred on all the tribes of animated nature whose spoil he could convert to his own uses, and he has not protected the birds which prey on the insects most destructive to his own harvests.

Purely untutored humanity, it is true, interferes comparatively little with the arrangements of nature,[2] and the destructive agency

2. It is an interesting and not hitherto sufficiently noticed fact, that the domestication of the organic world, so far as it has yet been achieved, belongs, not indeed to the savage state, but to the earliest dawn of civilization, the conquest of inorganic nature almost as exclusively to the most advanced stages of artificial culture. It is familiarly known to all who have occupied themselves with the psychology and habits of the ruder races, and of persons with imperfectly developed intellects in civilized life, that

although these humble tribes and individuals sacrifice, without scruple, the lives of the lower animals to the gratification of their appetites and the supply of their other physical wants, yet they nevertheless seem to cherish with brutes, and even with vegetable life, sympathies which are much more feebly felt by civilized men. The popular traditions of the simpler peoples recognize a certain community of nature between man, brute animals, and even plants; and this serves to explain why the apologue or fable, which ascribes the power of speech and the faculty of reason to birds, quadrupeds, insects, flowers, and trees, is one of the earliest forms of literary composition.

In almost every wild tribe, some particular quadruped or bird, though persecuted as a destroyer of more domestic beasts, or hunted for food, is regarded with peculiar respect, one might almost say, affection. Some of the North American aboriginal nations celebrate a propitiatory feast to the manes of the intended victim before they commence a bear hunt; and the Norwegian peasantry have not only retained an old proverb which ascribes to the same animal *"ti Mænds Styrke og tolv Mænds Vid,"* ten men's strength and twelve men's cunning; but they still pay to him something of the reverence with which ancient superstition invested him. The student of Icelandic literature will find in the saga of *Finnbogi hinn rami* a curious illustration of this feeling, in an account of a dialogue between a Norwegian bear and an Icelandic champion—dumb show on the part of Bruin, and chivalric words on that of Finnbogi—followed by a duel, in which the latter, who had thrown away his arms and armor in order that the combatants might meet on equal terms, was victorious. John Hay Drummond Hay's very interesting work contains many amusing notices of a similar feeling entertained by the Moors toward the redoubtable enemy of their flocks—the lion.

This sympathy helps us to understand how it is that most if not all the domestic animals—if indeed they ever existed in a wild state—were appropriated, reclaimed and trained before men had been gathered into organized and fixed communities, that almost every known esculent plant had acquired substantially its present artificial character, and that the properties of nearly all vegetable drugs and poisons were known at the remotest period to which historical records reach. Did nature bestow upon primitive man some instinct akin to that by which she teaches the brute to select the nutritious and to reject the noxious vegetables indiscriminately mixed in forest and pasture?

This instinct, it must be admitted, is far from infallible, and, as has been hundreds of times remarked by naturalists, it is in many cases not an original faculty but an acquired and transmitted habit. It is a fact familiar to persons engaged in sheep husbandry in New England—and I have seen of man becomes more and more energetic and unsparing as he advances in civilization, until the impoverishment, with which his exhaustion of the natural resources of the soil is threatening him, at last awakens him to the necessity of preserving what is left, if not of restoring what has been wantonly wasted. The wandering savage grows no cultivated vegetable, fells no forest, and extirpates no useful plant, no noxious weed. If his skill in the chase enables him to entrap numbers of the animals on which he feeds, he compensates this loss by destroying also the lion, the tiger, the wolf, the otter, the seal, and the eagle, thus indirectly protecting

---

it confirmed by personal observation—that sheep bred where the common laurel, as it is called [lambkill kalmia, or sheep laurel], *Kalmia angustifolia,* abounds, almost always avoid browsing upon the leaves of that plant, while those brought from districts where laurel is unknown, and turned into pastures where it grows, very often feed upon it and are poisoned by it. A curious acquired and hereditary instinct, of a different character, may not improperly be noticed here. I refer to that by which horses bred in provinces where quicksands are common avoid their dangers or extricate themselves from them. See Nicolas Théodore Brémontier, "Mémoire sur les dunes . . . entre Bayonne et la pointe de Grave" (1790), reprinted in *Annales des Ponts et Chaussées,* 5 (1833), 155–157.

It is commonly said in New England, and I believe with reason, that the crows of this generation are wiser than their ancestors. Scarecrows which were effectual fifty years ago are no longer respected by the plunderers of the cornfield, and new terrors must from time to time be invented for its protection.

Civilization has added little to the number of vegetable or animal species grown in our fields or bred in our folds, while, on the contrary, the subjugation of the inorganic forces, and the consequent extension of man's sway over, not the annual products of the earth only, but her substance and her springs of action, is almost entirely the work of highly refined and cultivated ages. The employment of the elasticity of wood and of horn, as a projectile power in the bow, is nearly universal among the rudest savages. The application of compressed air to the same purpose, in the blowpipe, is more restricted, and the use of the mechanical powers, the inclined plane, the wheel and axle, and even the wedge and lever, seems almost unknown except to civilized man. I have myself seen European peasants to whom one of the simplest applications of this latter power was a revelation.

the feebler quadrupeds and fish and fowls, which would otherwise become the booty of beasts and birds of prey. But with stationary life, or rather with the pastoral state, man at once commences an almost indiscriminate warfare upon all the forms of animal and vegetable existence around him, and as he advances in civilization, he gradually eradicates or transforms every spontaneous product of the soil he occupies.[3]

The Instability of American Life

All human institutions, associate arrangements, modes of life, have their characteristic imperfections. The natural, perhaps the necessary defect of ours, is their instability, their want of fixedness, not in form only, but even in spirit. The face of physical nature in the United States shares this incessant fluctuation, and the landscape is as variable as the habits of the population. It is time for some abatement in the restless love of change which characterizes us, and makes us almost a nomade rather than a sedentary people.[1] We have now felled forest enough everywhere, in many

3. The difference between the relations of savage life, and of incipient civilization, to nature, is well seen in that part of the valley of the Mississippi which was once occupied by the mound builders and afterward by the far less developed Indian tribes. When the tillers of the fields which must have been cultivated to sustain the large population that once inhabited those regions perished or were driven out, the soil fell back to the normal forest state, and the savages who succeeded the more advanced race interfered very little, if at all, with the ordinary course of spontaneous nature.

1. It is rare that a middle-aged American dies in the house where he was born, or an old man even in that which he has built; and this is scarcely less true of the rural districts, where every man owns his habitation, than of the city, where the majority live in hired houses. This life of incessant flitting is unfavorable for the execution of permanent improvements of every sort, and especially of those which, like the forest, are slow in repaying any part of the capital expended in them. It requires a very

districts far too much. Let us restore this one element of material life to its normal proportions, and devise means for maintaining the permanence of its relations to the fields, the meadows, and the pastures, to the rain and the dews of heaven, to the springs and rivulets with which it waters the earth. The establishment of an approximately fixed ratio between the two most broadly characterized distinctions of rural surface—woodland and plough land —would involve a certain persistence of character in all the branches of industry, all the occupations and habits of life, which depend upon or are immediately connected with either, without implying a rigidity that should exclude flexibility of accommodation to the many changes of external circumstance which human wisdom can neither prevent nor foresee, and would thus help us to become, more emphatically, a well-ordered and stable commonwealth, and, not less conspicuously, a people of progress.

---

generous spirit in a landholder to plant a wood on a farm he expects to sell, or which he knows will pass out of the hands of his descendants at his death. But the very fact of having begun a plantation would attach the proprietor more strongly to the soil for which he had made such a sacrifice; and the paternal acres would have a greater value in the eyes of a succeeding generation, if thus improved and beautified by the labors of those from whom they were inherited. Landed property, therefore, the transfer of which is happily free from every legal impediment or restriction in the United States, would find, in the feelings thus prompted, a moral check against a too frequent change of owners, and would tend to remain long enough in one proprietor or one family to admit of gradual improvements which would increase its value both to the possessor and to the state.

3

A Time for Reflection

The gods of the valleys are not the gods of the hills. The valley men stayed here, and made their valley culture. But the men of the Green *mountains* moved westward. Sometimes they only got as far as Stockbridge, say twenty miles westward. But generally speaking they kept going, carrying their household gods with them. Always a Bible and always a rifle. Sometimes somebody's picture, perhaps a lock of hair, sometimes a primer or a spelling book, occasionally a silver cup or spoon with initials on it. More often than you might think, a flute or a fiddle. If they were lucky, they had a Morgan horse, or a horse that could claim to be at least a kissing cousin to a Morgan, as guide, philosopher, and friend.

—Betty Bandel, *Amanda*

Sugar Making Rowland E. Robinson, courtesy of Rowland E. Robinson Memorial Association

Folk Songs and Ballads of Vermont

The Song of the Vermonters, 1779

Ho! all to the bor - ders! Ver- mont - ers, come down With your
breech-es of deer-skin and jack -ets of brown, With your red wool-en caps, and your
moc-ca - sins, come, To the gath-er - ing sum-mons of trum-pet and drum. Come
down with your rif - les! Let gray wolf and fox Howl on in the shadow of their
prim - i - tive rocks; Let the bear feed se - cure - ly from
pig - pen and stall; Here's a two- leg-ged game for your pow-der and ball.

Ho—all to the borders! Vermonters, come down,
With your breeches of deerskin and jackets of brown:
With your red woolen caps and your moccasins, come,
To the gathering summons of trumpet and drum.

Come down with your rifles! Let gray wolf and fox
Howl on in the shade of their primitive rocks;
Let the bear feed securely from pig-pen and stall;
Here's two-legged game for your powder and ball.

On our south came the Dutchmen, enveloped in grease;
And arming for battle while canting of peace;
On our east, crafty Meshech has gathered his band
To hang up our leaders and eat up our land.

Ho—all to the rescue! For Satan shall work
No gain for his legions of Hampshire and York!
They claim our possessions—the pitiful knaves—
The tribute we pay shall be prisons and graves!

Let Clinton and Ten Broek, with bribes in their hands,
Still seek to divide us and parcel our lands;
We've coats for our traitors whoever they are;
The warp is of feathers—the filling of tar:

Does the "old Bay State" threaten? Does Congress complain?
Swarms Hampshire in arms on our borders again?
Bark the war-dogs of Britain aloud on the lake—
Let 'em come; what they can they are welcome to take.

What seek they among us? The pride of our wealth
Is comfort, contentment, and labor, and health,
And lands, which as Freemen, we only have trod,
Independent of all, save the mercies of God.

Yet we owe no allegiance, we bow to no throne,
Our ruler is law, and the law is our own;
Our leaders themselves are our own fellow-men,
Who can handle the sword, or the scythe, or the pen.

Our wives are all true, and our daughters are fair,
With their blue eyes of smiles and their light flowing hair,
All brisk at their wheels till the dark evenfall
Then blithe at the sleigh-ride, the husking, and ball!

We've sheep on the hillsides we've cows on the plain,
And gay-tasselled corn-fields and rank-growing grain;
There are deer on the mountains, and wood-pigeons fly
From the cracks of our muskets, like clouds in the sky.

And there's fish in our streamlets and rivers which take
Their course from the hills to our broad-bosomed lake;
Through rock-arched Winooski, the salmon leaps free,
And the portly shad follows all fresh from the sea.

Like a sunbeam the pickerel glides through the pool,
And the spotted trout sleeps where the water is cool,
Or darts from his shelter of rock and of root
At the beaver's quick plunge, or the angler's pursuit.

Hurrah for Vermont! For the land which we till
Must have sons to defend her from valley and hill;
Leave the harvest to rot on the fields where it grows,
And the reaping of wheat for the reaping of foes.

From far Michiscom's wild valley, to where
Poosoonsuck steals down from his wood-circled lair,
From Shocticook River to Lutterlock town—
Ho—all to the rescue! Vermonters, come down!

Come York or come Hampshire, come traitors or knaves,
If ye rule o'er our land, ye shall rule o'er our graves;
Our vow is recorded—our banner unfurled,
In the name of Vermont we defy all the world!

And ours are the mountains, which awfully rise,
Till they rest their green heads on the blue of the skies;
And ours are the forests unwasted, unshorn,
Save where the wild path of the tempest is torn.

And though savage and wild be this climate of ours
And brief be our season of fruits and of flowers,
Far dearer the blast round our mountain which raves,
Than the sweet summer zephyr which breathes over slaves!

Stratton Mountain Tragedy

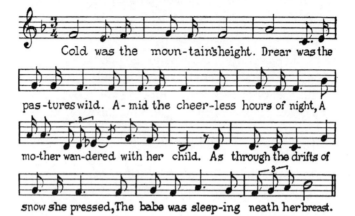

Cold was the moun-tain's height. Drear was the
pas-tures wild. A- mid the cheer-less hours of night, A
mo-ther wan-dered with her child. As through the drifts of
snow she pressed, The babe was sleep-ing neath her breast.

Cold swept the mountain high,
Dreary was the pathless wild.
Amid the cheerless hours of night
A mother wandered with her child.
As through the drifts of snow she pressed
The babe was sleeping neath her breast.

Bitter blew the chilly winds.
Darker hours of night came on.
Deeper grew the drifts of snow,
Her limbs were chilled, her strength was gone.
"O God," she cried in accents wild,
"If I must perish, save my child."

She took the mantle from her breast
And bared her bosom to the storm.
As round the child she wrapped the vest,
She smiled to think that it was warm.
One cold kiss, one tear she shed
And sank upon the snowy bed.

A traveler passing by next morn
Saw her neath the snowy veil.

The frost of death was in her eye
Her cheek was hard, cold and pale.
He took the robe from off the child.
The babe looked up and sweetly smiled.

John Grumlie

There was an old man who lived in the woods,
As you can plainly see.
He said he could do more work in one day
Than his wife could do in three.

"With all my heart," the old woman said,
"If you will me allow
You may stay at home today
And I will go follow the plow.

"But you must milk the Tiny cow
Less she should go dry,
And you must feed the little pigs
That are within the sty.

"And you must watch the speckled hen
Less she should lay astray,
And don't forget the spool of yarn
That I spin every day."

The old woman took her staft in hand
And went to follow the plow.
The old man, he put his pail on his head
And went to milk the cow.

But Tiny, she flinshed, and Tiny, she twinched,
And Tiny, she tossled her nose,

And Tiny, she gave him a kick on the shin
That sent the blood running down to his toes.

"Soe, Tiny, come soe,
Pretty, good cow, stand still.
If ever I milk you again in my life
It will be against my will."

Then he went to feed the pigs
That were within the sty.
He bumped his nose against a beam
Which caused the blood to fly.

Then he went to feed the hen
Less she should lay astray,
But he quite forgot the spool of yarn
His wife spun every day.

When the old woman came home from work,
He said he could plainly see
That she could do more work in one day
Than he could do in three.

And when he saw how well she plowed,
And made her furrows even,
He said she could do more work in one day
Than he could do in three.

The Wisconsin Emigrant's Song

Oh, hus-band, re-mem-ber that land of de-light Is sur-
round-ed by In-di-ans who mur-der by night. Your
Oh,
house they will plun-der and burn to the ground While your
stay on your farm and you'll suf-fer no loss, For the
wife and your chil-dren lie mur-dered a-round.
stone that keeps roll-ing will gath-er no moss.

"Since times are so hard, I've thought, my true heart,
Of leaving my oxen, my plough and my cart
And away to Wisconsin, a journey we'd go
To double our fortune as other folks do.
While here I must labor each day in the field
And the winter consumes all the summer doth yield."

"Oh, husband, I've noticed with sorrowful heart
You've neglected your oxen, your plough and your cart.
Your sheep are disordered; at random they run
And your new Sunday suit is now every day on.
Oh, stay on your farm and you'll suffer no loss.
For the stone that keeps rolling will gather no moss."

"Oh, wife, let's go. Oh, don't let us wait.
Oh, I long to be there. Oh, I long to be great!
While you some rich lady—and who knows but I
Some governor may be before that I die?
While here I must labor, etc."

"Oh, husband, remember that land is to clear
Which will cost you the labor of many a year,

Where horses, sheep, cattle and hogs are to buy
And you'll scarcely get settled before you must die.
Oh, stay on the farm, etc."

"Oh, wife, let's go. Oh, don't let us stay.
I will buy me a farm that is cleared by the way
Where horses, sheep, cattle and hogs are not dear
And we'll feast on fat buffalo half of the year
While here I must labor, etc."

"Oh, husband, remember that land of delight
Is surrounded by Indians who murder by night.
Your house they will plunder and burn to the ground
While your wife and your children lie murdered around.
Oh, stay on your farm, etc."

"Now wife, you've convinced me. I'll argue no more.
I never had thought of your dying, before.
To love my dear children, although they are small—
But you, my dear wife, are more precious than all.
We'll stay on the farm, etc."

Julia C. Dorr (1825-1913)

The Joy

The joy is in the doing,
   Not the deed that's done;
The swift and glad pursuing,
   Not the goal that's won.

The joy is in the seeing,
   Not in what we see;
The ecstasy of vision,
   Far and clear and free!

The joy is in the singing,
   Whether heard or no;
The poet's wild, sweet rapture,
   And song's divinest flow!

The joy is in the being—
   Joy of life and breath;
Joy of a soul triumphant,
   Conqueror of death!

Is there a flaw in the marble?
   Sculptor, do your best;
The joy is in the endeavor.
   Leave to God the rest!

Moon-Pictures

A slender crescent in the opal west,
Low-hung above a mountain's darkening crest—
A silent dream above a world at rest.

.   .   .   .

The bending curve of the horizon bar—
A silver boat moored high in depths afar,
Cradling in tender arms one lone bright star!

. . . .

An orchard close where wandering moonbeams strayed,
Weaving weird tapestries of light and shade,
And fairy paths for fairy footsteps made.

. . . .

A great white harvest moon, divinely fair,
Slow sailing through resplendent seas of air,
Over dark pine-trees, and a garden rare.

. . . .

A broad street flooded with the silver flow
Of the white moonbeams on new-fallen snow,
While, overhead, cloud shapes swept to and fro;

. . . .

A curtained window and a casement low,
And a fair woman in the radiant glow
On whom the king smiled, passing, long ago!

. . . .

What She Thought

Marion showed me her wedding-gown
    And her veil of gossamer lace to-night,
And the orange-blooms that to-morrow morn
    Shall fade in her soft hair's golden light.
But Philip came to the open door:
    Like the heart of a wild-rose glowed her cheek,

And they wandered off through the garden-paths
   So blest that they did not care to speak.

I wonder how it seems to be loved;
   To know you are fair in someone's eyes;
That upon someone your beauty dawns
   Every day as a new surprise;
To know that, whether you weep or smile,
   Whether your mood be grave or gay,
Somebody thinks you, all the while,
   Sweeter than any flower of May.

I wonder what it would be to love:
   That, I think, would be sweeter far,—
To know that one out of all the world
   Was lord of your life, your king, your star!
They talk of love's sweet tumult and pain:
   I am not sure that I understand,
Though—a thrill ran down to my finger-tips
   Once when—somebody—touched my hand!

I wonder what it would be to dream
   Of a child that might one day be your own;
Of the hidden springs of your life a part,
   Flesh of your flesh, and bone of your bone.
Marion stooped one day to kiss
   A beggar's babe with a tender grace;
While some sweet thought, like a prophecy,
   Looked from her pure Madonna face.

I wonder what it must be to think
   To-morrow will be your wedding-day,
And you, in the radiant sunset glow
   Down fragrant flowery paths will stray,
As Marion does this blessed night,
   With Philip, lost in a blissful dream.
Can she feel his heart through the silence beat?
   Does he see her eyes in the starlight gleam?

Questioning thus, my days go on;
    But never an answer comes to me:
All love's mysteries, sweet as strange,
    Sealed away from my life must be.
Yet still I dream, O heart of mine!
    Of a beautiful city that lies afar;
And there, some time, I shall drop the mask,
    And be shapely and fair as others are.

To a Late-Comer

(W. P. S.)

Why didst thou come into my life so late?
    If it were morning I could welcome thee
    With glad all-hails, and bid each hour to be
The willing servitor of thine estate,
Lading thy brave ships with Time's richest freight.
    If it were noonday I might hope to see
    On some far height thy banners floating free,
And hear the acclaiming voices call thee great!
But it is nightfall and the stars are out;
    Far in the west the crescent moon hangs low,
        And near at hand the lurking shadows wait;
Darkness and silence gather round about,
    Lethe's black stream is near its overflow,—
        Ah, friend, dear friend, why didst thou come so late?

The Armorer's Errand

A Ballad of 1775

Where the far skies soared clear and bright
From mountain height to mountain height,

In the heart of a forest old and gray,
Castleton slept one Sabbath day—
Slept and dreamed, on the seventh of May,
Seventeen hundred and seventy-five.

But hark! a humming, like bees in a hive;
Hark to the shouts—"They come! they come!"
Hark to the sound of the fife and drum!
For up from the south two hundred men—
Two hundred and fifty—from mount and glen,
While the deep woods rang with their rallying cry
Of "Ticonderoga! Fort Ti! Fort Ti!"
Swept into the town with a martial tread,
Ethan Allen marching ahead!

Next day the village was all astir
With unwonted tumult and hurry. There were
Gatherings here and gatherings there,
A feverish heat in the very air,
The ominous sound of tramping feet,
And eager groups in the dusty street.
To Eben's forge strode Gershom Beach
(Idle it stood, and its master away);
Blacksmith and armorer stout was he,
First in the fight and first in the breach,
And first in work where a man should be.
"I'll borrow your tools, my friend," he said,
"And temper these blades if I lose my head!"

So he wrought away till the sun went down,
And silence fell on the turbulent town;
And the flame of the forge through the darkness glowed,
A square of light on the sandy road.
Then over the threshold a shadow fell,
And he heard a voice that he knew right well.
It was Ethan Allen's. He cried: "I knew
Where the forge-fire blazed I must look for you!

But listen! more arduous work than this,
Lying in wait for someone is;
And tempering blades is only play
To the task I set for him this day—
Or this night, rather." A grim smile played
O'er the armorer's face as his hand he stayed.
"Say on. I never have shirked," said he;
"What may this wonderful task-work be?"

"To go by the light of the evening star
On an urgent errand, swift and far—
From town to town and from farm to farm
To carry the warning and sound the alarm!
Wake Rutland and Pittsford! Rouse Neshobè, too,
And all the fair valley the Otter runs through—
For we need more men! Make no delay,
But hasten, hasten, upon your way!"
He doffed his apron, he tightened his belt,
To fasten the straps of his leggings he knelt.
"Ere the clock strikes nine," said Greshom Beach,
"Friend Allen, I will be out of reach;
And I pledge you my word, ere dawn of day
Guns and men shall be under way.
But where shall I send these minute-men?"
"Do you know Hand's Cove?" said Allen then,
"On the shore of Champlain? Let them meet me there
By to-morrow night, be it foul or fair!"

"Good-by, I'm off!" Then down the road
As if on seven-league boots he strode,
While Allen watched from the forge's door
Till the stalwart form he could see no more.
Into the woods passed Gershom Beach;
By nine of the clock he was out of reach.
But still, as his will his steps outran,
He said to himself, with a laugh, "Old man,
Never a minute have you to lose,

Never a minute to pick or choose;
For sixty miles in twenty-four hours
Is surely enough to try your powers.
So square your shoulders and speed away
With never a halt by night or day."

'Twas a moonless night; but over his head
The stars a tremulous lustre shed,
And the breath of the woods grew strangely sweet,
As he crushed the wild ferns under his feet,
And trampled the shy arbutus blooms,
With their hoarded wealth of rare perfumes.
He sniffed as he went. "It seems to me
There are May-flowers here, but I cannot see.
I've read of the 'hush of the silent night';
Now hark! there's a wolf on yonder height;
There's a snarling catamount prowling round;
Every inch of the 'silence' is full of sound;
The night-birds cry; the whip-poor-wills
Call to each other from all the hills;
A scream comes down from the eagle's nest;
The bark of a fox from the cliff's tall crest;
The owls hoot; and the very trees
Have something to say to every breeze!"

The paths were few and the ways were rude
In the depths of that virgin solitude.
The Indian's trail and the hunter's tracks,
The trees scarred deep by the settler's axe,
Or a cow-path leading to the creek,—
These were the signs he had to seek;
Save where, it may be, he chanced to hit
The Crown Point road and could follow it—
The road by the British troops hewn out
Under General Amherst in fifty-nine,
When he drove the French from the old redoubt,
Nor waited to give the countersign!

The streams were many and swift and clear;
But there was no bridge, or far or near.
It was midnight when he paused to hear
At Rutland, the roar of the waterfall,
And found a canoe by the river's edge,
In a tangled thicket of reeds and sedge.
With a shout and a cheer, on the rushing tide
He launched it and flew to the other side;
Then giving his message, on he sped,
By the light of the pale stars overhead,
Past the log church below Pine Hill,
And the graveyard opposite. All was still,
And the one lone sleeper lying there
Stirred not either for cry or prayer.

Only pausing to give the alarm
At rude log cabin and lonely farm.
From hamlet to hamlet he hurries along,
Borne on by a purpose deep and strong.
Look! there's a deer in the forest glade,
Stealing along like a silent shade!
Hark to the loon that cries and moans
With a living grief in its human tones!
At Pittsford the light begins to grow
In the wakening east; and drifting slow,
From valley and river and wildwood, rise,
Like the smoke of a morning sacrifice,
Clouds of translucent, silver mist,
Flushing to rose and amethyst;
While thrush and robin and bluebird sing
Till the woods with jubilant music ring!

It was day at last! He looked around,
With a firmer tread on the springing ground;
"Now the men will be all a-field," said he,
"And that will save many a step for me.
Each man will be ready to go; but still,

I must confess, if I'd had my will,
I'd have waited till after planting-time,
For now the season is in its prime.
The young green leaves of the oak-tree here
Are just the size of a squirrel's ear;
And I've known no rule, since I was born,
Safer than that for planting corn!"

He threaded the valleys, he climbed the hills,
He forded the rivers, he leaped the rills,
While still to his call, like minute-men
Booted and spurred, from mount and glen,
The settlers rallied. But on he went
Like an arrow shot from a bow, unspent,
Down the long vale of the Otter to where
The might of the waterfall thundered in air;
Then across to the lake, six leagues and more,
Where Hand's Cove lay in the bending shore.
The goal was reached. He dropped to the ground
In a deep ravine, without word or sound;
And Sleep, the restorer, bade him rest
Like a weary child, on the earth's brown breast.

At midnight he woke with a quick heart-beat,
And sprang with a will to his throbbing feet;—
For armed men swarmed in the dim ravine,
And Ethan Allen, as proud of mien
As a king on his throne, smiled down on him,
While he stretched and straightened each stiffened limb.
"Nay, nay," said the Colonel, "take your rest,
As a knight who has done his chief's behest!"

"Not yet!" cried the armorer. "Where's my gun?
A knight fights on till the field is won!"
And into Fort Ti, ere dawn of day,
He stormed with his comrades to share the fray!

Ella Warner Fisher (1853-1937)

My Neighbor's Barn

My neighbor's barn is painted red
And so, I am sure, is his shed.
I thought some other color more
In accord with the green
That Nature wore.
> That the builder faced the gables east
> Should make no difference to any beast.

But the first faint beam
From the eastern skies
Caught the gables agleam
In the bright sunrise.
From my window's vista
Haloed in light,
My neighbor's red barn
Is a dream of delight,
And turning it over
In my mind,
A reason I find
For painting it red . . .
Even the shed!

The Cedars

On each side of the path
Straight and tall,
Bronzed by the weather,

Voices of the wind
Whispering among their branches.

Planted long ago
With children playing about them,
They were rooted in the soil.
They grew up together . . .
The children and the trees,
But the children went away!

Now, when the night falls early
And the windows shine out in the darkness,
There are long shadows on the white roadway
Cast by the cedars standing straight and tall . . .
Listening . . . listening for homing footsteps
With the wind whispering among their branches.

"All that tread the globe
Are but a handful to the tribes
That sleep within its bosom."

Nothing More

We stood on the rim of the world
Where all the graves are made
And watched the slow unheeding men
Fashion them with a spade.

And one yawned at your feet . . .
On its cold and empty floor
I spread your worn out garment . . .
You gave me nothing more!

My Prayer

To be snatched from life
When the days are sweet,
When the nights are full
With health replete . . .
Grant, I pray this boon to me
From Death my soul to wrest . . .
That joyous, living I may be
Snatched to Thy loving breast!

Daniel L. Cady (1861-1934)

Adam and Wife

Some folks demand such loads of proof
   On ancestorial points,
And stand so actively aloof
   They 'pear to have no joints;
But jest the reason for it all
   I never could conceive—
There's not a paper left to show
   That Adam married Eve.

No doubt the folks of folks I like
   Have had their ups and downs,
But who would call a social strike
   Because a high-hat frowns!
You've simply got to trust someone
   And make yourself believe,
For not a scrap is left to show
   That Adam married Eve.

Whence Came the Hankses—whence and when?
   Yet Nancy's gawming son
Set free more sad and hopeless men
   Than any king has done;
There's many strands in life's wild web
   That strangely interweave,
And 'tisn't odd that nothing shows
   That Adam married Eve.

A trick of Couer de Lion's face
   Saved Falconbridge his land,

And not the "records of his race"
  In some dead scrivener's hand;
Most every home and heart has lost
  Some gem it can't retrieve—
I think we'd better let it go
  That Adam married Eve.

When blood's too elderly or blue
  It's sometimes rather bad:
What kind of man am I, not who
  Was my great granddad's dad?
That there's the question, that's the point,
  At least so I conceive,
Especially as there's no proof
  That Adam married Eve.

A Vermont Pasture

You have to work your tillage land
  And mow and hoe and plow it,
But as for pasture, all you do
  Is jest to sheep or cow it;
And you can walk jest where you please,
  Instead of 'round the edges,
And Sunday you can go and set
  Upon the pasture ledges.

I've seen a lot of right good folks
  Whose names I ain't repeating,
Go through the bars on Sunday morn,
  Instead of off to meeting;
And when a preacher hits too hard
  With his dogmatic sledges,
You might be saved if you should spend
  A Sunday on the ledges.

You cross the brook on stepping stones
    You've hauled from out the mowing;
You own the stones and own the brook,
    Although it keeps agoing;
Then past the logged-off piece you climb,
    That's fenced with blackberry hedges,
And then you sight the butnut tree,
    And up beyond, the ledges.

At last you're there—you see your house
    And barn, and both your medders,
And 'way off north the other farm
    You rent to Elmer Cheddars;
You feel as fine as temperance tots
    Who've jest signed six more pledges—
The world, By Gol! is quite a place
    From Bagley's pasture ledges.

Your wife and boys are both along,
    And whilst you've been a-looking
They've fixed it so you'll all go snacks
    On mother's put-up cooking;
By George! that rozberry pie is good,
    Them great, big, bleeding wedges,
You don't feel wicked, none of you,
    For being on the ledges.

You stand up straight and give a stretch,
    And then go 'round by mother,
And quote from Waldo or from Walt
    Some out-door truth or other;
You're jest as full of nature thoughts
    As England is of hedges—
Thoreau, he loved the woods of Maine,
    But Bagley loves his ledges.

My! such a peaceful, fambly day,
    It makes you Congos Quakers;

You can't have no such day as that
   On top of tillage acres;
It beats a day on Woodstock Green,
   Or 'mongst the Highgate sedges;
There ain't no day that's like a day
   Upon your pasture ledges.

An Old Vermont Cellar Hole

To wander near a ruined home
   Upon a Springtime morning,
Informs the mind and charms the eye,
   But gives the heart a warning;
For, Oh! the sense of human change
   That such a scene discloses—
The roses 'round the fallen walls,
   And lilacs 'round the roses.

The hands that built the house were strong,
   The builded house was stronger,
The flowers, a wifely afterthought,
   But they are lasting longer;
We wonder in what grass-grown yard
   The tenant here reposes,
And she, as well, for whom they grew,
   The lilacs and the roses.

Some leaning wrecks of orchard trees
   Declare that life was pleasant;
They lived, as we are living now,

   Concerned about the present;
However dear, another day
   The dearest day deposes,
And after time binds up the wounds
   With lilacs and with roses.

Here children played about the door
    And here delayed the lover;
But now, not e'en the portal's site
    A stranger may discover;
We hope that no philandering Gad,
    No false Uriah or Moses,
Destroyed this home and only left
    The lilacs and the roses.

The highway once went winding by,
    But long ago was shifted
To follow through the intervale,
    Whereto "the world" had drifted;
The robins chirp about no more,
    A human chapter closes,
With just this fragrant finis piece
    Of lilacs set in roses.

Carcassonne

I'm sixty odd, my day is past,
    I've worked and worked until I'm tired,
Without attaining, first or last,
    The youthful wish my heart desired;
I see it's vain to try to build
    A house of hope and get it done;
My early vow is unfulfilled,
    I've never looked on Carcassonne.

"You see the city standing there
    High up, beyond the mountains blue;
To reach it five long leagues you fare,
    Of coming back the same is true;
The vintage, though, is my concern—
    Ah! if the autumn's work were done—

The wilful grapes refuse to turn,
   I shall not look on Carcassonne.

"On week days there they all parade
   As much as on a Sunday night;
You see them on the esplanade
   In fine new clothes and robes of white;
There's lofty towers and double walls
   As high as those of Babylon,
A bishop and two generals—
   And I know not fair Carcassonne.

"The vicar rightfully declares
   We're stupid to the last degree;
'Ambition,' says he in his prayers,
   'Destroys us, let its baubles be';
But if two days could be my prize
   Before the autumn rains come on,
I'd die content, for these old eyes
   Would then have looked on Carcassonne.

"Oh! if my prayer be deemed too bold
   And urgent, may God pardon me;
We see beyond ourselves when old
   No less than in our infancy;
My wife and little boy, Aignan,
   Have travelled even to Narbonne,
My grandson has seen Perpignan
   But I have not seen Carcassonne."

Thus sang an old man of Limoux
   To toil's deforming business born;
Said I: "My friend, I'll go with you,
   We'll start upon the morrow morn";
But, may the good God rest his soul,
   He died when we had halfway gone;
He never reached the longed-for goal,
   He never saw fair Carcassonne.

Rowland Evans Robinson (1833-1900)

The Fox and His Guests

A Fox, finding it becoming an irksome Labor to get a Living by his usual honest Methods, since it was a long Way from his Home to the nearest Poultry Yard or Goose Pasture, bethought him of a Plan to fill his Larder, and at once made Trial of it. He caused it to be noised about that nowhere in the whole Region could Turkeys find such Quantities of Beech Nuts as in his Wood, nor such Swarms of Grasshoppers as in the Pastures along the Woodside, where the Grass grew so thick and tender, with a wide Pond near at Hand for bathing and swimming, so that it would delight the Heart of any Goose. It was added that any Fowls wishing to get the Benefit of all these good Things were quite welcome to come and do so.

Some wise old Turkeys and Geese had no Faith in these fine Stories, saying that "they had heard of the Fox before, and doubted whether much tender Grass and many Grasshoppers held long together." But many less wise were taken by Host Reynard's glowing Representations, and flocked thither in great Numbers. But they found the Beech Nuts scarce, the Grasshoppers few in the poor Pastures, and the boasted Pond proved to be a mere Puddle. Meanwhile, however, the Fox had good Picking, and throve and waxed fat throughout the Season, for the few returning Fowls said Nothing of their Ill-Fare, and more kept going; and before the Summer had passed Feathers and Bones were plentier along the Woodside than Blades of Grass had ever been.

MORAL

Before thou believest a big Story of Fish and Game it may be well for thee to learn somewhat of its Source. Peradventure it may be a Tavern.

Gran'ther Hill's Pa'tridge

The September sun shone with summer-like fervor in the little valley of Danvis; not an afternoon of August had been hotter, or breathed a droughtier breath upon wilting forests and sered fields. Here and there among the dusky green of the woods, a tree nurtured by more sterile rootage than its neighbors was burning out its untimely ripeness in a blaze of red or yellow, from which the puffs of warm wind scattered sparks of color so intense that it seemed as if they might kindle the dry earth.

All nature was languid in the unseasonable heat and drought. The unrefreshing breeze blew in lazy puffs without even energy of direction, but listlessly trying this quarter and that, now bearing, now dropping, the light burden of a tree's complaining, the rustle of the rolled corn leaves, the faint whimper of tired brooks, the petulant clamor of the crows, and the high, far-away scream of a hawk that, level with the hazy mountain peaks, wheeled in slow circles, a hot brown speck against the bronze sky.

The same wearied air pervaded the precincts of Joseph Hill's home and the house itself. The hens lay panting with drooped wings under the scant shade of the currant bushes, whose shriveled remnant of fruit gave no promise of refreshing coolness; their half-grown progeny stalked aimlessly about the yard in indolent quest of nothing, while they grated out the discordant yelp which is neither peep nor cluck, and expresses nothing if it be not continual discontent; and the ducks waddled home, thirsty and unhappy, from the dried-up puddle.

The hollyhock stalks stood naked and forlorn among the drooping leaves, with only here and there a blossom too stunted to tempt a bumblebee showing among the browning buttons of seed vessels. The morning-glory leaves hung limp upon their twisted vines, that had evidently blown their last purple trumpet to call the bees, clutching their supporting cords only with a dying grasp. All the house-side posies were withered, "chiny asters," "sweet-williams," and "sturtiums"; nothing held up its head but the sturdy house-leeks—hens and chickens their mistress called them, and nursed them in their box in doors and out the year round, for their oddity and their repute for curing corns.

Even Gran'ther Hill, whom age might wither though it could not sap his vitality, showed little of his accustomed vigor, as he sat in the doorway with his bristly chin upon his staff, staring vaguely on the haze-bounded landscape, or at something beyond the filmy veil unseen by other and younger eyes, the past or the future. Battlefields of Revolutionary days, lonely scouts in the great wilderness, secret missions in the service of the old Green Mountain Boys—or was he looking forward to the paths of the unknown, which he must presently tread?

Whatever occupied his thoughts, it apparently was not what was said or done by those near him. In the same room was his son, who sat with his chair tilted against the wall; and a well-fed, self-satisfied man, who, slovenly clad, though his blue coat had not been long worn and its brass buttons were bright, sat across the table from Joseph, with a small hair trunk open before him, packed brimful of paper parcels and tin boxes. Joseph Hill's eldest daughter, a tired, overgrown girl of twelve in an outgrown frock, moved wearily about the household labors that had fallen on her, and her younger brother sat disconsolately in one corner, nursing an aching tooth that kept him home from school. Their mother, who lay in the bedroom beyond, had been ill for weeks with an intermittent fever, but was now "on the gain," thanks to the treatment of the keen-eyed, blue-coated man with the hair trunk full of roots and herbs and their tinctures.

He was a disciple of Dr. Samuel Thompson, a self-taught mediciner, who, many years before, had brought upon himself the wrath, bitterer than his own concoctions, of the regular physicians of New England by his unauthorized practice and his denunciations of their methods. In time they enlarged and improved their pharmacopœia by availing themselves of his discoveries, but gave him no credit, and few know to what "noted empiric" they are indebted for them. Joseph was conservative, and would rather have employed the old regular physician of Danvis than this innovator, or perhaps both, and his father was bitter "agin Injin an' ol' woman ways o' darkterin';" but this unlicensed practitioner had cured Maria's mother of "newrology," and him she was set upon having, and Joseph consented, according to his usual custom when "M'ri" insisted.

"Mis' Hill," said the doctor, looking over his spectacles and his trunk at Joseph, "is sights better. The reg'lar course we've gi'n her, lobele 'metics, steamin' an' sofuth, has hove off the agur spells an' the fever. All she wants naow is strenth'nin', suthin' tu give her an appetite t' eat, an' suthin' nourishin' t' eat. We're goin' tu leave her these here spice bitters, tu take a small spoo'f'l steeped up in a teacup o' hot water three times a day; an' you must git some popple bark, and steep up a big han'f'l on 't in a gallern o' water, an' hev her drink a ha' pint on 't most any time when she's dry, or a dozen times a day; an' it would be a good thing for her tu take a leetle pennyr'yal tea, say a teacupful three, four times a day, kinder 'tween times, an' then eat nourishin' victuals."

Gran'ther Hill turned his head and glowered savagely at him, but uttered only a contemptuous snort.

"I do' know," said Joseph, slowly easing the fore-legs of his chair to the floor and as slowly scratching his head, "but what M'ri kin hold some victuals arter she's took all them steepin's, but it don't seem's 'ough she could much, that is tu say, not a turrible sight. Ye see, Darkter, she hain't a turrible big womern, that is, not so big as some. But mebby she kin. I d' know."

"Ye'll draowned her wi' yer cussed slops!" Gran'ther Hill growled, turning in his chair and thumping the floor with rapid blows of his cane. " 'F you'd ha' gi'n her some callymill an' bled her 'n the fust on 't, she 'd ha' ben all right naow! You've roasted her an' biled her, an' naow yer goin' tu draowned her wi' yer pailfuls o' spice bitters an' popple soup, an' the Lord knows what tarnal slops!"

"Callymill is pizon, an' tew much bleedin' is what kills hawgs," said the doctor with calm emphasis.

"Pizon is good when it's took proper," Gran'ther Hill retorted, "an' folks hain't hawgs, not all of 'em hain't. I wish 't Darkter Stun 'ould come along an' gi' me a dost o' callymill an' bleed me;

I know it 'ould make me feel better this tarnal roastin' weather. It's a feller's blood 'at heats him. I c'n feel mine a chuggin' up ag'in the top o' my skull every beat o' my pult, an' I wish I was red of a quart on 't!''

"You don't look, Kepting Hill," the doctor said, after a brief survey of the old man's gaunt figure, "as if you hed a grea' deal o' blood tu spare."

"I know't I've shed lots on 't for my country," said Gran'ther Hill. "But I've got 'nough left tu fill up tew, three pepper darkters wi' better 'n they've got!''

"No daoubt on 't, Kepting, no daoubt on 't," the good-natured mediciner answered, "but you don't wanter waste it. Tew much good blood no man can't hev, an' aour remedies make bad blood good. You take some pepsissiway an' put it in some ol' Medford, an' take a swaller three times a day, a good big swaller, Kepting, an' see what it'll du for yer blood."

"That saounds sensibler 'n the water swash you was talkin' on, an' I begin tu think you know suthin' arter all. Jozeff, nex' time you go over tu Hamner's, you git me a quart, 'n' I'll gether me some pepsissiway, an' I'll put in three, four sprigs, an' try it."

"Reason is aour guide," said the doctor, "an' aour remedies is what Natur p'ints aout tu us. We don't make no secret o' what she tells us. Naow, these 'ere spice bitters is compaounded of sev-eral nat'ral plants, but the main ingrejencies is feverbush an' bay-berry. We hain't no secrets; all we're after is the trewth."

"Go t' thunder!" growled Gran'ther Hill. "You're arter yer livin', jes' as all on us is. Nothin' on this livin' airth riles me wus'n hearin' darkters an' preachers gabbin' 'baout the raslin' raound jes' for the sake o' duin' other folks good, when they an ev'ybody knows it's theirselves they're workin' for. Who they tryin' tu fool, —God amighty, or folks, or the' ownselves?"

"Sartainly, we 've got tu live whilest we 're raslin' for the trewth, Kepting. You drawed pay when you was fightin' fer your kentry, an' you fit a leetle better, proberbly, 'n you would for nothin' but glory. Starvin' fodder that is, for livin' on in this world. An' that reminds me 't Mis' Hill wants suthin' nourishin' t' eat. The' hain't nothin' better 'n pa'tridge meat, which it is victuals an' medicine to oncte, for a pa'tridge is continerly a-feedin' on a hulsome diet, fever-bush berries, wintergreen, pepsissiway, blackberries, popple-buds, and birch-buds, an' I do' know what all, of Nature's pharmy-copy, which is dissimerlated through the meat. You never knowed a man tu git sick eatin' pa'tridge, did ye, Kepting Hill, or you, Mr. Hill?" and while waiting for a reply the doctor dived into the depths of his tall Leghorn hat for a red bandanna handkerchief, with which he vigorously mopped his face and blew a trumpet-blast of his nose.

"Not me," said Gran'ther Hill, "I've lived on 'em for weeks when I was scaoutin' 'long wi' Peleg Sunderlan', an' the wolves had drove all the deer off."

"Not tu aour haouse, we don't," said Joseph; "ner scasely git a taste on 'em sen' father gin up huntin'. Wal, that is tu say, exceptin' when Sam Lovel brings us a mess, or oncte when bub killed one with his bow-arrer, or mebby ketched it in a snare, I d' know but he did."

"I did kill him wi' my bow-arrer," protested the boy, forgetting his toothache in his desire to assert his sportsmanship; "an' ol' he one he was, bigger 'n a rhuster, a thumpin' of a spreuce lawg I c'n show ye, an' I sneaked up julluk gran'ther tells o' Injins duin', an' I knawked him stiffer 'n a stake, 'n' I lit on him 'fore he—" Here a thump of the grandfather's cane reminded the boy of the often-repeated maxim that such as he were to be seen, not heard, and muttering that he could "show 'em the lawg," he subsided into silence and the nursing of his aching jaw.

"I s'pose you c'n shoot Mis' Hill a pa'tridge, can't ye, Mr. Hill? They say the woods is so full on 'em 'at they 're a stickin' aout o' the aidges."

"No, Darkter," said Joseph, going over to the stove hearth for his pipe and beginning a quest for his tobacco, "I hain't no knack for huntin' pa'tridge. They allers see me afore I du them, an' by the time I git my gun up the' hain't nuthin' left but a glimp an' a noise, an' afore I c'n git my mind made up tu shoot at them on-sartainties, as Sam does, an' father ustur, both on 'em is gone. I thought I left my terbarker on the mantel-tree shelf. Oh, there it is on the winder stool."

"Wal," said the doctor, bending a benign glance upon the boy, "bub c'n git his mar a pa'tridge with his bow-arrer, I know, an' if he will, I'll pull his tooth so 't won't ache again."

"I won't tech tu try fer no sech pay; but 'f they'd let me take Gran'ther's ol' gun, I'd git one. The' 's a hull litter on 'em stays up in the aidge o' the parstur."

"You shoot a pa'tridge wi' my gun?" growled his grandfather, glowering upon him. "Ye couldn't hol' it tu arm's len'th a secont, you hain't staout 'nough tu pull the tricker 'f you c'ld reach it, an' if ye could 't 'ould kick ye int' the middle o' next week! It's a man's gun, that is," pointing up to the long-barreled flint-lock that hung above the mantel, gray with all the dust which had fallen on it since the spring campaign against the crows, "an' it 's killed moose an' wolves an' bear an' Injins an' Tories an' Hessians an' Britishers, an' it c'ld tell who hel' it when it killed 'em. He hain't dead yit; an' 'f ye want a pa'tridge, he c'n git ye one, which his name is Josiah Hill. What ye say 'baout pa'tridge is sensibler 'n what ye say 'bout darkterin', an' Marier's goin' tu hev one. I'd be willin' fer you tu pick aout my victuals, but I'd ruther hev an' ol'-fashioned reg'lar larnt physician darkter du my darkterin'."

"Reg'lar licensed pizoners, they be, ign'antly killin' folks under kiver of the die-plomies," Dr. Wead protested in a discreetly low voice; then in a louder tone, "seem 's 'ough you was ruther along in years tu go huntin', Kepting. Better start aout some o' the young fellers, that aire Lovel, fer instance. They say he's a marster hand at huntin'."

"If ever I got sick o' anythin'," said the old man, bending his bushy brows in a savage frown and thumping the floor with his staff, "it's everlastin'ly hearin' tell o' that aire Sam Lovel's huntin'! Ye'd think, tu hear 'em talk, 'at me an' Peleg Sunderlan' wa'n't never nowheres 'longside o' him,—him 't was brung up on pa'-tridge an' foxes tu be sot up 'longside o' men 't was raised when the' was painters and Injins in the woods thicker 'n red squirrels be naow! I s'pose he ken shoot tol'able well wi' his cannern fer nowerdays, but I git almighty sick o' hearin' tell on 't. Jozeff here's allers braggin' secont han' o' what Sam Lovel's done, an' Jozeff do' know one eend of a gun f'm t'other. Took arter his mother, 'n' she wa' no hunter. Bub, here, ac's more like, an' 'f he 'd ben borned fifty years ago, when the' was suthin' tu hunt, he 'd ha' ben a hunter." Even such faint praise banished for a moment the torture of the aching tooth, as the boy cast longing looks up at the ancient gun, whose brass mountings were brighter and more precious to his eyes than burnished gold.

"I'm a-goin' tu git Marier a pa'tridge," the old man went on. "Good min' ter go right off. 'F I don't I will in the mornin'; I've heerd a gun every oncte in a while all the art-noon. There 't goes ag'in," as a flat report came faint and echoless through the sultry air from the lower slope of the mountain side. "He hain't killin' nothin', I know by the way his gun saounds, but he'll scare ev'ythin' aout'n the woods er over the maountin. Guess I'd better go right off an' git ahead on him."

"Better wait till the cool o' the mornin', father. They'll all git settled back in the' haunts by then," Joseph suggested; and then in a loud whisper to the doctor, "He'll fergit all 'baout it by then!"

"Wal, mebby; I'll see," said his father, settling back uneasily in his armchair, and again fixing his senile stare on the outer world.

"Naow, then," said Dr. Wead in a more cheerful tone than the proposal warranted, "naow, then, bub, 'f you seddaown in the door an' brace yer back ag'in' one post an' yer feet ag'in' t' other, I'll red ye o' that aire pesky tooth in a jiffy."

"I do' wanter hev it pulled!" the boy whimpered. "It don't ache a mite naow!"

"It's unly foolin' on ye, bub," said the doctor. "That's a trick the pesky things is allers up tu. I won't hurt ye more'n a minute, an' then you'll be tu play an' practicin' wi' yer bow-arrer fer to shoot yer mar a pa'tridge."

"Why, yes, Josie," urged his father, "jest seddaown an' hev her aout julluk a man, an' I'll git ye—le' me see, why, I'll git ye a jew-sharp nex' time I go t' the store."

"Can't play no jew-sharp when I hain't got no teeth, more'n Gran'ther can," the boy half sobbed.

"Couldn't ye give him suthin' tu kinder ease it up fer a spell?" Joseph asked, after puzzling his brains for a more tempting offer. "'F his mother was araound he c'ld stan' it better."

The doctor shook his head. "Nothin' but cold iron'll stop it."

"It'll hurt like Sam Hill!" howled poor little Josiah.

"Look a-here, bub," said his grandfather, turning his chair again to face the room. "It hain't a-goin' tu be said 'at a boy 'at wants tu go huntin' wi' a gun, an' which he's named arter his gran'ther that fit tu Hubbar'ton an' Bennin'ton, to say nuthin' o' takin' Ticonderogue, is a-goin' tu raise a rumpus 'baout hevin' a mis'able leetle tooth pulled aout. If ye don't come right stret here an' seddaown in the door an' open yer maouth an' shet yer head, I'll take ye up tu the leegislatur this fall, right afore them tew brass cannern 't we took f'm the Hessians tu Bennin'ton, an' hev yer name changed, the hull on't; Josier shall be Nosier, an' Hill shall be Holler, 'cause ye'll be so low daown, an' 'cause ye'll holler for hevin' a tooth pulled. An' if ye seddaown like a man an' say nothin', I'll let ye shoot my gun tu a mark, 'f it kicks ye furder'n ye shoot! There!"

The boy looked a moment into the relaxed sternness of his grandfather's face, and then, his own pale but resolute, he walked over and took the prescribed position on the threshold.

"Git aout yer cant-hook, Darkter, whilst his grit's up," said Gran'ther Hill, while Joseph retreated to the bedside of his wife, whither, with an appalled look dispossessing the wearied expression of her face, his daughter accompanied him.

The doctor, taking the terrible turn-key from his trunk, bestrode the boy, whose head he grasped between his knees, and in one brief but awful moment wrenched out the tooth and a suppressed groan.

"You'll make a hunter an' a sojer," said the doctor. "You stood it like a major, an' I'm goin' tu wrop up that tooth in a piece o' paper for ye t' show folks."

The old man gave his grandson a gentle punch in the ribs with his cane to express his approval. "Didn't hurt ye much naow, did it, bub?"

"The hole aches wus'n the darned tooth did," said Josiah the younger. "When ye gointer let me shoot yer gun, Gran'ther?"

"T'morrer, when I git back f'm huntin'," his grandsire promptly responded. "Say, bub, is that Mis' Purin't'n comin' up the rhud? Yes? Well, then, I'm goin' huntin' right naow 'f she's comin' here, 'n I'll bate she be." Arising with all the speed that his stiff joints could compass, he took down his gun, drew the iron ramrod and dropped it into the barrel, then measured the protruding end with his fingers, returned the rod to its pipes, threw the long barrel into the hollow of his arm, and critically examined flint and priming, before his son had come forth from the bedroom.

"Why, father, ye'd better not go this arternoon, you'll git your blood all het up!" Joseph expostulated.

"Your darkter says I hain't got no blood," his father answered, reaching up for the big powder-horn, the buckskin shot-pouch, and a wisp of tow for wadding, while he whispered loudly, "That aire Purin't'n womern 's a-comin', 'n' I'd ruther git het an' sun-struck 'n tu hear her gab. Wonder Purin't'n never took tu huntin'."

"She won't stay long, not so turrible long, I don't scasely b'lieve she will, an' you c'n go an' lay daown in yer room," urged Joseph; and the doctor also made some attempt to dissuade the old man from going abroad, though it was noticeable that he was hurriedly packing the little hair trunk and hastily preparing for his own departure.

"Don't you go a-huntin' no pa'tridge for me," pleaded Maria's feeble voice from the bedroom. "A chicken 'll du jest as well."

"I tell ye you're a-goin' tu hev a pa'tridge, an' I'm going tu git it!" the veteran protested.

"Wal," said Joseph, making search for his hat in all places but under his chair, where it was, "ef you will go ag'in all reason, I'll go 'long with ye, erless I'll hev bub go; er mebby we'll both on us go, tu kerry your game, ye know, an' yer gun, an' sech, an' mek it kinder comf'table fer ye."

"When I go huntin' I don't go 't the head of a army, wi' a fife an' drum a-playin'," cried Gran'ther Hill at the top of his cracked and whistling voice, "nor no lummuxes, an' no bubs a-taggin' tu my heels, a-scarin' all the game outen sight an' hearin' wi' the' crackin', an' snappin', an' sloshin', an' gabbin'! D' ye think I'm a five-year-ol' boy 't can't go nowheres by hisself? You stay 't hum an' tend t' your own business, an' I'll tend tu mine!"

Lowering the muzzle of his gun to clear the lintel of the door, he went out as Mrs. Purington entered. Dropping heavily into the nearest chair and puffing out a brief salutation, she cast back her green gingham sunbonnet, and began fanning her hot face with her checked apron held by its nether corners.

"It is tew orfle hot tu stir aou' door, but I thought I mus' come an' chirk up Mis' Hill a leetle mite, an' I tol' him I would come if it melted me. I declare tu goodness I b'lieve it hes! Whew! Who ever see sech weather for the time o' year? Hain't your caows s'runk the' milk orfle? An' aour cistern's mos' dry an' the spring hain't never ben so low sen' he c'n remember. I d' know what's going tu be become on us all 'f we don't git shaowers. It's enough tu make well folks sick an' tu kill sick folks, an' I p'sume tu say it will kill Mis' Hill. Haow is she anyway?" leaning forward to peer into the bedroom, her fat hands, still holding the apron corners, resting on her short lap.

"Gittin' wus an' wus, I s'pose?" then, with a sudden fear, " 'T hain't nothin' ketchin', I hope,—none of these ketchin' fevers?"

"No," Joesph assured her. "Intumittens, or some sech name, the darkter calls it. Suthin' like fev' 'n' aig; kinder wus 'n that, an' then ag'in, not so bad," he explained.

Her fears of infection set at rest, Mrs. Purington drew her chair to the bedroom door and set herself to comforting the sick woman.

"Wal, Marier, you du look peakeder 'n what I expected, an' it's a massy 't I come when I did, or I might not ha' seen you alive. Mis' Tarbell, his brother's wife's sister, was took jest the same way 'long in hayin', an' it hove her intu quick consumpshern, an' she died 'fore the graound froze up, which was some consolashern, 'cause 't wa'n't no such work diggin' the grave as 't 'ould ha' ben later. I du hope you feel prepared for the wust, Marier, I du."

"Ruby," said Mrs. Hill, as her eye caught the scared face of her daughter, "I wish't you'd gwaout an' see 'f you can't find that speckled hen's nest. No, Mis' Purin't'n, I hain't prepared for no wust. I've hed that, an' I'm better. All I want naow is some stren'th tu be up an' a-doin'. Poor Ruby!" as her eyes anxiously followed the girl's wearied footsteps. "It's ben tough on her, an' she's putty nigh tuckered aout."

The scared and tired girl got little comfort, except in escaping from the alarming and wearisome gabble of the visitor, in her list-less, rambling search for the nest of the Dominique among the withered currant bushes and the rampant weeds, that in spite of the drought still flourished in the fence-corners, to the delight of the yellow birds, who, too busy to sing, if singing days were not over, gathered the seeds of pig-weed and red-root. Nor was there more comfort in moping by her mother's posy-bed, whose neglected plants looked as tired as herself.

"That's allers the way wi' folks 'at's got consumpshern," continued Mrs. Purington, "a-thinkin' they're better when they're growin' wus—allers. An' that pepper an' steam darkter,—I met him as I was a-comin' int' the do'yard,—a mis'able cretur tu look at. They say he jest biles folkses' skins off, an' turns 'em inside aout wi' his lobele 'metics. Ef I wa'n't so beat aout wi' the heat, I'd turn tu an' help Ruby fix up things, for it does look dreffle run daown't the heel in the kitchin,—hain't ben int' the square room; but it does seem as if 't was all I c'ld du jest tu set here an' comfort ye all I ken. I will fix yer piller," and she set to beating the pillow close to the convalescent's ears, and twitching it to and fro under her head. "I'd ha' sent up sis tu help Ruby, but she's daown to Huldy's, an' they're fixin' up fer Uncle Lisher Peggs an' Aunt Jerushy, which they're expectin' on 'em back from the West nex' canal-boat 'at comes. A turrible senseless piece o' business all raound; but they will hev it the' own way,—Huldy an' Sam." And so she went on with her torturing gabble, which the sick woman was thankful only tired, but did not frighten her.

Meanwhile Gran'ther Hill was hobbling across the fields towards the woods, followed by the longing eyes of his grandson. Dr. Wead, watching the bent figure from the height of his sulky-seat rocking on its leathern thorough-braces, remarked to himself,

"A stronery tough ol' critter for a man 'at's ben pizened wi' cally-mill fer the Lord knows haow many year, an' as contrairy as he is ol' an' tough."

He was a pathetic old figure to look upon as, supporting his stiffened legs with his staff and trailing his long gun with the un-forgotten handiness acquired in years so far past that they were like a dream, he picked his slow way across the shrunken brook and into the skirt of the forest. The woods were very still, scarcely stirred by the light puffs of the breeze; the birds, their summer songs forgotten, so silent, and the feeble current of the brook bab-bling so faintly, that the continuous murmur of the bees among the woodside asters was the sound most audible, save when a locust shrilled its prolonged, monotonous cry that presently sank with an exhausted fall to the droning undertone of the bees.

The aged hunter made his way through the bordering thickets and over the dry matting of old leaves with a stealthier tread than many a younger man might have, and scanned carefully with slow, dulled gaze the shaded depths of low-branched young evergreens, sapling poplars and birches, and thorny tangles of blackberry briers.

Suddenly fell on his ears the noise of scurrying feet among the dry leaves, and the warning "wish, quit, kr-r-r, quit! quit!" of a grouse. Dropping his staff and bringing his cocked piece to a ready, he searched the thicket with eager eyes and presently discovered an alert dusky form skulking among the shadows. The long gun was aimed with almost the celerity if not with the precision of its ancient use in the boasted days when its owner scouted and hunted with doughty Peleg Sunderland. The trigger was pulled, the flint flashed out a shower of sparks, and the old gun bellowed and kicked in a way worthy of its renown, and mowed a narrow swath through the stems of saplings and briers. The booming report, so different from the flat discharges which at irregular intervals dur-ing the afternoon had cracked through the sultry air, came to young Josiah's ears, and almost shook him from his seat on the rail fence with the thrill of delight it sent through him.

Rushing into the house, he loudly proclaimed, "Gran'ther's fired. Yes, sir! I heard him!" and in the next breath, "I'm goin' t' see what he's got!"

"Don't you dast tu!" his father said with unwonted decision. " 'F he hain't killed nothin', an' 't ain't no ways likely 't he hes, though the's no tellin' but what he hes, he'll be madder'n tew settin' hens. Don't ye dast tu go, bub!"

"Jest's like's not his gun hes busted, er gone off't wrong eend, er suthin', an' killed him," said Mrs. Purington. "Guns is dreffle dang'ous things. It's 'nough tu dry up a feller's blood wi' col' chills tu hear father Purin't'n when he was alive, an' Uncle Lisher, tell o' the folks 'at got killed by 'em tu Plattsburgh fight, which they was both there. Don't ye go nigh, Bub Hill. 'T'ould scare ye t' death tu see your gran'ther a-lyin' in his gore."

"Hedn't you better go an' see, Joseph?" said Maria anxiously.

"Sho!" said her husband. "Father couldn't shoot hisself wi' the ol' gun erless he got someb'dy tu help him. It's longer'n a brook, an' it never busts, leastways it never did 's I knows on. Ketch me a-goin' nigh him 'f he's missed. He'll make things gee, a-blamin' it onter all creation but hisself."

Thus admonished, the boy went back to his perch on the top rail, to content himself with impatient watching for his grandsire's return.

It was well he did not seek him, for he would have found him then in his most peppery mood. Quicker than the echo of the discharge had come a rapid beat of wings and a brief scurry among the dead leaves. The old man stooped low and peered beneath the slowly lifting smoke, almost confident that he would see his victim fluttering out its last breath in or near the ragged path of the charge. But there was nothing to be seen astir but a sapling slowly bending to its fall from its half-severed stem, a sere leaf wavering to earth, and the eddying haze of rising smoke. Ah! the bird was stone dead, and lying there somewhere, waiting to be picked up without casting one reproving glance upon his slayer from his glazing eyes. Gran'ther Hill was glad of that, for like all old hunters he had grown tender-hearted toward his prey.

First he reloaded his gun, measuring powder and shot in his palm with scrupulous care in spite of his haste to go forward, and then, stooping low, groped his way into the thicket. Scanning the ground foot by foot, often misled this way and that by some semblance of what he was in quest of, objects that upon poking with his staff proved but gray and russet stumps or clots of old leaves, he crept on far beyond the range of his gun, growing less hopeful with each more wearied step. Then he retraced his course, zigzagging across it, peering into hollow logs and probing brush heaps with his staff, and then took his bearings anew from the place where he had shot, and went over the ground again and again, rewarded only by finding one mottled tail-feather, which he thrust in his hat to disprove a total miss, and grew more rebellious against fate with every unsuccessful attempt to find his bird, which, in fact, sat unscathed amid the branches of a fir, recovering from the terror of the sudden storm of lead that had so lately hurtled past it.

"What tarnel dodunk loaded that aire gun, I wonder?" he growled, glaring savagely into space. "Didn't put no wad top o' the paowder, I'll bate, er the shot was tu big er tu small er suthin'! Er 't was some of that cussed paowder o' Chapin's; 't won't burn no quicker 'n green popple sawdust, an' the pa'tridge seen the flash an' dodged! But I hit him, I know I did! I never missed a settin' shot in my life, an' he lays right here clus tu, deader 'n hay, on'y I can't see him! Blast my darned eyes, a-failin' on me jes' naow, arter eighty-six, goin' on eighty-seben year! I wish 't I hed my specs; I wish 't I 'd let Jozeff's boy come 'long wi' me, he's sharper eyed 'n a lynk; he'd ha' faound him. I'll fetch him here an' hev him look, an' ef he don't find him I'll skin him. 'F I thought 't was you 't made me miss him," shaking his gun till the ramrod rattled in its pipes and wooden casing, "ye ol' wore aout, goo'-for-nothin' iron hole, I'd wallupse ye raound a tree, darn ye! But I didn't miss him, he's lyin' dead clus tu, 'mongst some o' these cussed rhuts an' bresh. Darn yer cussed hidin' tricks!" addressing the trees and shaking his staff at them, "can't ye let an ol' man 'at fit fer ye when you wa'n't knee-high tu a tudstool hev one leetle, nasty, mis'able pa'tridge fer his sick darter? Darn ye, I wish 't ye 'ould all burn up an' roast yer cussed pa'tridges inside on ye!"

For answer came a rustle of feet suddenly grown careless where they trod, and then appeared through the parted branches the tall form and good-natured face of Sam Lovel. The old man stared half-angrily, half-ashamed, at the apparition.

"Why, Gran'ther Hill, you a-huntin' this hot day?" Sam asked.

"Yis, I be," the old man answered testily. "I do' know but I got jes' 's good right tu go a-huntin' hot days as other folks."

"Sartainly, Gran'ther, sartainly; but I didn't s'pose the' was nob'dy else but me sech a fool as tu go huntin' sech weather. Ye know some on 'em calls ev'rybody fools 'at goes huntin' any time. Wal, what luck be ye hevin'?"

"The cussedest luck I ever see. I come tu git a pa'tridge fer Jozeff's wife 'at's sick, an' I shot one fust thing, an' I can't find the darned thing, an' it hain't tew rod off f'm where we be."

"Wing broke, an' hid?"

"No, sir, killed deader 'n hay, jest one kerflummux an' still; an' I can't find it nowhere, nothin' but this tail feather."

This Sam examined, but did not suggest the patent fact that it was not cut out by a shot, nor the possibility of a miss. "Wal, naow, mebby I c'n help ye find him; four eyes is better 'n tew sometimes. I s'pose you hain't shot a pa'tridge afore for a good spell, an' you wouldn't ha' ben tryin' naow only tu git one for M'ri. Wal, le' 's see, you sarch in there, an' I'll try up this way. He's flummuxed inter some bresh heap er holler, I bate ye. An' they look julluk the dead leaves 'f they don't lay belly up, anyway."

Searching intently in one direction while the old man pottered in another, Sam presently shouted gleefully, "Here he is, Gran'-ther! Deader 'n a mallet, lyin' in a bresh heap 't you've trod onter! You most took his head off an' knocked him gally west. It was jest the stren'th o' the shot 'at hove him here!" and Sam reappeared, holding a rather rumpled partridge, whose head dangled from the ruffed neck by a film of skin.

The old man, more pleased than a child with a coveted toy,

took the bird and smoothed its rumpled feathers, so absorbed that he did not notice the softened thud, mixed with the careless scuff of Sam's foot, of something that fell between them.

"Wal, I'll be darned!" Sam ejaculated in suppressed surprise; "ef here ain't another 'at we're most treadin' onter!" and stooping, he picked up another partridge, that with its life had almost lost its head.

"Tew tu one shot, by the gret horn spoon! Wal, Gran'ther, you beat the hull caboodle!" and he patted the veteran's shoulder tenderly. "I never done that but oncte, an' I've bragged on 't ever sence."

Gran'ther Hill's blank stare of astonishment relaxed into a toothless grin of supreme delight, and his bleared eyes were dim with unaccustomed moisture.

"I knowed the' was one a-lyin' here somewheres, but I never 'spected the' was tew," he said, his voice trembling with the swelling and throbbing pride of his heart. "Young eyes is sharper 'n ol' ones, an' I'm a thaousan' times obleeged tu ye fur findin' my pa'tridges. I'd abaout gi'n up, an' was goin' hum tu git Jozeff's boy tu help me find the one 't I knowed I killed; he's got eyes julluk a lynk, an 'ould ha' made a hunter 'f he'd ben borned soon 'nough, when the' wus suthin' wuth huntin'. These 'ere'll jest set Marier right up, an' fore they're gone, I'll git her another. They thought I couldn't git nary one, but 't ain't nothin' tu kill a pa'-tridge when ye know haow;" and all the while he was slowly turning the birds before his admiring eyes.

"Naow 'f I c'n find me some lutherwood, I'll tie them pa'tridge laigs tugether an' sling 'em crost my gun an' g' hum. You don't see some handy, du ye?"

Yes, Sam saw a sprawling moose-wood or wicopy close at hand, and presently fitted the old man out with a thong of its tough bark, wherewith the birds were tied together, ready for slinging on the gun barrel.

" 'Tain't every day 't ye see a man goin' huntin' wi' a gun in one hand an' a cane in t' other," Gran'ther Hill chuckled; "but the ol' gun an' me hain't forgot aour ol' tricks 'f we do go wi' a cane. It 's kinder cur'ous 't I hit 'em both in the neck an' nowheres else 'cept knockin' aout one tail feather, an' there it is, a-missin';" but he did not notice that the feather in his hat did not correspond in length or markings with those in the tail of the bird that he was inspecting.

"The ol' gun kerries turrible clus," Sam exclaimed, "an' jes' one stray shot hit the tail—glanced on a twig like's not."

"An' hain't you killed nary one?" the old man asked, only now noticing that Sam carried no game in sight. "I swan, I'd ort tu divide wi' ye," making a feeble motion toward untying one of his birds.

"Wal, yes, I got tew, three in here," patting the pocket of his striped woolen frock.

"Wal," the old man said, slipping the birds on to his gun and shouldering it, "I s'pose I mus' be a-moggin'. Do' know haow I'm goin' tu make up ter ye for findin' my pa'tridge, erless I go 'long wi' ye some day an' show ye haow tu hunt pa'tridge."

"That 'll jest du it," said Sam heartily. "Some cool day, t' rights, 'fore they git wild wi' the fallin' leaves, we'll go. I want tu see ye kill tew't a shot."

And so they parted, each going his way, the young man skirting the woods, the old man homeward, picking his way across Stony Brook with a lighter step and a lighter heart than he had come with. He minded nothing of the hot, droughty weather; no day could have seemed finer than this in its decline, its warm air laden with the odor of the firs, and the "cheop" of the crickets beginning to thrill through it, while the purple of the asters grew darker in the blurred, lengthening shadows. As he crossed the pasture he began to whistle toothlessly, "We're marching onward toward Quebec," and his rheumatic footsteps fell to the time of the old martial air.

Then he saw his grandson running to meet him.

"Oh, Gran'ther!" cried the boy breathlessly, as he caught a glimpse of the old man's swinging burden, "ye got one, didn't ye?"

and then, as he walked puffing and eager-eyed alongside, "Tew on
'em! Oh, my sakes, tew! I never hearn ye shoot but oncte. You
never killed 'em both tu one shot, gran'ther?"

"Sho, bub, that hain't nothin' for a man 'at onderstan's it," said
his grandfather lightly.

"Oh, Gran'ther! you c'n jest beat 'em all, you can. Say, Gran'-
ther, le' me kerry 'em, won't ye? Gran'ther, say?" the boy pleaded.

"Jullook a-here, bub," said the old man, sinking his voice to a
husky undertone, "you le' me kerry 'em, an' I'll let ye shoot the
gun tu a mark right naow! Hey?"

"Oh, my sakes! Will ye, naow, t'-night?"

"Yes, sir, I will. You go an' set that aire busted cap ag'in the
fence, ten rod off, an' come back here an' rest crost this 'ere stump
an' let 'er hev!"

Away the boy ran, never minding a stubbed toe or a heelful of
thistles that waylaid his course, and, setting the broken fence-cap
against a rail, came panting back.

"Git ye breath fust," Gran'ther Hill said, as the boy reached
eagerly for the gun, which the old man took slowly from his shoulder, depressing the muzzle till the partridges slipped to the ground.
"Ye couldn't hit a barn-door tew rod off whilst ye're a-puffin' that
way. Naow," as the boy's breathing became regular through hard
restraint, and he gave the gun into his hands, "p'int below the
mark, an' raise her up slow, an' when ye git aimed atween the tew
holes, onhitch!"

Kneeling and resting the long barrel across the stump, the boy
slowly elevated the muzzle till it hid the lower auger hole, and
then pulled with might and main, shutting both eyes in expectation
of the flash and recoil, but neither came.

"I can't pull her off," he whined, in half-tearful disappointment.

"Ye can't pull her off when she hain't on'y half cocked, ye
gump!" said the old man impatiently, and reaching out he pulled
the heavy hammer to full cock. "There, naow, when ye pull the
tricker, I guess ye'll hear from her!"

Again the boy essayed, pulled manfully at just the right moment, and there was a shower of sparks, a blinding flash of ignited priming, a deafening roar, and with it a kick that tumbled the young marksman on to his haunches.

"You hit it!" the old man cried, "I seen the splinters fly! Naow run over 'n' fetch the cap here."

The boy made all haste to get upon his feet, and ran wildly over to the fence, rubbing, as he ran, his shoulder, that ached with a more universal pang than his tooth had done. But it was a delightful pain, and borne with a triumphant smile when he saw the weather-worn surface of the wood brightened with fresh splinters and punctured with a half dozen dark holes, and as many half-embedded shot staring at him as if in astonishment at his skill.

"Ye done well, bub, so ye did!" said his grandfather, when the target was brought to him and inspected. "She scattered more'n she did when I shot the pa'tridge, but I s'pose I got in a leetle tew much paowder; but you done almighty well." So they went home, the one as proud as the other, the old man with his birds, the boy with his target, he running ahead to proclaim the wonderful achievements of the twain. It was a pleasure added to the old man's triumph, another reward of his afternoon's outing, to see the departing form of Mrs. Purington waddling homeward along the highway.

The two were welcomed with all the honors they could desire; even Mrs. Hill came forth from her bedroom to view the trophies, and the youngsters home from school were dumb with admiration of the feats of their grandfather and brother. Gran'ther Hill recounted all the details of his afternoon's adventure, and ended by saying:—

"I don't b'lieve I'd ha' faound one of 'em 'f 't hadn't ben for that aire long-laiged Sam Lovel;" and Joseph, picking the birds, unmarked but by the bullet holes in their necks, remarked with a twinkle in his eyes that no one saw:—

"I don't scarcely b'lieve ye would, father; don't seem's 'ough ye would."

Dorothy Canfield Fisher (1879-1958)

The Bedquilt

Of all the Elwell family Aunt Mehetabel was certainly the most unimportant member. It was in the New England days, when an unmarried woman was an old maid at twenty, at forty was everyone's servant, and at sixty had gone through so much discipline that she could need no more in the next world. Aunt Mehetabel was sixty-eight.

She had never for a moment known the pleasure of being important to anyone. Not that she was useless in her brother's family; she was expected, as a matter of course, to take upon herself the most tedious and uninteresting part of the household labors. On Mondays she accepted as her share the washing of the men's shirts, heavy with sweat and stiff with dirt from the fields and from their own hard-working bodies. Tuesdays she never dreamed of being allowed to iron anything pretty or even interesting, like the baby's white dresses or the fancy aprons of her young lady nieces. She stood all day pressing out a tiresome monotonous succession of dish-cloths and towels and sheets.

In preserving-time she was allowed to have none of the pleasant responsibility of deciding when the fruit had cooked long enough, nor did she share in the little excitement of pouring the sweet-smelling stuff into the stone jars. She sat in a corner with the children and stoned cherries incessantly, or hulled strawberries until her fingers were dyed red to the bone.

The Elwells were not consciously unkind to their aunt, they were even in a vague way fond of her; but she was so utterly insignificant a figure in their lives that they bestowed no thought whatever on her. Aunt Mehetabel did not resent this treatment; she took it quite as unconsciously as they gave it. It was to be expected when one was an old-maid dependent in a busy family. She gathered what crumbs of comfort she could from their occasional careless kindnesses and tried to hide the hurt which even yet pierced her at her brother's rough joking. In the winter when they all sat before the big hearth, roasted apples, drank mulled cider, and teased the girls about their beaux and the boys about their sweethearts, she shrank into a dusky corner with her knitting, happy if the evening passed without her brother saying, with a crude sarcasm, "Ask your Aunt Mehetabel about the beaux that used to come a-sparkin' her!" or, "Mehetabel, how was't when you was in love with Abel Cummings." As a matter of fact, she had been the same at twenty as at sixty, a quiet, mouse-like little creature, too timid and shy for anyone to notice, or to raise her eyes for a moment and wish for a life of her own.

Her sister-in-law, a big hearty housewife, who ruled indoors with as autocratic a sway as did her husband on the farm, was rather kind in an absent, offhand way to the shrunken little old woman, and it was through her that Mehetabel was able to enjoy the one pleasure of her life. Even as a girl she had been clever with her needle in the way of patching bedquilts. More than that she could never learn to do. The garments which she made for herself were the most lamentable affairs, and she was humbly grateful for any help in the bewildering business of putting them together. But in patchwork she enjoyed a tepid importance. She could really do that as well as anyone else. During years of devotion to this one art she had accumulated a considerable store of quilting patterns. Sometimes the neighbors would send over and ask "Miss Mehetabel" for such and such a design. It was with an agreeable flutter at being able to help someone that she went to the dresser, in her bare little room under the eaves, and extracted from her crowded portfolio the pattern desired.

She never knew how her great idea came to her. Sometimes she thought she must have dreamed it, sometimes she even wondered reverently, in the phraseology of the weekly prayer-meeting, if it had not been "sent" to her. She never admitted to herself that she could have thought of it without other help; it was too great, too ambitious, too lofty a project for her humble mind to have conceived. Even when she finished drawing the design with her own fingers, she gazed at it incredulously, not daring to believe that it could indeed be her handiwork. At first it seemed to her only like a lovely but quite unreal dream. She did not think of putting it into execution—so elaborate, so complicated, so beautifully difficult a pattern could be only for the angels in heaven to quilt. But so curiously does familiarity accustom us even to very wonderful things, that as she lived with this astonishing creation of her mind, the longing grew stronger and stronger to give it material life with her nimble old fingers.

She gasped at her daring when this idea first swept over her and put it away as one does a sinfully selfish notion, but she kept coming back to it again and again. Finally she said compromisingly to herself that she would make one "square," just one part of her design, to see how it would look. Accustomed to the most complete dependence on her brother and his wife, she dared not do even this without asking Sophia's permission. With a heart full of hope and fear thumping furiously against her old ribs, she approached the mistress of the house on churning-day, knowing with the innocent guile of a child that the country woman was apt to be in a good temper while working over the fragrant butter in the cool cellar.

Sophia listened absently to her sister-in-law's halting, hesitating petition. "Why, yes, Mehetabel," she said, leaning far down into the huge churn for the last golden morsels—"why, yes, start another quilt if you want to. I've got a lot of pieces from the spring sewing that will work in real good." Mehetabel tried honestly to make her see that this would be no common quilt, but her limited vocabulary and her emotion stood between her and expression. At last Sophia said, with a kindly impatience: "Oh, there! Don't bother me. I never could keep track of your quiltin' patterns, anyhow. I don't care what pattern you go by."

With this overwhelmingly, although unconsciously, generous permission Mehetabel rushed back up the steep attic stairs to her room, and in a joyful agitation began preparations for the work of her life. It was even better than she hoped. By some heaven-sent inspiration she had invented a pattern beyond which no patchwork quilt could go.

She had but little time from her incessant round of household drudgery for this new and absorbing occupation, and she did not dare sit up late at night lest she burn too much candle. It was weeks before the little square began to take on a finished look, to show the pattern. Then Mehetabel was in a fever of impatience to bring it to completion. She was too conscientious to shirk even the smallest part of her share of the work of the house, but she rushed through it with a speed which left her panting as she climbed to the little room. This seemed like a radiant spot to her as she bent over the innumerable scraps of cloth which already in her imagination ranged themselves in the infinitely diverse pattern of her masterpiece. Finally she could wait no longer, and one evening ventured to bring her work down beside the fire where the family sat, hoping that some good fortune would give her a place near the tallow candles on the mantelpiece. She was on the last corner of the square, and her needle flew in and out with inconceivable rapidity. No one noticed her, a fact which filled her with relief, and by bedtime she had but a few more stitches to add.

As she stood up with the others, the square fluttered out of her trembling old hands and fell on the table. Sophia glanced at it carelessly. "Is that the new quilt you're beginning on?" she asked with a yawn. "It looks like a real pretty pattern. Let's see it." Up to that moment Mehetabel had labored in the purest spirit of dis-interested devotion to an ideal, but as Sophia held her work toward the candle to examine it, and exclaimed in amazement and ad-miration, she felt an astonished joy to know that her creation would stand the test of publicity.

"Land sakes!" ejaculated her sister-in-law, looking at the many-colored square. "Why, Mehetabel Elwell, where'd you git that pattern?"

"I made it up," said Mehetabel quietly, but with unutterable pride.

"No!" exclaimed Sophia incredulously. *"Did* you! Why, I

never see such a pattern in my life. Girls, come here and see what your Aunt Mehetabel is doing."

The three tall daughters turned back reluctantly from the stairs. "I don't seem to take much interest in patchwork," said one listlessly.

"No, nor I neither!" answered Sophia; "but a stone image would take an interest in this pattern. Honest, Mehetabel, did you think of it yourself? And how under the sun and stars did you ever git your courage up to start in a-making it? Land! Look at all those tiny squinchy little seams! Why the wrong side ain't a thing *but* seams!"

The girls echoed their mother's exclamations, and Mr. Elwell himself came over to see what they were discussing. "Well, I declare!" he said, looking at his sister with eyes more approving than she could ever remember. "That beats old Mis' Wightman's quilt that got the blue ribbon so many times at the county fair."

Mehetabel's heart swelled within her, and tears of joy moistened her old eyes as she lay that night in her narrow, hard bed, too proud and excited to sleep. The next day her sister-in-law amazed her by taking the huge pan of potatoes out of her lap and setting one of the younger children to peeling them. "Don't you want to go on with that quiltin' pattern?" she said; "I'd kind o' like to see how you're goin' to make the grape-vine design come out on the corner."

By the end of the summer the family interest had risen so high that Mehetabel was given a little stand in the sitting-room where she could keep her pieces, and work in odd minutes. She almost wept over such kindness, and resolved firmly not to take advantage of it by neglecting her work, which she performed with a fierce thoroughness. But the whole atmosphere of her world was changed. Things had a meaning now. Through the longest task of washing milk-pans there rose the rainbow of promise of her variegated work. She took her place by the little table and put the thimble on her knotted, hard finger with the solemnity of a priestess performing a sacred rite.

She was even able to bear with some degree of dignity the

extreme honor of having the minister and the minister's wife comment admiringly on her great project. The family felt quite proud of Aunt Mehetabel as Minister Bowman had said it was work as fine as any he had ever seen, "and he didn't know but finer!" The remark was repeated verbatim to the neighbors in the following weeks when they dropped in and examined in a perverse silence some astonishingly difficult *tour de force* which Mehetabel had just finished.

The family especially plumed themselves on the slow progress of the quilt. "Mehetabel has been to work on that corner for six weeks, come Tuesday, and she ain't half done yet," they explained to visitors. They fell out of the way of always expecting her to be the one to run on errands, even for the children. "Don't bother your Aunt Mehetabel," Sophia would call. "Can't you see she's got to a ticklish place on the quilt?"

The old woman sat up straighter and looked the world in the face. She was a part of it at last. She joined in the conversation and her remarks were listened to. The children were even told to mind her when she asked them to do some service for her, although this she did but seldom, the habit of self-effacement being too strong.

One day some strangers from the next town drove up and asked if they could inspect the wonderful quilt which they had heard of, even down in their end of the valley. After that such visitations were not uncommon, making the Elwells' house a notable object. Mehetabel's quilt came to be one of the town sights, and no one was allowed to leave the town without having paid tribute to its worth. The Elwells saw to it that their aunt was better dressed than she had ever been before, and one of the girls made her a pretty little cap to wear on her thin white hair.

A year went by and a quarter of the quilt was finished; a second year passed and half was done. The third year Mehetabel had pneumonia and lay ill for weeks and weeks, overcome with terror lest she die before her work was completed. A fourth year and one could really see the grandeur of the whole design; and in September of the fifth year, the entire family watching her with eager and admiring eyes, Mehetabel quilted the last stitches in her creation. The girls held it up by the four corners, and they all looked at it in a solemn silence. Then Mr. Elwell smote one horny hand within the other and exclaimed: "By ginger! That's goin' to the county fair!" Mehetabel blushed a deep red at this. It was a thought which had occurred to her in a bold moment, but she had not dared to entertain it. The family acclaimed the idea, and one of the boys was forthwith dispatched to the house of the neighbor who was chairman of the committee for their village. He returned with radiant face. "Of course he'll take it. Like's not it may git a prize, so he says; but he's got to have it right off, because all the things are goin' to-morrow morning."

Even in her swelling pride Mehetabel felt a pang of separation as the bulky package was carried out of the house. As the days went on she felt absolutely lost without her work. For years it had been her one preoccupation, and she could not bear even to look at the little stand, now quite bare of the litter of scraps which had lain on it so long. One of the neighbors, who took the long journey to the fair, reported that the quilt was hung in a place of honor in a glass case in "Agricultural Hall." But that meant little to Mehetabel's utter ignorance of all that lay outside of her brother's home. The family noticed the old woman's depression, and one day Sophia said kindly, "You feel sort o' lost without the quilt, don't you, Mehetabel?"

"They took it away so quick!" she said wistfully; "I hadn't hardly had one real good look at it myself."

Mr. Elwell made no comment, but a day or two later he asked his sister how early she could get up in the morning.

"I dun'no'. Why?" she asked.

"Well, Thomas Ralston has got to drive clear to West Oldton to see a lawyer there, and that is four miles beyond the fair. He says if you can git up so's to leave here at four in the morning he'll drive you over to the fair, leave you there for the day, and bring you back again at night."

Mehetabel looked at him with incredulity. It was as though someone had offered her a ride in a golden chariot up to the gates of heaven. "Why, you can't *mean* it!" she cried, paling with the intensity of her emotion. Her brother laughed a little uneasily. Even to his careless indifference this joy was a revelation of the narrowness of her life in his home. "Oh, 'tain't so much to go to the fair. Yes, I mean it. Go git your things ready, for he wants to start to-morrow morning."

All that night a trembling, excited old woman lay and stared at the rafters. She, who had never been more than six miles from home in her life, was going to drive thirty miles away—it was like going to another world. She who had never seen anything more exciting than a church supper was to see the county fair. To Mehetabel it was like making the tour of the world. She had never dreamed of doing it. She could not at all imagine what it would be like.

Nor did the exhortations of the family, as they bade good-by to her, throw any light on her confusion. They had all been at least once to the scene of gayety she was to visit, and as she tried to eat her breakfast they called out conflicting advice to her till her head whirled. Sophia told her to be sure and see the display of preserves. Her brother said not to miss inspecting the stock, her nieces said the fancywork was the only thing worth looking at, and her nephews said she must bring them home an account of the races. The buggy drove up to the door, she was helped in, and her wraps tucked about her. They all stood together and waved good-by to her as she drove out of the yard. She waved back, but she scarcely saw them. On her return home that evening she was very pale, and so tired and stiff that her brother had to lift her out bodily, but her lips were set in a blissful smile. They crowded around her with thronging questions, until Sophia pushed them all aside, telling them Aunt Mehetabel was too tired to speak until she had had her supper. This was eaten in an enforced silence on the part of the children, and then the old woman was helped into an easy-chair before the fire. They gathered about her, eager for news of the great world, and Sophia said, "Now, come, Mehetabel, tell us all about it!"

Mehetabel drew a long breath. "It was just perfect!" she said; "finer even than I thought. They've got it hanging up in the very middle of a sort o' closet made of glass, and one of the lower corners is ripped and turned back so's to show the seams on the wrong side."

"What?" asked Sophia, a little blankly.

"Why, the quilt!" said Mehetabel in surprise. "There are a whole lot of other ones in that room, but not one that can hold a candle to it, if I do say it who shouldn't. I heard lots of people say the same thing. You ought to have heard what the women said about that corner, Sophia. They said—well, I'd be ashamed to *tell* you what they said. I declare if I wouldn't!"

Mr. Elwell asked, "What did you think of that big ox we've heard so much about?"

"I didn't look at the stock," returned his sister indifferently. "That set of pieces you gave me, Maria, from your red waist, come out just lovely!" she assured one of her nieces. "I heard one woman say you could 'most smell the red silk roses."

"Did any of the horses in our town race?" asked young Thomas.

"I didn't see the races."

"How about the preserves?" asked Sophia.

"I didn't see the preserves," said Mehetabel calmly. You see, I went right to the room where the quilt was, and then I didn't want to leave it. It had been so long since I'd seen it. I had to look at it first real good myself, and then I looked at the others to see if there was any that could come up to it. And then the people begun comin' in and I got so interested in hearin' what they had to say I couldn't think of goin' anywheres else. I ate my lunch right there too, and I'm as glad as can be I did, too; for what do you think?"—she gazed about her with kindling eyes—"while I stood there with a sandwich in one hand didn't the head of the hull concern come in and open the glass door and pin 'First Prize' right in the middle of the quilt!"

There was a stir of congratulation and proud exclamation. Then Sophia returned again to the attack. "Didn't you go to see anything else?" she queried.

"Why, no," said Mehetabel. "Only the quilt. Why should I?"

She fell into a reverie where she saw again the glorious creation of her hand and brain hanging before all the world with the mark of highest approval on it. She longed to make her listeners see the splendid vision with her. She struggled for words; she reached blindly after unknown superlatives. "I tell you it looked like——" she said, and paused, hesitating. Vague recollections of hymn-book phraseology came into her mind, the only form of literary expression she knew; but they were dismissed as being sacrilegious, and also not sufficiently forcible. Finally, "I tell you it looked real *well!*" she assured them, and sat staring into the fire, on her tired old face the supreme content of an artist who has realized his ideal.

Zephine Humphrey Fahnestock
(1874-1956)

Is This All?

"Suppose," began Peter, embarking on his Sunday morning sermon, "you knew you were to die next week, and you sat down to
write a last letter to your best friend."

"Oh, Peter!" I thought, looking up from my pew, "that's a tech-
nical mistake. How can you expect us to listen to your sermon
when you throw out such an arresting challenge in the first sentence?"

Youth, however, especially youth of the present generation, is
lavish with challenges; and, after all, no preacher can desire a better success than to set his hearers thinking. It was therefore with
no real sense of compunction or disloyalty that I obeyed the well-
nigh irresistible impulse and, hearing no more of the sermon, devoted myself to a rough mental draft of the suggested letter.

Not that I expected to die in a week. But one can never tell.
And anyway how much better to compose such a letter in cold
blood, as it were, than in all the haste and confusion of imminent
demise. For my part, I was not even sure that I should be capable
of telling the truth if I had only seven days in which to do it, with
of course a great many other things to think of at the same time.
Emotion, to be valid, must sometimes be anticipated as well as
"recollected in tranquillity."

The idea itself seemed to me admirable, and I thought everyone
might do well to put it in practice not only once in a lifetime but
repeatedly during the decades, perhaps at the close of each cycle
of development. Surely such a wholesome and fruitful exercise
must result in an increase of personal and mutual significance.

The particular act of imagination must be strengthening too, the resolute laying hold on a fact of experience which is the only one we can all infallibly predict but which we seldom face. Moreover, the pausing and summing up of life's meaning must be clarifying.

For all these reasons, but chiefly of course because the notion "intrigued" me, I arranged my features in what I hoped was an intelligent expression and left them with eyes fixed on Peter while I retired behind them and, projecting myself to the portals of death, turned right about.

My first reaction was a memory: that of an aging acquaintance who once, by some occurrence or other, was brought up short and reverted. Looking back over his nearly spent life, "Is this all?" he had cried.

At the time (I was then in my twenties), the remark had seemed to me a deplorable admission of failure and incompetence; but I had never forgotten it. What is more, it had made a place for itself in my mind as one of the authentic utterances of humanity which I should understand some day if I did not then. And now suddenly, sitting in our country church and making my own volte-face, I did understand so poignantly that I echoed the cry: "Is this all?" And quick on its heels came the reverberation of Solomon's "Vanity! vanity!"

It was strange that this should have been the first effect of Peter's challenge on me; for I knew at once, knew even before-hand, that I did not mean what I said. The two outcries were racial, part of our human heritage of tragedy and humor, sponta-neous expressions of universal stupefaction and chagrin. But, though I echoed them, I did not make them mine.

In fact, as I pondered their meaning, frowning and smiling over the frustration they implied, their very inevitableness seemed to me to dispute their finality. There must be some deep reason why people are so dismayed and astounded by the brief fragmentari-ness of life, and it may very well be that the surprise is more im-portant than the failure.

Where, if not from some cosmic source, do we all get the con-fident expectation that life is going to give us ample opportunity? We start out in youth with a vast design which we do not hurry to put into execution. Instinctively we understand that hurry is fatal to excellence; and, as we seem to have all time before us, we work patiently. Closely considered, youth is more patient than age. Then suddenly we awake to the fact that, for us, time is almost over, and, turning to see what we have accomplished, we find nothing there, or hardly anything, never, never by any chance what we had intended. Checkmate! No wonder we feel duped. The thing is not our fault; we simply have not had half a chance.

Moreover, youth assumes, unwarrantably—unless, here again, is some deep-lying reason—that life has a purpose and a unity. Everything else has. Stars and seasons meet punctual appointments, harvests grow and mature, evolution pursues an inscrutable but none the less deliberate course. Must not each human history fulfill an ordained cycle?

Not at all. Not the least in the world. Human histories are like nothing so much as sky rockets, soaring straight and swift and immensely determined for three quarters of their career, then suddenly stopping and bursting into irrelevant sparks. They finish nothing, they get nowhere, they arrive at no conclusion. The sparks vanish and a dull stick comes flatly back to earth.

In the light of these cogitations it might have seemed that "Is this all?" would do very well as my own comment on life. But, though it hit the target of my assent, it missed the bull's-eye. There was, I felt sure, something more to the human experience than those sparks and that stick.

The mere intention perhaps, "all we have willed or hoped or dreamed of good." "Abt Vogler," then, or "Rabbi Ben Ezra." A quotation from Browning might save me the trouble of writing my letter.

But no, this was still not the bull's-eye. There was a difference between Browning's reason and mine. Thoroughly sealed now to all outside admonitions and influences, I stared at the pew rack before me and strove to coordinate my belief.

Man's expectation seemed to me a deeper, more cogent thing than his intention. Where, as I questioned before, did he get it if not from some authoritative principle? It was as much born in him as his early confidence in his mother's breast. Could such an intrinsic, spontaneous faith be a fallacy?

Surely not. This, I thought, was my bull's-eye, the central reason why, looking back over my life and distressfully realizing its fragmentary incompleteness, its pitiful futility, I was yet not ready to cry, "Is this all?" I trusted my early hope more than my later experience.

As a matter of fact, what is hope but a kind of experience, a high adventure of the soul? No one who remembers (and can anyone ever forget?) the exultation with which he stood on the sunrise crest of his youth and faced the forward road, doubts that in that exultation pulsed verity. There was the meaning of life, there in that summons and ringing response. The soul's consummation triumphed before it failed.

Wordsworth instead of Browning, then, the "Intimations of Immortality." No, not entirely; I must still insist on finding and expressing my own point of view. For, just recently, in the midst of middle-age, with youth left behind me and old age not far ahead, I have felt a revival of that early rapture, that sure victory. Again I have stood on the heights and bared my head to the sun, exulting in the summons of the road. It is not so long a road now as it once was and not nearly so well defined. After an indeterminate period of checkered sun and shadow it runs into a shining cloud. But I love it as much as ever and trust it even more confidently. And in that love and trust I think I find the one great, sufficient, enduring significance of life.

We human beings do not know what nor why we are. The more thoroughly science investigates the nature of our essence, the more at a loss we become. The physical universe disintegrates around us, the psychic entity dissolves within. We are not even sure any more that anything exists. Instead of "I think, therefore I am," the accepted philosophical formula runs simply, "There is thinking." But, so far, nothing has conquered the inalienable faith with which man embarks on his adventure nor the tenacity with which he pursues it, and these deep native impulses are perhaps his best credentials, the passports to eternity which will bring him through the welter of his present temporal agnosticism.

Life itself seems to me, then, its own answer to its riddle, its own excuse for being. So far, so good in my final testament. Now what about the nature of life? Are there outstanding characteristics which I should like to proclaim as recognizable?

Well, looking back over my own brief span and surveying what I can see of the lives about me, I seem to discover that the salient quality of the human experience is beauty.

Oh, I know there is plenty of sheer ugliness, too: disease, frustration, impotence, fire and famine, accident, war, selfishness, cruelty and greed. But surely those things are at bottom our fault and mark the abuse of a gift. Life never meant to involve us in such miseries.

Its setting is marvelously lovely, at least such portions of it as we have not spoiled. The vast depths of space, with its lusty sun by day and swarming stars by night; the wonder world of clouds; the miracles of light and color; mountains, seas, woods, rivers, fields; sunrise and sunset; rain, frost, wind and snow: who among us could have devised anything so endlessly, variously beautiful as the common daily scene? It strikes the keynote, gives the clue to the intention of our destiny.

And the raw material of the latter is lovely too: the affection we feel for each other, our prevailing desire to do some work which shall be worth while, our instinctive worship of God, our impulse to learn and grow. We are part of the whole noble process of creation, and our very discontent with its present development shows that its idealism is inherent in us, has in us perhaps for the first time come to self-consciousness. We have made and are making some quite hideous mistakes, but we are ready to do and undo and do over again.

Beauty is God, too, and perhaps God and life are one. Certain people are accustomed to say nowadays that they do not believe in God. Well, of course, his existence cannot be proved; and some of us who feel most sure of him are less and less ready to define him. But personally I have never been able to see how anyone can account for the miracle of beauty without recognizing divinity.

What else is it that lurks in the evening shadows, hushing the heart? What else lays a spell upon the awakened spirit in the early dawn? What else thrills the soul with rapture in the rushing wind, subdues it in the quiet rain, or awes it in the silence of the woods?

Not just sensuous pleasure; the quality of that is distinctly different. Beauty transcends the senses and relegates them often enough to forgetfulness. Its effect on the human spirit is a mystery which those of us who believe in God find no difficulty in ascribing to him. It is his language, his most direct way of speaking to us.

If our human lives are our language, our way of speaking back to him, we have ample cause to lament the barbarity of our dialect but not to be entirely ashamed of it. For, uncouth and strident though we often are, there are notes and accents of sheer loveliness in our mutterings. Our cathedrals, our great pictures and poems, our symphonies, our philosophies and sciences, our philanthropies: all these are admirable responses to God. So are our personal loves and compassions, our beautiful human relations in which soul calls to and answers soul across chasms of circumstances, while all the time remaining hid securely each in each. If man had done nothing but echo the note of love back to God, he would have justified his existence. For love is the keynote of all excellence. Rather, it is the seed which cannot choose but grow into the very Tree of Life whose leaves are for the healing of the nations.

Of course, this growth is not always, perhaps not often easy; and many a perverse, pernicious choice may delay the ultimate beatitude. For love causes suffering, and suffering taxes the will. Indeed, it may be questioned whether man did not do more to defeat than to fulfill his quest for happiness by the cultivation of love. Jealousy, pride, suspicion, misunderstanding, morbid sensitiveness, even hatred and cruelty may choke the tender plant. But, if it springs from a true seed, they cannot kill it. Again and again it will push its way to the sunshine of freedom and peace. Even the pain it causes is part of its significance. As Æ sings in a couplet recently printed by "The Yale Review,"

> "The fragrance and the glow were born
> From its own agonies."

Expiation is what it feels like, this mysterious anguish of love; and those who suffer it cannot fortify themselves better than by remembering the bitter bliss of the atoning souls in Dante's

Purgatorio. The purifying process may be personal, a decree of Karma; or it may subserve the whole destiny of the race. Perhaps indeed human love is nothing more nor less than expiation of the vast greeds and cruelties of evolution. This theory would go far to explain the cosmic necessity for Christ.

Does life not, then, seem to me happy? No, not essentially. Moments, even hours it has of triumph and ecstasy, flashings of glory, breathings of peace, pauses of holiness; but all so precarious, so evanescent that the dominating impression they make is that of the beating of wings.

Life seems to me mostly a matter of discipline, stern, inexorable. Character cannot be forged except with straight blows, at white heat. This may be one merciful reason why all our experience is so brief and fragmentary. Just as our physical bodies cannot stand more than a few hours of wakefulness at a time, so our spirits may need a swift anodyne of death. Doubtless we all of us know moods in which seventy years seem too many, moods in which we wonder if we can endure another day. But for most of us the longing for death cannot be even temporarily sincere unless we believe in our hearts that beyond lies a sequence of other lives.

Do we not really all of us thus believe? I know that I do. Rationally, when challenged to deliver an honest opinion concerning death, I declare for agnosticism; but practically, observing my actions and reactions, I find myself always proceeding on the assumption that I have countless opportunities ahead of me. Sometimes I am even deliberately lax enough to decide that I like a certain unspiritual weakness of character well enough to keep it through another incarnation or astral cycle or whatever lies "beyond." There is plenty of time; or, rather, there is no time at all but always, everywhere, eternity.

A steadfast necessity, however, stands at my elbow waking and sleeping, day in and day out. Spiritual I must become sooner or later. Moreover, the process, though delayed and retarded, must never be interrupted, never come to a halt. Out of self-indulgence or out of sheer love of the process, I may postpone the eradication of this vice or that; but some vice I must be always digging at. If

I do not do it for myself, life will do it for me, confronting me with the same temptation over and over until I am thoroughly familiar with its tricks and wiles and with its consequences. Stern, did I say? Relentless! Imperative! But so wise, so sure in its dealings, so deeply humorous, so merciful that, if defeat were possible, it would come near defeating itself through the appreciation of those who feel it at work on them. Make me not perfect for ages, dear Life, that so I may feel thee forever constraining me. The keenest and purest joy possible to human hearts lies in the recognition of discipline.

It thus appears that our human life is unsatisfactory and unsatisfying. No matter when a person dies, he leaves his work undone, the work for which he was born and to which he was just about to put his hand. Heart-breaking verity! Unless, indeed, in the very dismay of the realization, the bitter disappointment, lies the chance of another life. For modern psychology agrees with the Christian gospels in stating that what one demands one gets; and it may be that frustrated souls, arriving at the portal of death and crying out against its finality, do then and there create their own immortality. That would be a generous arrangement, kind to those rare people who, now and then, here and there—perhaps because they have become more nearly perfect than they suppose—desire to have done with the process and put on the ample peace of annihilation. New life to those who crave it; beautiful nescience to those who have had enough.

A friend of mine, refreshing to talk with in these disillusioned days, says she has loved her life so well that she would gladly go back and live it right over again. I cannot share this enthusiasm. Not only because of the sins and mistakes which I could not bear to repeat, but also because in going back I should feel that I was interrupting a sequence. I want to go on and on. But I do like to go back over my life in thought now and then, picking up stitches, following strains of development, pondering problems and issues, seeing how this led to that and that other resulted. Not infrequently, in so doing, I seem to divine a sort of troubled unity.

Another friend of mine, given to meditation on the nature of things, once had a dream that seemed to us both significant. She thought she had been sewing a long, long time on a shapeless mass of cloth and had at length grown weary and discouraged. What was the use of such aimless drudgery? Then someone had come and lifted the cloth, holding it up before her, and lo! it fell into the perfect lines of a beautiful garment, all finished but one sleeve.

It may be that this garment, or something like it, is the fourth dimensional aspect of the sky rocket stick. Saint Paul knew what he was talking about much more accurately and scientifically than was supposed in his day when he said that we "see through a glass darkly" and that "it doth not yet appear what we shall be." Everything on our three dimensional plane is fragmentary and un-satisfying, but it may all have its eternal place in a glorious fourth dimensional fulfilment.

At any rate, the hope is the thing, "the earnest expectation," to quote Saint Paul again. Once more I fall back on that. We could not so desire unity if it were not already implicit in us; we could not know what consummation means if we had not blindly antic-ipated it. Life's need is its own best promise.

The sermon was nearly over. Through my preoccupation I became obscurely aware of the approach of the benediction and bestirred myself to gather the ends of the mental threads I had followed into some sort of knot.

I was glad I had lived, then, was I not? Yes. Very few things had turned out as I had expected; in fact hardly anything had turned out at all. I had failed far oftener than I had succeeded; I had been disappointed, chagrined, humiliated. I had sinned and re-sinned and behaved like a fool. The sorrows and mistakes of the world had vastly disillusioned me. Nevertheless, there was something in the mere naked gift of life which I had found pre-cious. Suppose I had never known it, never known this beautiful valley, these beloved people, this home, this work, these books, these enterprises? The obvious answer is that, not having known them, I should also not have known the difference they make; but negative answers are unsatisfying. I know the difference now anyway, and it is all the difference in the world.

This seed of life germinating in me has entirely limitless potentialities. To what extent it is going to realize them, or when, or how, I have no idea. But I trust it as I trust God. Perhaps, as I suggested before, God and life are one.

Arthur Goodenough (1871-1936)

The Fir Wood

I feel a sense of opulence when I
  Behold a wood of fir-trees green and fair,
With tops against the blue floor of the sky;
  I know no fairer vision anywhere!

For they are rich in beauty and romance,
  In sylvan dreaminess and poetry;
And in the days of mythic Pan perchance
  Dryad and Satyr may have fared thereby!

Beauty and grace peculiarly its own
  Has the fir-forest in its garb of green;
The tempered wind speaks there in monotone,
  And oracles assert themselves unseen.

A strange and splendid Brotherhood of Trees,
  Sharing life's stress as human souls should share;
Guarding their vague fraternal mysteries
  With gravity and exceeding care!

Were I a hermit I would dwell therein
  Untouched by earthly discord or dismay;
And shutting out, meanwhile, insidious sin,
  Their swaying arms should warn the world away!

Wendell Phillips Stafford (1861-1953)

Song of Vermont

My heart is where the hills fling up
    Green garlands to the day;
'T'is where the blue lake brims her cup,
    The sparkling rivers play.
My heart is on the mountains still
    Where'er my steps may be;
Vermont, O maiden of the hills,
    My heart is there with thee!

Oh, you may find a prouder dame,
    With jewel at the ear
And richer robe and louder fame,
    But never face so dear!
No queen has had for followers
    A bolder train of men;
And when again the need is hers
    They shall be hers again!

My heart is where the hills fling up
    Green garlands to the day;
'T is where the blue lake brims her cup,
    The sparkling rivers play.
My heart is on the mountains still;
    My steps return to thee,
Green-hooded maiden of the hills,
    Lady of Liberty!

4

Vistas Old and New

I love Vermont because of her hills and valleys, her scenery and invigorating climate, but most of all, because of her indomitable people. They are a race of pioneers who have almost beggared themselves to serve others. If the spirit of liberty should vanish in other parts of the union, and support of our institutions should languish, it could all be replenished from the generous store held by the people of this brave little state of Vermont.

—Calvin Coolidge,
"Address at Bennington, 9/19/1928"

Haying—Old and New Methods Rowland E. Robinson, courtesy of Rowland E. Robinson Memorial Association

Robert Luther Duffus   (1888-1972)

The Stingiest Man

I cannot speak for the other two Duffus children, my older brother and my younger sister; but I myself could not be called devout and I don't recall that the others were, either. We liked church suppers, whether they provided baked beans, oyster stews, or maple sugar on snow, with pickles and doughnuts; we liked anything good to eat; we also liked sociability within certain limits.

For this reason I think we, all of us, at one time or another, went to the Wednesday evening prayer meeting with my mother. Once we even had a religious cat, which followed my mother to church and up the stairs to the Sunday School room, where the prayer meeting was held, and sat on her lap, purring loudly, throughout the service. This must have been during the Reverend Blake's time, because the Reverend Jasper Pell, the old war horse who followed Mr. Blake, would have regarded the presence of a cat as sacrilegious.

But Mr. Blake, as I am sure it was, stopped and petted the cat as he came down the aisle after saying the benediction. "That's a good Congregational mouser," he said.

My mother was reassured. "Of course," she protested, "I didn't know he was following me."

"He wouldn't make noise in the snow," chuckled the Reverend Blake, for this was, indeed, a snowy evening, and we could see cat tracks all the way home in the almost untraveled road.

This was a pleasant incident, but things were always happening at prayer meeting. Once in a while somebody would start to, as we said, get religion; but neither Mr. Blake nor Mr. Pell, unalike though they otherwise were, cared much for emotionalism.

We were expected to take our religion soberly and seriously, and not to shout about it in public.

The best way to stop anybody from getting religion too loudly at a prayer meeting in the Congregational Church in Williamstown was to call for a hymn. If Mr. Ainsworth was present, and he usually was, there was noise enough then.

Still, a prayer meeting was different from the regular Sunday morning service. It was more informal. In theory, anyhow, anybody present could offer a prayer or a personal statement, which he couldn't do, of course, Sunday mornings. The minister became a sort of moderator. I found this interesting, the way a play was, or an adventure book, because you never knew what would happen next.

So I would remember, even if there were not other reasons, the night Deacon Slater got up and said he had been doing a lot of praying lately. He was, he said, a naturally stingy man, maybe the stingiest man in town. He had been praying to the Lord to help him overcome this weakness, and he thought he was making some progress.

There was quite a silence when Deacon Slater sat down, because the truth seemed to most persons about as he had stated it. He really was a stingy man, perhaps the stingiest man in town.

Mr. Blake promptly called for a hymn.

I asked my mother on the way home what Deacon Slater meant and if he really was as stingy as he said.

She debated with herself for a while. Finally she shook her head. "If he was," she concluded, "he wouldn't say so."

2

I didn't then know much about Deacon Slater's story. A boy of ten doesn't—or didn't—know much about any adult's story. It seemed to a boy of ten that an adult had always been an adult. I knew my father and mother couldn't have been born at their present ages, as of 1898, but I couldn't believe with my heart and emotions that my parents had ever been ten years old.

So I thought of Deacon Slater as having always been Deacon

Slater, even with the title of deacon tacked to him like a set of whiskers. But people said Albert Slater had once been a hired man, and I did know a hired man or two.

I knew a humorously self-pitying hired man named Blaine Stillson, who worked for Ed Gorham on the Gulf Road. The Gorham farm was pretty good land, and Ed did well by his wife and daughter. Mrs. Gorham chose to dress her daughter in styles of about ten years back, but that was not Ed's fault—he couldn't tell one style from another.

Ed's attitude and Mrs. Gorham's attitude toward the hired man seemed to be different. The hired man said he got eleven dollars a month for working between twenty-two and thirty-two hours a day. He was a serious young man, and I didn't dare question his figures. He also said he reminded himself of a hired man he knew who worked for a family where the lady of the house cut the bread so thin you could read the Bible through a dozen slices of it. The hired man watched me carefully as he said this, and I didn't express any doubt.

This hired man didn't look undernourished, and I thought maybe he got more to eat than he would admit. The customary complaint made by hired men, and sometimes by school teachers who taught in district schools and boarded around up in the hills, was not that there wasn't enough to eat, but that it wasn't good. I hesitate to tell about one teacher and what he found in the milk gravy with which the lady of the house surrounded the fried salt pork; I hesitate to do this, and I will not, though when I heard about it at the age of ten, I was glad I boarded at home.

But what I am trying to make clear is, that if this hired man with whom I was speaking had succeeded in saving enough money out of his wages to make a payment on a farm, and had then married a hired girl with a little less money than he himself had, and then acquired four or five children, he would have had to be stingy if he were to stay alive and keep his family alive. A generous man simply couldn't have existed under those circumstances. I suspect that the poor house and the cemetery had a large surplus of generous men.

So, although I could not think of Deacon Slater and Blaine Stillson as being alike, and they were not alike, I may have connected them in my mind without ever realizing it. I can do so now, at any rate.

The only men who got their land easy in Williamstown were those who inherited it. There were a few of these, the substantial old families. I suppose Mr. Ainsworth's land, which he did not farm except as he sold his hay on the stalk once or twice a year, was an inheritance. But even those who inherited farms couldn't sit around and let nature pour bounty in their laps. They had to work. Even if they had hired men to help them, they had to work.

Some farmers cut down their maple trees—their sugar bush, as we called them—for timber, and then sat around in late winter when they should have been sugaring. We didn't respect such men.

But there were also young men on their way up; and now I see that Deacon Slater must have been one of these when he was in his prime. To understand Deacon Slater one has to understand that this was no affair of buying for a certain sum and selling for a larger sum. What the young man who was to become Deacon Slater had for his earthly possession was what he produced out of the land with his own labor. Some of this he and his family ate, and some he sold; but it was his sweat and ache that gave it value.

That was what a dollar or a dime was to Deacon Slater: aching and sweating, doing more than he wanted to do, stumbling late into the kitchen after the chores were done, eating enough to make him sleepy and soggy but not eating for fun, the way we boys did, the way village folks who didn't work too hard seemed to do.

I could understand this situation at the age of ten. We village boys were really the only leisure class Williamstown had. We alone ate without sweat on our brows, we alone reaped where we had not sowed.

It was different for the farm boys who did their chores before coming to school and after getting home from school, and who all winter long got up by lamp-light. They knew what hard work was, they knew what a dollar or dime meant in terms of hard work, just as Deacon Slater did. My brother and I learned this, too, but not so thoroughly—not at that time.

I suppose this was how Deacon Slater lived when he was a boy. Still, I couldn't get it clear in my mind that Deacon Slater had once been ten years old, then had gone through all the ages up to twenty or so, then had got married and become what he was now. Deacon Slater was Deacon Slater, that was all there was to it, just as Stevens Branch was Stevens Branch, always had been, and always would be.

My maternal grandmother, marrying a second time after Josiah Graves' death, took for her husband a man who had started life as a bound boy—or apprentice. At the age of twenty-one, I think it was, he had been given a new suit of clothes and a hundred dollars. That was what he had in the world.

He was successful, according to his opportunities and the standards of his time. He was so successful that when the time came for me to be born my mother went home to her mother on a prosperous farm in Waterbury, on the Winooski River below the village, and made this my birthplace. Thus I could always say that I was born on a farm, though it was not until I was earning my way through college that I learned to milk a cow.

As Luther Davis (my step-grandfather) got ahead in life, he left the farm and moved into Waterbury village to a house where I later lived with my grandmother and my aunt, my mother's sister, during my high school days. My brother and sister also fondly remember this house.

Such was the achievement of a man who started with nothing but a suit of clothes and a hundred dollars. I think he valued money, as well he might have done; but he had a kindly disposition, and whenever he and my grandmother and my aunt came to visit us in Williamstown, which they did once or twice, I always wept at the parting and wanted to go back with them.

I remember my grandfather in his coffin, the first such sight I had ever seen. I remember, too, my grandmother saying that during his final delirium, in the crisis of the pneumonia that killed him, he thought he was driving his horses in the woods and was talking to them. He died working, so it now seems, leaving my grandmother with a modest competency. All this life of hard work had not, however, made him a stingy man; he merely knew what it was that gave value to a dollar.

Stingy and *mean* were words you used when you didn't like a man. If you liked him, or respected him, or owed him money, or expected to inherit from him, you said he knew the value of a dollar.

My grandfather Davis knew the value of a dollar, but people didn't use harsh adjectives about him, not that I ever heard of. The question was, however, whether Deacon Slater was or was not a stingy man, and maybe the stingiest man in town. When the Deacon had mentioned this matter in prayer meeting he had no doubt done it on the spur of the moment, and with a desire to humble himself and please the Lord. He hadn't meant to make an issue of it.

But he did. Not much was happening just then. There weren't any scandals worth talking about. The outside world didn't matter too much, even though some persons in New York and Washington were even then planning a war.

Maybe Deacon Slater wished he had kept his mouth shut before the Lord. But he couldn't unsay what he had said. He couldn't unpray what he said he had prayed.

3

One not too cold dreamy afternoon about this time, some of us were woods-roaming on an off Saturday, or maybe during one of those frequent vacations that come in a twenty-eight-week school year. There was a thaw, and snow melting, and a drip of water. I suppose Ralph Stevens and Jim Nutting were along, and perhaps my brother, and maybe one or both of the Linton boys. We weren't roaming for any definite purpose, although I believe the theory among us was that we were Indians, or pioneers looking for Indians. The theory didn't matter too much. It was wonderful just to be alive and out of doors. I shall never forget the utter freedom of those days; there is no such freedom now, anywhere. We weren't even hampered by a sense of guilt, for we didn't intend to steal apples, butternuts, or even turnips; and anyhow, the sense of guilt hadn't yet been invented.

We came unexpectedly out of the woods into a level pasture clearing, then into a meadow with some hummocks and bunch grass at the lower end and a cow or two grazing on withered grass from which the snow had melted; next we came to the hay barn and the cow barn, beside which was a neat brick house. At one side were the corn cribs, with open, out-slanting slats to let the corn dry, and nearby was the hen yard, with its white-washed coops and sharp but not unpleasant smell.

As we came up, a rooster crowed, a hen announced that she had just laid an egg, and there was an aimless, happy clucking from other hens that were doing nothing in particular except enjoy life. We boys understood that—we weren't doing anything in particular, either.

I had a sensation of utter peace, such as I rarely had even then, and have never had as an adult—except, perhaps, on an occasional camping trip.

I stood still for a long moment. I think we all did. I can still see, hear, and smell everything that came to my senses in that interval of time. Years later I went back to see if all I imagined was true: it was. Some of the magic had gone, but a red fox loped silently across the pasture and under a rail fence.

"He's a good farmer, anyhow," said one of the boys, Jim Nutting, maybe.

"Who is?" I asked, for I hadn't paid much attention to where we were going and didn't recognize the farm. Indeed, perhaps I wouldn't have recognized it in any case, for the dream lay hazy on it, and it was not a real farm at all, but a farm out of a story book.

"Deacon Slater," retorted Jim Nutting, giving the words a scornful intonation.

And in fact there was the Deacon himself, coming out of the cow barn with a pitchfork in his hand. He was not a smiling man, but he looked pleasant enough and greeted us in friendly fashion.

Is he really the stingiest man in Williamstown, I wondered. There wasn't anything stingy about the farm and its buildings, unless he had discovered that neatness and thrift go together.

We hung around for a while. On some farms the farmer would have called out to his wife, who would be working in the kitchen, to give us some doughnuts or cookies, or at least a drink of buttermilk. I didn't like buttermilk, but I preferred it to nothing at all. We eyed Deacon Slater somewhat hungrily, I imagine. But he didn't call Mrs. Slater. After a while he waved goodbye to us, with the remark that we'd better be getting home if we expected to be there for dinner, and went back into the cow barn.

Maybe that was stingy, I thought. But did it make him the stingiest man in Williamstown? After all, he hadn't been talking about giving doughnuts, cookies, or buttermilk to boys that evening at the prayer meeting; he had been talking about foreign missions and other good works to which he thought he ought to contribute.

Suppose he saved money by not giving us anything to eat, and then gave the money to foreign missions? Would that be stingy?

The other boys didn't debate this subject, at least not out loud. If they couldn't get anything to eat at the Slater farm, they intended to go where they could.

What I got out of that sunny winter day was a conflict of impressions: first, the deep sense of peace that brooded over Deacon Slater's land and buildings; second, the care he took of everything in them and on them. Whether or not he felt any peace was another question. I couldn't imagine him stopping his work long enough to look up at the sky and wonder about it.

Next day, when I went up to the Linton store to see what was going on, I heard that the boys at the livery stable had been putting up bets about Deacon Slater's remark at the prayer meeting. The only trouble was, they couldn't decide just how to prove who was the meanest and stingiest man if Deacon Slater wasn't.

My father asked my mother just what Deacon Slater said to stir up all this commotion, and she told him.

"He wanted to impress people," said my father. "He knows very well there are stingier people in town than he is." He gestured toward Mr. Ainsworth's side of the house. "Do you remember the time he gave what he called a party and served small green apples for refreshment?"

My mother did. "That was all he had, maybe," she commented. "He was taking his meals at the Monument House."

"He could have bought a bag of candy," my father said. This made him recall a man he had known when he was a young granite cutter in New Brunswick for a while. This man would have a fit of generosity and buy a large box of candy on a Saturday night to share with my father and perhaps one or two others. Then he would sit nibbling at it, after passing it around once or twice, and eat practically all of it himself.

"He probably had a craving for sugar," my mother remarked.

I asked what made people stingy.

My father said they were born that way. There were just as many stingy people in Scotland as there were in Vermont—more, because Scotland was bigger.

My mother kept still for a while, and then suggested that people were stingy because they hadn't had enough when they were children and were afraid they wouldn't have enough when they were grown-up.

My father replied that this couldn't be true of Jim Beckett, who squeezed every penny he could out of everybody he had dealings with, and never let go of a single cent if he could help it. Jim might have been poor when he was a boy, but so was his brother George, in that case, and George Beckett would give the shirt off his back if anybody really needed it.

My mother thought you could be saving without being stingy. There was Mrs. Gorham's mother, for instance, Mrs. Caldwell, a lovely old lady who spent a lot of time rolling pieces of old newspapers into spills that could be lighted at the stove and thus save matches. There hadn't been enough matches when Mrs. Caldwell was young, and they had cost too much.

There were elderly people in our town who saved string, old nails, old newspapers—George Ainsworth practically cut his living space in half by the old newspapers he didn't read and wouldn't throw away—odd pieces of lumber, and clothes that nobody would ever wear again. This was what attics were for; they weren't good for anything else, except for the chimneys to run through and perhaps to keep the lower floors from getting too cold in winter or too hot in summer.

My father said it was a good thing for young people, especially boys, to learn the value of money by hard work. My brother and I did learn this lesson, in moderation. My brother once worked all day in a farmer's hayfield and received twenty-five cents in exchange. I suppose my father would have said about this that my brother learned the value of money, but that the farmer didn't have to—he knew it already.

All this set me to thinking of the time my brother and I contracted to deliver wild raspberries for canning to a shrewd neighbor of ours, at ten cents a quart. The berries were dead ripe and as we picked in the hot sun, they softened and sank a little in the pails. The result was that each quart we delivered came to maybe a quart and a quarter.

But this wasn't the way Mrs. Mims saw it. She said the berries were second-rate, and paid us eight cents a quart. We were too young to argue this matter with her, for in our world adults were generally held to be right. But I still think Mrs. Mims was a stingy woman, although she never got up in prayer meeting and said so.

The Slater farm wasn't far from the village, except, of course if you were a boy and found a lot to look at on the way. You cut across an end of Mr. Ainsworth's meadow, stopping in certain seasons of the year to eat black raspberries from a bush near the hay barn and get your teeth full of seeds, but they weren't too bad when they were full ripe; or maybe you found a gooseberry bush and if you had the patience to get the spines off the gooseberries, if they were of that sort, you could stand it to eat some; then you crawled under the fence and went up the hill to the left of the falls, and you might find some spruce gum if you looked carefully, and you could chew it if you hadn't any loose teeth at the time; slippery elm bark was also good to chew, though it was thought best not to swallow it; and if you didn't intend to drink any milk right away you could eat a chokecherry or two if there were any such; and at the right time there could be beechnuts, which tasted all right but required a lot of work to get at a tiny morsel of meat; and the brook came down and was worth looking into in case there might be a frog or two in sight, or a small trout hustling under a stone; or sometimes a small green or brown snake, though I didn't care for even harmless snakes myself.

The Slater farm wasn't far, but a boy might be delayed getting there. Yet I did go past there quite frequently, sometimes with other boys, as on the occasion I have already mentioned, and sometimes on a scouting expedition of my own.

Once Mrs. Slater came to the door, I think with a pail of kitchen scraps for the pigs. She looked neat and gray, thin and very tired, but friendly enough. It seemed to me that both the Slaters were friendly, but didn't have much time to work at it.

She said, "Hello, Robbie," though I was surprised that she knew my name.

I said hello, and stood still and fidgeted, wondering what to say or do next.

"Are you all alone today?" she asked.

I said I was. She seemed to think hard for a moment, then made up her mind. "You come into the kitchen and I'll give you a doughnut," she said. "And some buttermilk."

My spirits rose, then sank, but there wasn't anything to do but follow her into the kitchen. She laid out the doughnut on a clean table, with oilcloth shining on the top. Then she got the buttermilk.

"I always said," she remarked, "that if buttermilk was good for pigs, which it is, it ought to be good for growing boys." She drew a long breath. The Slater boy had grown to be a young man and had drifted off, nobody seemed to know just where.

"Yes, mam," I said, and gulped the milk down as fast as I could.

"Do you always shut your eyes when you drink?" asked Mrs. Slater with a faint smile.

I said I didn't know. I wasn't sure that the milk wouldn't be right back up again.

"Could I take the doughnut with me?" I said.

"If you want to. I'll have to be getting the washing in."

I thanked her and went out, carrying the doughnut like a big ring over the forefinger of my right hand. I wondered why she suddenly laughed, the first time I had heard her do that, as I left.

The buttermilk finally made up its mind to stay inside me, and in a few minutes I reached the hill above the village and sat down to eat the doughnut, pretending it was a strip of jerked venison.

Maybe she was trying not to be stingy, I thought. Or maybe it was just the Deacon who was stingy. I wondered if he was still praying to get over this fault and if his prayers were having any results. My own prayers usually didn't, but maybe, I reflected, that was because I prayed for solid things, such as a horse to ride, and not just to be a better boy.

I wanted to be a better boy, that was certain. What I was afraid of was that if I got too good I wouldn't have much fun. A really good boy wouldn't steal apples. Yet this might mean that a slightly bad boy would get more apples than a really good boy. What was the sense of it?

Yet I did get an apple not long afterward, without being a bad boy. I got an apple, free, from Deacon Slater. I had again drifted up to the Slater farm on a solitary ramble, without really intending to go there, and perhaps balancing the disadvantages of having to drink a big glass of buttermilk against the advantages of getting a doughnut or maybe some cookies. I suppose I was still worrying about Deacon Slater, and what kind of man he really was.

It was again about the middle of the morning and the Slater farm seemed as peaceful as ever, with the hens talking softly to themselves about what they had done or meant to do, and a rooster bragging at the top of his lungs, but not as though he really thought he would get any votes out of it.

Deacon Slater was sitting in the sun on a pile of sawed chunks of wood. This surprised me, and I stopped short. I had believed that when Deacon Slater was at home and not eating or sleeping, he was working. But he wasn't working. He looked puzzled and thoughtful.

I waited for him to speak. "I'm taking it easy today," he said, as if he were apologizing. "Something is wrong with my insides. I've got a pain. I couldn't eat my breakfast." He stopped. "I guess you ate yours. What did you have for breakfast?"

I had had twelve griddle cakes, with maple syrup. "Griddle cakes," I said.

Deacon Slater clasped his stomach and groaned a little. "I'd give a million dollars, if I had a million dollars, if I could eat something that tasted as good to me as those griddle cakes tasted to you."

"A million dollars?" The words jumped out of me. A man as mean as Deacon Slater said he was couldn't be talking in sums like that.

The Deacon corrected himself. "Well, make it a thousand dollars. I could raise that much on this farm. I've done a lot to this farm. It's worth a good deal more than that."

He got up painfully and began to walk me around as though he were a guide showing people the sights. "I painted the house," he said. "It hadn't been painted for years. That was after Gil went away, but I thought he might come back. I built that barn from the bottom up. Before that there was just one barn, with the cows down below and the hay up above, but it didn't hold all the hay we could cut and we had to buy some."

"I see," said I. I was interested but embarrassed.

He turned sharply. "No, you don't," he cried. "Nobody sees." He was talking to me as though I were a grownup. "Some people think I'm made of money, and don't have to work for it. When I say it's hard for me to give money away, they laugh."

We went on talking, he lumbering ahead, myself following

with shorter and quicker steps. "There!" he indicated the stubby pasture land. "I cut the trees off that with my own hands—beech and birch and pine and an elm or two. I didn't cut my sugar bush, the way some men around here do. And I didn't have a hired man, and she didn't have a hired girl, except once, a long time back, when Gil was born. I owed that much to her; but she agreed she wouldn't want money we could save for Gil being spent for a hired man, or a hired girl, either. We've both worked hard, but she's never complained about it."

"I see," said I. I didn't know what I saw, but those were the only words I could think of.

"When a man is stingy," Deacon Slater went on, "he is stingy on account of something. He isn't just stingy. You remember that when you grow up, Robbie."

We walked on a little further, going up the slow rise of the pasture until we could look back at the house and the barns. A thin wisp of smoke was rising from the kitchen chimney.

I made the only original remark I had made that day—or for several days. "It's kind of quiet, isn't it?" I ventured.

He nodded. "Yes, it is. It's real quiet. I like it that way. Real quiet." He was still for a few moments. "Would you like to be a farmer when you grow up, Robbie?"

"No," I replied promptly. "I want to be an engineer."

"A what?" demanded Deacon Slater.

I was sure my answer hadn't pleased him. "An engineer," I repeated. "Like Mr. Webb."

Deacon Slater snorted in an un-Christian fashion. Then he sighed. "Gil must have felt that way," he said. "I don't know that he wanted to be an engineer and sit around all day pulling a throttle and blowing a whistle. Gil had some sense. But he didn't want to be a farmer." He paused, looking over his land and buildings with a sad sort of proudness. "Maybe he was right. When Ma and I are gone this farm as likely as not'll go back to woods again. I can raise good apples, but not as cheap as those from New York State, and they say they're bringing them in now all the way across from the State of Oregon. We can raise our own eating vegetables. I can sell some milk to the creamery, or I can peddle it at five cents a quart; but that's a hard way to get cash money." He shook his head. "Maybe Gil was right. And maybe it's no use trying to save a little for him, the way Ma and I have been doing for about five years. It gets to be a habit, saving." He turned abruptly. "Were you at prayer meeting when I said that?"

I nodded.

"Drinking liquor is a bad habit," said Deacon Slater, "and smoking is a bad habit, and women—but you wouldn't know about that—they're all bad habits and they're all sins against the Almighty, but maybe saving is a bad habit, too. That was what I meant."

"I see," I said.

"You're a good boy," the Deacon resumed. "You make me think a little of Gil at your age. I'm going—" he drew a long, resolute breath—"I'm going to give you an apple for yourself and one each for your brother and sister. Big red Astrachans. Would you like that?"

"Oh, yes," I said.

I walked home slowly, eating one of the big red apples, with their thin skins and the white pulp, full of juice, underneath.

A few days later Mr. Ainsworth told my mother that Deacon Slater had been pretty sick and had had to have Dr. Watson come to see him. He got well, but I don't know how well. His voice in prayer meeting never boomed as much as it had once done, and Mrs. Slater, when she came with him, looked more tired than ever.

I don't know whether or not they ever heard from their son Gil. When I last saw the Slater farm, and that was years later, when the red fox seemed to feel at home on it, the house and barns were in disrepair and the land had long been out of cultivation.

4

When the livery stable boys had what they thought was a good joke, they treated it like a dog with a bone. They buried it and dug it right up again. They pretended to forget it, and then came back to it with a pounce. This habit of theirs can be understood, for they had little but their own slim wits to amuse them. Anyhow, this was what they did with the joke about the meanest and stingiest man in Williamstown—the one Deacon Slater unintentionally started.

One of their bright ideas about this time was to elect a stingiest man at the next town meeting, just as, in those days, many towns elected timber reeves, hog reeves, and other honorary but unnecessary officials.

Sheridan Dabney, who was a sort of spokesman for the livery stable hangers-on, took the idea around town. "Do you get it?" he would ask. "We elect him. Maybe the Deacon would win and maybe somebody else would."

Dab, as he was called, would then laugh uproariously, and as he hadn't any chin to speak of, and a big mouth, this was something to look at as well as listen to. He didn't seem to mind that most of the laughing that was done at his jokes was done by himself.

In another day or two he changed his mind. Maybe someone had told him he shouldn't make fun of town meeting and its elected officials.

"What we've decided to do," he declared, "is to offer a prize. Maybe J. K. will let us set up a box with a slot in the top in his store and then anybody who wants to vote can pay one cent and do it. The man who gets the most votes gets the prize." He added, as he had done before, "Maybe the Deacon wouldn't win, maybe somebody else would. We've got a lot of mean men around this town. There'd be some competition if they all really went after that prize.

"What are you fixing for the prize to be?" somebody asked.

Dab guffawed again. Of course there was only one sort of prize he could think of; that was the sort of mind he had, as I perceived. "Hand-painted," he explained, "with roses on it, and a lid."

"Too bad you don't stand a chance for it yourself," said the man who had spoken before. "It seems to please you so much. But a man can't be mean without having something to be mean over, and that lets you out."

Dab didn't like that remark, but he didn't say much. He had never exercised enough to get up enough muscle to be any good in a fight. Besides, he was too lazy.

I didn't like Dab's kind of conversation, but it fascinated me. It reminded me of what I could find under a flat stone in a pasture if I turned it over, white worms and beetles and other unattractive forms of life. But I kept turning over stones in pastures, and I kept listening to Dab's kind of conversation whenever I heard him trying it out on a group of men in the store or around the stable. I couldn't always keep away from the stable, because I did like horses and kept dreaming of having one of my own.

But I didn't want Dab and his friends to send Deacon Slater, if he was the man they decided on, a thunder jug with hand-painted roses on it, and a lid. If he was a mean man, which I doubted, he was still a better man than Sheridan Dabney. I kept thinking of what it was like to stand beside Deacon Slater's barnyard and hear the hens clucking and the roosters crowing, and how Mrs. Slater had given me a doughnut, which I liked, in addition to a mug of buttermilk, which I didn't like, and how the Deacon had given me those Red Astrachans, and how the Deacon had talked about his absent son Gil.

I didn't want Dab, or anybody at all, to do anything to hurt the feelings of Deacon and Mrs. Slater.

And in the final outcome he didn't.

One day Philander Milton, as I shall call him, came down, in one of his rare visits to Williamstown Village, from his rocky farm around the far corners of the East Hill. Philander was the sort of man who wouldn't let his wife come to church more than once a month because the horses needed rest on Sunday, and ate too many oats if they were overworked. Mrs. Milton was a ghost of a woman, with unkempt graying hair and a lost and mournful look. How she got her husband to accept her mother as a boarder, nobody ever knew. Maybe Mrs. Milton had the strength that the meek often do have.

Philander grumbled about the arrangement but it continued until his wife's mother died. The funeral was as simple and cheap as it could be. The next time Philander came to the store somebody said, with an undertone of sarcasm, that it was generous of him to take the dying old woman in.

Philander coughed apologetically. "Well, I'll tell you," he said. "She never did eat much, all the time she was with us." A slow smile spread over his face. "And the last two weeks she didn't eat nothing at all."

He looked around. Nobody spoke, though the story would be all around town by next morning and would be a tradition in Williamstown as long as any of the old timers lived there.

I thought of Deacon Slater and Mrs. Slater, and now they had a shining quality. I don't remember that after that anybody ever called the Deacon stingy—not even the Deacon himself, though, when he was well enough, he kept coming to prayer meeting.

Alton H. Blackington (1893-1963)

Human Hibernation

Everybody has heard about "dead" birds picked up after a blizzard and revived in a warm room, and fishermen by the hundred recall occasions when a frozen-solid pail of pickerel was melted, and the fish started swimming; and there have been several cases where humans revived, and survived, after being pronounced dead by freezing.

These occurrences have a certain aura about them—is it supernatural? miraculous?—which makes them always fascinating. When a Russian scientist announced a few years ago that he had found fungi, bacteria and moulds buried for centuries in the vast Siberian deep-freeze, and had successfully brought them back to life, newspapers all over the world gave his discovery a big play. Readers of all ages, in all walks of life, everywhere, saw these articles and pondered over them.

Up in the Green Mountain State of Vermont, Elbert S. Stevens of Bridgewater Corners, when he read these reports, puffed on his pipe and drawled, "I guess them Rooshians never heard 'bout freezing the old folks up back of Montpelier. When Marm told us that story of a winter's night, us kids got goose-pimples."

The boys at the General Store kicked the spittoon out of the way and moved in close. "Tell us abaout it, Elbert."

Mr. Stevens hitched his thumbs comfortably under his galluses. "Seems there was a famine round here, and to save grub and firewood, some of the old folks who couldn't work for their vittles was given a good big supper and put outdoors to FREEZE! By midnight they was stiff as stovepokers. Next morning they was piled in a box, covered with straw and sledded out under a big ledge. There they stayed, under them snow-drifts, all winter!

"Come spring, they was dug out and put in warm water. Soon's any of 'em showed signs of coming to, they give him a slug of brandy, wrapped him in blankets and took him home. After a few good feeds they was fit as fiddles and them that was able set to work planting corn."

Mr. Stevens pulled at the tarnished ends of his handlebar mustache and added, "It was all printed in the paper and I have the clipping Marm pasted in her scrapbook. I've read it hundreds of times."

The General Store Boys shook their heads, some sidewise, some up and down, and without much conviction either way. Not long afterward, the curious tale came to the ears of a staff reporter of the Rutland *Herald*. Hunting up the aged Mr. Stevens, he borrowed the old scrapbook, and on May 24, 1939, the whole eerie yarn came out in his paper. The following is a verbatim copy of the yellowed clipping.

"A Strange Tale"
By A. M.

"I am an old man now, and have seen some strange sights in the course of a roving life in foreign lands as well as in this country, but none so strange as one I found recorded in an old diary, kept by my Uncle William, that came into my possession a few years ago, at his decease. The events described took place in a mountain town some twenty miles from Montpelier, the Capital of Vermont. I have been to the place on the mountain, and seen the old log-house where the events I found recorded in the diary took place, and seen and talked with an old man who vouched for the truth of the story, and that his father was one of the parties operated on. The account runs in this wise:

" '*January* 7.—I went on the mountain today, and witnessed what to me was a horrible sight. It seems that the dwellers there, who are unable, either from age or other reasons, to contribute to the support of their families, are disposed of in the winter months in a manner that will shock the one who reads this diary, unless that person lives in that vicinity. I will describe what I saw. Six persons, four men and two women, one of the men a cripple about 30 years old, the other five past the age of usefulness, lay on the earthy floor of the cabin drugged into insensibility, while members of their families were gathered about them in apparent indifference. In a short time the unconscious bodies were inspected by one man who said, "They are ready." They were then stripped of all their clothing, except a single garment. Then the bodies were carried outside, and laid on logs exposed to the bitter cold mountain air, the operation having been delayed several days for suitable weather.

" 'It was night when the bodies were carried out, and the full moon, occasionally obscured by flying clouds, shone on their upturned ghastly faces, and a horrible fascination kept me by the bodies as long as I could endure the severe cold. Soon the noses, ears and fingers began to turn white, then the limbs and face assumed a tallowy look. I could stand the cold no longer, and went inside, where I found the friends in cheerful conversation.

" 'In about an hour I went out and looked at the bodies: they were fast freezing. Again I went inside, where the men were smoking their clay pipes, but silence had fallen on them; perhaps they were thinking of the time when their turn would come to be cared for in the same way. One by one they at last lay down on the floor, and went to sleep. It seemed a horrible nightmare to me, and I could not think of sleep. I could not shut out the sight of those freezing bodies outside, neither could I bear to be in darkness, but I piled on the wood in the cavernous fireplace, and, seated on a shingle block, passed the dreary night, terror-stricken by the horrible sights I had witnessed.

" '*January 8.*—Day came at length, but did not dissipate the terror that filled me. The frozen bodies became visible, white as the snow that lay in huge drifts about them. The women gathered about the fire, and soon commenced preparing breakfast. The men awoke, and, conversation again commencing, affairs assumed a more cheerful aspect. After breakfast the men lighted their pipes, and some of them took a yoke of oxen and went off toward the forest, while others proceeded to nail together boards, making a box about ten feet long and half as high and wide. When this was completed they placed about two feet of straw in the bottom; then they laid three of the frozen bodies on the straw. Then the faces and upper part of the bodies were covered with a cloth, then more straw was put in the box, and the other three bodies placed on top and covered the same as the first ones, with cloth and straw. Boards were then firmly nailed on the top, to protect the bodies from being injured by carnivorous animals that make their home on these mountains.

" 'By this time the men who went off with the ox-team returned with a huge load of spruce and hemlock boughs, which they unloaded at the foot of a steep ledge, came to the house and loaded the box containing the bodies on the sled, and drew it to the foot of the ledge, near the load of boughs. These were soon piled on and around the box, and it was left to be covered up with snow, which I was told would lie in drifts twenty feet deep over this rude tomb. "We shall want our men to plant our corn next spring," said a youngish looking woman, the wife of one of the frozen men, "and if you want to see them resuscitated, you come here about the 10th of next May."

" 'With this agreement, I left the mountaineers, both the living and the frozen, to their fate and I returned to my home in Boston where it was weeks before I was fairly myself, as my thoughts would return to that mountain with its awful sepulchre.' Turning the leaves of the diary, the old man recounts, the following entry was found:

" '*May 10.*—I arrived here at 10 A.M., after riding about four hours over muddy, unsettled roads. The weather is warm and pleasant, most of the snow is gone, except here and there drifts in the fence corners and hollows, but nature is not yet dressed in green. I found the same parties here that I left last January, ready to disinter the bodies of their friends. I had no expectation of finding any life there, but a feeling that I could not resist impelled me to come and see. We repaired at once to the well remembered spot, at the ledge. The snow had melted from the top of the brush,

but still lay deep around the bottom of the pile. The men commenced work at once, some shoveling away the snow, and others
tearing away the brush. Soon the box was visible. The cover was
taken off, the layers of straw removed, and the bodies, frozen
and apparently lifeless, lifted out and laid on the snow. Large
troughs made out of hemlock logs were placed nearby, filled with
tepid water, into which the bodies were separately placed, with
the head slightly raised. Boiling water was then poured into the
trough from kettles hung on poles over fires near by, until the
water in the trough was as hot as I could hold my hand in. Hemlock boughs had been put in the boiling water in such quantities
that they had given the water the color of wine. After lying in this
bath about an hour, color began to return to the bodies, when all
hands began rubbing and chafing them. This continued about
another hour, when a slight twitching of the muscles of the face
and limbs, followed by audible gasps, showed that life was not
quenched, and that vitality was returning. Spirits were then given
in small quantities, and allowed to trickle down their throats.
Soon they could swallow, and more was given them, when their
eyes opened, and they began to talk, and finally sat up in their
bathtubs. They were then taken out and assisted to the house,
where after a hearty dinner they seemed as well as ever, and in
nowise injured, but rather refreshed, by their long sleep of four
months.' Truly, truth is stranger than fiction."

Four days later, on May 28, 1939, the Boston Sunday *Globe*
carried this headline: "HUMAN HIBERNATION IN VERMONT
CENTURY AGO."

"Montpelier, Vt. May 27—Recent experiments with freezing
of humans so that all bodily functions were suspended for hours,
described at the sessions of the American Medical Association in
St. Louis, were merely the beginning of possibilities in this direction, according to goings-on in a tiny village near here nearly a
century ago.

"A recent issue of the Rutland *Herald* carried a reprint of a
clipping taken from an old scrapbook belonging to Elbert S.

Stevens of Bridgewater Corners in which he described the strange adventures of a traveler in Vermont in the 90's." Then followed the reprint, "A Strange Tale, by A. M."

Yankee magazine printed the grisly tale in 1940 and it created so much speculation, from far-afield points, that Publisher Robb Sagendorph included the story of "Frozen Death" in the 1943 edition of the famous *Old Farmer's Almanac.*

B. A. Botkin borrowed the chiller from the *Almanac* for his *A Treasury of New England Folklore.*

The story was now well on its way to becoming a classic, and all over the country youngsters shuddered delightfully while old and feeble folks were understandably repelled.

Charles Edward Crane, distinguished Vermont author and historian, gave the story a place in his book, *Winter in Vermont* and to answer innumerable questions, he broadcast, not once but several times, over Montpelier's radio station. I also broadcast the story.

Anxious to see the clipping and interview Mr. Stevens, and photograph them both before anything happened to them, I had driven to Vermont and found the old-timer in his accustomed corner of the general store. He said if I didn't mind walking down the "rudd" a piece, I could see the scrapbook.

"Don't mind the mess," he puffed, leading me up a rickety flight of stairs on the outside of a rambling, unpainted two-story structure. "Since my last wife died, I've kinda let things go."

The living room was a clutter of old clothes, dishes and pile upon pile of books, papers and magazines. On a shelf, two carved female faces stared woodenly from under the brims of old-fashioned headgear. "My late wives," Elbert explained. "Dead and gone a long time. I carved 'em out of a chunk of pine. Keeps me from being lonesome."

Reaching into a closet, he held up a pig's head, also whittled from wood. *"He* was a good pal too."

While I returned the stares of the wooden wives and the pig, Mr. Stevens did considerable rummaging, finally handing me the scrapbook—a bulky, heavy, leather-bound volume entitled: *Mes-*

sages of the President of the United States to the Two Houses of Congress at the Commencement of the Thirty-Seventh Congress. 1862. Vol. I.

Originally this voluminous report had contained 910 pages, but Mother Stevens had clipped a few pages here and there to allow room for the births, marriages, deaths, recipes, poems and local doings which had taken her fancy. On page 62 was "A Strange Tale, by A. M." but there was nothing to show when it had been published, nor by what newspaper. After a cursory examination of the dusty book, I made a few photographs and then turned my attention to Elbert Stevens.

"Do you believe that story?"

He exploded. "Course I do! My mother told me about freezing them old people!"

Back in Boston I prepared my radio script, never dreaming that this tale of "Frozen Death" would arouse so much interest, indignation and speculation. Immediately following the broadcast we were flooded with phone calls and letters.

"Missed your hibernation story; please repeat it."

"Don't tell me you fell for such a hoax."

"Who was Uncle William and where is his diary?"

The prize and not-so-serious letter came from a listener up in Cal Coolidge's country. "After reading how the Washington experts (?) got the farmers to plow under their crops, kill their hogs, and dump thousands of bushels of potatoes to rot, I'm worrying for fear they'll start freezing us old folks to conserve food and fuel." It was signed, "Lifelong Republican."

Concurrently, as this story rolled along, gathering momentum, newspapers and magazines printed other stories of *FREEZING,* and in several instances the Vermont episode was quoted as fact.

Dr. Gregory Pincus of Clark University described an experiment in which the male cells of a man, a bull, and frogs were plunged into liquid nitrogen, frozen solid, and later thawed gradually, and to everyone's astonishment 50 per cent of the cells were alive.

A new treatment for cancer was being tried. An item from

Springfield, Illinois, stated: "A man was restored to life after having been frozen in an unconscious sleep for five days and nights in an amazing experiment to rid his body of deadly cancer." The patient was placed in a tub and packed with ice until his body temperature was reduced to 84 degrees. Whether or not the cancer was cured, a serious heart condition apparently was, and doctors suggested that hibernation might be employed in the treatment of cardiac patients. Anyway, the man awoke from his iced sleep smiling and feeling fine.

Bernarr MacFadden in *Physical Culture* helped matters along by writing that "frozen sleep" treatment for cancer was not really so revolutionary—six persons had once been frozen for the winter up near Montpelier, Vermont. This was quite in accord with a long-held theory of his, that human bodies could be frozen and brought back to life in the same manner as certain animals.

Describing the use of low temperature, which numbs the nerve ends, as a local anaesthetic, more than one medical man anticipated a time when the entire body might be frozen and revived "as was done in Vermont many years ago." Dr. Fay of Temple University, who performed early cold-therapy experiments with cancer patients, was quoted as saying he accepted the story as fact.

I, myself, confronted a famous New York diagnostician, and asked him point blank if he thought the scrapbook story was possible. He was a long time answering. "While I doubt if any such event ever took place as described in this story, so many remarkable experiments have been conducted along this line that I hesitate to say it is impossible."

Scientific progress was all around me, and *FREEZING* seemed to be in the very air. By this time, and not alone by any means, I began to wonder if "A Strange Tale, by A. M." could be true!

Among the many with whom I discussed this mystery was Roland Wells Robbins, a local archeologist with a penchant for digging up facts. Mr. Robbins had just settled a fifty-year-old controversy concerning the exact location of the hut in which Thoreau lived and wrote at Walden Pond. For years visitors had been piling stones on a cairn in Concord, Massachusetts, believing it was the site of Thoreau's cabin. Robbins spent two years reading, probing, measuring and digging until he unearthed the actual foundation of the cabin; this was fascinating business for Robbins.

After that he turned to pre-restoration archeological work at the site of the First Iron Works, at Saugus, Massachusetts, for the American Iron and Steel Institute. I was interviewing him on location when suddenly he changed the subject.

"That story about freezing old folks up in Vermont. . . ." he began.

"Yes," I said, "that is a puzzler. I've never known a story to get such a hold on people."

"I'm going up to Vermont and solve that mystery if it takes ten years. Will you tell me all you know about it?"

I hesitated. I was fond of the tall tale and it had done well for me as it had for quite a few others, and I rather disliked having it debunked. But of course I was anxious to learn who had written the story originally, what paper had printed it, and what had inspired the strange tale.

Robbins began, as I had ten years before, with a trip to Bridgewater Corners, but Elbert Stevens, now over eighty, wasn't living there any more. "You'll find Elbert," drawled one of his neighbors, "over ter Woodstock in the County Jail. But 'tain't as bad as it sounds; he's jest boarding there for the winter."

By the time Robbins reached Woodstock, Elbert had moved to a better boarding place, up in Rutland. Bundling the old fellow into his car, Robbins drove over slippery, snowy roads to the cold, empty house in Bridgewater Corners. Elbert produced the scrapbook, and Robbins took it to his hotel.

On the fly-leaf was written "Hannah F. Stevens, Bridgewater, Vermont, July 24th, 1895." But the earliest clipping was dated 1879, so Robbins concluded that the article about Frozen Death had been clipped from some local newspaper between those dates. But which newspaper?

Examining the clipping carefully, he noted that a thin black line ran down the left side of the column but not down the right, indicating that it had appeared on the right hand side of a page. A decorative space line below the story showed that it didn't quite fill the column, and, by measuring, Robbins found that the newspaper had used wider and longer columns than most papers of those days.

His next step was to visit the State Library at Montpelier where he examined files of old newspapers. Only one used the same width of column—the Montpelier *Argus & Patriot.* So far, so good, but as the task of going through bound volumes of the *Argus* for sixteen years seemed hopeless, he "split the difference" between 1879 and 1895, and began with the file for 1886. No luck. He examined the file for 1885. Nothing there.

He had reached the last few pages of the 1887 file when his heart leaped! "A Strange Tale, by A. M." had first been printed on Wednesday, December 21, 1887!

Above the title was the line (which had been snipped off the clipping in the Stevens scrapbook), "Written for the *Argus & Patriot.*" Evidently, then, "A. M." was a regular contributor, and it should be easy, Robbins figured, to find other stories bearing that by-line. But a search of the entire newspaper files for 1887 and 1888 proved fruitless. The nearest he came to it was one poem by "A. H. Mills of Middlebury."

Stranger still, he found no reference to the freezing episode in later editions. Had the story excited no interest, no curiosity, in that generation?

Baffled, but unwilling to give up his research, Mr. Robbins toured the towns within a twenty-five miles radius of Montpelier, where the freezings were said to have taken place. Almost everyone knew the story, but no one could add anything new.

Hoping someone would yet come forward with the information he wanted, Robbins prepared a lengthy article which was published in the 1949 winter edition of *Vermont Life,* the official publication of the State of Vermont. The following (spring 1950) issue said editorially, "The article on 'Human Hibernation' evoked an avalanche of letters, phone calls and newspaper comment. One columnist suggests that 'A.M.' might have been some member of the Atkins family, who owned and published the *Argus & Patriot* in 1887. Several members of that family have initials 'M. A.' which might simply be reversed."

But Robbins had already interviewed Miss Elaine Atkins, editor and publisher of the Montpelier *Argus* (now a daily) and reached another dead end. Old office records had been destroyed by flood or by fire; there was nothing left to identify old-time contributors.

Among the letters which Robbins received, one from Florida seemed promising. Mrs. Mabel E. Hynes wrote, "The A. M. you are looking for was my grandfather, Allen Morse." Robbins would have liked to have jumped a plane that very day, but his duties at the Iron Works kept him in Saugus, and impatiently he sweated it out until Mrs. Hynes returned to her home in Massachusetts where he could talk to her.

This is what he learned: Allen Morse was born in Woodbury, Vermont, on December 21, 1835. The family moved to Calais, Vermont, in 1840, and there he lived most of his life. He had four children, three girls and one boy. The eldest girl, Alice May Morse (Mrs. Hynes' mother), secured her first employment in the *Argus & Patriot* office in Montpelier and "took board and room" with the publisher, Hiram Atkins.

Like most Vermonters, Allen Morse devoted much of his time to farming, but he was also of a literary bent and frequently wrote pieces for the *New England Homestead* and for *Farm & Fireside.* That he was progressive and thrifty is shown by his purchasing the first parlor organ and the first sewing machine in that section of Vermont. The organ was used freely for Sunday night gather-ings, but neighbors were charged by the yard when they borrowed the sewing machine.

Allen Morse was noted as story teller, and no family reunion or Christmas party went by that he wasn't called upon to spin a few yarns. Benjamin Morse, his cousin, was runner-up, and con-siderable rivalry existed between A. M. and B. M. to see who could tell the tallest tale.

Benjamin's favorite spell-binder concerned a grave which burst into flame, and not to be outdone, Allen Morse concocted his freezing story, using familiar local spots to make it sound real. The cabin where the bodies were prepared was an old deserted log house near the Morse farm, and the ledge where they lay under the snow was Eagle Ledge, on the road between Calais and East Elmore. And incidentally, the snow has been known to drift to a depth of twenty feet and more at that particular place.

The "Uncle William," mentioned was a brother-in-law, William Noyes.

Mrs. Hynes explained, "My mother left the *Argus & Patriot* after she married and moved to Connecticut, but she frequently came back to Vermont for short visits. Around the middle of December, 1887, she called on her former employer, Hiram Atkins, and suggested he print her father's favorite story on his birthday."

Editor Atkins read over the handwritten pages about the alleged freezings and smiled. "I'll print it if you'll set it." So, borrowing an apron and a composing stick, Allen Morse's daughter set the type from which "A Strange Tale, by A. M." was printed on her father's fifty-second birthday, December 21, 1887.

Over in Bridgewater, Mrs. Hannah Stevens, interested by the story, cut it out and pasted it into her scrapbook, never dreaming that half a century later, authors, editors, newspaper reporters and photographers would be pestering her son Elbert for just a peek at the old clipping. And how surprised "A. M." would have been to read in all the books and papers and magazines this tall tale he had invented in his effort to tell a bigger lie than his cousin!

In spite of the fact that this famous Vermont legend has been debunked, it will still be told when Yankee families gather round their firesides on future winter nights. Fiction though it was, it caught the public's interest, and fooled not a few. And, considering what has been accomplished since that time with low-temperature treatments in medical research, who can say that it was not prophetic?

Walter Hard (1882-1967)

Always Hollerin'

When the neighbors heard Charlie Barney
Whistling about his place,
And saw him playing with his black Spaniel
They used to say:
"Hello. Guess Charlie's havin' a vacation."
They meant that Mrs. B.
Had gone over the mountain
To visit her sister.
The only affection in that household
Existed between Charlie and his dog.
Between Charlie and his wife
There was an armed truce
Not infrequently broken.
One Monday morning they were doing the washing.
Charlie had brought in the tubs,
Filled the boiler on the stove,
And built a good hot fire.
He was slowly turning the wringer
His thoughts outside the window
Where the hens were having a party
In "her posey bed."
Suddenly the wringer turned hard
And he put on more steam.
A wild yell demanded his attention.
He had turned Mrs. B's arm into the wringer
Half way up to the elbow.
A few days later, he was getting some groceries
When someone asked him about the accident.

He told the story briefly, without feeling.
"But didn't your wife make an outcry?"
He picked up his packages
And turned toward the door.
"O yes. She hollered.
But Lord—she's always hollerin'."

Youth of the Mountain

Sap dripped from a broken twig.
Here and there a green spike showed
Through the mat of leaves,
Pressed flat by the winter snows.

Along the road by Roaring Branch
Rob was driving a pair of steers
Hitched to a home-made, rattling cart.
He was past eighty, yet his step was firm,

And he easily kept pace with the fast walking cattle.
He broke a twig from a birch
And chewed the sappy bark.
He looked with eager eyes
At the mountains rising on either side.
When the team stopped to rest
He squared his shoulders
And took in deep breaths of the fragrant air.
He was going home to his mountains.

He stood in the door of the mountain farm house,
Watching the sun through the spruces.
—*They say I'm too old to stay up here.*
Old?
Mebbe I am old down thar in th' valley
With all the rushin' and new fangled idees
Clutt'rin things up with what they call civ'lization.
But up here . . .

He came out to the edge of the porch,
—*Y' see old Stratton through the gap yonder?*
Been thar you tell how long.
Hear th' Branch aroarin' back th' house?
How many hundred year has it been acuttin'
T' make this valley here?
Thar's that stand o' spruces yonder
That never felt an axe;
They was good timber when I was born
Right here in this house
Eighty three year ago come July.
He heaved a sigh full of contentment.
—*Mebbe down thar*
I ain't nothin' but an old man,
But up here where I b'long . . .
There was exultation in his voice—
—*Up here,*
I ain't nothin' but a yearlin'.

A Monument

Rob put a maple chunk into the stove,
And turned the pipe damper.
—*There's another reason,*
I want t' be buried under that pine.
He went to the sink
And drank from the dipper.
The night wind
Rattled the window.
Away off on the mountain
An owl hooted and another answered.

—*I ain't sayin' there is or there ain't,*
But 'sposin' there is a day comin'

When we all resurrect.
I don't want t' be mixed up
With a lot o' queer tomb stuns
And a mess o' strange folks.

He opened the door.
The candle flickered and went out.
The moonlight drifted in
On the mountain mist.

—I want to come to,
Right there b' that pine.
I want t' be alone fer a spell
And hev time t' think things over.

The tall pine
Stood out against the sky,
Gently beckoning.

The Deserted House

Since Rob went,
The old house seems to have given up.
The two had grown old and gray together.
Rob had kept the roof sound
And the windows tight.
The old house had made Rob a home.
Each seemed to need the other.

Now that Rob has gone
The old house has nothing to hold it.
The doors stand open,
Swinging and slamming when the wind
Roars through the gap in the mountain.
A shutter hangs by one hinge;
A loose clapboard

Slants over a broken sash;
Weeds are growing between the worn stones
That lead to a door which gives no welcome;
There are patches of green moss
On the rotting roof.

The winter snows, piled deep,
Will break the sagging ridge-pole.
Tumbled bricks will choke the cold chimney
And cover the hearth.
The howling of shivering winds,
The cracking of frost-bound timbers,
And the rasping of a hedge-hog,
Gnawing holes in the salty kitchen floor,
Will be all the old house hears.

Some spring,
When the fresh green is creeping up,
Along Roaring Branch,
You'll find the woods
Have taken the old house back.
There'll be only a bush-grown cellar hole . . .

And memories.

Arthur Wallace Peach (1886-1956)

Weasel in the Wall

Flames in the night, and thunder far,
Cities dustward reeling,
Fatal bloom of death across
The red skies stealing—
Out of the dust a mortal sighing,
Deep in the mist the children crying.

Is there a Word I must obey
Out of the jungle's distant day,
Rising out of the ancient slime,
Ruling me in this later time?

Bright eyes of death that turn away,
The meaning in your eyes is clear:
I wish my fellowmen could see
Your sneer!

Bright eyes of death that stare at me,
Suppose we set our fancy free:
What think I of you?
What think you of me?

Swift and clean is the death you deal,
Your lean strength blocking
All escape, and in the throat
Your white teeth locking.

Out of the past the quick Word comes
With no gainsaying—
And you at the ancient call
Obeying.

Robert Frost (1874-1963)

The Runaway

Once when the snow of the year was beginning to fall,
We stopped by a mountain pasture to say, "Whose colt?"
A little Morgan had one forefoot on the wall,
The other curled at his breast. He dipped his head
And snorted at us. And then he had to bolt.
We heard the miniature thunder where he fled,
And we saw him, or thought we saw him, dim and gray,
Like a shadow against the curtain of falling flakes.
"I think the little fellow's afraid of the snow.
He isn't winter-broken. It isn't play
With the little fellow at all. He's running away.
I doubt if even his mother could tell him, 'Sakes,
It's only weather.' He'd think she didn't know!
Where is his mother? He can't be out alone."
And now he comes again with clatter of stone,
And mounts the wall again with whited eyes
And all his tail that isn't hair up straight.
He shudders his coat as if to throw off flies.
"Whoever it is that leaves him out so late,
When other creatures have gone to stall and bin,
Ought to be told to come and take him in."

The Onset

Always the same, when on a fated night
At last the gathered snow lets down as white
As may be in dark woods, and with a song

It shall not make again all winter long
Of hissing on the yet uncovered ground,
I almost stumble looking up and round,

As one who overtaken by the end
Gives up his errand, and lets death descend
Upon him where he is, with nothing done
To evil, no important triumph won,
More than if life had never been begun.

Yet all the precedent is on my side:
I know that winter death has never tried
The earth but it has failed: the snow may heap
In long storms an undrifted four feet deep
As measured against maple, birch, and oak,
It cannot check the peeper's silver croak;
And I shall see the snow all go down hill
In water of a slender April rill
That flashes tail through last year's withered brake
And dead weeds, like a disappearing snake.
Nothing will be left white but here a birch,
And there a clump of houses with a church.

Good-by and Keep Cold

This saying good-by on the edge of the dark
And the cold to an orchard so young in the bark
Reminds me of all that can happen to harm
An orchard away at the end of the farm
All winter, cut off by a hill from the house.
I don't want it girdled by rabbit and mouse,
I don't want it dreamily nibbled for browse
By deer, and I don't want it budded by grouse.
(If certain it wouldn't be idle to call
I'd summon grouse, rabbit, and deer to the wall

And warn them away with a stick for a gun.)
I don't want it stirred by the heat of the sun.
(We made it secure against being, I hope,
By setting it out on a northerly slope.)
No orchard's the worse for the wintriest storm;
But one thing about it, it mustn't get warm.
"How often already you've had to be told,
Keep cold, young orchard. Good-by and keep cold.
Dread fifty above more than fifty below."
I have to be gone for a season or so.
My business awhile is with different trees,
Less carefully nurtured, less fruitful than these,
And such as is done to their wood with an ax—
Maples and birches and tamaracks.
I wish I could promise to lie in the night
And think of an orchard's arboreal plight
When slowly (and nobody comes with a light)
Its heart sinks lower under the sod.
But something has to be left to God.

A Drumlin Woodchuck

One thing has a shelving bank,
Another a rotting plank,
To give it cozier skies
And make up for its lack of size.

My own strategic retreat
Is where two rocks almost meet,
And still more secure and snug,
A two-door burrow I dug.

With those in mind at my back
I can sit forth exposed to attack,
As one who shrewdly pretends
That he and the world are friends.

All we who prefer to live
Have a little whistle we give,
And flash, at the least alarm
We dive down under the farm.

We allow some time for guile
And don't come out for a while,
Either to eat or drink.
We take occasion to think.

And if after the hunt goes past
·And the double-barreled blast
(Like war and pestilence
And the loss of common sense),

If I can with confidence say
That still for another day,
Or even another year,
I will be there for you, my dear,

It will be because, though small
As measured against the All,
I have been so instinctively thorough
About my crevice and burrow.

On Being Chosen Poet of Vermont

Breathes there a bard who isn't moved
When he finds his verse is understood
And not entirely disapproved
By his country and his neighborhood?

Vrest Orton (1897-   )

What Else Had Failed

I

Hardly a man comes up this far
Without asking me the same question:
How can I live so far away!
Since you didn't pose the question,
You'll be the first to have my answer.

II

I came up here to see how man had failed!
Down country he seems to have won all his wars;
He's littered land and befouled water.
He's a stranger to peace and the clean heart.
The fear of God is not in him.
Up here, I thought, maybe someone else
Might have the upper hand.

III

Just a minute, Robert. You know the Bible says
. . . The Lord put Man in the Garden of Eden
To dress it and keep it.
Do you think he's done well in Vermont?

IV

I don't know as he's had a chance.
But I'll let you in on something . . .
I wanted to get back far enough
To learn what else had failed.

Dorothy Canfield Fisher (1879-1958)

Tourists Accommodated

Written by Dorothy Canfield Fisher and worked out with a small group of her Arlington neighbors, Tourists Accommodated *makes use of typical experiences that Vermonters have with the summer tourists. Much of the humor derives from the contrast between the manners, customs, speech, and dress of the native Vermonters and the accommodated tourists. After a lengthy discussion of the merits of the project, the Lymans decide to take in summer boarders. In the following scene they receive their first guests.*

A play in six scenes and one setting

CAST OF CHARACTERS

Sophia Lyman. About forty years old, neat, clean, self-respecting, plainly dressed country-woman, who makes her own clothes, but following good patterns.

Lucy Lyman. Her daughter, pretty, brisk, attractive girl about eighteen years old, simply dressed but very trim and neat.

Phillip Lyman. Her twelve-year-old son.

Aunt Jane. The deaf old Great-aunt.

Aunt Nancy Ann. Another Great-aunt, but much younger than Aunt Jane, very vigorous and vital.

First Group of Tourists. A man and his wife and two children. They are dressed as are all the tourists in these scenes, in city clothes, but not expensively so, the kind of people, not rich, who would naturally stop over night in a farmhouse and not a hotel. Second Group of Tourists. Two women and a lot of children— there must be five at least, but you can have as many more as you like.

SCENE II

Time: *Decoration Day.*

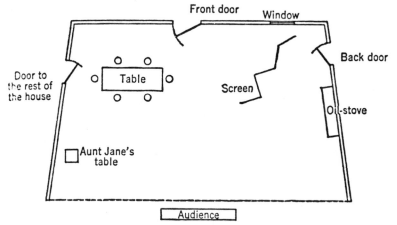

Scene: *The stage is laid at each scene in the same place—the living-room-kitchen of a comfortable farmhouse. Furniture taken out of any house will do if it is plain and somewhat old-fashioned. One good old chair is necessary. Some old-fashioned chromos or "God Bless Our Home" mottos, etc., on the walls. There is a window at the back, and a door. A door at each side, right and left. A table at the back. At the right (as you look up at the stage) an oil cooking-stove, with kitchen utensils hanging up back of it. At the left (also as you look at the stage from the audience) as old-fashioned a telephone outfit as you can find, set on a small stand. There is a large screen across the right-hand side of the stage as you look up from the audience. As the curtain goes up,* SOPHIA *is pulling the screen in place to conceal the cookstove and back door from the room (but not from the audience). She and* LUCY *flutter nervously about, picking up and laying down things.* AUNT JANE *sits at her telephone table, knitting.* PHILLIP *sticks his head in the*

back door, back of the screen but visible to the audience, and asks eagerly in a loud voice: "Has anybody come yet? What do they look like?" *They fly at him, suppressing him with voice and gesture.*

Sophia. Sh! Sh! No, there haven't. But suppose somebody had. What would they think! Suppose somebody *was* here!

Phillip [*impertinently*]. Aunt Nancy Ann said you weren't to do so much supposing. [*His mother rushes at him to box his ears and he vanishes, slamming the door. She returns to the center of stage, and begins again to pick up and set down chairs, twitch picture frames, etc.*]

Lucy. Goodness, I'm too nervous to live. I wish to goodness somebody would come and get it over! Say, Mother, what do you say we practice! You be a stranger and I'll be me. Come on!

Sophia [*getting the idea, snatches up a dish towel, wraps it around her shoulders like a shawl, advances from the door looking very haughty, nose in the air, and says in a high, squeaky, affected voice and accent:*] Do you 'commodate tourists here?

Lucy [*rattling her learned-by-heart phrases off in a rapid monotone*]. Yes, ma'am, we have five good bedrooms, with double bed in each and a cot for children to put up extra if you like. A dollar a person for each bed, and fifty cents for a cot. [*She pauses, laughs, says in her natural tone:*] Nothing charged for the use of a bureau drawer for a cradle for the baby. [*Goes back to her mechanical recital.*] Thirty-five cents for fruit, coffee and toast breakfast— fifty cents for a 100% American meal with pancakes and maple syrup! [*They both laugh and then with a shout* LUCY *says:*] Mother! There's a car slowing down! Somebody is going to stop. [*They both rush to the window, stare through it, clutching hard at each other's hands, and then draw back.*]

Lucy. No, they just slowed down for the turn in the road. *My!* That gave me a scare!

Sophia [*anxiously*]. What *will* we do when somebody really *does* come? [*The telephone rings. Usual business of* AUNT JANE.]

Lucy [*hopefully*]. Perhaps nobody will.

Sophia [*desperately*]. They've *got* to! All those new sheets and pillow-cases we've bought! My goodness, if they don't— [*She gives a start and says nervously:*] Seems as though I heard a car drawing up. Look out the window, Lucy. [LUCY *goes to the window, drawing aside the curtain a very little to see. The children open the back door and troop in behind the screen, watching from that place what happens. They are hidden from* LUCY *and* SOPHIA *on the stage but plainly seen by the audience, as they look through the crack of the screen.*]

Lucy [*over her shoulder*]. Yes, it *is* somebody stopping. A Chevrolet. A man and a woman. Some children in the back seat. And an old person. Yes, the man *is* coming in. [*She turns back in a panic.*] Oh, Mother, *you* open the door. [*During this time* SOPHIA *has been slyly moving towards the back door, and now she opens it.*]

Sophia [*over her shoulder*]. I've got to get my clothes in from the line. *You* do it, Lucy. [*She slips out.*]

Lucy [*running back towards the back door, in an agonized voice*]. Mother, you've *got* to come. I *can't* do it! [*She returns towards the center of stage.*] I can't remember a thing we were going to say. [*Her voice rises to nervous heights.*] I can't remember even what we were going to ask them. [*She flies towards the back door, calling:*] Mother! [*A loud knock at the front door. She turns back, rolling up her apron nervously, stopping, as if she were ready to run away, looking around the room for help.* AUNT JANE *is listening at the telephone, her hand over the mouth-piece. Another impatient knock.* LUCY *goes shyly to the door, opens it a very little and stands there, hanging her head.*]

A Man's Voice from Outside. Is this the road to Manchester?

Lucy [*rebounding into naturalness, flings the door wide open, says eagerly:*] My! Yes, it is! Straight ahead for a mile and a half and then turn to your right. [*She looks out of the door as if at the car, smiles, waves her hand, shuts the door, and sinks into a chair.*] Well . . . ! [*The children come in around the screen and begin to play tag, racing around the stage.* AUNT JANE *hangs up the receiver, takes up her knitting.*]

Aunt Jane [loudly, above the children's voices]. They say Ed Wentworth has bought himself a new car, but I don't believe a word of it. The old one wa'n't more than five years old. *[The back door opens a crack.* SOPHIA *sticks her head in.]*

Lucy [calling cheerfully]. Is that you, Mother? Come right in. It was only somebody asking his way. [SOPHIA *comes in, looking shame-faced.* LUCY *asks ironically:]* Were your clothes dry?

Sophia [honestly, abasing herself]. No, child, you know as well as I do I didn't go out for my clothes. I just lost my head. It's the Perkins coming out in me. You know the Perkinses never were any hands to get on with strangers. *[With a long breath]* I'll just have to get my Searles blood going good. The Searleses are as bold as brass with anybody. *[A knock on the door. They jump from their chairs and stand still, staring at each other.]*

Lucy [in a loud whisper]. Get out your Searles blood! *[The children scurry behind the screen, and watch the proceedings through the crack.]*

Sophia [going to the door resolutely, opens it wide and says with an effort to be natural that makes her sound disagreeable]. Good afternoon. *[Man in plus fours enters, followed by wife and two children.]*

Man [matter-of-factly]. Can you take in four for over night? And what are your prices?

Sophia [in a learned-by-heart monotone]. A dollar a person for the beds. Thirty-five cents for a light breakfast. Fifty cents for a hundred per cent—I mean for a heartier breakfast. *[She speaks a little defiantly as if expecting them to protest. Dumb show from* LUCY *of admiration for her mother's courage.]*

Woman [suspiciously]. Do you give an extra cup of coffee with the thirty-five-cent breakfast?

Sophia [swallowing, looks at LUCY *who nods her head repeatedly].* Yes, yes, we do.

Man [walking around the room, looking things over, leans down to pass his fingers over chair, and then looks at them for dust]. Have you got a *clean* place to leave the car over night? That locks? And that I can have the key of?

Sophia. Well, we've left the lower part of the hay barn empty for cars. You can't lock it. But you won't need to. Nobody around here would take anything. And you can lock your car. [*She speaks firmly and looks hard at the man who retreats.*]

Woman [*suddenly, belligerently*]. Do you boil your drinking water?

Sophia [*very much astonished*]. What would we *boil* it for? [*After an instant's pause:*] No, we drink it raw.

Woman [*throwing up her hands*]. Oh, how unhygienic! [*To her husband in a loud aside:*] But I suppose off in the wilderness in this way we'll have to put up with utter ignorance of hygiene. [PHILLIP *behind the screen sticks out his tongue at her.*]

Aunt Jane [*hanging up the receiver and speaking loudly over her shoulder*]. Well, Joel and Emmeline say they're goin' to get married—and high time, too. [*Her loud voice makes the tourists start. They turn towards her.*]

Woman [*in a mincing voice*]. I *beg* your pardon! I didn't catch what you said.

Aunt Jane [*pushing her glasses up to look at her, and speaking cordially with a smile*]. Well, warmer for this time of year than I really like it. [*The tourists stare.*]

Sophia [*coming forward to explain*]. She's my husband's great-aunt. And she's stone deaf. Only she *can* hear over the telephone. You know some deaf persons can. It's such a comfort to her. She gets all the news that way. I don't know what she'd *do*, if 'twa'n't for the phone.

Woman [*full of horrified disapproval*]. Do you mean to say she *listens* to what other people say to each other? Why, I think that's terrible! It's against the law, too, I'm sure.

Sophia [*nettled, standing protectingly before* AUNT JANE]. Well, I don't know what kind of laws they have where you come from, but nobody in *our* town is going to grudge a poor old deaf woman the only satisfaction she has.

Man [*breaking in from behind*]. What kind of mattresses have you on the beds?

Sophia [*after a moment's astonished pause*]. Well, I don't know how to *tell* you very well. Why don't you come and look at them?

Woman [*nodding her head very hard*]. Yes, we *will*. And at the *sheets*, too. [*They go out, all together, the woman talking steadily, her voice continuing to come back long after they are off the stage.*] And I don't want skim milk with my berries in the morning—I want *cream*. And paper napkins are a thing I abominate! Are the window shades dark colored? I can't sleep mornings a minute after four o'clock unless the window shades are dark colored. I hope you haven't any crowing roosters around the place. [LUCY *is left in the room with* AUNT JANE. *The children now storm out from behind the screen and run to her.*]

Lucy [*indignantly*]. Of all the stuck-up people! If that's the kind of tourists we're going to have— [*A knock at the door. The children scurry to cover behind the screen.* LUCY *goes with some alarm to open the door. Enter two women tourists with four or five little children.*]

First Woman [*speaking in a strong Scotch accent, or with any other kind of odd mannerism*]. Have ye room for a party of five—and what do ye ask?

Lucy [*shyly, a little breathless, twisting the corner of her apron and looking down*]. Yes, we have room. A dollar a person for a bed. If you want breakfast, thirty-five cents for a light breakfast, and fifty cents for a heavy one.

First Woman. How much for a double bed?

Lucy [*looking surprised*]. Why, twice what it is for one person, I suppose. Two dollars. [*The two women walk past her to the center of the stage to discuss ways and means.* LUCY *goes back of screen. The telephone rings and* AUNT JANE *takes down receiver.*]

First Woman [*to the other*]. Sandy and James and Robbie can sleep three in a bed and she can't charge but two dollars because she's told us that. And we can say Elspeth and Nettie have stomach trouble and can't eat any breakfast, so three breakfasts will do for the five of us easy. One look at that girl would tell you she has no head for business. She'd never get up the nerve to object. [LUCY *reappears and the women turn back to her.*]

First Woman. Well, show us what you have. [*They all start towards the exit on left.*]

Second Woman [*with pity*]. You must find it *terribly* lonesome here winters, don't you, with everybody gone back to the city? [LUCY *looks volumes but says nothing. They go out. There is a moment's pause, during which* AUNT JANE *hangs up the receiver.*]

Aunt Jane [*loudly to empty stage*]. Mrs. Henning is a-selling strawberry preserves to city people and a-asking thirty cents a jar—a nawful price, I call it. [*She does not notice that there is no one to hear her news, and takes up her knitting contentedly. The first group of tourists return with* SOPHIA.]

Man. Well, all right, we'll stay—if you can *guarantee* there won't be any whip-poor-will yelling his head off all night, the way one did *last* year when we stopped at a farmhouse.

Phillip [*sticking his head around the screen*]. I'll get up and throw stones at it, mister, if it gets going. [*The tourists are startled and the man looks sternly at* PHILLIP *who hastily draws back behind the screen.* AUNT NANCY ANN *comes in through the back door and stands with the children listening behind the screen to what goes on. The second party of two women comes in with* LUCY.]

First Woman. All right, we'll stay. But the two little girls have summer complaint, so they won't need any breakfast but a glass of milk each. I presume you'd throw that in, wouldn't you, without extra charge? [*Facetiously*] There's always more milk on a farm than people know what to do with. You'd be *glad* to have a couple of glasses just taken off your hands, *I* know.

Second Party Woman [*without waiting for an answer they pounce on a whatnot (or table or chair) standing in the corner, crying out:*] "Oh, the *lovely* old antique!" [*The man and his wife turn to look. The wife rushes to the other side of the antique and seizes it, calling out:*] "Why, that's just like the one I saw in an antique shop in Lenox." [*As she wrestles with the other tourist for it, pulling it back and forward, she shouts to* LUCY:] "What do you want for it? What do you want for it?" [LUCY *looks bewildered at her mother. Her mother looks dumbly at the antique.*

The man tourist lights his cigar with elaborate indifference.]

Sophia [*hesitatingly, to the two panting women, each clutching one side of the antique*]. Well, I don't know rightly what *to* answer. That was bought so long ago—it's part of my grandmother's things. I don't believe there's anybody who'd remember what *was* paid for it. Would you think I asked too much if I said we'd want— [AUNT NANCY ANN *flings her sunbonnet off her head on the floor behind the screen and advances rapidly to the front, talking in her masterful, bossy, self-confident way and dominating everyone on the stage as usual.*]

Aunt Nancy Ann. Seeing that that's a genuwyne antique and a family relic, the price would be thirty dollars, not a penny less. One was sold up Granville way the other day to a Mrs. Sweeney from East Orange, New Jersey, and she paid thirty-five for hers and it had one less shelf in it, and big dents on the side where it had knocked against the door jamb when the family moved. You know what moving will do to furniture. [*The wife of the man tourist has been looking in her purse and as* AUNT NANCY ANN *pauses for breath, she quickly presses some bills into* SOPHIA'S *hand.*]

Woman. There, I'll take it. [*To the woman tourist, belligerently*] I've *paid* for it. [*To her husband, grimly*] We can tie it on the luggage-carrier behind the car. [SOPHIA *looks in silent astonishment at the money in her hand, showing it to* LUCY.]

Aunt Nancy Ann [*turning to the two women tourists, firmly*]. But you'll have to *pay* for those glasses of milk. Five cents apiece. You don't see taxicabs offering you free rides in the city. We country folks don't call it being *"near,"* when we ask a fair price for what has cost *us* a fair price in work and worry.

Aunt Jane [*in a loud voice as she hangs up the receiver*]. Well, what do you think? That red cow of Harmon Higgins is sick again.

CURTAIN

William Hazlett Upson (1891-   )

Botts Runs for His Life

Earthworm Tractor Company
Earthworm City, Illinois
Office of the President
Wednesday, January 10, 1951.

Mr. Alexander Botts
Sales Manager Earthworm Tractor Company
Waldorf Astoria Hotel
New York, N.Y.

Dear Botts: While you are traveling around calling on the trade I hope you will have time to contact one of our old customers, Mr. James Jorgensen, who is now engaged in a big logging project in the Green Mountains near Middlebury, Vermont. He has purchased a sawmill and lumber yard and is cleaning up several million feet of timber which blew down in a severe wind storm last November. He is using fifteen of our Earthworm tractors, and for the past month has been having continuous mechanical difficulties.

Several service mechanics, sent up last week by our Albany dealer, were unable to remedy the trouble. And Mr. Jorgensen became so enraged that he ordered them off the job and at the same time announced that he was going to transfer all his business to the newly reorganized Superba Tractor Company.

Following the departure of the service mechanics, one of our district representatives called on Mr. Jorgensen and attempted to smooth him down by pointing out that the Superba tractor is one of the worst-built machines in the field. Unfortunately, Mr. Jorgensen did not believe this fact. And, after a bitter argument, he ejected our representative bodily from his sawmill and threw him down an icy slope with such violence that he was painfully bruised and lacerated.

We have considered complaining to the police, and also filing a civil suit for damages. Since we do not like to take legal action against a customer, it occurs to me that you might be able to call on Mr. Jorgensen and work out some solution—provided you are not afraid to tackle such a violent customer.

> Most sincerely,
> Gilbert Henderson,
> President Earthworm
> Tractor Co.

> Waldorf Astoria Hotel
> New York, N.Y.
> Saturday evening,
> January 13, 1951.

Dear Henderson: You don't have to worry about my being afraid to tackle a violent customer like Mr. Jorgensen. I have already gone into action. Immediately after receiving your letter last night, I took the 10:30 P.M. train from Grand Central, and arrived early this morning right in the lion's den, so to speak, at Middlebury, Vermont. At once I began making inquiries. I learned that Mr. Jorgensen is regarded as a rough character, but completely honest and a good businessman. If I could approach him in exactly the right manner, I was sure that our meeting would mark the beginning of a truly beautiful friendship, and that I would have no trouble at all in convincing him of the folly of replacing his splendid Earthworms with any such mechanical atrocities as are perpetrated by the Superba Tractor Company.

To make the best possible first impression, I felt I should know something about Mr. Jorgensen's present mental attitude. I therefore decided to interview a man called Harold Quincy, who is a representative of the Superba company, and who, I was told, had been spending the last two days with Mr. Jorgensen. It was reported that Mr. Quincy was leaving on the 12:22 P.M. train for New York. As I was unable to contact him beforehand, I resolved to travel back to New York with him. I took a taxi to the railroad station, where the taxi driver pointed him out.

He was strutting up and down, swinging a brief case marked in big gold letters: "Harold Quincy. Superba Tractor Company." He wore a Tyrolean hat with a shaving-brush ornament, a checked overcoat and yellow gloves.

At once I sized him up as a typical low-grade salesman—smart aleck, conceited, and not too bright. He was, in short, just the opposite of the typical high-grade salesman—well bred, modest and intelligent—which is so well represented by myself. I knew this man would be as putty in my hands.

When the train pulled in I let him get on board first. He entered the smoking lounge. At the last moment I boarded the day coach, where I remained until the conductor had punched my ticket. Then I walked forward to the lounge, where I found my quarry. He had removed his overcoat and hat, revealing a rather loud suit and an even louder necktie. Timidly I sat down beside him.

"Do you mind if I sit here?" I asked in a mournful tone of voice.

"It's a free country," he said.

I pointed to his brief case. "Are you Mr. Harold Quincy?" I asked.

"That's right."

"And you're a tractor salesman?"

"You said it, big boy. I'm the best tractor salesman in the country."

This palpable falsehood—uttered, ironically enough, in the very presence of the man who really is the best tractor salesman in the country—gave me exactly the opening I needed. As long as Mr. Quincy was wandering so far from the truth, I felt that a few minor inaccuracies on my part would be entirely justified.

"My name is Ebenezer Boggs," I said.

"Pleased to meet you, Mr. Boggs," he said heartily.

"I'm a salesman, myself," I continued. "I've been up in Montreal, trying to sell candy bars for a firm in New York. But I didn't make a single sale. Maybe you could help me, Mr. Quincy, by telling me the secret of your success."

At this flattering approach, the man's chest swelled with pride. "Always glad to help a fellow salesman," he said. "What seems to be your main trouble?"

"I don't know," I said hopelessly. "I call on a candy-store proprietor. I give him what I think is a wonderful sales talk. But he always says he's perfectly satisfied with the candy bars he's already handling. So I never get anywhere. Maybe you could tell me what to do. There must be times when you have to sell one of your tractors to a man who is completely satisfied with some other kind."

Mr. Quincy smiled with smug satisfaction. "As a matter of fact," he said, "I am right now engaged in selling a whole fleet of Superba tractors to a man who has always used machines called Earthworms, and who, until I met him, was completely satisfied with them."

"It looks like a tough proposition," I said. "It would take a better sales talk than anything I ever heard."

"That's exactly the point, Mr. Boggs. You second-rate salesmen try to do everything with a sales talk. Me—I go beyond that. I am constructive. I manipulate the various factors in the situation so as to create an atmosphere that will be favorable to my plans."

"I don't understand," I said.

"Of course you don't. You're just a small-time operator. In this deal I started to tell you about, I found myself up against a stubborn old bird called Jorgensen. He runs a sawmill near Middlebury, Vermont. He had been using Earthworm machinery so long he wouldn't consider anything else. When I first met him, about a month ago, he was in such a rut, mentally, that he wouldn't let me even start a sales talk. I could see that I had no chance, at the time, to create in his mind a desire for Superba tractors. So I changed my tactics. I decided to make the old fool dissatisfied with his Earthworm tractors."

"Wouldn't that be pretty hard to do?"

"Not for a practical man like me. I stopped wasting my time on mere sales talks. I went out in the woods. I looked over his tractors. And especially I looked over his tractor operators."

"What was the idea of that?"

Here Mr. Quincy got very confidential. "In any tractor sale, Mr. Boggs, the important thing is not the tractor. It's the human element. If you want to be a successful salesman, always concentrate on the people—not on the product."

"Mr. Quincy," I said, "I think maybe you've got something there."

"Of course I have. And this basic principle has been of vital importance in the deal I am promoting in Middlebury. About noon of the second day I found a young man named Oswald who was highly dissatisfied with his job as a tractor operator. So right away I started working on him. I got him talking about himself."

"How did you do that?"

"Get him talking about himself? It's easy if you know how. All you got to do is flatter the guy, ask him just enough questions to draw him out, and then listen while he sounds off."

"I never thought of that," I said. "What did this man Oswald tell you?"

"It was the usual line of a typical sorehead. He said he was the finest mechanic in the state of Vermont. Old Jorgensen should have put him in charge of all the repair and maintenance work of all the tractors. He should have doubled his salary. But he didn't appreciate him. So I sympathized with the poor sap and led him on, and pretty soon he began telling me about his girl."

"This Oswald had a girl?"

"Yes. They wanted to get married. They had picked out a little dream of a house in Middlebury that was for sale for only fifteen thousand dollars. But, as long as he was being exploited by this old tightwad Jorgensen, he couldn't even scrape together enough money for a down payment. By this time the setup was so simple that even you, Mr. Boggs, could guess how I handled it."

"I wouldn't have the slightest idea," I said.

"Well," said Mr. Quincy, "I made this man Oswald a proposition. 'Oswald,' I said, 'you don't have to worry any more about what these boobs and nitwits think about you. I'm going to make you an offer. I am planning to open a Superba tractor dealership right here in Middlebury. I'll have a big service and repair shop. I'll need a first-class man in charge. So I'll give you the job, at $7500 a year. And, as an extra bonus, if you'll sign a five-year contract with me, I'll buy that $15,000 house and give it to you and your wife as a wedding present.' "

"That certainly was a generous offer," I said. "Pretty near sensational."

"That's what young Oswald thought," he said. "I could hardly keep him quiet long enough to explain the conditions."

"Oh," I said, "there was a catch to this offer?"

"Of course there was. I explained it to Oswald like this: 'Before I establish the dealership in Middlebury,' I said, 'I've got to make at least one big sale around here. The only big prospect is Jorgensen. I'm trying to get him to turn in his fifteen old Earthworms, and buy fifteen new Superbas. So far, he has refused to do this because he claims he's completely satisfied with the Earthworms. So, Oswald, you've got to make old Jim dissatisfied with his Earthworms.' "

"How could he do that?" I asked.

"As I explained it to Oswald, the answer is obvious. 'You are a regular employee around here,' I said. 'You have access to the fuel and the oil and the tools and supplies. You can go in and out of the repair shop and the equipment shed any time you want. Nobody spies on you. Nobody would object if you stuck around to work on your tractor after hours.' "

"Wait a minute," I said. "You weren't suggesting, were you, that you wanted this man to sort of sabotage those Earthworm tractors?"

"I wasn't suggesting anything, Mr. Boggs. All I did was set forth the facts. And I went on to explain that if the Earthworms accidentally started to have all kinds of mechanical breakdowns, it would be possible that old Jim might decide to switch to some other make of tractor. Does that sound logical to you?"

"It certainly does."

"It also sounded logical to Oswald. I had sized him up right. He has just enough low cunning so that he caught on to what I wanted. And he could figure out exactly how to do his dirty work so nobody would suspect anything."

"Just what did he do?"

"I don't know. And I don't want to know. All I care about is the way things are working out. It is now a month since I had that little talk with Oswald. And all through this month those Earthworm tractors have been breaking down and getting so little work done that Jorgensen is about frantic. I have been spending the past two days with him, and when I left, he asked me to bring up a Superba tractor. He said if I could prove in a competitive demonstration that my machine is better than the Earthworm he would trade me all his Earthworms for half what he paid for them and buy a whole fleet of Superbas."

"Say, that's wonderful," I said. "I suppose you're going to ship a tractor to Middlebury right away?"

"I have already ordered it. It should be there early next week. I will be busy with some important conferences in New York for several days, but I go back to Middlebury and put on a demonstration for Jorgensen next Friday. I can probably finish the demonstration in the morning. And in the afternoon the old boy will sign up to turn in his Earthworms and buy fifteen of my machines."

"If the Earthworms are in such bad shape," I said, "I shouldn't think you would want to take them in on trade."

"Don't worry about that. Young Oswald has pulled off nothing but minor breakdowns. Fundamentally they're as good as ever. As soon as I get hold of them they'll start running fine, and I can resell them at a handsome profit."

"And you're really going to give Oswald a house and a job?"

"Certainly not. Whatever gave you that idea?"

"That's what you told me you were going to do."

"Oh, no. That's not what I told you. That's just what I told Oswald. But you are forgetting that this man is a crook. If I gave him a house or paid him a big salary for what he did to those Earthworm tractors I would be rewarding a dishonest act. You wouldn't want me to do anything as immoral as that, would you?"

"No, I suppose not," I said. "But won't Oswald make a big row when he finds out you've let him down?"

"He can't prove anything against me, and the more he hollers the more he'll be telling everybody how crooked he is. Not only would he lose the job he's got but he'd have a tough time getting a job anywhere else. So there won't be any trouble from young Oswald. And I'll put the sale through like the high-powered sales-man that I am."

"Mr. Quincy," I said, "you don't know how educational your talk has been. I feel that it is going to help me a lot in my own business. I thank you."

"Mr. Boggs," he said, "it has been a pleasure." He reached into his brief case and handed me a lot of Superba advertising literature and a large lapel button labeled "Superba Tractors."

From here on, our talk drifted about through various subjects. Mr. Quincy explained to me exactly why business ethics are so much higher in America than in other parts of the world. I came back with a few of my best Swedish jokes. And when we finally parted at Grand Central Station I thanked him again. I then came to the hotel where I have been writing this report.

I have given you this very full account of my activities so that you may realize how well I am handling the problem you have assigned me. Even though I went all the way to Vermont and came back without seeing Mr. Jorgensen, I have accomplished far more than if I had barged in after the manner of our district repre-sentative and, like him, succeeded only in getting myself thrown out.

As things now stand, the difficult case of Mr. James Jorgensen is, for all practical purposes, in the bag. Such being the case, I will spend next Monday, Tuesday and Wednesday taking care of sev-eral urgent matters here in New York. I will return to Middlebury on the Wednesday night train—arriving on Thursday, one day ahead of Mr. Harold Quincy. I will then prove to Mr. Jorgensen that Quincy and Oswald have been playing him for a sucker. As soon as he understands what has been going on, he will throw Mr. Quincy out on his ear, and fire young Oswald. From then on, his

Earthworms will run perfectly. And harmony and justice will prevail.

Yours, with keen satisfaction for a job well done,
                              Alexander Botts,
                              Sales Manager
                              Earthworm Tractor Co.

                              Earthworm Tractor Company
                              Earthworm City, Illinois
                              Office of the President
                              Monday, January 15, 1951.

Mr. Alexander Botts
Waldorf Astoria Hotel
New York, N.Y.

Dear Botts: Your letter is here. I am very much disturbed over your plans. In your final paragraph you say that on Thursday you will arrive in Middlebury and "prove to Mr. Jorgensen that Quincy and Oswald have been playing him for a sucker." At first sight this may seem like a plausible method of approach. Unfortunately, however, you have nowhere in your letter given the slightest indication that you are in a position to prove anything to Mr. Jorgensen. Please remember that Jorgensen has been having trouble with the Earthworm company. From the very moment you meet him, he will be violently prejudiced against you. On the other hand, his relations with the Superba company have, as far as we know, been completely friendly. Jorgensen will therefore be definitely prejudiced in favor of Mr. Quincy.

To deal with this adverse situation, I fail to see that you can present anything in the way of facts or figures or concrete evidence. All you have is an incredibly fantastic story involving the most serious accusations against a trusted employee and against a rival tractor salesman. These accusations will undoubtedly be denied by Mr. Harold Quincy and this man Oswald. As you have nothing to offer in rebuttal except your own unsupported word, you cannot hope to get anywhere. If you approach Mr. Jorgensen in the manner indicated you will succeed only in getting yourself thrown out in exactly the same way as our district representative was thrown out.

I would suggest, therefore, that you refrain from accusations which you cannot back up. And when you meet Mr. Jorgensen, I feel that you should:

1. Keep the conversation on a high plane.

2. Prove to him the superiority of Earthworm tractors by giving him a straightforward, scientific discussion of the obviously superior qualities found in our product.

Most sincerely,
Gilbert Henderson.

Porter Hospital
Middlebury, Vermont
Friday, January 19, 1951.

Dear Henderson: Your letter arrived before I left New York. And I regret to inform you that it has been impossible for me to follow your advice. How could I keep the conversation on a high plane with all the low and slimy skulduggery that has been going on? And how could I convince Mr. Jorgensen of the superiority of Earthworm tractors by a mere scientific discussion, when Mr. Jorgensen's Earthworm tractors were breaking down all over the landscape? Merely to ask these questions is to answer them; your suggestions were absolutely and obviously impractical.

However, you may perhaps derive a little wry satisfaction in learning that at least one of your predictions has come true. Owing to a slight miscarriage in my plans, Mr. Jorgensen became violently enraged under circumstances which caused him to throw me out even more violently than he threw out our district representative, and to send me skidding down the same icy slope with such force that I have been in the hospital ever since.

Fortunately, it is a good hospital. My injuries are not critical. I expect to be out tomorrow. And I am pleased to report that I am not in any way discouraged. To the end that you may understand how much better I have handled this situation than would have been the case if I had followed your advice, and in order that you may realize how I would have achieved a complete success unmarred by any hospital interlude if it had not been for the unforeseen presence of a fire escape outside the window. I will now give you a full account of my activities since I arrived in Middlebury yesterday morning.

After a good breakfast at the Middlebury Inn, I hired a taxi and drove to Mr. Jorgensen's sawmill at the foot of the mountain. I did not, however, introduce myself as a representative of the Earthworm company. The plan which I had evolved was much more subtle. I had decided that I would pretend I represented the Superba Tractor Company. I would persuade Oswald the mechanic to tell me all about his sabotage operations. He would suppose the conversation was confidential. But all the time Mr. Jorgensen would be listening around the corner of a building or from some other vantage point. Thus Oswald would be convicted out of his own mouth, the fat would be in the fire, the Superba company would be in the doghouse, and the Earthworm would be on top of the heap.

This plan, of course, was not complete. I had not yet worked out any technique for enticing Mr. Jorgensen into a concealed position and keeping him quiet while I attempted to trick young Oswald into giving himself away. These questions, however, were unimportant. I had created a grand master plan. And I could follow my usual custom of leaving the minor details completely fluid so they could be altered according to changing conditions.

Upon arriving at the sawmill I told the taxi driver to wait. I put on the "Superba Tractor" button Mr. Quincy had given me. I picked up my brief case in which I had a lot of the Superba advertising folders, and I accosted a couple of men who were piling boards. I asked them where I could find Mr. Jorgensen. They said he was in his office on the second floor of a long wooden storage building beside the mill. I entered the building. I tiptoed up a flight of stairs, along a hallway, and around a corner to an open door. I peered into the room beyond. Mr. Jorgensen, a man of powerful build, was seated with his back to me. He was working with some papers at his desk. The setup seemed favorable. So I quietly withdrew.

I returned to the men who were piling boards. I asked them where I could find a mechanic named Oswald. They said he was behind the sawmill, moving some logs with his tractor. I went around and found him. I told him he was to report to Mr. Jorgensen's office. He said he would be there in five minutes. I went back, climbed the stairs and waited in an upper hall around the corner from the door of Mr. Jorgensen's office. Here, according to my plan, I would intercept the treacherous mechanic and trick him into a discussion which would reveal all of his nefarious activities to Mr. Jorgensen—provided, of course, that Mr. Jorgensen remained quietly in his office, listening to what went on.

Unfortunately, however, Mr. Jorgensen turned out to be the kind of man who likes to spring to action at the slightest excuse. I had hardly taken my position when I inadvertently shifted my weight onto a loose floor board. The board squeaked.

There was a yawp from the office. "Who's that out there?"

I decided I had better try to smooth down the old guy. I walked around the corner and into the office. "Are you Mr. Jorgensen?" I asked.

"I am."

"I represent the Superba Tractor Company," I said glibly. "Mr. Harold Quincy sent me up to make a thorough study of your job here so that we can give you the best possible demonstration when our tractor arrives. It has been nice meeting you. And now, if you will excuse me, I will be on my way." I started out.

"Wait a minute," said Mr. Jorgensen. "Mr. Quincy gave me a Superba catalogue, and there's something about the drawing of the power take-off that I don't quite understand. I want you to explain it to me."

"I will do my best," I said modestly.

Mr. Jorgensen continued: "My bookkeeper has the catalogue in his office at the other end of the building. I'll call him and ask him to bring it over."

He flipped a switch on a metal box on his desk. The box bore a name plate: "Signal Corps—U. S. Army—Interphone Amplifier BC-605-D."

"This," he explained, "is surplus Army equipment that I picked up a while back. It's a great convenience—even though you have to wait for the tubes to warm up."

"Very interesting," I said. "How does it work?"

"There's a mike and a speaker in a little box over in the book-keeper's office," he said. "It's connected to this thing here by a pair of wires. When I want to call the bookkeeper I throw this other little switch to the position labeled 'Talk.' When I want to hear what he has to say, I change it to the position labeled 'Listen.' Do you hear that faint humming?"

"Yes."

"That means the tubes are warmed up." He moved the switch to "Talk" and began yelling, "Hey, there, George! Are you there, George?" Then he flipped the switch to "Listen," and waited. Nothing happened. "I guess George is out somewhere," he said. "I'll have to go and get that catalogue myself." He rose and started down the hall.

The situation was getting out of hand. Oswald, the mechanic, was due to arrive at any moment. I began to think fast. How could I keep this energetic Mr. Jorgensen quiet and in one place long enough so he could hear the conversation I was hoping to stage with Oswald? I kept on thinking—faster and faster. And gradually, in the back of my mind, I began to get a sort of vague hunch. Possibly that Army interphone contraption might fit into my plans.

I followed Mr. Jorgensen down the hall for several hundred feet to the far end of the building. He opened a door marked "Bookkeeper," walked into the room, and started pawing through a pile of pamphlets and catalogues on a desk.

I stood in the hall outside and sized up the situation. On the desk was a metal box—obviously the other end of the interphone system. The room had one window. As we were on the second floor, I did not think this window would provide a practical means of exit. There was one door. I examined it closely. I saw that it was of stout construction. And then I noticed something that caused all my half-formed ideas and hunches to crystalize suddenly into a complete and beautiful plan of action. The door was equipped with a heavy hasp. On the jamb there was a heavy staple. And hanging on the staple was a heavy open padlock. "Eureka!" I said. "This is it!"

"What's that?" asked Mr. Jorgensen.

By way of reply I slammed the door, removed the padlock, shoved the hasp over the staple and replaced the padlock.

The old boy was safely locked in. I was safely outside. I raced back to Mr. Jorgensen's office. Oswald had not yet arrived. I made a quick test. With the little toggle switch pushed up to the position "Listen," I could hear everything that went on in the bookkeeper's office. There was a great pounding, and the sound of Mr. Jorgensen's voice yelling, "Open this door, you fool!"

I threw the switch to the position marked "Talk." I could no longer hear anything from the bookkeeper's office. But Mr. Jorgensen could hear everything that went on at my end of the line. Or, at least, that is what I hoped.

I settled myself quietly in the chair behind the desk. A moment later Oswald, the mechanic, came in.

"Oswald," I said, "Mr. Jorgensen has stepped out for a few minutes, so this is a good chance for us to have a serious confidential talk. I represent the Superba Tractor Company. Mr. Harold Quincy sent me here to find out why you are falling down so badly on the job which you agreed to handle for him."

Oswald looked startled. Then he asked suspiciously, "What job?"

"You can speak frankly," I said. "I know the whole story. Mr. Quincy says he hired you to sabotage Mr. Jorgensen's Earthworm tractors so thoroughly that the old guy will become completely disgusted with them and will buy a fleet of Superba tractors. Mr. Quincy says you promised to do this. But so far, he says you have accomplished practically nothing. What's the matter with you?"

Young Oswald looked uncomfortable. He went to the door and

glanced up and down the hall. "I was afraid somebody might be listening," he said.

"You can see we are alone," I said. "Come on—speak up."

"I don't like to discuss this thing with strangers," he said.

"But I'm not a stranger. I'm Mr. Quincy's confidential adviser. Unless you can give me some reasonable assurance that you will go through with this thing, the deal is off. You won't get the $15,000 house, and you won't get the $7500 job."

"But I'm doing the best I can," Oswald whined. "I got to go slow and cover my tracks, or I would spoil the whole thing."

"Have you done anything so far?"

"Sure I have."

"It can't be much. I notice your own tractor seems to be running all right."

"Of course it is. If I louse up my own machine I would get fired. And that would spoil everything."

"Have you wrecked any of the other machines?"

"I'm not supposed to wreck them. Mr. Quincy plans to take them in on trade, so he doesn't want any serious damage. He just wants a lot of minor breakdowns."

"And you claim you've actually accomplished something along that line?"

"Sure I have."

"What, for instance?"

"Well, for one thing, I've been working on the radiators. I sneak around at night. I drive a nail into the radiator core and plug the hole with chewing gum. The next day, when the tractor is way off in the woods, the chewing gum works loose and all the water runs out. They lose a lot of time bringing in the machine or sending a man out to solder it. And they always think, just because they first noticed it in the woods, that the damage must have been done out there. So they never suspect me. They figure the hole must have been punched by a branch of a tree or something, and they decide the Earthworm radiators must be poor quality. And that's not all."

"You have other tricks?"

"I'll say. I stole all the solder out of the repair shop and replaced it with some trick solder out of a toy chemistry set that a friend of mine bought for me down in New York. This trick solder melts in boiling water. When they use it to repair a leaky radiator, it lasts only till the engine gets well heated up. And the mechanics around here are so dumb they never notice the difference. They have nothing but trouble and more trouble. But one of my best ideas is putting potatoes in the cooling system."

"Potatoes in the cooling system?"

"Sure. I've fixed up ten or twelve Earthworms that way. I do it at night when nobody is around. I take off the water manifold and I wedge several raw potatoes into the manifold or into the water jacket around the cylinders."

"What's that for?"

"The potatoes cut off part of the circulation in the cooling system. The engine heats up. The radiator starts to boil. So the operator shuts down. He looks in the radiator. He takes off the radiator cap. He looks inside. There is plenty of water. So he checks the fan. He checks the water pump. He checks everything. He calls the chief mechanic. And by that time the potatoes have all boiled away, and the cooling system is full of a kind of potato soup that is so thin that it looks practically the same as water. So they finally get the machine running again. But a lot of time has been wasted. And they never find out what was the matter."

"Oswald," I said, "permit me to congratulate you. You have given a very convincing account of your activities. I am sure you will be suitably rewarded. And now I think you had better be getting back to your tractor before Mr. Jorgensen arrives. Good-by."

Oswald departed. As soon as he was out of earshot, I flipped the switch on the interphone amplifier and listened intently for any audible reaction that might come from Mr. Jorgensen over in the bookkeeper's office. There was none. The silence was complete.

This was disturbing. If the violent-tempered Mr. Jorgensen

were still trapped in the bookkeeper's office, he most certainly would be yelling his head off. The ominous silence indicated that he must have escaped. If he had escaped before he had a chance to hear my conversation with Oswald, he would undoubtedly want to beat me up for having locked the door on him. On the other hand, if he had escaped after hearing the conversation, he would probably want to beat me up for conspiring against him. In any case, he would be after me—and with blood in his eye.

I decided I had better get out of there before he caught me. I ran down the stairs and out the door. But I was a little late. Just as I emerged into the open air, Mr. Jorgensen came charging around the corner of the building with all the fury of an enraged rhinoceros. I ran in the opposite direction. I circled around the building.

At the far end I caught a brief glimpse of a fire escape with an open window at the top. Then I knew how Mr. Jorgensen had escaped so easily from the second-floor room.

I kept on running. Three times I circled that building—with Mr. Jorgensen in hot pursuit. At the beginning of the fourth lap he caught up to me and gave me a shove which sent me down what must have been the same icy slope which had been previously traveled by our unfortunate district representative. Mr. Jorgensen did not continue the pursuit.

I was eventually rescued by the taxi driver and brought here to the hospital, where I have been treated for a sprained ankle, a sprained wrist, and various cuts, bruises and contusions.

That was yesterday. This morning Mr. Jorgensen arrived at the hospital. He had learned my true identity from various papers in the brief case I had accidentally left behind when I departed so hurriedly from his office. He had learned of my plans and of the duplicity of Mr. Quincy from a carbon copy of the letter I sent you last week, Henderson. Any lingering doubts were removed by the conversation between Oswald and me. He had heard the whole thing. And he told me somewhat regretfully that Oswald had taken alarm and disappeared before he had a chance to fire him in his usual forcible manner. He stated further that he was through forever with the Superba Tractor Company, and he said he would stick with Earthworm the rest of his life.

"Has Mr. Quincy shown up yet?" I asked.

"Yes, indeed," he said pleasantly. "Mr. Quincy arrived this morning and promptly departed down that same icy slope." He glanced out the window and continued, "Just as I expected. The ambulance has arrived and they're bringing him in now. So the only thing that worries me is the unnecessarily rough treatment I handed out to you, Mr. Botts, before I realized that you were helping me so much. Can you ever forgive me?"

"Not only do I forgive you, Mr. Jorgensen," I said, "but I have a feeling that this is the beginning of a beautiful friendship."

Most sincerely,
Alexander Botts.

Murray Hoyt (1904-   )

Trout Fishing in Vermont

Trout season and the Hoyts arrived back in Vermont in pretty near a dead heat.

Why trout fishing gets such a death grip on fishermen I've never been able to figure out, but it does. It doesn't make too much sense that a fisherman will take more pleasure from a twelve-inch brook trout on a fly rod than he will from a seventy-five-pound tarpon on a star drag reel. He'll go from catching huge fish that it takes a winch to lift over the side of the boat, to catching eight-inch brook trout in a tiny stream high in the Green Mountains. And he'll appear to be getting more kick out of the brook trout. This is crazy on the face of it; nobody in his right mind could feel this way.

Well, there are a lot of fishermen who aren't in their right minds. And, like Abou Ben Adam, Abou Ben Hoyt's name led all the rest.

In order to get trout fishing from our cottage on Lake Champlain you either had to paddle across the lake to Mullen Brook on the New York side of the lake, or you had to drive at least eighteen miles over to the brooks and rivers of the Green Mountains.

Back in the days when I'd had a New York state license because I was coaching in Waterville, I'd paddled over and fished Mullen Brook a lot. Once I paddled the three-and-a-half miles across the lake, reached into the canoe to take out and set up my rod, and found that both rod and reel were still reposing on the Vermont shore.

Well, I had no intention of paddling across and back again, seven weary miles, so I found a wadded-up mass of old line right where I'd noticed it caught on a fence the last time I'd been over there, and I managed to untangle about eight feet of it. I cut an alder pole and attached the line to it. My hook case, creel, worms, landing net, I had.

I caught a number of nice brookies in the course of the day, but what I remember best was the double-take of the fishermen I met. You can understand their feelings. Here was a sportsman pretty nattily got-out with fishing jacket, fishing boots, fisherman's vest, creel, and landing net hanging from the shoulder. And he was fishing with an old alder pole with the knots showing where the branches had been hastily cut off. There were a number of kinks in the thing, because perfectly straight alders seemed hard to come by. And at the end of this monstrosity had been tied a frayed piece of line with one knot in it where two smaller pieces had been made into one. The line was just wound around a couple of times and tied, that was all. There was no reel, no extra line.

When we'd meet I'd ask them blandly what they'd caught, show them the brookies in my creel, say nothing about the pole on which I was leaning and on which their bugged-out eyes were riveted. I'd say good-bye and pass along. I'd look back out of the corner of my eye at the next pool, and they'd still be standing there, their mouths dangling slightly. The situation would, I've thought lately, be a natural for *Candid Camera.* Anyhow, I had a fine day. And when I was through I stashed the outfit where I could find it if I ever did a stupid thing like that again. It's an example of what I was saying earlier about extenuating circumstances.

But when we got back from Florida that first year of our married life, I had no New York license. I chose to go over to the East Middlebury River, at the foot of the Green Mountains, for the May First opening of the season.

The only drawback was that Marg had a meeting in Addison, Vermont, that day and needed the car. However, a good resourceful trout fisherman who has made up his mind to go fishing is seldom stymied by so trivial a matter as this. We decided that Marg would drive me over to the stream, dump me off, and then go about her business. Late in the day, after her meeting, she would return to the stream and pick me up.

We rose while it was still dark and unbelievably cold. We ate breakfast, made me a couple of sandwiches, and started out. I wanted to be on the stream with the first streaks of dawn.

I fished for a while and got nothing. It was way too cold for trout fishing (or anything else), but Opening Day is a ritual, and neither snow nor sleet nor dark of night will stay the trout fisherman from paying homage on this occasion.

It was so cold that there was a skimming of ice on the stagnant water at the bottom of the big pools. It was so cold that ice built up on the line, and inside the guides of the rod. You couldn't fish decently with gloves on, and your fingers got numb if you fished without gloves. You got to shaking because you needed at least two more sweaters than you already had on.

But I had the day to spend, and it was Opening Day, and I tried. I knocked the ice off the guides, and stripped it off the line. A couple of times I had to hold the line in my hand to melt the ice enough so I could strip it off and get rid of it. And greater dedication hath no man than that. I fished grimly.

I came to a deep pool where I had always had good luck. It eddied against a sloping rock. I dropped the worm into the eddy— I was using worms since no fly in his right mind would hatch out under such conditions, and no fish in his right mind would venture up after him if he did—and steered it through the eddy carefully.

I reached out to bring it around just right, and suddenly I felt my feet going out from under me. The moss and the rock had been wet, and the wet had frozen into some of the slipperiest ice it has ever been my bad fortune to encounter.

I sat down hastily and grabbed at everything in the neighborhood. Nothing I could get my hands on had any permanency. I began to slide, slowly at first, the way a giant tree starts its fall under the woodman's ax. Then faster and faster.

Clawing and breaking fingernails on everything near me, I slid majestically down and into the pool.

I have heard it said that under these conditions your boots, full of water, will weight you down and pull you under and drown you. Maybe this is what happens to the Simon-pure Sportsman. I guess I'll never be able to do things right. That drowning bit didn't appeal to me at all. I set myself for the shock of going under and to the bottom. I prepared myself to walk on the bottom if it was necessary, until I could get the short distance to where my head would poke out.

The shock never came. I never got really under. The straps on my boots were pulled tight around my legs, and a lot of air was trapped inside my heavy pants and my jacket and all the clothes I had on.

I went under only about halfway between my waist and my armpits. For one split second I didn't even feel the water until it got through all that clothing. When it did, *that* was a shock, believe me.

I was buoyed up there by all that air like a fat old lady with an innertube around her. I couldn't even start swimming the way you normally would. I had to reach down to paddle. As more and more water got inside and dispelled the air, I sank lower and lower. But the shore was only a few yards distant. Majestically, sticking up there like a cork, I floated myself over to it and waded out.

Obviously this was a sticky situation. I had no car, it was miles to a telephone. Besides, I wanted to fish.

I repaired to the most sheltered place I could find. I took off my boots first and that wasn't easy. Did you ever try to take off a pair of boots half-full of water? The water forms some sort of vacuum and the resulting suction makes the task fit right along with getting your leg out of a quicksand or walking across a barnyard in a rainstorm.

I then took off the socks, the jackets, the sweaters, and the long-handled underwear. After that I stood there in that icy morning air, just as I had been when the doctor held me upside down and slapped my bottom, only larger and right side up.

I emptied out the boots. Then I started wringing everything else out. I wrung every last drop out that I could, for two reasons; I wanted it out of there, and wringing it hard kept my blood circulating.

Years later this happened to a friend of mine on a warm pleasant Opening Day when we'd both arrived on the stream in my car. He made me drive him all the way home.

In this case there was nobody to drive me home, even if I'd wanted to go, which I didn't. I got myself as dry as I could, and I put everything back on. It was unbelievably cold and clammy at first, but your body warmed things up shortly. And at least the clothes acted as wet insulation.

I went back to fishing, testing all rocks for ice before I trusted myself to them. I still had miserable luck. I might very well be catching cold, but it was a cinch I wasn't catching anything else.

Then I met a friend of mine named Ed. He had had the same luck I had had, but he was dry.

"What we need to do is fish a lake," he told me. "In a lake the water temperature wouldn't have dropped as low with this sudden freeze, after the good weather we've been having. What do you say we try Lake Pleiad?"

I didn't mention that I felt I was an authority on the water temperature of that particular brook. I said, "I got no car."

"Come with me."

Lake Pleiad is a gem of a little lake, set high in the ring of Green Mountain peaks, at the very top of the ridge. It is stocked heavily, and the Long Trail, part of the Appalachian Trail System, passes beside it.

We drove up the mountain on Route 125. As we neared the top there began to be snow beside the road. Right below Lake Pleiad is the Middlebury Snow Bowl ski area, and it will have maybe fifty inches of snow up there when there won't be any down in Middlebury.

We had taken for granted that with the warm spring we'd had, all snow up there would be gone. We'd been pretty naïve.

"Anyhow, we can hike through the snow for half a mile; that's the distance in there. It will be worth the hike to get some fish."

We found that the cold of the night before had made a crust

atop some four feet of snow on the Trail. We started along the Trail toward Lake Pleiad.

You'd take three steps on the crust, and when you took the fourth step your leg would go through and drop practically the length of it. If you weren't on the alert, this would snap your head forward like the knot on the end of a whip.

You'd retrieve your leg, go a couple more steps. And just when you were lulled into a false sense of security, the other leg would drop in and your head would snap again, jarring your teeth and maybe making you bite your tongue.

We traveled a long, long half-mile in this manner, buoyed up only by the thought of the fine fishing that awaited us. There were no recent tracks, so we knew we would be the first ones to fish the lake.

As we traveled we developed a cunning in that matter of neck-snapping. If you held your neck constantly rigid enough, it lessened the snap. But it gave you a headache right then. And we later found that it made your neck sore for about four days afterward.

There was, too, one other little matter I had to contend with but that Ed didn't. When you have wrung out your clothing and put it back on, you can never get all the water out. It's impossible. So a drop here and a drop there, from your socks, your pants, your shirts and sweaters, and that heavy underwear, finds it way down into the bottom of your boots by force of gravity.

Ordinarily this isn't bad. Your body heat warms it up, and it isn't too uncomfortable. But when, every few steps you take, your boot goes into snow all over, snow packs around it, immediately the water inside starts to cool down like champagne in an ice bucket. When your legs aren't deep in snow, snow is clinging to the outside of your boot, and the sole of the boot is on crust.

By the time we were halfway in there, I was walking in a quart or more of ice water. To a person reading in a nice warm room with his feet dry, this may not seem like much of a disaster. Let me assure you there is nothing quite like it in the world for exquisite torture. The Inquisition would most certainly have used it if they'd thought of it or if they'd been able to pick up a pair of hip boots and four feet of snow.

But I buoyed myself, as I say, with anticipation.

And then we made the last turn in the trail, and Lake Pleiad lay there before us—a solid sheet of ice. Not just anchor ice. This was the winter's solid stuff. It never had melted up high that way, as we had assumed it had; the way all the lakes down in the valley had melted long since.

We never wet a line. You couldn't have, short of owning an ice chisel. And then there was the trek out with the boot water getting nearer and nearer thirty-two degrees. I felt like yelling out loud from the extreme torture of the last hundred yards.

I sat on the car seat with my legs stuck out while Ed worried my boots off for me. I wrung out the socks again and the bottoms of my trousers, and put everything back. I felt better after that. We drove back down into the valley.

It was still only about nine-thirty in spite of all that had happened. We began to fish the huge pool at Big Bend. No luck.

The long rock at the head of the pool was comfortable though, and we were loath to leave the place. Our stomachs had for some time back been assuring us with more and more authority that our watches were wrong and that noon had come, so we broke out a sandwich apiece. While I was wringing some of the water out of my sandwiches and the rest of my lunch, Ed let the current carry his worm deep into the pool. And when it stopped and would go no further, he laid the rod down beside him on the rock and we attacked the sandwiches. Ed ate his and I drank mine.

When we were ready to start on, Ed began to reel in. There was a pleasant tugging at the end of his line, and he landed an eleven-inch brookie.

He threw back, and I threw in my line. This time we tightened up on the line when the bait stopped. Nothing happened. We just sat there. After a long time I felt a tug, and I landed a nice brookie. Ed landed one shortly thereafter.

So we settled ourselves on the rock and just allowed our baits to lie on the bottom where the current deposited them. They'd stay there quite a few minutes, then there'd be a bite.

Ed said, "Looks like all the fish in this pool are in one bunch, and we're letting our bait lie there among 'em until looking at it makes even a half-frozen trout hungry."

I'd never fished brookies that way before. But we hadn't found any fish biting anywhere else, so we just sat there. And the fish kept on coming in—not fast, but steadily.

A couple of times other fishermen came up or down the stream. And when they did, Ed and I just reeled in before they got there and sat on the rock, not fishing. They'd ask if they could fish the pool, we'd tell them to go ahead. They'd fish it the orthodox way, get nothing, and pass on. When they were out of sight we'd go back to fishing it our way. The black clouds in the sky increased, but we fished on.

You'd be surprised how rapidly fish mount in your creel under such circumstances. The limit at that time was twenty. We passed ten each and it began to snow. Still we sat there.

When we reached twenty apiece it was snowing hard.

I now had my limit, and it was still morning. Marg wasn't due till after five o'clock that afternoon. Somehow I couldn't cozy up to the idea of sitting around there nearly six hours in a blinding snowstorm, my clothes wet below the armpits, doing nothing.

So I cadged a ride into Middlebury with Ed. And from Middlebury I started to walk toward Addison, where the car would be. It's nine miles from Middlebury to Addison.

I walked. I walked and walked. The boots, and some more seeped-down water in them, got heavier and heavier. Both heels began to chafe in the wet socks and the spots got to feeling as if somebody were holding a match against them. When you're walking a brook to fish, you don't even think about it. When you're walking just to get somewhere, you think about nothing else.

The twenty brook trout in the creel, which had seemed only pleasantly heavy when I first picked them up back at the brook, more and more began to take on the weight of a dip net full of mullet as I walked with them. From approximately the weight of twenty small fish, they went rapidly through various stages until I'd have sworn each fish was eight times its size and made of lead, and that my shoulder under them was listing forty-five degrees on that side.

I walked six miserable miles, and only the first one held itself down to a mere 5,280 feet. As for the rest of them, somebody began to play jokes on me and stretched them out to double and triple that footage. I got a ride the last three miles, and only the fact that the driver who stopped and picked me up was sitting in his car kept me from dropping to my knees and kissing his feet.

But the strange part is that after I got dry, and the blisters healed, I found that I'd had a wonderful time. I wouldn't have missed it for the world. In the years to come it took its place as one of the nicest days I ever spent. This doesn't seem either reasonable or sensible. But that's how it is.

Ralph Nading Hill (1917-   )

Steamboating to New York with Brian Seaworthy

The Voyages of Brian Seaworthy, *a freshwater saga of the 1870's,
tells of the struggles of the teen-aged Brian Seaworthy aboard
the* Republic *and the* Bennington. *After his father is killed in a
boiler-room explosion, Brian comes of age in a series of dramatic
episodes which exhibit the glamor, excitement, and danger of
steamboating on Lake Champlain. In the following episode Brian
and his friend Barney Barnaby find adventure as they travel to
New York City via the canal and the Hudson River.*

The Chief was wrong in his prediction of fair weather. As we entered the first lock early the next morning, water was pouring in
as relentlessly from above as below. To rise twelve feet in such a
deluge seemed like magic. One cannot appreciate a lock's mecha-
nism until the gates close behind him and those in front presently
open as he floats into a higher world.

The Chief asked if we knew we'd lost elevation and gained it
at the same time. There was a catch in this, as in much else he
said. To pass under the canal's low bridges, sailboats had to step
their masts, as did small steam vessels their funnels. The *Gloria's*
had been designed with hinges that permitted us to lower it with
block and tackle. In doing so we had obviously decreased her
elevation!

The roar of water from the canal tumbling into the rocky basin
soon faded away and we found ourselves on a peaceful creek
aimlessly wandering among steep ledges and verdant hills. The
cows in their misty pastures, the rows of cornstalks in the fields,
and the dripping woods cast a spell. We were not accustomed to
willows brushing the pilot house, leaves fluttering to the deck, or
pigs and geese so close we could touch them with our pike poles.

Every so often mules appeared along the bank with their pre-posterous burdens in tow. When two of these passed abreast it was often possible to cross the canal by jumping from one to the other. The bargemen's families lived in odd-shaped cabins open-ing on to awning-covered back porches where laundry flapped over the stern. Though the cargo was their children's only playground, I thought them fortunate indeed to have seen more of the world from their moving front yards than had Barney and I—the world of the canal and the Hudson from Troy to the sea.

So that the wash from our propeller would not erode the banks, our speed between the locks was limited to five knots. No tug without a special permit could navigate the canal, nor any barge drawing more than four and a half feet, since the depth of the water scarcely exceeded that. Though sailing vessels might raise their masts after passing under the bridges, they were still at the mercy of the wrong wind, or none at all. Thus mules prevailed on the hard-trodden towpaths. Near the bank we saw a competitor of the days before the railroad: the hulk of an old passenger barge that still revealed the cabins where travelers slept while teams of horses in relays hauled them the sixty-six miles from Troy to Whitehall.

The shape of this country was as different as its traditions, and we had almost passed Fort Edward before I thought of Jane McCrea, whom Parson Bugbee never mentioned in his lectures because she lived south of the lake, but whose fate Mr. Lampwood had discussed with us in school the previous winter. She was en-gaged to a young British officer with General Burgoyne's army that sailed from Canada in 1777 and disembarked at Skenesboro, as Whitehall was then called. But the reunion near Fort Edward where Jane awaited her lover never took place. She was taken captive by the Iroquois who killed her in an argument among themselves. Later they appeared at headquarters with her blond scalp. General Burgoyne would have executed the murderer, one of his own troops, had the Iroquois not warned him that if he did so they would all desert his army. The guilty Indian was par-doned instead and the name of Jane McCrea echoing through the

woodlands spelled the defeat of ten thousand Redcoats. A tangle
of trees felled by local axemen and swarms of giant mosquitoes
in the swamp now traversed by the canal delayed them nearly a
month. Shortly thereafter, outside the town for which the *Bennington* was named, a detachment of this ponderous cavalcade
fell victim to the White and Green Mountain militia, foreshadow-
ing the later eclipse of Burgoyne's whole army at Saratoga.

The motley crews and cargoes fascinated us as they lined up at
the twenty locks, all opened and closed by hand. The bridges, too,
claimed special attention, for we had to lower the funnel for
nearly every one. We failed to count them but there must have
been nearly a hundred and fifty, some of iron, some of iron and
wood, and some entirely of wood roofed over. Most, however,
were humble open ramps with tranquil processions of cows crossing from pasture to pasture each morning and evening.

We spent two days on the northern canal. On the third, early
in the morning near Waterford, we met puffing tugs and deep-
laden barges just off the Erie Canal from Syracuse, Rome, Utica,
Herkimer, Little Falls, Amsterdam, and other fabled places toward the Great Lakes. Barney thought we ought to forget the
Bennington, the *Republic,* and Cap'n Bullard and follow this
silver ribbon westward into another life; but the Chief said a
Yankee could no more swap Champlain for Erie water than a
catfish could shed its whiskers.

Our excitement quickened as we descended the deepening Hudson. Three cups apiece of the *Gloria*'s blackest coffee and the
swells of a line steamer half again as long as the *Republic* opened
our eyes so wide the Chief was worried they'd leave their sockets
by the time we got to New York. Ruffled by a faint breeze from
the south, the grey river turned blue and the rain-washed shores
glistened in the sunrise.

Our stop for coal among all the ships and boats at the great
smoking port of Albany was brief because the Chief was anxious
to keep going; the sooner we got to Hoboken, the sooner they
could measure the old filler piece against the new one being cast.

Yet the sooner our arrival, the easier it would be for Barney and me to catch the returning night boat as we had promised. If we reached New York after six we would be too late and of course have no alternative but wait until tomorrow. This pleasant possibility we discussed in whispers.

Five minutes after leaving Albany, the *Gloria*'s little engine began to relax with falling steampressure.

"What's the matter?" asked the Chief. "Too much excitement?"

"Nope," said Barney. "The shovel's too heavy."

"And I just got this awful crick in my back," I complained.

"Well then, supposin' you open the boiler door and set down and make a game of who can hit the fire with the most coal."

"We can try, but my arm feels heavier'n lead."

"And my crick goes right into my finger tips."

We opened the door to the boiler, sat down, and each picked up a lump of coal. Barney held his up and turned it around, inspecting it from every angle. "Nice shape to this piece of coal," he said.

"No two of 'em alike," I agreed.

Barney threw his at the boiler but it hit the edge of the door and dropped back. "That was a rotten shot. Now you try." Mine was so wide of the mark it missed the door by a foot. The steam pressure, down several pounds, was falling steadily.

"What's come over you two?" asked the Chief, looking back from his perch on the pilot house stool. "Ten minutes ago you was busier'n a cow's tail in fly time."

"Too much to take in, I guess," said Barney, throwing another hunk of coal at the boiler. This one glanced off the door and into the fire. "Oops!" he laughed, "that was a mistake." We started giggling as more bad shots rained against the side of the furnace. "We've been pushin' the engine pretty hard, Father. What difference does it make if we get to New York at five or seven?"

"Now I see!" nodded the Chief. "You got me over a barrel. S'posin' you was to hear we got a tide to buck in the North River and couldn't make New York by six if we burned pitch pine?"

"Funny thing," said Barney. "My arm don't feel as heavy as it did. How about your crick?"

"It comes and goes. I think it's going!"

The fire quickly revived and as the pressure rose the cranks resumed their lively pace. The sun having dispelled the fog that clung to the eastern bank, and warmed the breeze, we spent much of the morning on deck watching the pageant of sail and steam on the deepening river. Though I had never been north or south of Lake Champlain, I had often sailed the Hudson in my dreams, and excitedly identified the mouth of the Katz-Kill which tumbled out of the craggy Katzburgs where Rip Van Winkle slept, and the ghostly crew played at nine-pins. Fact and fancy were all jumbled together. Aboard the high-pooped *Half Moon* Henry Hudson was searching for the Northwest Passage, and Captain Kidd was rowing ashore to bury his strong box. Robert Fulton's *Steam Boat* was weighing anchor at Clermont on her way to Albany. Athens, Hudson, Saugerties, Kingston: I had heard of them all between blows at the forge during the long winters at the shipyard.

Square foot for square foot the little port of Rondout was the busiest on the river, for it was the outlet of the Delaware and Hudson Canal that led from the mountains of Pennsylvania. Since no berth was available, we tied the *Gloria* to a canal boat and stumbled over piles of flagstone as we carried coal from the dock. As at Albany, we protested shoving off so quickly; we wanted to explore every inch of waterfront and inspect all the boats. The Chief assured us that their vertical beam engines were all like ours, and that New York was the place to keep our eyes peeled. Manhattan had 360 degrees of shoreline. There'd be clippers and other windjammers along South Street and blocks of wharves thick with steamships and steamboats. The definitions of a ship and a boat now being called for, the Chief observed that while ships were supposed to belong to salt water and boats to fresh, steamboats longer than most ships were abundant on Long Island Sound, which was "saltier than the pork that came out of Aunt Agatha's brine."

Our excitement in the evening as the *Gloria* entered the incoming tide in the lower river beneath the lofty Palisades was beyond reckoning. Nothing in our experience compared with a panorama so wondrously new. Barney, who enjoyed posing as an experienced, if not indifferent, man of the world, looked like a little boy, his brown eyes wide with awe as the great *Drew* of the People's Evening Line swept past on her way to Albany, her white bulwarks as long as a city block, her twin funnels high as factory smokestacks. She was gone almost as soon as she appeared, the windows in her turtle deck glimmering in the twilight, her immense wheels laying white water on the darkening river. Were it not for her mountainous swells rolling shoreward, almost tipping our coffee pot off the cylinder head, it would have been easy to dismiss her as a huge jeweled phantom in an outlandish dream.

The sky was dark when we reached New York, but the shores were aglow and the river's shadowy shapes flickered far and near like fireflies. Neither Barney nor I would have steered even if the Chief had asked us to. Familiar water is baffling enough at night without ferries darting from a dozen slips, tows crossing one's bow, and tugs backing and filling in every direction. But the Chief didn't mind.

"We're scared of what we don't know," he said, taking a broad swing north of the Battery before crossing to Hoboken. "My first trip I felt like a pullet in a cockfight. Know your rules, hold your course, and don't let 'em bluff you." He searched his pockets for a cigar, but they were all gone. "Sightseein's poor at night," he said at length. "The *Gloria's* tired."

"We aren't," said Barney.

"You wouldn't admit it if you was. When you roll out at sunup you'll look like the last of pea time. I know what you boys are thinkin'. You want me to turn you loose in the city, but the waterfront's no place at night. Shanghaiin' ain't dead. There's still many an old bucket with a crew that was blackjacked."

"How old do I have to be to take care of myself?" asked Barney.

"Seventeen up on the lake and seventeen down here is two

different things," said the Chief. "You're strong, all right, and smart, but you ain't wise enough. Remember the pickle you got into at Whitehall?"

"That wa'nt our fault. We were mindin' our own business."

"But others ain't. That's just it. Tomorrow you can spread your wings all over New York. Long as you're at the People's Line pier at five-thirty."

Barney and I couldn't fall asleep until after midnight, and our condition at 5 A.M. was accurately prophesied. After calling us twice with no response other than a faint stirring, the Chief emptied the water jug on Barney's face. He rose up sawing the air as if he had gone down for the third time. The Chief, good as his word, suggested we immediately cut loose and take the ferry for New York.

"You got no fish to fry here. Leave your carpet bags with me. I'll bring 'em to the pier at five."

From the moment the creaking double-ender disgorged us at 14th Street in New York until it was time to start for the People's Line pier we could never recall how we got where we went. We must have walked five miles before we climbed on a horse car headed in the wrong direction just so we could sit down. Our objective was the Battery, which we reached by way of the fish market. No spectacle real or imagined could compare with the flotilla of steam and sail on the lower East and North rivers— nor any music with the slushing of their paddles, the chuffing of their exhausts, or the "Yo-heave-ho" at their capstans.

The blackened painting of the square-rigger on the *Bennington*'s donkey-room wall and the clipper model in Captain Hawley's stateroom came startlingly to life, their bowsprits reaching clear over the street, their shabby figureheads and weathered spars confirming the fading age of sail. As if in defiance of steam, a few industrious masters were directing their crews at caulking and painting, which gave the breeze the familiar fragrance of oakum and turpentine. The cool doorways of the ship chandlers facing the piers smelled of manila cordage, and some of the freight piled along the bulkheads was redolent of spices and tobacco.

"Avast there, you swabs! Clear the poop deck!" Barney commanded an imaginary crew. "You in the crow's nest!" he shouted looking up and cupping his hands to his mouth. "Wake up! This ain't no flop house!" From Captain Grizzlegruff he reverted to Barney Barnaby. "I wouldn't mind shippin' out on one of those."

"Not me," I said. "You could be gone six months or a year."

"What's the matter with that? Think of all the places you'd go."

"I'd feel lost."

"I'd rather be lost than found," said Barney.

"But sooner or later you'd want to come back," I allowed, "and you have somebody to come back to."

"So do you."

"I mean your parents, your grandfather, and your aunt. All I have are Mrs. Mayberry and Uncle Reuel."

"Don't forget me," said Barney, sensing I was having one of my lonely spells. He put his hand on my shoulder.

"I mean the lake is enough of a world for me," I said. "It's too big here, and all these people. Anyway, I like steam better than sail."

"That's because you know more about steam."

"You don't know anything about sail, either."

"And prob'ly never will," admitted Barney, "because it'll all be gone, the way things are goin'."

"I thought you wanted to be an engineer," I said.

"I do. I'm just kiddin'. Except it must be excitin' to sail way off somewhere."

"Exciting! Who needs more excitement than we've had? First the *Republic*'s pressure went to eighty-three pounds and we got thrown off for fighting. Then we hit the dock at Bluff Point, then the *Bennington*'s filler piece cracked, and now they're building an opposition boat."

"Just the same I get these wanderin' pains," said Barney, "and sometimes they really hurt. Prob'ly they'll go away. I know there ain't a boat in the world to compare with the *Republic,* or even the *Bennin'ton.*"

"Supposing you were an engineer at sea," I said. "You wouldn't get to handle the engine because you'd just be going and going and all you'd see is water every day. There's always something doing on the lake because we land so often."

"I s'pose I'll be married and live on the Point and never leave the lake again."

"Who do you suppose the fair damsel will be?"

"Dunno. She ain't appeared yet. One thing, no barns for me, emptyin' all those damm cows mornin' and night. Grandfather likes it. But he ain't ever smelled steam and hot cylinder oil."

"I thought he was on one of the old boats."

"Yup. Hall boy one summer. But the equinoctial storm hit and he puked all the way from Basin Harbor to Cumberland Head and that was the end of it."

When we reached the People's Line pier at the foot of Canal Street we could not have walked another foot if our lives had depended on it. It was half an hour until we were due to meet the Chief, and we lay down on an empty wagon where we tried to believe we would soon be boarding the largest vessel in the world, other than the *Great Eastern.* Her name was the *St. John* and she was 420 feet long, longer even than the pier, the most astounding sight of a day filled with wonders. But the senses can absorb just so much; all we had the power to do was gaze at her from our backs and try to count the windows in her lofty turtle deck four stories above the water. We failed in this, for there were so many that it proved impossible to keep track of those already counted. We didn't fall asleep but were only half conscious of the hubbub on the pier which, more than an hour before sailing time, already bustled with carriages and drays. The cries of newsboys rose above the road of steam and the insistent clanging of a bell. Peddlers beset arriving passengers as they tried to thread their way toward the line at the gangplank.

"I'll be jiggered if it ain't the two tourists, all humped up like burnt boots! You two look like you got some mileage on you. New York ain't all beer and skittles, is it?"

Barney was obviously disappointed not to have spied the Chief first so he could pose as an experienced traveler, wise in the ways of the city. "No," he said, jumping from the wagon and dusting himself off. "It's all boats, 'least the part we saw." My legs felt like stumps as I swung them over the edge of the cart.

"See anythin' you liked better'n in the *Republic?*"

"Barney thinks he'd like to ship out on a clipper."

"You'd think different after eatin' the wallpaper paste they feed their crews."

"I didn't partic'ly have a clipper in mind. I just thought I'd like to ship out," grinned Barney.

"I want to hear everythin' you seen," said the Chief, handing us our carpet bags, "but that'll wait. If you don't get in line you'll stand as much chance of hirin' a state-room as a one-legged man in a rump-kickin' contest."

"Is it true," I asked, "that the *St. John* is the biggest thing afloat since the *Great Eastern?*"

"She's a monster. She's got a seventy-six-inch cylinder, a fifteen-foot stroke, and forty-foot wheels. I used to know her engineer but he's not on her now. Wish I could go aboard but they're workin' on the filler piece tonight and I want to get back to Hoboken. Tell your uncle I'll be startin' back tomorrow or the next day and extend to Cap'n Bullard my warmest greetin's."

As the line moved past the ticket window we dug into our jeans for our meager savings to purchase the cheapest stateroom on the boat. We didn't care a fig that it was barely large enough for the double bunk, the washstand and the pitcher, and our disappointment that there was no outboard window was mild compared to the thrill of boarding the queen of the Hudson. Scrambling into our suits we felt like men of the world as we stepped out into the richly carpeted hall.

For once we ignored the engine room, heading instead for the news and tobacco stand where Barney bought and lit a large cigar. It was the first time I had seen him smoke, but such a minor vice seemed fitting for such a major occasion. We had always supposed the stateroom hall of the *Republic* to be the finest afloat, and so it was for its size. Nothing, however, could rival the *St. John*'s embellishments in carved mahogany, in plush, and gilt. The lobby of the American Hotel in Burlington would be lost in her grand saloon, a yawning expanse as high as the boat and half as long, with stateroom galleries curving round the sides, like the balconies of an opera house, and huge pillars supporting the dome in the center. The man in the newsstand told us that the grand staircase of carved mahogany inlaid with white holly had cost twenty-five thousand dollars. Though this was hard to believe, its beauty was such as to remind me of the stairs to Heaven, of which I had often dreamed.

Most of the people were decorated as elegantly as the surroundings. In such company plain suits were barely adequate, providing they didn't look so tight as to suggest hand-me-downs. Apparently to dispel any possible suspicion of our country origin, Barney was assuming the airs of a gentleman.

"I say, theah," he commanded in a voice not quite loud enough to be heard by a hall boy. "Fetch me my tea and crumpets!" He made quite a show of his cigar, smoking it little but removing it from his mouth with exaggerated motions. "I do hope James will be on time with the carriage at Albany. Such a nuisance, these public hacks!" With this he removed his cigar with a sweep of his arm so wide that it collided with the bouquet of a girl about to pass us, knocking some of the flowers out of her hand.

"Oh!" said Barney, scrambling to pick up the roses on the carpet. "I'm sorry!"

The girl's eyes were smiling. "That's all right. Accidents will happen."

"They always seem to happen to me!" complained Barney, his face quite flushed.

The girl had a small dimple in her chin and when she smiled two others appeared in her cheeks. Though she could not have been older than Barney or younger than I, she looked much more at home in her long satin skirt and organdy waist than I felt in my suit. In her dark hair she wore a peach-colored ribbon exactly matching the color of her cheeks. I had never seen a prettier girl.

Breaking an awkward silence during which we didn't know

whether to move on or stay, she asked, "What other accidents have you had?"

"Oh," said Barney, regaining his composure, "nothin' important—just bumpin' into things. This is sure a nice boat, isn't it?"

"Yes, I love it."

"Do you travel much?"

"Yes, quite a lot. Do you?"

"Oh yes," said Barney. "We've been in New York on business."

"What business are you in?"

"Transportation. Steamboats."

"Oh, how interesting! Boats like this?"

"Yes, on Lake Champlain." The *St. John*'s whistle blew. Ordinarily wild horses could not have dragged us from the engine room while getting under way, but this was an extraordinary circumstance.

"I've always heard Lake Champlain is so beautiful. Do you have many boats?"

"Three," said Barney (I presumed he was counting the *Gloria*). "We're in the engine department."

"Gracious, you look so young to be engineers!"

"We started young," Barney explained, holding to his dangerous course. Responding to further questions, he went on at length about the awesome responsibilities of an engineer and the perils of the pilot house. The *Republic* and *Bennington,* as he talked, grew longer, more luxurious, and more difficult to handle by the minute.

"Do you live in New York?" I inquired at last.

"Part of the time," said the girl. "But mostly on the *St. John.*"

"On the *St. John*!" said Barney. "How does that happen?"

"My father is the Captain." The deepest blush imaginable started over Barney's collar and rose to the roots of his hair. "And I think," she continued, "he'd enjoy visiting with you. Would you like to go up to the pilot house?"

"Would we!" I replied. "I'll say we would!" The springing of the trap he had set for himself left Barney at a complete loss for words. While we climbed the stairs and passed through the state-room hall with its succession of paneled doors, he appeared to be reassessing what he had told the girl compared to what he might now tell the Captain. The girl never hinted that she knew as much about steamboats as we, which was probable, and seemed delighted that on one of her hundreds of trips to Albany she had met two boys with whom she had something in common.

Even the lofty lookout I had built into the tree on the Point was not as high above the water as the pilot house of the *St. John*. We entered to the creaking of her huge steering wheel as the quartermasters swung her into her course upstream. Through curved windows of glistening plate glass the pilot was surveying one hundred and eighty degrees of river, of New York and New Jersey. The Captain and another man were seated in two ornate chairs under the clock and barometer. The pilot house was no less resplendent with brass than the grand saloon was with gold leaf.

"Father," said the girl, "these boys run steamboats up on Lake Champlain. I thought they'd enjoy coming up here and meeting you. This is . . . I'm sorry, I don't know your names."

"I'm Brian Seaworthy. And this is Barney Barnaby."

"Very glad to see you . . . Lake Champlain . . . did you say Seaworthy?"

"Yes, sir."

"You wouldn't be kin to Jacob Seaworthy, would you?"

"Yes, sir, he was my father."

The Captain shook his head as he took hold of both my hands. "Would you believe it! I knew him well! I suppose you know he was responsible for the design of several boats here. We all had great respect for him." I managed to smile, though momentarily the victim of one of my lonely spells. Immediately sensing this, the Captain changed his tack; he said he'd never seen the *Republic* but was aware of her reputation as the finest of her class.

"We think the *St. John* is pretty fine," I said.

"So she is. But the *Republic* has some features the *St. John* hasn't, such as boilers in the hold. That's the coming thing. How fast does she turn up? Close to twenty knots, doesn't she?"

"Yes, sir," said Barney, finding his tongue. "My father's Chief on her and he once clocked her at exactly twenty."

"There aren't many faster," observed the Captain, "unless they're running the tide." He turned to his daughter. "This is quite a coincidence, isn't it, Jeanie?" He now introduced us to his friend, a Mr. Burnside, and to the pilot and quartermasters, who proved equal to all of our questions. Did they often run on compass course? Did they have trouble figuring the wind and the tide? Had their bell system always been the same? It wasn't like ours. How the minutes raced! We stayed the better part of an hour, fascinated with a vantage point which dwarfed everything else on the river.

Presently the Captain looked at his watch. "Well, boys, I have to go below, but Jeanie and I would like you to join us for dinner at eight-fifteen. Is that too late?"

"Oh no, that would be fine."

"By the way," said the Captain, "what stateroom do you have?" He rang the bell for the purser, who shortly appeared. "Is the Presidential suite occupied?"

"No, sir."

"Good. I want these boys moved into it. My compliments."

"Very well, sir."

Jeanie's smile would have warmed the coldest heart on the river. "You have a surprise coming," she said. "That's the nicest room on the boat." This was so startling a development we could think of nothing appropriate to say as we descended to the hall, where Jeanie and her father left us in care of the purser. Insisting that a hall boy fetch our carpet bags, he unlocked the door to the Presidential suite with his pass key, ushered us in, expressed the hope that we would be comfortable, and left.

"Holio Rolio!" exclaimed Barney.

"It's true," I said. "It must be!" The chairs were of gold, the curtains, the carpet, the picture frames, the leather on top of the desk, even the waste baskets. Three people could have slept comfortably on each of the ornate brass beds draped with gold plush. Imposing as all this was, no occupant of the Presidential suite could have failed to be even more impressed by the adjoining bathroom. It had a six-foot tub supported by iron lion's paws, and towels the size of rugs warmed on polished brass racks piped with steam. Having tried out all the chairs and bounced on the beds, laughing uproariously at our good fortune, we flipped a coin to determine who should have the first bath. Barney, winning the toss, had no sooner stepped into the tub than there was a knock on the door, which I opened.

"You rang, sir?"

"No, I didn't ring."

The valet—that's what he appeared to be—looked puzzled. "Beg your pardon, sir." He left, but in a few moments was back. "Sorry, sir, but someone here has rung."

"It's only my friend and me, and he's taking a bath."

"Then it is your friend who has rung." Crossing to the bathroom door, he knocked, went directly in, and stood stiffly in front of the bathtub. "You rang, sir?"

"Rang! Rang what?" Barney's face was a study in bewilderment.

"The board shows someone rang."

"No, I didn't ring."

"Beg pardon, sir, you have hung your coat on the bell-pull. Kindly excuse the intrusion, sir." He backed out the door, bowing. Removing Barney's coat from the bell-pull he had mistaken for a hook, I had another fit of laughter as did Barney on recovering from his embarrassment.

Of all the day's events the dinner was perhaps the most memorable. Sandwiches were all we had had since morning, and when we sat down to the Captain's table, decorated with fresh flowers and glistening with sparkling glass and silver, our problem was how to eat everything we could lay our hands on without appearing greedy. But an impasse presented itself, the Captain's special menu:

POTAGE DE VOLAILLE

HORS-D'OEUVRE

POISSONS GRILLÉS
À LA MARSEILLAISE
TOURNEDOS DE BOEUF
MAÎTRE D'HÔTEL
POMMES DAUPHINE
QUARTIERS D'ARTICHAUTS
ÉTUVÉS AU BEURRE
SALADE DE SAISON
BAVAROIS AUX FRAISES
PATISSERIE
CAFÉ

I could understand scarcely a word of it, and Barney's expression, while pondering such choices as "grilled poison," was one of utter consternation. It was only by observing what the others did with their finger bowls that I followed suit and removed mine to the left. His menu so preoccupied Barney that when the waiter removed his service plate he had first to set aside his finger bowl. This went unnoticed, but the menu was a dilemma of larger proportions.

"What would you boys like to have?" asked the Captain. In a rare moment of resourcefulness, I said, "It's hard to decide." The pressure was off, for the Captain then turned to his wife, to Jeanie, and to Mr. Burnside, who made their choices in English, which allowed me to say: "I think I'll have that too," and Barney to follow up with: "I'll have the same."

Fortunately the several glasses filled with water and wine took care of themselves, and the problem of which forks and spoons to use at what time was solved by observation. It was the most elaborate dinner I had ever sat down to; Delmonico's could not have catered with greater style. Actually there was little to distinguish the dining room of the *St. John* from that of a large hotel on shore.

Barney was having a gay time with Jeanie but was now far more reserved about his boating experiences, for she had had a few herself, as I had surmised. Listening attentively to our trials in the boiler room, Mr. Burnside, who proved to be the agent supplying coal to the People's Evening Line, confirmed what I already knew: that there was no substitute for the best coal for the simple reason that all of it burned, producing more heat and therefore greater economy. He expected to go to Lake Champlain within a few months and I invited him to call at the Point.

After dinner we toured the engine and boiler rooms, then sat with Jeanie in the grand saloon until after eleven. Scarcely able to keep our eyes open when we returned to our suite, we moved the gold chairs to the windows and watched the river for nearly an hour as we recalled our experiences. All that we had seen and done might well have been a dream. Even Jeanie appeared as a kind of Cinderella, though of course our roles were reversed: it was we, tomorrow, who would exchange this world of fantasy for the northern lake in the lap of mountains that also encircled our lives.

Sarah Cleghorn (1876-1959)

The Golf Links

The golf links lie so near the mill
    That almost every day
The laboring children can look out
    And see the men at play.

Comrade Jesus

Thanks to Saint Matthew, who had been
At mass-meetings in Palestine,
We know whose side was spoken for
When Comrade Jesus had the floor.

"Where sore they toil and hard they lie,
Among the great unwashed, dwell I.
The tramp, the convict, I am he:
Cold-shoulder him, cold-shoulder me."

By Dives' door, with thoughtful eye,
He did tomorrow prophesy:—
"The Kingdom's gate is low and small:
The rich can scarce wedge through at all."

"A dangerous man," said Caiaphas,
"An ignorant demagogue, alas.
Friend of low women, it is he
Slanders the upright Pharisee."

For law and order, it was plain,
For Holy Church, he must be slain.

The troops were there to awe the crowd:
Mob violence was not allowed.

Their clumsy force with force to foil,
His strong, clean hands he would not soil.
He saw their childishness quite plain
Between the lightnings of his pain.

Between the twilights of his end
He made his fellow-felon friend.
With swollen tongue and blinded eyes
Invited him to Paradise.

Ah, let no Local him refuse!
Comrade Jesus hath paid his dues.
Whatever other be debarred,
Comrade Jesus hath his red card.

Nightfallen Snow

These nights of snow are loving to the air
As the still mother of a grieving boy;
For so they fill the air with soft concern,
Imponderable, irresistible,
And draw the numbing hardness slowly out,
And slowly weave a gradual sweetness in;
So spending, on its harsh and hungry gloom,
The last calm silver penny of reckless love.

O perfect strength of soft, unstrenuous snow!
O mouth of beauty whispering in the night!
Eolian snow, that thrills against the wind,
That drifts on hidden grace, and lights it up
With shreds of many rainbows blending white!
O wild and revolutionary snow!
That tosses utter newness round the world,
And lays it on the nations in their sleep.

Ann Batchelder (1885-1955)

Warum?

I would poise my arm for the discus throwing,
   I would be a swimmer in the strong deep sea;
Here must I stop and sit at my sewing,
   Hemmed in by four walls that frown on me.

I would fare away on the world's broad highways,
   I would hear the alien winds singing through the sails;
Here must I stay and roam the dusty byways,
   Looking for berries to fill my berry-pails.

Why should the wild things cry to me forever?
   Why should the green hills seem like prison walls?
Why should the echoes answer "never, never, never,"
   When through the darkness my eager spirit calls?

Never for me to see the shore-light burning,
   Not for me to portage by undiscovered streams;
Mine to hoist the weary task at the days returning,
   While I bake the corn-cake at the camp-fire of my dreams.

East of Bridgewater

I

On Woodstock Green the summer's past,
Even there it could not last,
Even there the leaves must lie
Prone beneath an autumn sky.
And through the park the scuffing feet

Of children find the dead leaves sweet,
As once I found them, on my way
With playmates of another day—
Playmates long unheard, unseen,
Forever gone from Woodstock Green.

II

This is the trysting place,
Where the long road goes down,
Where the branches interlace
Above the path to town.

Here we would meet and stay
Through many an afternoon,
And watch at the end of day
The cold, indifferent moon.

Years have unset these stones,
Bent with great age this tree,

Scattered the crumbling bones,
And made no friend of me.

Genevieve Taggard (1894-1948)

To Ethan Allen

Sleep, Ethan, where you belong,
Allen of the little clan,
Clan of large men on lavish continent,
In the place of uncut trees and the trackless green.
Sleep to the thrush's tranquil, seasonal song.
Vermont itself is your big monument;
And also those who sing of wilderness and man;
Of intelligence and hardihood and the keen
Struggle. Song is for heroes in their time of rest.
Sleep in your granite bed under the mountain tent,
Beside your lakes and rivers; near falls that splash and flare.
Vermont was wild frontier and still contains the West.
Daily your turbulent spirit delights this air.
Sleep well in your wedge-shaped bed,
Under the slanted snow, or in spring's frequent
Vehement thunder. Sleep. A poet said,
Nature is never spent.
Neither are we, nor were you, Old Heart of Oak.
I heard your tone when first the thunder spoke.
The toil of men and women, the excited feet
Stamping at country dances, and Town Meeting Day
Chiming their biblical notes of *yea* and *nay*,
And many customs sweet
Prolong an enduring impulse this citizen took
To be his passion: to be Freedom's servant rude.
A man no Tory conclave could undo,
Founding a state and writing a troubled book.
Prisoner, freeman, leader and strategist,

Sagacious creature with uplifted fist
Against all tyrants . . . Those who remember you
Wish never to outgrow such servitude.
Sleep, Ethan Allen of the little clan.
Vermont in its quiet way recalls this man.
Sleep, Ethan, in the mountains where you belong.
Sleep to the thrush's tranquil, seasonal song.

The Nursery Rhyme and the Summer Visitor

Green Mountain Mary, Green Mountain Mary
What does your garden grow?

Violets, moss, ground pine, goldenrod, briars,
Strawberries, spirea, wintergreen, ferns,
And a little bit of grass, alas.
Will you sell me your meadow?
                              Oh, no.

Who crops it?

            Deer.

See, here, Green Mountain Mary, you people are very,—
Excuse me—
Queer.

On the Trout Streams

Crystal-white and bottle brown, seal-brown, sunny
the simple streams. Glacid curves, sliding over
into up-toss,—mazed crystal and foam,
between banks of vertical pine, spruce, hemlock,
solemn, dim-scented, loaded with evening dew;
timber, heavy and sleepy, where we tune

heart and ear to quiet entire, quiet, quiet . . .
. . . the wood-thrush, listen, the articulate bird.

In Flame Over Vermont

Green state where edging moss covers the poor
In graves; where hardship moves with moss an inch a year,
Your air holds claps of thunder and quick end—
Sons falling foremost, planes that shadow graves
Skimming the lichen on the hill of stones.

He fell
Out of a cloud.
Flame took him as he fell.
Flying from state to state for daily wage
Over Vermont, over a double wind
He spiraled.
   All the graves
Plushy with moss, the sunken and homely graves,
Vermont's old rural center of the dead
Were lit by honey-fire as he fell
Out of a cloud into a cup of flame.

Green state where edging moss covers the poor
In graves; where hardship moves with moss an inch a year,
Your air holds claps of terror and quick end—
Sons falling foremost, planes that shadow graves
Skimming the lichen on the hill of stones.

Mari Tomasi (1909-1965)

Stone

Maria Dalli shivered in the cold wind. Her full lips tightened grimly as she studied the stonecutters gathered about the open grave of Italo Tosti. Her husband's ruddy cheeks were sunk in sorrow. He could not conceal his pain, her Pietro. He and Italo had grown up together in the old country. But it was Pietro who had come first to this Vermont granite town. It was he who had written glowing letters telling of the splendid wages in the stonesheds, who had said, "Come over to this fine country, Italo. Marry your Lucia and cross the ocean."

The black cassock flapped at the ankles of young, red-headed Father Carty. *"Requiescat in pace,"* he intoned to the wind. He turned from the coffin, touching his hand to Lucia Tosti's in futile comfort.

So. Another *paesan'* stonecutter laid away. Maria breathed deeply. "Come Lucia," she ordered gently.

The widow had stopped her sobs. She was rigid now, staring at the coffin, heedless of Maria's words.

Pietro blinked his eyes and tugged at his silky mustache. "You go now, eh, Lucia?" he begged. "We will stay—the six of us—to see that everything is all right." He hesitated. Then, "Yes?" he inquired of the other five bearers.

They nodded—Gerbati the shed boss, Uey Olsen the polisher, Jose Santioz the smithy, Vitleau the sawyer, and the sadfaced Ronato, most skilled of the carvers in Granitown.

Fumbling awkwardly with his cap, Gerbati spoke. "You need not worry about a memorial, Lucia Tosti. I will give the stone, free. And Pietro and Ronato, they have agreed to carve it in their spare time." He shifted his great weight clumsily.

"You are generous, Gerbati," Lucia said.

But as Maria led her away, she spat bitterly. "Stone! Stone! The dead wear granite memorials at their heads. Dead stonecutters like my Italo wear granite in their lungs. Stonedust!" Her voice was low, tense. "Only eight years he cut stone. Only eight years to catch the sickness." Her fingers dug into Maria's arm. "You are a fool, Maria, to let Pietro stay in the sheds. Make him quit now —before you find yourself a widow with five little ones. Like me. . . . What shall I do now? I will not take charity! Shall I then turn *strega,* like Granitown's Josie Blaine? Shall I throw open the doors of my home to anyone who wishes to buy a glass of wine?"

"Hush," Maria murmured.

Tonight she would try again. Tonight, after having seen his closest *paesan'* laid in the ground from the sickness, perhaps Pietro would listen.

Maria and Pietro closed Lucia's door behind them at midnight. They knew she would sleep, fatigue and grief had so obviously conquered her flesh. Under the wavering light of the one street lamp they walked the frozen ruts of Willow Hollow Road to Main Street. The morning's wind had spent itself. The night was still, cold. Maria's eyes lifted westward across the town to the gaunt bulk of Quarry Hill. If it were day, the shattered slope would show the vast pockmarks of its quarries, the towering gray pyramids of grout that were its wasted entrails.

Strange how the Hill dominated the town. Two-thirds of Granitown's men eked out a living, one way or another, from stone. The Hill was vindictive, merciless to the quarriers who drilled into its rock-ribbed sides; most merciless toward the stonecutters in the sheds, the men who finished the granite blocks into carved memorials. The Hill stood quiet as they gouged out its stone, yet it was not without revenge. In the end stone took its toll of all stonecutters. . . .

Now Maria saw Pietro's breath in the chill night air and heard him say, "Tomorrow night we must make our grappa. We have had the wine removed from the mash these three days. If we wait much longer, age will rot it, steal the goodness—"

Her mind was not on the grappa. "Pietro," she pleaded, "have you not seen enough? Eight of our *paesani* taken in five years— Edo, Jo-Jo, Luigi, Rico, Almo, Toni, Pino. And now Italo. Ah, Pietro, quit the sheds while your chest is still free of dust!"

He was silent.

She moved her dark head toward his. "Our fourth baby, Pietro. Will this one, too, be born with a father who is a stonecutter?"

He spoke shyly, sorrowfully. "But it is foolish to give up my work now, when no other job presents itself. We must have money for you, for the new baby—"

Her patience snapped. "Four times I have heard this. With each of the other three I have heard, 'After it is born.' Promises!"

His hand sought hers. She would never understand. He liked the gray stone with its small, black, twinkling flakes, its strength under his hands. Here was ageless stone, born perhaps at the world's birth; and here were his hands carving into it. Ah, good *Dio,* what a feeling! True, the great Creator gave life to man. But eventually He took away that life. And when death came, it was Pietro and other stonecutters who perpetuated that life in stone. . . . Surely the granite he carved into beauty would not repay his love with death.

He said quietly, "It is a bad time to quit now. All those Canadians who pushed in during the strike—bakers, clerks, farmers— they cannot carve. They are not artists. Their work is plain, plain. They will ruin the stone industry. Some of us must stay—"

"Stone industry!" she cried fiercely. "Do you own it? They wanted to lower your pay, they welcomed those unskilled strikebreakers with open arms! Treated them royally, gave them police protection against you. And now you talk 'loyalty'!"

He was empty. All his excuses limped beside the real one—his love for his work. But he tried again. "I know only my trade. Granitown offers few other jobs."

"We could open a store! In our own home. In our living room! With groceries and fruit and a little bell on the door to tinkle a warning when a customer enters." Her voice lifted. "Think, Pietro, what clean, wholesome work! Selling bread that makes for life —not cutting stones for the dead. See how happy my sister Vanna is since Hugo left the sheds. They do well in their store!"

But Pietro would make no promises.

They made grappa the following evening. Pietro's short stocky figure busied itself in the kitchen, fitting out the old washboiler with copper coils. He turned the grape mash into the boiler and set it on the stove. When the first transparent drops of distilled liquor trickled from the tube, Maria packed the children off to bed in the attic bedroom, away from the alcoholic vapors that filled the lower house. The teasing piquancy irritated the nose to deep, deep breaths, and left one as giddily warmed as two long draughts of wine.

Ronato came to help. And Vanna and Hugo, passing by, decided to wait and sample the new spirits. Vanna, glowing from the grappa vapors and the wine, boasted of their new venture, the store.

"Our happiest moments in Granitown began when the first customer walked in. Yes, Hugo?" she prompted, and her elbow nudged him sharply.

"*Si, si,*" Hugo agreed. *Dio,* why must Vanna flaunt their good fortune! He saw the shadows of envy and discontent in Maria's eyes, Pietro's shrinking. He tortured his brain to interrupt the sudden silence. "Eh, Pietro," he said at last, "Ronato tells me you are carving a fine memorial!"

"The best these hands have ever cut," Pietro admitted. "Yet, if it were our Ronato's work," he supplemented humbly, "I would judge it the least of his masterpieces. It is a cross, standing just so high—smothered under an intricacy of vines. The best job I have yet undertaken, and it will be finished next week."

Maria started. *The best job . . . finished next week.* The words revolved in her mind, meaningless at first. Then her hands trembled. She remembered the day a month ago when Vitleau had been threatened with dismissal if his rheumatic hand slipped again to spoil the stone he was working on. Better still she remembered Pietro's fervid, "If by accident my hand should sometime err with the chisel, just let any boss give me hell! I would throw the job in his face and quit! *Dio!*"

The best job I have yet undertaken. . . . I would throw the job in his face and quit. . . . Maria's heart pulsed in quick hope.

"More wine," she urged and poured a brimming glass. Ronato, watching her face ripen a joyous red, murmured, "Your cheeks, Maria, are as red as the skirt you wear!"

Not until Pietro's cheeks bloomed and his words stumbled thickly one upon the other, did Maria close the door behind her three visitors.

When his deep breathing bespoke a half-drugged sleep, she rose from their bed, dressed quickly, supplied herself with a flashlight and chisel, and stole from the house. This plunge into the frosty air nipped at the confidence she had enjoyed in the grappa-vaporized kitchen. A moment of indecision held her to the porch. Then her lips tightened and she stepped swiftly across the granite chip walk and ran in quiet flight down the road in the harsh moonlight.

She breathed more easily after she had crossed the bridge and tracks to the shadows of Shed Row. A darkened car was parked beneath a sprawling river willow and from its interior came a woeful quartet: "Show me the way to go home—" Maria gained the sheds and kept to their backyards. Under moonglow the weathered structures loomed gaunt. Strewn pieces of grout lay on the ground like whiting bones. Here and there an oblong block of granite became an overturned tombstone. Her feet pressed harshly for reality on the granite chips; each step was a sharp reminder what stone could do to flesh.

The great front doors of Gerbati's shed were strongly barred. She tried to raise one after another of the high windows but succeeded only in loosing thick showers of gray dust. A wire ripped open her thumb and she sucked at it for a moment. Then the muscles of her arms strained to aching agony and a window gave an inch. With her index finger she explored the inside sill. A bent spike was holding the window. She poked at it with the chisel until it turned in its socket.

The quartet's drunken voices drowned the creaking of the window. She climbed into the room. Gerbati's office. The flashlight grew a bright circle on the floor and revealed dust-filled cracks between the floor boards. Even Gerbati, boss though he was, got his share of dust. A door opened into the dark wet-room, cluttered with giant saws and polishing machines. Here was the earthy chill of some subterranean cave, and, cloyed with it, a dank smell of rust and oil that constricted her body. What was it Pietro said? The machinists hated water because it rusted their well-oiled machines . . . the carvers hated oil because it stained the granite. . . . Yet in this machine room, water had to be fed, she knew, in steady cold streams to prevent the metal saws from melting as they cut hotly into stone. If granite could thus destroy metal, how easy then to break flesh and blood. . . . Stone, the implacable. Stone, the victor. Her mouth twisted into a grim sly smile: stone could not reason, could not plot as did her brain.

She pushed open another door, to the dry chalky air of the finishing room. Here she was blind to everything but Pietro's corner where his little masterpiece stood under a stiff covering. She pulled off the tarpaulin, studied the cross dispassionately, and set the chisel to a corner leaf design where a chip might appear a slip of Pietro's hand. She hammered, and the lofty room echoed with hollow sound. Another blow. A small edge of the cross chipped off and fell to the hard earth-packed floor. Again. The leaf pattern dwindled to half a leaf. She straightened breathlessly. Now that the deed was accomplished, its magnitude appalled her. Her heart thrashed wildly against her ribs.

For the first time since she entered the barnlike finishing room, she looked about her. A half dozen moonlit memorials stared back. On the boxing platform three little markers, ALMA, JOHN, and ALICE, accused her. She shook a fist at them and fled back to the office window, clambering out in such haste that when an outside wire caught at her skirt she tore it loose frantically, eager only to put the river once more between herself and Shed Row.

Maria Dalli never stinted a healthy sleep-appetite with worries. Night was for rest. So it was tonight. The deed was done. She crept into the house and once more beside the deeply-breathing Pietro promptly fell asleep.

But she was no longer mistress of her mind. Before the seven o'clock shed whistle could awaken her to reality, a shrill police note had called miles of blue-coated police who marched toward her from the four corners of Granitown. Hundreds of stern eyes were riveted to her hand which clutched a chisel and hacked away at the lifeless face of the man for whom Pietro was carving a cross.

She tossed in bed, struggling to wakefulness.

"Yours is a big head, too, this morning?" asked Pietro. He sat in his nightshirt on the edge of the bed massaging his temples.

"Big head?" she murmured sleepily. Ah, the grappa vapors. The wine. She smiled ruefully. "*Si,* we were much too generous with the wine last night. . . ."

As soon as Pietro and his dinner pail had disappeared down Pastinetti Place, she fed the children and sent them to school. "Now he enters the shed," she thought. "He chats a moment with Ronato. . . . Now the shed whirrs with a deafening din, the men are at work. . . . He draws off the covering. He stares with unbelieving eyes. . . . Now comes Gerbati. Gerbati storms. The workmen gather around. Pietro is shamed before them. . . . 'Go to hell!' he shouts to Gerbati. 'I quit!' And he stalks away, leaves the shed forever!" She must prepare his favorite dinner: he would soon be home, dinner pail and all. He would be saddened, perplexed, enraged. He would enjoy *salsigi,* perhaps, and a fine *ensalata* of endive, tomatoes, and eggs.

The children ate the noonday meal and left again for school. No Pietro. Was he fine-combing Granitown this minute for another job. *Si,* that was it.

He came in shortly after four, his round face thoughtful, his head bent. He had neglected to slap the stonedust from his clothes. True, his heart must be heavy at leaving this work he loved, but she felt little sympathy. *Dio,* suppose an infant was attracted to red—would she not remove a red-hot poker from its reach, even though the babe screamed as if its heart were breaking? She waited patiently for his "Well, Maria, I did it. Today I quit the sheds." But he only muttered with a preoccupied air, "The days are getting too brisk for just a kitchen fire." And in a few minutes he was in the cellar, cleaning out the furnace.

After supper when the children were abed, he shrugged into his coat, explaining briefly, "I promised to help Rossi with his grappa tonight."

Pietro is Pietro, Maria consoled herself; he will say nothing until he has found a new job. He does not want me to worry. . . .

She was alone in the kitchen darning socks when Ronato entered, his long face drawn to extreme melancholy. He hung back, ill at ease. Despite the cold evening, his brow shone with sweat. He handed her a small square of red and white checked cambric. "Last night you wore a skirt of this cloth. The skirt was whole and pretty. Last night Pietro's stone was mutilated. This morning this piece of cloth waves accusation from a wire outside Gerbati's office window. And this morning, I wager, your skirt lacks this little square." He shook his head. An artist, he could find no rhyme to this outrageous act. His lean shoulders tried to shrug off the fury in him, and he turned to leave.

Maria's fingers clenched the square until her nails, cutting into the palms, smarted her to action. Her voice was fiercely anxious. "Does Pietro know?"

He shook his head.

"Gerbati?"

"No. I chanced to be searching the yard for a flat stone. I saw the cloth—and I remembered." He finished coldly, "Don't fear— I won't tell."

Even his contempt could not stop her from gripping his arm and pleading in wild hope and despair, "What happened, Ronato? What did Gerbati say? What did Gerbati do?"

"Do? Pietro did not tell you?"

"No, no. Not one word has he spoken!"

"Nothing happened, Maria."

Her hands fell rigidly to her sides.

"Gerbati did not give him hell?" Toneless words. "Pietro did not rebel and—quit?"

Ronato's slow eyes widened. He asked gruffly, "And why should Gerbati give him hell? Anyone could see it was no accident. It was the intentional butchering of some malefactor. Gerbati respects Pietro's love for stone. He had only to see his stricken face to know he was innocent."

Her shoulders drooped. Only her black eyes were defiantly alive.

He moved uncomfortably under their blaze. *Dio,* to have a woman love him as Maria loved Pietro. . . .

She whirled away. Never had a *paesano* seen a tear glisten in Maria Dalli's black eyes. Nor would Ronato see one tonight.

Marguerite Hurrey Wolf (1914-   )

Pig in a Bucket

I should no longer be surprised that our pleasure in raising pigs is not an emotion widely shared. In any group there are those who champion tropical fish, Labrador retrievers, or tuberous begonias, but not pigs. This wouldn't surprise me in Manhattan, or even in Westchester. But in northern Vermont even those who live in the country but earn their living in the nearby city, suffer sporadic attachments to saddle horses, a small flock of sheep or some bantam chickens. This attachment, however, does not seem to extend to pigs, even among our neighbors, most of whom are dairy farmers.

When a recent guest, a psychiatrist, explained in great detail that his success in trout fishing was based on his ability to think like a trout, I exclaimed happily, "Of course! The same thing is true in catching pigs."

The ensuing silence and tolerant glances in my husband's direction indicated that in the minds of the other guests, the psychiatrist's time in our home would be better spent professionally than socially.

On the way to thinking like a trout, the psychiatrist used many years and half the equipment in L.L. Bean's catalogue. The same thing has been achieved by intuitive country boys with garden worms and a willow wand.

Twice a year the psychiatrist escapes from the demands of his work and renews his strength with a fishing vacation. Twice a year we cannot escape from the fact that our two pigs are large enough to be butchered, and that we must renew the diminishing stock of pork in the freezer. We share two things in common with the psychiatrist. Both he and we can eat the products of our efforts, and both he and we backed into our respective skills through learning how NOT to catch our quarry.

There are all sorts of books on trout fishing, some with yellow sou'wester waterproof covers, so that you may go right on reading when you step into a deep hole and begin feeling like a trout. I have never seen a book on catching and loading pigs into a half-ton truck. It probably wouldn't be a fast moving item in most book stores.

We keep two pigs all the time for a variety of reasons. We have a large barn at a good distance from the house. They save us money in food bills. They require a minimum of care, and most important but least understood, we like pigs.

However, twice a year they must be loaded into the truck and taken to the slaughter house. A seven-month-old pig weighs about two hundred and fifty pounds, which is distributed in such a streamlined fashion that there is nothing to hang on to. Even if you could put a halter on a pig, it cannot be pulled. The harder you pull the harder the pig pulls the other way, and the pig has the edge on most of us in weight. Shoving won't work either, even if you have another pig fancier pulling on the front end. The pig, screeching in blood-curdling tones, whether you are holding a leg or an ear, will thrash and twist out of your grasp.

The first time we were faced with this problem was ten years and forty-six pigs ago. The memory of that morning is still too painful to describe objectively. We tried to fasten ropes around the pigs, but they slithered loose. We chased them through the garden and fields. Finally, by luck rather than skill, we cornered the two pigs in the barn where they were confined, though far from being loaded in the back of the Jeep station wagon. Shaken and bruised from head to foot, George leaned against the barn door and threatened to shoot the pigs. Only the fact that he was too exhausted to move postponed their doom. Hours later, we finally dragged the shrieking floundering pigs up a wooden ramp into the wagon and set off on a limp journey to town.

In true Vermont fashion, none of our neighbors offered unsolicited advice to George. But when I described our struggle to one friend, he told me that all you had to do was put a bucket over a pig's head and back it to whatever destination you had in mind. When he added that it helped if someone else grabbed the tail and steered the pig, I suspected that my city-bred leg was being pulled once more, and dismissed his words from my mind.

It was not until the next summer that I remembered his suggestion and offered it tentatively to George. Softened by the memory of bruises and a sprained knee, my husband agreed to let me try. I put a little grain in the bottom of a pail and climbed into the pen with the pigs. While George knocked off the boards on one side, I enticed the pig to try a bite. The moment her head was in the bucket, George grabbed her tail, while I pushed from the bucket end, and all three of us sailed out of the pig pen, up through the barnyard and were inside the Jeep in three minutes!

It couldn't be true. It was too easy; just luck. So with some doubts, the next season we once again started to load pigs.

This time it was early morning and George and I were going to load the pigs before he went to his office. We had only a half an hour. When neither pig showed any interest in the pail, George lunged at them and all was lost. He and the two pigs chased each other around making angry noises. We gave up and went in for breakfast.

After breakfast, with George at work and the children at school, I began to wonder. The Jeep was still parked half-way in the barn door. The ramp was in place on the tail gate. Could I . . . ? Would it be possible to load those two pigs by myself? When, if I got one in the station wagon, could I keep it there while I loaded the other? With pounding heart, I planned my strategy. First I put an appetizing mound of lettuce leaves in the back of the Jeep. Then I mixed some grain and water in the pail. Singing Brahms' lullaby with words improvised for pig loading, I held the pail in the pig pen and tried to act disinterested. Immediately one pig thrust her snout in the pail. I jammed it farther onto her head and backed her out of the pen. The ramp was narrow, and without George's guiding hand on the curly rudder, she backed off the side on to the barn floor. But I stayed with her, keeping the pail over her head and shoving with all my strength. The air was limited in the pail. She was gasping. So was I. The thought that she was weakening gave me second wind and we plunged up the ramp into the Jeep. She immediately became engrossed in the lettuce, as I had hoped, and I crawled out to find the other pig.

He was grunting curiously at the tail gate. I slammed the pail over his head and backed him in a wide arc so that his rear end would come around to the wooden ramp. There's a lot of strength in a pig. I was losing mine rapidly along with the skin from several knuckles. My arms were quivering from exertion. Halfway up the ramp he began to fold his hind legs under him and sit down.

"Please . . ." I gasped. "PLEASE get in there!"

I shut my eyes and strained till little lights danced before my eyes. Miraculously, the pig backed up the ramp and into the Jeep. With shaking hands I closed the tail gate and leaned against it, panting. I was dripping wet. I was also streaked with a gruel of grain and water. I staggered into the front seat and slowly drove off with my shifting grunting cargo.

It wasn't necessary to go past George's office to get to the slaughter house; in fact it was quite a bit out of the way. But there are times when the shortest distance is beside the point. The driveway at the Medical College went right under the windows of George's office. I pulled up beneath the windows and serenaded him with the horn. The pigs added their hoarse baritones. No response, so I leaned on the horn with more than necessary fervor. I had hoped to see George, but in a moment four heads appeared at the windows. A family affair was one thing, but I was hardly dressed for an executive committee meeting. Four jaws dropped. Four noses were grasped between thumb and forefinger, and four mouths burst into laughter.

There are a few moments in life which are too tightly packed with emotion to allow space for words. The laughter was applause, and I was giddy with pride.

Noel Perrin (1927-   )

Steam Coming Out the Vent

For some reason, town meeting day in Vermont—the first Tuesday after the first Monday in March—is almost always warm and sunny. Winter has by no means ended. It is going to snow again at least three or four times. Fields won't be starting to green up until mid-April. Lilacs and apple blossoms won't be out until May. But when you get home from town meeting at two or three in the afternoon, the temperature is up to sixty. Snow water is dripping from all the eaves, and you can almost hear the maples pumping sap. It is irresistible to hang a few buckets. Even though you remember clearly from last year that the sap ran only one day, and then the temperature stayed below forty for a week and you didn't get another drop, the afternoon is just too nice to waste.

Town meeting day in 1970 was like the rest: blue skies and a cunning semblance of spring. A little after three P.M. my daughters and I emerged from the barn. I was carrying a brace and bit, a hammer, and a clean sap bucket containing a pile of freshly washed spouts. Lily, the nine-year-old, was staggering behind me with a stack of buckets; and Margaret, the six-year-old, came last with the lids. It was hard walking, because there was still two feet of snow on the ground, and the crust had completely rotted since morning.

We were heading for a row of hundred-year-old maples along the road in front of our house. They are fortunately on the higher side of the road, so that only a little highway salt gets to them. With luck, they won't be completely killed for another twenty years. (I have already started their replacements: a row of saplings dug up in the woods, set halfway between each of the old trees and ten feet further back from the road. They should be ready for tapping soon after the year 2000. I hope to be sitting on the front porch, quavering advice.)

When our procession reached the first tree, I went around to the south side, where sap usually runs best, and found a place directly under a big branch where there was no scar from an old tap. I drilled the first hole, and hammered in a spout. A few seconds later sap began dripping out, the drops in such quick succession that it was almost a tiny stream. A fraction of a second after that, all the buckets and all the lids were in the snow, and the girls were fighting over who would be the first to put her mouth up to the spout and get the year's first drink of new sap. I have often wondered if the settlers, with eight or ten children each, and their troughs just sitting on the ground, didn't lose a lot of sap. Parental discipline must have been sterner then.

By four o'clock we had eighteen buckets up, two on the southerly side of each front tree. Even from the house you could hear one of the nicest of all spring sounds, which is the ping of sap dripping into empty buckets. You don't get that with plastic tubing. I don't suppose you got it with the old wooden buckets, either.

The rest of my buckets I planned not to hang until mid-March. I didn't have them all washed, anyway. But if there was a good early run, I'd at least get some of it. And there was. Thursday and Friday were both warm after freezing nights, and by Saturday most of the buckets were full, and the rest at least half. These were sixteen-quart buckets from Messer, which means that I had sixty-some gallons of sap to play with. By kitchen standards, this is a formidable quantity.

Saturday was another blue and gold day, and the minute I stepped outside, I knew I was not only going to gather but to try my first boiling. I had had Mr. Illsley's tank soaking since Tuesday, and it was now fully taken up and ready to use. Also remarkably heavy. By tipping it up on one side and then using my thighs as a fulcrum, I was just able to hoist it into the back of the truck.

Even with the girls to help, it took longer than I had expected to empty eighteen buckets. A truck, of course, won't come when called, and I was constantly in and out of the cab driving it another few feet down the road. Furthermore, a full sap bucket is impossible for a small girl to carry, and not easy even for a grown man. It has no handle, it weighs about thirty pounds, and it sloshes terribly. (That's why I've since been back to Grimm's and bought two flare-lipped gathering pails for $9 each.) We probably spilled six or eight gallons in the process of gathering.

To my dismay, the tank had only about a foot of sap in the bottom when we were done, and the thought did cross my mind that it would be prudent to wait a few days before boiling. I could use today to wash the rest of the buckets, and maybe paint the Illsley ones. I firmly repressed the thought, though, and we drove on down the hundred feet from the last tree to the sugarhouse. The sun was high, and the rapid ping of sap dripping into the newly empty buckets sounded reassuring. There'd be a few more gallons by noon, if I needed them.

I had worked out my plans long before. Not having a storage tank, I intended to run sap into the evaporator directly from the truck. The dirt road where it goes past the sugarhouse is about eighteen inches higher than the house site. (If you'd asked me that morning, I would have said three feet.) With the added elevation of the truck, I could easily park at the edge of the road and pipe in by gravity. An hour's boiling, and I'd have a gallon of syrup—the pale delicate fancy grade that you get from the very first sap. Other years I thought I'd done well to get three or four babyfood jars of first-run.

In actual fact, it took more than an hour just to get the sap flowing. I had long ago bought twenty feet of one-inch plastic pipe ($3.60 at Nichols Hardware in Lyme, New Hampshire) and attached one end to the intake valve of the evaporator. It took about a minute to fit the other end into a coupling and the coupling into the new hose on my tank. When nothing at all happened, my first thought was to unhook the evaporator end and try sucking on it, as people do when siphoning gas. Again nothing happened. It was Lily who found the ice plug where the pipe sagged lowest in the middle, and she and Mag who worked an eight-inch lump of ice out with their hands. The next suck got me a mouthful of sap (it beats gasoline), but no stream followed. Not enough elevation. Eventually I worked a couple of old beams under the tank, raising it another six inches. Then at last the evaporator began to fill with a steady gurgling sound. While it filled, the girls and I laid a fire in the grate, chiefly of alder branches and barn boards. Then I opened the steam vents and lit the fire.

You get a superb draft with an evaporator, and about two minutes later the first wisp of steam arose from the sap. A minute or two after that, the red paint began to blacken on the furnace doors, and at the same instant the first little wave of boiling began. Shortly thereafter the whole back pan went into a rolling boil, and a continuous eight-square-foot cloud of white steam began ascending to the steam vent and out both sides of it. I rushed out the door to see what it looked like from outside. What it looked like is hard to describe. For some reason the sugarhouse reminded me of a Viking helmet, the great plumes of steam, now gold-colored in the sunlight, being the horns. This mass of steam coming out in perfect silence and then floating away on the wind also reminded me by an even looser association of a clipper ship leaving port with sails just up. But all it actually looked like, I suppose, is a sugarhouse in the spring.

Shrieks from Lily brought me back in. Both pans were now boiling at high speed, and a thick, yellowy-white foam had formed all over the surface and was beginning to mount rapidly in the corners. I was prepared for it. Included with the evaporator had come a tin skimmer—an instrument like a trim, very narrow dustpan, with perforations all over the bottom. For the first time I skimmed the pans. Some sugar makers fling the foam on the floor, but I was (and am) too proud of my sugarhouse, and sent it flying out into the snow. The sap had already taken on a faint tinge of color, and enough was going out as steam so that the float valves had opened, and a steady stream was flowing in from the truck to the first pan and from the first pan to the second.

Just after I finished skimming and putting a little more wood on the fire, I learned a new social fact about Vermont. I see no truth at all to the myth that New Englanders are taciturn—they love gossip as well as anyone I ever knew—but the talk takes place mostly on neutral ground: in stores and barnyards, at auctions and church suppers. Your house is private. Vermonters are less likely to drop in unannounced for coffee than most other Americans, or to have you over for the evening. There are about two hundred people in Thetford Center, and I would guess I know a hundred and ninety of them. But I have not been in more than a dozen houses, and most people have never been in mine.

A different custom prevails for sugarhouses. Steam had been rolling out for about fifteen minutes now, and people in the village had had time to see it. I don't say they came pouring out of their houses and down to visit, but one or two at a time, a remarkable number did appear. First came Gordon Fifield, who lives just across the covered bridge, with stories about sugaring when he was a boy. Then Rob Hunter. Then a man, actually not from the village at all, who delivers milk for Billings Dairy. (He's not the same milkman I bought two pigs from a few years ago, but his successor.) Then Russell Jamieson—Mickey's father—who happened to be passing in his truck. I am clear that if I ever build another sugarhouse that's visible from a traveled road, I will make it considerably larger than eight feet by eleven. Ken Bragg's, which I was in for the first time just recently, is probably about right. There's room in his, on one side of the evaporator, and not crowding it any, for a row of armchairs.

It was Russell who pointed out to me that I was just about to have an emergency. I was so busy talking and skimming and keeping Margaret from opening the draw-off tap that I hadn't noticed that the stream of new sap had ceased coming in. The level in the back pan was sinking fast. Most sugar makers keep a bucket of water standing by for such cases, and I had one, too. But you hate to thin your sap that way; and while Russell opened the grate doors to chill the fire, I rushed out to check the tank. There was about three inches of sap left in the bottom, but not a drop flowing. I tipped it up on its side and held it long enough to run most of the remaining sap in, and then I let my fire go out and closed down for the day, without having made any syrup at all. What I had in the back pan was about twenty gallons of a pale amber fluid, perceptibly thicker and sweeter than sap, but nothing like syrup. In the little flat-bottomed front pan I had a couple of gallons of some stuff sweet enough so that Maggie and Lily each drank a cupful with relish (you set the cup on a snowbank for a couple of minutes first to cool it), but probably no more than half-way to syrup. I had been boiling for just over an hour. That afternoon it snowed a little, the temperature dropped, and the sap quit running.

I hung the rest of my buckets the next Saturday. That is, I hung another twenty-two, since I never had got the Illsley buckets painted, and one Messer bucket was down in the sugarhouse full of water. It was good sugar weather, and the sap was running briskly. Four days after that I had a day off from school and spent it boiling again. Willis Wood, the student who had come with me to buy the evaporator, worked with me. This time the gathering tank was full to the top when we started, which meant we had 125 gallons.

The partly boiled sap in the pans had been sitting there eleven days, but it was frozen solid. I don't believe it had deteriorated much—any more than frozen orange juice does in a grocer's counter. It was not only thawed but steaming within six or seven minutes of the time we started the fire. It soon did more. I had been content the previous time to keep the surface of the pans at a brisk rolling boil. But Willis is more adventuresome. He said his cousin Augustus down in Weathersfield, who is eighty-two and who has sugared every spring for seventy years now, kept the sap in *his* pans leaping up like storm waves breaking on a rocky coast. Otherwise you're just fooling around, said Willis.

With my reluctant consent, he began stuffing barn boards into the fire as fast as they'd go. A sort of low murmur went over the pans, the column of steam visibly thickened, and for the first time a cloud bank began to build up under the sugarhouse roof. All the windows misted over simultaneously. Then the whole surface of boiling sap surged up, something like fifty pots on a stove all boiling over at once. (This is no exaggeration, but a slight understatement. I checked. My wife's pots range from saucepans five inches in diameter to one big ten-incher for cooking corn on the cob. Her two favorites are sixes. When one of them boils over, a twenty-eight-square-inch surface surges up. With the evaporator, 1,728 square inches of boiling surface are involved, or sixty-one pots' worth.) Just before there was a flood, Willis slammed the draft shut, and the whole surface gradually sank down again, still boiling hard. He opened it part way, and it started back up. We seemed doomed to fool around.

At that point something Russell Jamieson told me popped into mind. I had known all along that syrup pans sometimes surge up, though I hadn't realized it was quite so dramatic. I knew from Grimm's catalogue that there was a chemical on the market called Atmos 300, which is supposed to prevent this. But I had no idea of putting Atmos 300 in my sap, any more than I would plant stilbestrol pellets under the skin behind a calf's ear to force him to grow faster. That's not farming, that's outdoor chemistry.

I also had heard of a nineteenth-century technique for keeping pans from boiling over, which is to suspend a little piece of pork fat from a rafter, so that it dangles over your back pan, just below the rim. When the boiling sap leaps up and touches it, just enough gets melted to stop the high boiling. It can't really make maple sugar taste like pork fat, or Vermont sugar wouldn't have kept its good reputation. But I wasn't attracted to the pork-fat system, either.

Russell, though, was a dairy farmer for thirty years, and he knows a lot of dairy tricks. He had described the magical effect when you let one drop of cream fall onto the stormy surface of an evaporator. While Willis stayed to tinker with the draft and keep skimming, I hurried up to the house. We turned out not to have any cream, but we did have a pint of Billings Coffee-Cereal Special. When I came back with it, we opened the draft full, waited until the upward surge began, and then I stuck my finger in the Coffee-Cereal Special, and let one drop fall into the pan. It does look like magic. The whole pan quits tossing at once, and even the humming sound dies away, though the column of steam rises as thickly as before. I always keep a little jar of cream on a handy snowbank now.

This being a weekday morning, there were fewer visitors than there had been the first time. But one of the town listers—in most of America they're called tax assessors—did show up in mid-morning. He said he wanted to ask me some questions about a piece of land I had sold. I think he also wanted to watch a little sugaring, and reminisce. It was no moment to sit down and chat, because with our new fast-boil system we were getting to have something very close to maple syrup in the front pan. Willis and I were just hesitating whether to draw the first batch off. In other years, making a half-pint at a time on the kitchen stove, I had judged the product by taking a little out in a teaspoon and seeing if it tasted right. It always tasted delicious, and the syrup fairly often turned out later to be a little thin. No harm when it's for home consumption, but now I was a commercial producer. All the same, we had some in the scoop now, and were tasting.

The lister watched for a moment, and then asked us if we knew about aproning. Neither of us did. (Cousin Augustus has an ancient hydrometer.) So he took the scoop, dipped it in the finishing pan, and then held it vertically over the pan until the last drops were trembling on the edge. Then they aproned. Instead of falling, they slowly merged until there was a little curving apron across the rim of the scoop, looking rather like maple taffy. "Draw her off, boys," he said triumphantly, and we did. We got a gallon and a half of fine first-run syrup.

Mr. Bisbee back in 1872 would have left the syrup standing a couple of days to let the nitrates and the sugar sand settle out, and then canned it cold. (Or, more likely, he would have taken it on down to maple sugar, which formed 90 percent of the crop in those days.) Willis and I ran ours through a double filter: an inner paper one and an outer felt one, both of which I had bought at Grimm's. $3.25 for the felt, 35 cents for the paper. The felt will last indefinitely; some people throw away a paper one after using—and washing—it no more than eight or ten times. Then we canned the first gallon on the spot, put a quart in a jar for Willis to take home as pay, and left the last quart still slowly dripping through. Before lunch we made another gallon.

I had a good supply of cans ready, having saved them up for five years from all the syrup we had bought, which was a couple of gallons a year. The one to three quarts I had been making myself each spring never even lasted until summer. I have a feeling you're not supposed to reuse Vermont Sugarmakers Association cans, but I have been careful never to ask. Anyway, I am not alone in reusing them. There used to be a hardware store in White River Junction—a tall old store full of parts for plough harness and big wooden hayrakes—that always had a whole tableful of them for sale, rather like the bookstores on Fourth Avenue in New York that sell slightly used review copies of new books at half price.

When the season ended on April sixteenth, I had made eight and a half gallons from forty buckets. A little low, but then I got half the buckets up late. Three gallons I kept for my family, and one I gave away. Willis Wood got a quart for pay, and so did Gary Fifield, a Thetford Academy senior who is roughly Gordon's second cousin. He dropped in at the third boiling, and stayed to work. That left four gallons to sell, all of which I sold in half-gallon cans at $4 each, for total cash receipts of $32. In each case the buyer was someone I knew who was aware he was getting his syrup in a secondhand though spotless can. I didn't grade it, because I didn't have a state grading set. In my opinion, what I sold was all Grade A. The Fancy grade I either kept or gave as presents; and the one gallon that was clearly Grade B I also kept, because Lily loves it strong and dark.

As against total expenditures of $508.23—I have now added in the plastic pipe and the filters—$32.00 is a fairly poor return. It would be even worse if I figured in any value for the several hundred hours of my time I put in building the house and sugaring, or counted truck time to Royalton, Randolph, and Rutland. Furthermore, most of the profit I immediately spent on the two gathering pails and the hydrometer. But I have three lines of defense against critical comment.

First, this was my prentice year. I expect to do better in the future. This year I expect to hang sixty buckets (an evaporator the size of mine will handle up to two hundred) and to get a full quart from each. That will be fifteen gallons, of which I expect to sell ten or eleven. Even granting that this time I'll be paying for new half-gallon cans at 38½ cents each, net receipts will be in the neighborhood of $75. In time, as Lily and Margaret get stronger and we hang more buckets, they may reach $100 and even more.

Second, there is the question of what I would be doing if I weren't sugaring. I observe that many of my fellow teachers put in *their* spare time in March getting in a little late skiing, going to the movies, and watching hockey on television. Their receipts are invariably $0.00, and what with lift tickets and Head skis and one thing and another, their expenses often exceed mine. Nor do they wind up with a year's supply of syrup. On the contrary, most of them feel they can't afford decent syrup for their own pancakes, and are getting supermarket stuff which is 6 percent maple or 5½ percent maple or—this is superstition, not flavor—2 percent maple. The ones who mostly watch movies, as a matter of fact, don't even dare eat pancakes, because they are afraid of getting fat. Whereas if they were getting out the frock and milking stool, or hanging a few buckets, they could eat what they pleased.

But my last line of defense is the one I put most stock in. Sugaring, even on a much larger scale than mine, is not really a commercial operation. It is that happiest of combinations, a commercial affair which is also an annual rite, even an act of love. I will quote two old sugar makers as evidence. One is a man named L. C. Davis of South Reading, Vermont. In 1878 he gave a speech to an audience he addressed as "Brother Farmers." He began by quoting Thomas Jefferson on farming in general ("Tillers of the soil are the chosen of the Lord"), and then he launched into sugaring techniques—about as much from the point of view of the maple tree as that of the farmer. Mr. Davis felt, for example, that no maple, even the biggest, should be asked to handle more than one spout. But he had noticed many of his neighbors putting in three or even four, just as I do. (I go by a rule which says don't tap a tree until it's ten inches in diameter. One spout from there to eighteen inches, then two, and so on up to a maximum of four.) Mr. Davis could not have approved less. "To such I would say: you ought to have a guardian put over you, and if the trees could speak, they would have it done. Why will you abuse this most noble of trees, the sugar maple?" These are not the words of a businessman—though Mr. Davis made good money out of sugaring—but of a lover.

My other witness, Lyman Newton of Fairfield, was not so much in love with maple trees as he was with Vermont itself. But he expressed his love through the spring rites at the evaporator. In 1885 he gave a speech before the State Board of Agriculture. He started by talking about sugar in general, dwelling on its plebian origin. (Beets! Sorgo grass!) Then he turned to sugar in its lordly condition. His style rises—slightly—to the occasion. Echoes of the King James Bible can be heard in his normally flat storekeeper prose.

"Here in Northern Vermont we neither raise the Southern cane nor the Western sorghum, neither do we make beet sugar; but we are credited with making a superior article of maple sugar, a kind of sweet that when made with care retains its moisture and rich aromatic flavor, rendering it more acceptable to consumers than the most refined and highly-scented candies of the confectioner; and where introduced is almost always sure to sell, and especially is this the case among those who spent their childhood and youth in a maple sugar country. Hence the West has become to us a market for maple sugar. Vermonters have gone everywhere, and when spring comes they remember, like the children of Israel, not the leeks and garlics but the sugar works of their native hills. . . . And they attempt, although many times vainly, to satisfy their appetite by going to the grocery, where they inquire of the proprietor if he has Vermont maple sugar on hand, and they are informed that "he has a small lot of *new* direct from the

East,' and without waiting to investigate, they make a purchase. They get about as near Vermont maple sugar as oleomargarine is like Vermont butter."

When you're producing a sacred article, you don't have to maximize your cash return.

Frances Frost (1905-1959)

Advice to a Trespasser

There are several ways of crossing barbed-wire fences
According to your inner differences
On various occasions. Seize a post
And climb and teeter, and if something's lost
From hand or leg in jumping, say that skin
Is minor penalty for that bright sin
Of trespassing. Another way's to spread
The wire, bend double, get your graceless head
Through first. The rest of you will follow after,
Severely scratched and panicky with laughter.

In search of stargrass or blackberry plunder,
I always drop to earth, roll quickly under,
And come up sandy, grass-stained, nearly whole.
But he who trespasses must heed his soul,
Find his own devilish and delightful knack
For crossing fences—and for getting back.

The Inarticulate

I laid my forehead on a rock
Ice-floods had chiseled deep and broken,
And suddenly I was aware
The inarticulate had spoken.

I heard what frantic fires were loosed
In boulders, now stern-locked and narrow,

What blazing yields were flung from stone,
Burned out to black and long unfallow.

I learned the agony of ice,
The gaunt despair of granite clinging
To orchard slope and hill and field,
Beneath a dark hawk's carven winging.

I laid my forehead on a sun
Spent and frozen, scarred and broken.
By my stone heart I was aware
The inarticulate had spoken.

Little Poem for Evening

The dusky sound
Of a heifer's bell
Told me when
The evening fell
With a windy sigh
Across the cool,
Starry, swiftly
Shaken pool;
Told me with
A darker note
When a star went down
A tawny throat.

Language

This is a country of little rivers—
Dog river, Mississquoi, Otter creek—
Slicing villages with gold at sunrise,

Looping them with silver on yellow afternoons,
Putting them to sleep with cloud-purple and mountain-purple at
    dusk.
This is a country of small rivers running north and west—
Winooski, Lamoille, Ottauqueechee;
And the Connecticut going south and keeping the maples of
    Vermont
From burning with the maples of New Hampshire.
Apple trees on a slope say what a man cannot say
And ask questions a man cannot ask,
Knowing he will not be answered.
A grindstone under apple trees by a white house,
Old wagons under apple trees by a deserted barn,
A scythe hung in the low crotch of an apple tree east of a rocky
    hill—
These are the stunted speech of a country
Slow to live and equally slow to die.
Stone walls in the South,
Piled along hill-ridges and through the woods,
Stone walls up as far as Dorset and Chelsea.
Split-rail fences in the North,
Zigzagging between fields,
Running beside the roads.
Barbed-wire fences in the North, for pastures,
Barbed-wire for hay-fields and river-lots.
In the North we leave the stones where they grew . . .
Wetly out of brook bottoms,
Jagged and dark out of the hills.
Stone walls, fences, rivers, apple trees—
These speak of a slow country,
Of white-spired villages between two hills
And the loves and hates and passions between two hills.
These talk of abandoned farms and abandoned lives
And of men who ask no questions of the earth,
Knowing earth will not answer.
Stone walls, rivers, fences, apple trees—

These are the language of a slow country,
The curious speech of a rock-bitten,
Inarticulate heart.

The Children

When I grow up, I want to be . . .
Why do the great-eyed children
still have faith in us whose brows are marked
with the blood of our human kill? Do they not know
we'll kill them too—they with their sun-browned knees,
their tree-scratched legs and impudent small noses?

We lean to them, with secret mirth we ask,
slyly hiding death behind our backs,
What do you want to be when you grow up?
and eagerly, with candor and with faith
in some strange dream they've picked up God knows where,
they answer us as if the world were fair,
as if they *could* grow up!

The boy with fiddle fingers, and the girl
with a thrush's throat,
the sturdy one who wants a grocery store
and all the licorice sticks that he can eat
and a tiger cat to drowse in the Sunday window,
the scientist, the doctor, and the farmer,
the one who takes apart and reassembles,
the little girl whose doll has feeding schedules,
the pilot and the poet and the builder,
the pigtailed Einstein and the freckled Christ . . .
they answer us with certainty as if
we were on their side in their growing up.

Don't they know that we intend to stop them?
Don't they know we have the bombs and gas?

Don't they know we've won the sky? It's ours,
and we can put an end to all this growing.
Sometimes I have a feeling that they know:
times when they look at us with fearless eyes
and say, *When I grow up, I want to be* . . .
and turn away and gaze into the evening
with calm light in their faces. Oh, they know
we're not on their side, and they mean to fight!
They're brave and tough and beautiful, they know
some of them will grow up, in spite of us.

Footnote

What can I say of the death of the russet vixen,
her young in her belly, of the beautiful and shy
and breaking heart of the young buck brought to his knees?
What can I say when the lean bell-throated hound
closes upon the spent hare's throat?
                                        I seize
the meaning of the poet's suicide
and the refugee's, I annotate the breath
turned fire in the airman's lungs, or torn from what
was once a soldier's mouth.
                                But there is neither
proportion nor equality in death:
what can I say of the dying of the vixen,
what can I say of the fawn on the spattered ground?

Tide of Lilac

From the Kennebec to Casco,
from Lebanon to Dover,

from Champlain to New Bedford,
lilac has taken over.

On roads to Narragansett,
by Cornwall cellar holes,
the lilac spires are clustered
to plague New England souls.

Purple in clean-swept dooryards,
guarding the worn doorstones,
lilac invades the marrow
of reticent strong bones.

And careful housewives shiver,
and cautious men bite lips,
when they, with no one looking,
touch blue with their fingertips.

James Hayford (1913-   )

Processional with Wheelbarrow

With every move I've made today
Four lambs paired up to lead the way,
Or follow, in high-tailed array.

To an unheard overture
We're marching with manure
In rites that seem obscure.

What are we out to celebrate—
The Force that makes seeds germinate,
Or the Grace that makes men meditate?

From the arch look on the features
Of four of us five creatures,
I'd say the day was Nature's.

On the Opening of a Superhighway

They are almost all gone who can recall
How any range of hills was once a wall,
And a hollow was a room and not a hall.

A change was a half-day's walk to the opposite range;
A wonder was a visit to the Grange
In the next hollow—strange street, new and strange.

A treat was local talent playing parts,
Dressed up and mannered so to steal our hearts,
Which seldom had the comfort of the arts.

And from these separate rooms a few went forth,
On bands of gravel winding south and north—
The few that glorified their place of birth.

Leland Kinsey (1950-   )

Deep in the Sleep Gorged Side

The snow voice vibrates
To the weight of the stoneboat
Crossing the stiff-banked white,
Bearing my father's body
Home to its life's last night,
Home to the couch in the house's bowels.

I sit by his side as the night slips in,
Sunlight drawn to the hawk's sharp wings,
Compass to the tangent moon
As they slice across traceways of field mice,
The hare's deep run,
To spring from the sullen sky
Leaving all to owl-light.
The voice of the hyla is far in the wood.

He cries for his father
Dead in the war,
Dead at Salonika, malarial underbelly
On the sea's blue shore.
His father was a telegram.

The house is couched in humid leaves
The trees spewed months before
And left to lie rotting here.
The water that ran in their veins
Fumes in the stream's white race,
The stream where I hunted salamanders has gone
Hurtling all landward or seaward.
The salamanders that I caught all died,
Still paler bellies to the sun.

The night is done.
Earth protrudes its belly sunward.
Stalks stand still,
Winter-killed weeds with lost heads.
Skunk cabbages spear the snow
With spathes as purple as the sky.
There is a fire of thorns
Deep in the sleep gorged side of my father
As he holds his hands to his ribs and cries
For the long lost.

An owl dives its one last time
Before it hies homeward
To be replaced by the circling hawk.
Far below them a salamander rises from its muddy bed;
I too am dumb
Beside the hollow shell of my father.

We will bury him at the side of his mother
Under the stone bearing the text she chose
When she knew that she could not survive.
"Now is the accepted time; behold,
Now is the day of salvation."
He has no horses or they would be killed,
Throats slit, and buried on the granite-backed hill
Where grandfather's horses are bone in harness
Remembering still the true and steady hand.

The horses are moving,
I can smell the carrion air they breathe,
But the coach and four has been replaced.
Far off, an early morning train whistle;
A lone traveller embarks
Upon this mechanical amphibian sliding north
On its whitened paunch,
Swimming in the year's last snow.
It will travel far today, but it will fare well,
Farewell proud father.

Howard Frank Mosher (1942-   )

Alabama Jones

I should have known better than to stop when I saw her standing there by the side of the road in a dress as red as the maple tree she was standing under. I should have taken just one look at that short red dress and gunned Frog LaMundy's log truck on by as fast as she would go. But it was four o'clock on a bright October day, and I was headed home with nothing but chips and dust in my rig and cold beer frosting my insides and Kingdom Fair to go to that night and the next. I began to shift down.

First she was standing under the tree as still as a deer watching you go by from the woods' edge of a meadow at dawn. Then she was running like that same deer would run if you started to slow down, running on the gravel shoulder alongside the road with her bare legs moving as brown and fast and slim as a deer's, it seemed, and jumping onto the running board and up into the cab before I had any more than shifted down into first gear. Before I could even reach out and swing open that heavy door for her, she was inside the cab, talking.

"I don't believe it. Now that I am here I still don't believe it. It is like a color postcard, I reckon, like my brother used to send us. No, not a color postcard, but a round card with little films pressed onto it that you put into a machine to look at. One was of a palace in India with water in front, and one was mountains, the Alps, I believe, and one of the Empire Building in New York City, so high it made you dizzy if you looked at it too long. And one like this. Underneath it said *Autumn in the White Mountains*. Since this morning I have been saying it put me in mind of a color postcard when that is not it at all. Because a postcard is flat. But when I looked into that picture machine at *Autumn in the White Moun-*

tains it was like looking at these trees and hills through a pair of field glasses, with every tree standing out separate. With every leaf standing out separate even."

She was different from what I had expected. Without actually thinking of the words, I had just naturally expected that she would be hard and quiet, and maybe resentful of me that had a truck to ride in. I had expected her to have suspicious eyes, too, but when I looked at them they were only blue, pale blue, and her hair was black and straight and long. She had an arch of freckles spattered over the bridge of her nose, and she was about my age, twenty or so.

"Say, you got beer," she said. She was not exactly asking. It was more like the idea of me having beer or maybe the idea of the beer itself pleased her. Like she had not had time to think about beer for some time, and now thinking about it again pleased her. I reached under the seat where I had put the sixpack and got out a bottle and handed it to her. She twisted off the cap, tipped back her head, and drank half of it. I could see the cords in her throat ripple as she drank, almost the way a man's neck moves when he is chugging down beer after working all day in the woods, only with a man it is his whole neck that moves and not cords rippling.

"So this is what you are running," she said. "I reckon maybe you are running this up to Canada. I reckon maybe this is what half the people in this state do for work, the way they have passed me up on the road for the past two days. Like they had a secret they didn't want me to find out. Men and all. Passed me up like they never saw me at all, even the truckers. Except for you I believe I would be back there by that tree all night. They just passed by me like I wasn't even there at all, like I was part of the tree. I never see such a hard place to get a ride on the road as up here in these White Mountains."

"This is Vermont," I said. "Kingdom County. The White Mountains are across the river in New Hampshire."

"I reckon this is the White Mountains, all right," she said. "I can remember that picture machine. *Autumn in the White Mountains,* it said. It din't say nothing about any Vermont. Capital of which is Montpelier, by the way. But this ain't it. I reckon there couldn't be two places on earth like *Autumn in the White Mountains.*"

She tipped back her head to drink, and then there was a clatter. I looked over past her legs where her empty bottle was rolling back and forth on the coiled log chain on the floorboard. Her legs were brown and slim and hard. You could see where the road dust left off above her knees.

"It is plain to see why you stopped for me," she said fast. "You was looking at my legs, the way you are now. Well, go ahead. If I can look on your White Mountains I reckon you can look on my legs. If I din't want folks to look I reckon I could cover them with a sack."

I reached out two more beers from under the seat and gave one to her and opened one for myself. They were still quite cold.

Her name was Alabama Jones and she was a singer in her brother's traveling show. On the last night of Chittenden Fair she had been carried unconscious in an ambulance to a Burlington hospital with appendicitis which for three days she had thought was stomach grippe. The doctors had said she would be in the hospital two weeks. Six days after undergoing an emergency operation for the ruptured appendix she had left the hospital in the night wearing her red dress and sandals and started walking north on roads she did not know to rejoin her brother's show at Caledonia Fair. She walked all the first night. The second night she slept in the back seat of an abandoned Chevrolet on a mountain road. She had gotten to Caledonia that morning, two hours after her brother had left for Kingdom Fair, forty miles north. That was now her destination.

"He will for sure be surprised when I show up tonight," she said. "He told Pappy he would look out for me before Pappy would leave me go off with him to sing. And then he went off and left me alone in that building with all those people I din't know. I see you got a radio. You mind?"

She turned on the switch and got the country and western station from Sherbrooke. Loretta Lynne was singing *Wine, Women, and Song.* When the song ended Alabama switched off the radio and began to sing it herself, exaggerating the country twang.

"Wouldn't you know," she said. "Wouldn't you just know that is the kind of earwash they play over the radio up here. I grew up hearing this stuff on the radio morning till midnight, and now I have to hear the same thing every place we go. Every place we go they have got some tonedeaf jake with what he believes is a southern accent that has never been south of New York playing country over the radio until you can smell it. Having to listen to them whine and moan like a cow in heat is one of the main reasons I left home." She was pressing her hand against her side now and her lips were pulled in tight against her teeth.

"Can I stop?" I said. "So you can rest?"

"No," she said. "No, go on. I will be all right soon. It was just that singing on the radio that done it. I have got to sing tonight at that Kingdom Fair, I reckon. I din't know it was showing." She curled up her legs under herself and put her head back on the seat and went to sleep.

I took the county road up the back side of the lake instead of going on up the state road through the Common the way I usually go, telling myself that I would leave Frog's truck up home and take Alabama down to the fair grounds on the edge of the Common in the car, telling myself that I didn't want to get into the traffic snarl around the grounds with the truck, and knowing all the time that it was a lie. It was getting toward evening when I turned off the county road into our lane at the top of the lake and came through the sugar maples, as polished and yellow as hard butter, out onto the pasture. The sun slanted low across the grass and it shone as green as early April. The milkers were strung out in the barbwire lane between the barn and the pasture, so I knew that Lucien had already finished chores.

She sat up straight and opened her eyes just as we came into the dooryard. I put Frog's truck by the barn. "Here we are," I said.

"Here we are," she said, and I saw that her forehead was wet and her eyes were bright. She did not open her door.

"Come on," I said. "Come on in and meet my father. Then I'll drive you down to the fair in the car."

"I reckon I will wait on you here," she said. "You go in and meet him yourself. Maybe your father will not want to meet a girl you have picked-up on the road that sings in a show."

"You do not know Lucien," I said. "He is half French and will be pleased to meet any girl."

"Sure. I reckon I will wait on you here," she said.

I got out and went up to the house. Lucien was sitting at the kitchen table looking at a girlie magazine. "Home at last," he said, not looking up. "I thought you was laid over drunk in a roadhouse again."

"There is the French in you," I said. "Unlike some of my near relatives, I do not drink on the job."

"No, nor girl-it neither you will tell me next," he said, looking at the pictures in the magazine. "Who is that woman out in the truck?" From where he was sitting Lucien could not possibly have seen the truck. He will surprise you every time. Just when you think there is some little thing he does not know, he comes up behind you and says it in your ear. That is Lucien for you.

"Her name is Alabama Jones," I said. "I picked her up outside of Lyndon. She is traveling to Kingdom Fair to rejoin her brother, who runs a show."

"That would be Jones' Shows," Lucien said. He wet his left thumb and turned a page. "I was to that show with Frog this afternoon. They could take some lessons from the French shows, you better believe. In the French shows they begin without no clothes. They is only one show worth your money this year. That is the French show from Sherbrooke. Frog and I see that one three times this afternoon. Is it polite to let her set in that truck all night? She cannot help what show she works in."

"She is a singer," I said. "Not what you think."

"I would advise her to go with the French show if she is any good," Lucien said as I went out.

At first I thought that she was gone. I began to run toward the truck, and when I opened the door I saw her on the seat. She had passed out. I lifted her out and was running again, toward the house.

"Put her on the daybed," Lucien said, holding the door open. I carried her into the downstairs bedroom and laid her on the bed. Her forehead was very wet now, and her hair was damp on the bedcover. Lucien was by the bed with a cold cloth for her head and a blanket. "Cover up her legs with this," he said. "It ain't decent to let a girl lay unconscious with her legs showing like that." He began to talk French, saying what a sin it was that a girl with legs like those was only a singer.

First she was breathing fast and light, but as Lucien applied the cold cloth to her forehead, her breathing evened out, and after awhile she was breathing deep and sleeping easy. Lucien sat in a chair by the bed smoking his pipe. Outside it was twilight.

"Call the doctor," I said. "I will drive down to the Common and notify the brother."

The brother was sitting alone at a hinged table that folded out of the wall of a camper parked behind the show tent. He was about forty, with thick greying hair brushed straight back. He was drinking beer, well along on his way into a sixpack.

"You had better have yourself a drink," he said, opening me the last bottle. "This does not surprise me. Trust her for a trick like this. I cannot turn my back on her for five minutes. Do you think any of the Joneses ever caught appendicitis before? No, they did not. Nor Twists, neither. We are Twists on the other side. Trust her to be the first. Trust her to ruin me with hospital bills and then leave in the night like a man that owes money and tramp the highways to give me a bad name. And then up and faint on strangers in order to make me beholden to them. I will have to visit her, I reckon."

He stood up, not too steadily, and put on his hat. When we got to the door, he put his hand on my shoulder and said, "Look, boy. I can't go tonight. I have an important business to run here, and I can't go. I don't worry about her because I see she is in good hands, and if you want the truth she is tough as a rattlesnake. All them Twist women was and is. I reckon it would take more than a walk in the country and a little case of the appendicitis to do for a Twist, all right. Fresh air is good for a singer. Put this in your pocket for the doctor. Never take to drink, boy; it will ruin you. I am forty-three years old come November twenty-first, and I do not have a stomach. Tell her I will be up to see her tomorrow. Tell her to get some bedrest."

Up home the doctor had come and gone and left some sleeping medicine for Alabama. He had looked at the incision and said that it was clean for a wonder. Lucien and I sat in the kitchen until late, drinking beer and talking.

"Maybe the brother will take you in as partners," Lucien said. "Then you can get away from this forsaken land."

"Yes," I said. "Just the way you did, you mean."

"You could get him to hire some of them little Frenchies you take out Saturday nights and bring him in a fortune. Have I told you about the French show Frog and I see this afternoon? They was this blondheaded girl that couldn't have been a day over sixteen—"

"I thought that was last year. Can't you get your stories straight?"

"You shut your mouth, boy. I intend to sell this miserable farm and get me a French show that gives one performance a night that lasts five hours with me alone for audience. Now, what do you say?" He began to go on in French. After awhile I pretended not to understand what he was saying and got up and looked in on Alabama, breathing deep and easy, and went on up to bed.

She was sitting at the table when I came into the kitchen at eight o'clock the next morning after chores.

"I reckon I took too much sun yesterday walking them roads," she said. "I am obliged to you." She was not apologizing, any more than you would apologize to a man that pulled a tree off your leg because the tree fell on you in the first place. It was just a statement. She was obliged.

"I saw your brother last night," I told her.

"I am obliged. Did you inform him that he can depend on me to sing tonight?"

"He said he would be up to see you today."

"Well, when he comes I will tell him myself. No doubt his business has fallen off already. I am the main one, I reckon, and I don't take off that much, neither."

Lucien came into the kitchen in his barn suspenders and I introduced him to Alabama, because she had never opened her eyes once the previous evening to see him, and while I scrambled eggs and fried bacon and made the coffee they sat at the table telling stories and laughing like they had known one another over the years. After breakfast Lucien said he and Frog were going to a cattle auction in Canada.

"Why don't you and Miss Alabama Jones put up a lunch and drive up to the top of the lane," he said. "I will stop on the way to the auction and tell the brother she is well again and will be in this evening."

"Only I reckon I would as soon walk," Alabama said.

I put up sandwiches and a quart of beer, and we started out through the meadow behind the house. The sun was well up and hot, but the meadow was still wet from the dew. When we crossed through the high grass at the lower end, she held her dress high so the dew would not soak through it. The sun glistened on her legs above her knees where the wet grass brushed against them. At the very top of the meadow under the scattered beech trees that Lucien had left standing we turned around and looked back. We could see down through the meadow to the back of the house and the barn, on past the buildings to the lower pasture where the cows were grazing, spread out small and still in the grass, below the pasture to the bright yellow sugar maples, and beyond them to the county road winding thin out of the trees down to the lake. We could see the whole length of the lake, five miles, and the mountains sheering up out of the water on both sides, and in places the county road cutting thin and winding along the east side. The mountains were red with soft maple and yellow and white with birches a thousand feet up their sides, then blue-green with firs rooted tight into the cliffs where you would say trees could not grow. For maybe a whole minute Alabama looked at the lake and the mountains.

Even after I had sat down in the grass under a beech tree she kept looking. Finally she spoke. "I reckon," she said, "that is so much more than any picture machine that I about have to believe it."

She sat down beside me without taking her eyes off the view, as though it might disappear if she looked away for even a second, like something you are watching go across the sky at night or like a buck that you cannot quite get a good line on through the woods. After awhile she said, "I reckon this is why you stay here. Because any time you want, you can just step out of the door and see all these colors."

"For a few days in October I can."

"A few days? That is as long as they last?"

"Until the first fall rain. That will turn them brown, and then the wind will blow them away in a night."

"Then I reckon it must be that girl that keeps you here."

"What girl?"

"The one that's picture is down there in the front room. I won't ask her name. She is a nice girl, no doubt?"

I nodded.

"She wouldn't like me then, I reckon," Alabama said. "What does she do? Sing country and western over the radio?"

"She goes to school."

"High school? I thought that was her high school picture down there. That she was already graduated and out singing. Well then. I reckon she is going to school to be a nurse. That is what the nice girls do, all right. Like them nice girls at the hospital that was so nice to me when they found out what I done for work."

"She isn't nice like that," I said. "She doesn't sing country and western or even like it much, and she isn't in nursing school. She is going to state college to be a teacher."

"I reckon she likes children then," Alabama said. "Well, everybody to their own taste, I always say. What does she call you?"

"Bill."

"I reckon I will call you William. I do not intend to call you what she does. Besides, I have knowed a boy named Bill once or twice. Well, William, I am not what you would call a nice girl, and I do not stand up well under children. It is thinking about children, plus my singing, that keeps me as nice as I am. Children was the one thing besides country singing we had too much of in our family."

"I see other girls," I said. "She knows that. She has dates at college."

"What have you got in the sack?" Alabama said.

Sitting with our backs against the smooth grey beech trunk, listening to the little yellowing leaves click together in the wind and to a buzz saw cutting somewhere high on the mountain, we ate the sandwiches and drank from the quart of beer. When we had emptied it Alabama began again.

"All right," she said. "If it ain't the colors. And if it ain't that girl. Then what is it that keeps you? Why don't you go to college too? Or the city? Is it Lucien?"

Maybe it was the food and the beer, or the warm sun coming down through the clicking beech leaves. Maybe it was that she had figured out that there would have to be something more than hauling logs and milking cows. Maybe it was just that she had pretty legs.

"It isn't Lucien," I said. "It isn't any girl, and it isn't the colors. Least of all the colors. Because they're like Kingdom Fair. They come once a year for less than a week; then they're gone. And even while they're here they aren't quite real. You can't paint them. I've tried, and they always come out like a picture postcard. It's when they go that's the best time to paint this country. After the rain and wind have torn down the leaves and left the hills and farms bare. Then maybe you can paint it like it is. I have not heard that they teach you to do that at college."

"So that is it," Alabama said. "I be dog." Her legs were curled under her, and she was looking straight at me. "And that picture on the wall in the little room where I slept. The one that looks like you seen it before in a bad dream, with the white trees sticking up dead out of the water the brightest things in it. That is real?"

"I could show you where in half an hour," I said.

"I reckon you couldn't," she said. "Not in the White Mountains, I reckon."

She stood up and we started back down through the meadow. The grass was dry now.

"I reckon it is good, all right," she said halfway down to the house. "But it ain't in no White Mountains."

She slept all afternoon. I took my shotgun and went for partridge. I missed two easy shots, both straight away and clear. Lucien was not back from his auction in time to do the milking, but when I came in from the barn at six he was sitting at the table teaching Alabama a dirty French duet and pounding a can of beer in time with the song.

"Where did you say that auction was held?" I said. "The Common Hotel?"

I got supper and afterwards we drove down to the fair. Kingdom Fair is held after the summer people have gone back downcountry, and you will see everybody in Kingdom County there. We parked behind the grandstand in Wheeler's haylot, and on our way down to the midway Warden Kinneson stopped us in front of the Women's Floral Building. He was electioneering for sheriff on the platform that he would close down the girlie shows at the fair. He gave me a campaign button that said *Stamp Out Smut—Vote R. W. Kinneson.*

"Bill," he said, "do you want your girl walking past painted women standing in plain view on the midway, enticing husbands and fathers and schoolboys into a dark tent full of sin?"

Alabama laughed.

"How do you know what those tents are full of?" I said.

"How does he know?" Lucien said. "Because he spends half his time down there, that's how. Says he is investigating. He spent this afternoon investigating that French show four times. Leave us pass by, Warden. You had better stick to shocking fish."

"I thought you were at an auction all day," I said to Lucien.

"I was delayed at the brother's," he said. "They was a fight in his tent and the troopers closed him down for the afternoon, so him and Frog and me went to the French show."

The brother was sitting in his camper at the foldout table drinking beer. "Here I am," Alabama said. "Ready to go work."

"Your father and I have had a day of it," the brother said to me. "I have been closed down for six hours and lost at least two hundred dollars. I am opening up again in a few minutes. She is a good singer if I can keep her fit."

Alabama went behind a curtain to change and the brother stood up heavily and said, "I am too tired to be doing this." He walked out of the camper and around to the platform in front of his tent, where there were two women dressed in satin robes open down the front. They were swaying automatically to music coming out of two loudspeakers on poles. Climbing heavily up onto the platform, the brother began to advertise the show. In a few minutes he had a crowd and began to sell tickets. He passed us in free.

Inside the tent we sat down on one of the rough wooden benches. There was no band, just the same music that was being piped outside. The two women came out looking bored and took off their clothes like they were tired and getting ready for bed.

Alabama was the main attraction. She sang hot rock in a black bikini and enjoyed it, and except for the few women that had come in with their husbands, so did the audience. You could see her incision plainly. After the show she was holding her side, and the brother said he had already lost so much he might as well close for the night and call Kingdom Fair a total loss. They were leaving for Tunbridge in the morning.

Lucien invited them all up home for a party, but the strippers said they were tired. Alabama and the brother came alone, following along behind us in the camper. When we arrived Lucien got out the last quart of Fish White's whiskey and we sat on the porch, Lucien and the brother sitting in straightback chairs with their feet on the rail, Alabama and I sitting on the stoop. It was warm, and the wind was coming up from the south. When the quart had gone around twice, the brother began talking to me.

"It is not much of an offer," he said. "But if you wanted to come in with me. It is not the hardest kind of work, and you would have the days to yourself mostly. With her and some new girls we could likely stay in the black. These we have will not be going south with us. If we was all satisfied after six months, I reckon there would be a partnership in it, though Lord knows it is no great offer. Lord knows what it has done to me."

"There is your golden chance, boy," Lucien said. "There is your chance to get away from this forsaken land once and for all."

Looking off down the valley, I could just make out the dark bulks of the October hills. The sky above them was starless, and I could not see the shapes of the mountains beyond. I felt the warm wind on my face and knew it would rain that night. In the morning the hills would be brown. In a week grey. Then white.

Alabama stood up. "Well," she said, "you have been right good to me. This has been two good days in my life. I will always remember autumn in the White Mountains and Lucien and William."

She walked across the dooryard to the camper and got in. The brother wrote down where he would be for the next month in case I changed my mind and shook hands with us. We watched their taillights disappear down the lane where it went into the sugar maples. We finished the quart. For once Lucien was quiet.

It was raining hard when I got up the next morning. Frog's truck started slow, and the overhead wipers did not move fast enough to keep up with the water streaming across the windshield. I drove slowly down the slick lane to the county road, then up along the river toward the Common. When I came to the pulloff where we were loading I shut off the motor and sat in the cab smoking cigarettes while they stacked the pulp in the back and chained it down in the rain. It was still raining hard when I drove through the Common. The fair ground was empty, and the hills around it were brown in the rain.

Biographies

Ethan Allen, hero of the Revolutionary War, was born in Litchfield, Connecticut, on January 10, 1738. He came to the New Hampshire Grants in 1766 and quickly established himself as a leader of the Green Mountain Boys in their opposition to the rule of New York. On May 10, 1775, he and his company captured the historic fortress of Ticonderoga on Lake Champlain. During an ill-planned attempt to take the city of Montreal in the autumn of 1775, Allen was taken prisoner by the British. He relates his experiences during his three-year imprisonment in the *Narrative of Colonel Ethan Allen's Captivity*. In addition to being a prolific pamphleteer on political matters, Allen was also much interested in philosophy and theology. His book *Reason the Only Oracle of Man* clearly demonstrated his antagonism to Calvinistic theology. He died February 12, 1789, at his farm in Burlington.

Ira Allen, the youngest of the sons of Joseph and Mary Allen, was born May 1, 1751, in Roxbury, Connecticut. He followed his brother Ethan to the Grants in 1772. With a vested interest as a land owner, he joined with other settlers to defend the Grants against the Yorkers. Ira, a lieutenant in the Green Mountain Boys, participated in the capture of Ticonderoga and fought in other battles in the Revolution. After the War, he became treasurer of Vermont and its first surveyor general. He played an important role in the Haldimand Negotiations with Britain while Vermont tried to gain admission to the Federal Union. Allen firmly believed in the value of education and was instrumental in securing a charter for the University of Vermont in 1791. A prolific pamphleteer, Allen also wrote *The Natural and Political History of the State of Vermont, One of the United States of America*. Largely as the result of some intriguing episodes and disastrous reversals, Ira Allen died penniless on January 15, 1814, in Philadelphia.

Ann Batchelder was born on March 21, 1885, in Windsor, Vermont. She was a student at the University of Vermont and campaigned for woman's suffrage in the state for a number of years. A newspaper reporter in Boston and New York, she later became food editor for the *Ladies Home Jour-*

nal, which also published dozens of her poems. She returned to Vermont and made her home at Woodstock where she died on June 18, 1955.

Alton Hall Blackington was born in Rockland, Maine, on November 25, 1893. His first loves were photography and writing. He was photographer and feature writer for the *Boston Herald* and the *Boston Globe.* In addition to producing an extremely popular radio program, "Yankee Yarns," on station WBZ in Boston, he lectured widely on New England folklore. The folk materials that he collected from a lifetime of experience and research appear in his two books, *Yankee Yarns* and *More Yankee Yarns.* He died April 24, 1963, at his home in Beverly Farms, Massachusetts.

Daniel L. Cady was born in West Windsor, Vermont, on March 10, 1861. After graduating from the University of Vermont, he studied law, then established a practice in New York City. When he retired to Burlington, Vermont, in 1913, he took a wife and devoted himself to the writing of poetry. In the two decades left to him, he developed a distinctive homespun style that belied his sophistication and learning. His three volume *Rhymes of Vermont Rural Life* is richly evocative of older times and ways. Before he died in 1934, Cady had become Vermont's most celebrated poet.

Sarah N. Cleghorn, a native of Virginia, was born on February 4, 1876. When she was still a child, her family moved to Manchester, Vermont, where she attended Burr and Burton Seminary. After two years at Radcliffe College, she taught English at Pawling, New York, for several years. She lived with a maiden aunt in Manchester until 1943, when she moved to Philadelphia. She died in 1959. Miss Cleghorn's life was more active and varied than a brief outline might suggest. A suffragette, pacifist, and humanitarian, she joined the Socialist Party at the age of thirty-five. Her volume of what she called "burning poems," *Portraits and Protests,* reflects her deep desire for social reform, while the other side of her poetic temperament found expression in her "sunbonnet poems," treating life in rural Vermont. In addition to hundreds of poems, she published two novels and an autobiography.

Julia C. Dorr was born on February 13, 1825, to a Southern mother and a Vermont father. After the untimely death of her mother and her father's remarriage, the family returned to Middlebury, Vermont, when she was six years old. Her education was unusually good for a young woman of the time, and she early learned to love books and reading. After her marriage at twenty-two to Seneca Dorr, the couple relocated in Ghent, New York, where they lived for ten years. But the pull of Vermont exerted itself on the young family, and they returned to Rutland to build a permanent home, The Maples. Mrs. Dorr's writings—stories, novels, travel sketches as well as poetry—achieved for her an excellent reputation among the famous: Emerson, Holmes, and Longfellow were her friends. She died on January 18, 1913.

Robert Luther Duffus was born in Waterbury, Vermont, on July 10, 1888. After taking both his A.B. and M.A. at Stanford University, he embarked on a career in journalism as a reporter and editorial writer in the San Francisco area. After 1937 he was with the *New York Times* until his retirement. His more than two dozen books include *Roads Going South; Books: Their Place in a Democracy; Night Between Rivers; Williamstown Branch; The Waterbury Record: More Vermont Memories; Nostalgia, U.S.A.;* and *Jason Goode.* Death came to him in 1972, in Palo Alto, California. Vermonters fondly remember him for his now famous editorial "Flag Day."

Charles Gamage Eastman, authorities agree, was born in Fryeburg, Maine; they disagree about whether it was in 1813 or 1816. The family moved to Barnard, Vermont, where the boy grew up. After attending the University of Vermont, he went into newspaper work, spending the last fifteen years

of his life as editor and co-owner of *The Vermont Patroit and State Gazette* in Montpelier. His verse received national recognition and earned him the epithet "The Burns of New England" from British reviewers. He died in 1860.

Zephine Humphrey Fahnestock, an accomplished essayist, was born in Philadelphia, Pennsylvania, on December 15, 1874. She attended Smith College and was graduated in 1896. After her marriage to Wallace Fahnestock, she resided in Dorset, Vermont, until her death in 1956. She was very active in Vermont literary circles and was a member of the Committee on Traditions and Ideals, organized in 1929, under the Vermont Commission on Country Life. Her numerous publications include *Over Against Green Peak; The Edge of the Woods; The Homestead; Mountain Verities; The Story of Dorset; Winterwise; The Beloved Community; Green Mountains to Sierras;* and *A Book of New England.*

Thomas Green Fessenden—satirist, editor, lawyer, and inventor—was born in 1771 in Walpole, New Hampshire. He worked his way through Dartmouth College by writing and teaching. After studying law in Rutland, he was admitted to the Vermont bar. The rest of his life is a remarkable patchwork of enterprises: he publicized a bogus medical "marvel" through his satire "Terrible Tractoration"; he edited newspapers in New York, Philadelphia, Brattleboro, Bellows Falls, and Boston; he invented a "portable steam and hot water stove." Death came to him in 1837 at the age of sixty-six.

Dorothy Canfield Fisher was born in Lawrence, Kansas, in 1879. She received her A.B. degree from Ohio State University and studied for her doctorate at the Sorbonne and at Columbia University. In 1907 she, with her husband John Fisher, established residence upon the Canfield family's ancestral property just outside of Arlington, Vermont. Her extremely prolific career was interrupted when she accompanied her husband to France in 1916 to participate in the war effort. Her novels, stories, and non-fiction reflect her wide experience and diversified interests; they include *Gunhild; The Squirrel-Cage; The Montessori Mother; The Bent Twig; Hillsboro People; Home Fires in France; The Brimming Cup; The Deepening Stream; Rough-Hewn; Made-to-Order Stories;* and *Why Stop Learning?* She was appointed to the Vermont State Board of Education in 1921 and served on the Editorial board of the Book-of-the-Month Club from 1926 to her death. Her *Vermont Tradition* is an invaluable contribution to the state's literature —the final production in a brilliant career. She died in 1958.

Ella Warner Fisher was born in Ferrisburg, Vermont, on January 29, 1853. She was a teacher before her marriage to Henry P. Fisher. Thereafter she lived in Vergennes, Vermont, writing and publishing poetry regularly. Among her volumes of verse are *Green Mountain Echoes* and *Homeland in the North*. She died in 1937.

Helen Hartness Flanders, daughter of a Vermont governor, was born in 1890 in Springfield, Vermont. Educated in Massachusetts, she returned to her native state and married Ralph E. Flanders, later U.S. Senator. Her sensitivities and skills as poet and musician proved invaluable as she devoted herself to collecting and editing several volumes of Vermont songs, among which are *Vermont Folk Songs and Ballads; The New Green Mountain Songster;* and *Ballads Migrant in New England.* Mrs. Flanders died at the age of eighty-two in Springfield, Vermont.

Frances Frost was born on August 3, 1905, in St. Albans, Vermont. After graduating from Middlebury College, she taught creative writing and studied for a Bachelor of Philosophy degree at the University of Vermont. *Hemlock Wall,* her first book of poetry, was published in the distinguished Yale Series of Younger Poets when she was only twenty-four. It was followed by, among others, *Blue Harvest; These Acres;* and *This Rowdy Heart.* A versatile and prolific writer, Miss Frost wrote a number of novels and children's books as well. Her first marriage ended in divorce in 1931; two years later she married a second time and relocated in Charlestown, South Carolina. She later moved to New York City, where she died on February 11, 1959.

Robert Frost, born in San Francisco in 1874, came to Vermont late in life. Reversing the usual pattern of American migration, his family moved east to Massachusetts when the boy was ten. He wrote poetry in high school; after graduation he attended Dartmouth College, then Harvard College, but finished neither. In 1900 he became a farmer and English teacher in Derry, New Hampshire, where he stayed until he and his wife moved to England in 1912. During those years he continued to write, but recognition was delayed until his residence in England, when he published two books of verse, *A Boy's Will* and *North of Boston*. He returned to New Hampshire, remained four years, then moved to a farm near South Shaftsbury, Vermont, in 1919. In the years that followed his teaching took him to Michigan, Massachusetts, Connecticut, and New York, as four Pulitzer Prizes for poetry and other honors came his way. During the time that he resided at Ripton, Vermont, he was instrumental in the founding of the Bread Loaf School of English. In 1961 he read his poem "The Gift Outright" at the presidential inauguration of John F. Kennedy. Frost died in 1963.

Arthur Goodenough was born on November 11, 1871, in West Brattleboro, Vermont, where he lived for his entire life. For several years beginning in 1889 he published a magazine, *The Sieve*, printing it himself by hand. Called "The Vermont Whittier," he composed verse prolifically, contributing to numerous magazines until his death on September 15, 1936.

Walter Hard, born on May 3, 1882, in Manchester, Vermont, graduated from Burr and Burton Seminary and Williams College. Returning home, he took over the family drugstore in Manchester and later, with his wife Margaret, herself a poet, operated a bookstore for many years. In addition to writing a column in the Rutland Herald, he served several terms in the state legislature. His pungent wit permeates his collection of verse portraits such as *Some Vermonters; Salt of Vermont;* and *A Mountain Township*. He died on May 21, 1967.

James Hayford was born in Montpelier, Vermont, in 1913. He took his B.A. from Amherst College and his M.A. from Columbia University. He has taught such varied subjects as English, history, and music at all levels from elementary school through college. At odd times he has been farmer, carpenter's helper, gardener, taxi-driver, waiter, office worker, textbook editor, organist and choirmaster, and piano teacher. *Harper's* and the

New Yorker are just two of the magazines that have published his poetry. His books of verse are *The Equivocal Sky; Our Several Houses; A Personal Terrain;* and his latest, *Processional with Wheelbarrow.* Recently retired from teaching at Winooski High School, he lives in Burlington and continues to write.

Ralph Nading Hill was born in 1917. A native and resident of Burlington, Vermont, he has authored numerous historical and biographical books; his specialty is Lake Champlain and the history of steamboating. The books produced by this Dartmouth College graduate include *Sidewheeler Saga; Contrary Country; Window on the Sea; The Mad Doctor's Drive; Yankee Kingdom;* and *The Voyages of Brian Seaworthy.* Mr. Hill is a senior editor of *Vermont Life* magazine and a trustee of the Shelburne Museum.

Murray Hoyt, a native of Worcester, Massachusetts, is presently a resident of Middlebury, Vermont. After graduation from Middlebury College and a brief coaching career in New York state, he and his wife operated the successful Lake Champlain resort of Owl's Head Harbor for twenty-five years. He is the author of *Does It Always Rain Here, Mr. Hoyt?* and *The Fish in My Life;* his humorous articles and stories have appeared in *Vermont Life, Reader's Digest, The Saturday Evening Post,* and *Ladies'*

Home Journal. He is a senior editor of *Vermont Life* magazine.

Leland Kinsey was born on May 2, 1950, in Barton, Vermont, a small community in the Northeast Kingdom. He prepared for college at Craftsbury Academy and Lake Region Union High School. At the University of Vermont, where he earned his degree in English in 1972, he presented a collection of his poetry and fiction as an honors project. Married, he is now living in Burlington, "writing and trying to earn a living."

Cornelius Ambrosius Logan was born in Baltimore, Maryland, in 1806. As a popular actor and playwright, he is remembered for his ingenious comic roles and his perceptive, sensitive creation of Yankee characters. His farces were widely performed and received much acclaim. They include *Yankee Land, or, The Foundling of the Apple Orchard; The Wag of Maine;* and *Chloroform, or, New York a Hundred Years Hence.* In *The Vermont Wool Dealer,* Logan develops the Jonathan character, the wise Yankee rustic, first introduced by Royall Tyler in *The Contrast.* He died in 1853.

George Perkins Marsh was born in Woodstock, Vermont, on March 15, 1801, into one of the state's first families. After preparing at Phillips Andover Academy, he studied at Dartmouth College and taught in a local school for several months after graduation. But like so many bright and versatile men of his time, he was attracted to the legal profession and was admitted to the Burlington bar in 1825. He later became a congressman and minister to Spain and to Turkey. Throughout his life, however, he maintained the scholarly interests that were awakened at Dartmouth, and he derived much satisfaction from his work as linguist and bibliophile. But it is for his efforts in conservation that he is best known today. His *Man and Nature* (1864), revised and republished as *The Earth as Modified by Human Action* ten years later, has been called "the fountainhead of the twentieth-century conservation movement." Marsh was on a visit to his beloved city of Florence, Italy, when he died in 1882.

Howard Frank Mosher, a native of Vermont, was born in 1942. After graduation from the University of Vermont, he traveled to California. Like many another Vermonter, he returned to his native state; he lives with his wife and son on a farm in Orleans. His stories have appeared in *Epoch, Colorado Quarterly, South Carolina Review,* and *Cimarron Review.* Currently he is writing a novel about his experiences working in the woods.

Vrest Orton, born in Hardwick on September 3, 1897, left Vermont in his early teens and completed

his education in Massachusetts. After attending Harvard, he traveled extensively and served in World War I. Later he did advertising and public relations work with *The Saturday Review of Literature, The American Mercury,* and the publishing firm of Alfred A. Knopf. After his return to Vermont, he was the founder and general editor of the Stephen Daye Press in Brattleboro. In 1945 he began The Original Vermont Country Store in Weston. Long associated with the Vermont Historical Society, he founded *Vermont Life* magazine. Among his numerous books are *Dreiseriana: A Book About Theodore Dreiser* and *Afternoons with Robert Frost.*

Arthur Wallace Peach was born in Pawlet, Vermont, on April 9, 1886. He graduated from Middlebury College and served as chairman of the Department of English at Norwich University for many years. Although he achieved excellence as teacher, scholar, and poet, his greatest contribution was probably as general editor of *The Green Mountain Series* (1932). This four-volume collection of Vermont poetry, prose, folk songs, and biographies has stood for four decades as the standard work on Vermont letters. He was also a founder and the first president of the Poetry Society of Vermont. He resigned from Norwich in 1952 to become director of the Vermont Historical Society, a post he held until his death on July 21, 1956.

Noel Perrin is a resident of Thetford Center, Vermont, and a Professor of English at Dartmouth College. He was born in New York City in 1927. He is a regular contributor to *The New Yorker.* Other essays of his have appeared in *Harper's Magazine, Punch, Vogue,* and *Vermont Life.* He has published three books, *A Passport Secretly Green; Dr. Bowdler's Legacy;* and *Amateur Sugar Maker.* The last of these reflects his interest in activities that bring him close to the land.

Rowland Evans Robinson was born at Rokeby, the Robinson family homestead, in Ferrisburg, Vermont, on May 14, 1833. After a brief period in New York City, where he worked as a draughtsman, Robinson returned to Vermont to pursue his career as an artist and writer. He contributed sketches of all aspects of New England life to *Moore's Rural New Yorker, Forest and Steam, Atlantic Monthly,* and *Youth's Companion.* Robinson's sensitive and accurate powers of observation, interest in the tales and legends of pioneer Vermont, and love of life of the forest and field are best exhibited in his collections of fiction, *Uncle Lisha's Shop; Sam Lovel's Camps; Danvis Folks; Uncle Lisha's Outing;* and *Out of Bondage and Other Stories.* Robinson was also an historian of some note; his active and sustained interest in early Vermont history resulted in *Vermont: A Study of Independence; A Hero of Ticon-*

deroga; In the Green Wood; A Danvis Pioneer; and an unpublished biography of Ethan Allen. Although blind for the last eight years of his life, Robinson's work reflects his interest and unfailing spiritual energy. He died at Rokeby on October 15, 1900.

Thomas Rowley was born in 1721—like many of Vermont's early settlers, in Connecticut. At the age of forty-seven he took up and cleared two hundred acres of farmland in Danby, Vermont, and held a variety of town offices. As a member of the Green Mountain Boys, he shouldered arms with Ethan and Ira Allen, Remember Baker and Seth Warner. But his role as versifying propagandist and "Ministrel of Vermont" looms larger than his feats of arms. He was especially proud of his ability to improvise a verse on a moment's notice. Rowley spent the years before his death in 1796 in Shoreham, Vermont.

John Godfrey Saxe was born in Highgate, Vermont, on June 22, 1816. After graduating from Middlebury College, he studied law in St. Albans and was admitted to the Vermont bar. He mixed the job of editing the Burlington *Sentinel* with law and politics and ran twice for governor of Vermont. Yet all the while he was writing poetry, usually light and humorous, that achieved great popularity. His collected *Poems* (1850) went through forty editions. Despite a full and rich life, his last years were unhappy, and he suffered severe bouts of depression before his death in 1887 at the home of his son in Albany, New York.

Wendell Phillips Stafford was born on May 1, 1861, in Barre, Vermont, where he grew up. He studied law at Boston University but returned to Vermont to set up practice in St. Johnsbury. His legal skill was acknowledged by appointments to the Vermont Supreme Court and the Supreme Court of the District of Columbia. Perhaps better known in his own time as an orator, he nevertheless managed to write and publish several volumes of poetry, including *The Land We Love* and *War Poems*. Judge Stafford died in 1953.

Genevieve Taggard was born in Waitsburg, Washington, on November 28, 1894, and raised in Hawaii. When her family returned to the West Coast, she entered the University of California and became editor of the college literary magazine. After graduation she taught at Bennington College in the early 1930's and thereafter summered on Lake Champlain. One of over a dozen books by Miss Taggard, *A Part of Vermont* celebrates her love for her adopted state. Some of her poems have been set to music by such noted composers as Aaron Copland and William Schuman. She retired from teaching to her home in Jamaica,

Vermont, and died on November 8, 1948.

Daniel Pierce Thompson was born in Charlestown, Massachusetts, on October 1, 1795. At the age of five, he moved with his family to a farm in Berlin, Vermont. He was graduated from Middlebury College in 1820 and subsequently studied law in Virginia. Several years later he began a law practice in Montpelier. Although he was an incorporator of the Vermont Historical Society, editor and proprietor of the *Green Mountain Freeman*, and, for two years, Secretary of State of Vermont, he is best known as an author. An antiquarian and accomplished storyteller, Thompson turned for his subjects to local legends and to the grand stories of the Revolution and Vermont frontier life. Among his novels are *May Martin, or the Money Diggers; The Green Mountain Boys;* and *The Rangers, or, The Tory's Daughter*. In addition, Thompson wrote a *History of Vermont, and the Northern Campaign of 1777* and a *History of the Town of Montpelier*. He died on June 6, 1868.

Zadock Thompson, historian and naturalist, was born in Bridgewater, Vermont, May 23, 1796. He received his degree from the University of Vermont in 1823. Later he studied theology and in 1837 was ordained deacon in the Episcopal Church. Annually, Thompson published the almanac known as

Thompson's Almanack. Other publications include *The Youth's Assistant,* an arithmetic textbook, and *The History of Vermont.* He is best known, however, for his *History of Vermont, Natural, Civil, and Statistical,* which is still considered an excellent primary source book for the region. He died in Burlington in 1856. At the time of his death, he was Professor of Natural History at the University of Vermont.

Mari Tomasi was born in Montpelier, Vermont, on February 9, 1909. After attending Wheaton College and graduating from Trinity College, she taught grade school in the Montpelier area. A Vermonter of Italian extraction, Miss Tomasi is the author of *Deep Grow the Roots,* voted one of the outstanding first novels of 1940. The novel is set in Italy and tells the story of the farming soil and the people whose lives are bound up with it. *Like Lesser Gods,* set in Granitown, Vermont, concerns the fortunes of the Italian community and the granite industry. Miss Tomasi has had her short fiction appear in *The Catamount, Hill Trails, American Prefaces,* and *Common Ground.* During the Second World War, she worked for the Montpelier *Evening Argus.* Later she was active with the Vermont Historical Society and the Poetry Society of Vermont, and she edited three volumes of *Vermont, Its Government.* Death came to her in November, 1965.

Royall Tyler was born in Boston on July 18, 1757. After graduation from Harvard, he practiced law and played a role in suppressing Shays's Rebellion. While in New York for a short visit, he had the opportunity to see a production of Richard Sheridan's *The School for Scandal.* Within three weeks he had written his social comedy *The Contrast,* the second play and the first comedy to be written by an American. Tyler wrote at least six other plays, four of which survive in manuscript. In 1791 he moved from Boston to Guilford, Vermont, where he pursued his legal career, eventually becoming Chief Justice of the state supreme court and Professor of Jurisprudence at the University of Vermont. In collaboration with Joseph Dennie, Tyler contributed satirical, witty verse and light essays to the *Farmer's Weekly Museum* and other journals. He is known for a novel, *The Algerine Captive* (1797), and for *Yankey in London* (1809), a series of letters. His complete poems, *The Verse of Royall Tyler,* were published in 1965.

William Hazlett Upson was born September 26, 1891, in Glen Ridge, New Jersey. Currently, he is a resident of Ripton, Vermont. After graduation from Cornell University, Upson was employed for a short time in the service department of the Caterpillar Tractor Company, experience that provided the basis for the stories of Alexander Botts, Earthworm Tractor salesman. Since that time he has had a successful career as an author and lecturer. He is a member of the League of Vermont Writers. In addition to numerous stories in *The Saturday Evening Post* and other magazines, he has published *The Piano Movers; Earthworm Tractors; Keep 'em Crawling; How to be Rich like Me; Earthworms Through the Ages; No Rest for Botts;* and *The Best of Botts.*

Marguerite Hurrey Wolf was born in Montclair, New Jersey, in 1914. After graduation from Mount Holyoke College and the Bank Street College of Education, she taught at the Bank Street Nursery School and at Sarah Lawrence College. She is married to Dr. George Wolf, former Dean of the University of Vermont College of Medicine. After an absence of nine years in Kansas, the Wolfs returned to Vermont with their two daughters. Mrs. Wolf has written four books, *Anything Can Happen in Vermont; How to be a Doctor's Wife without Really Dying; Vermont is Always with You;* and *That Book About Vermont*—and has contributed many articles to *Vermont Life, Yankee, The Saturday Evening Post,* and *Ski.* Presently, she is a resident of Jericho Center, Vermont.

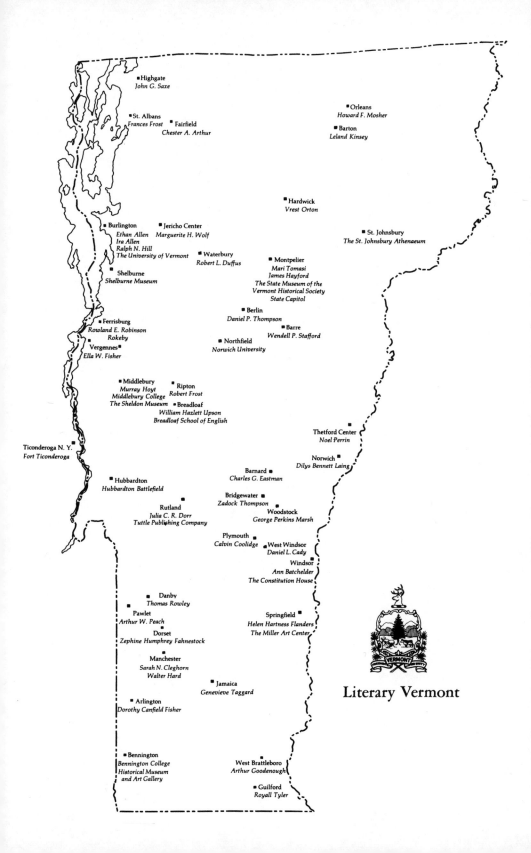

■Highgate
John G. Saxe

■Orleans
Howard F. Mosher

■St. Albans
Frances Frost ■Fairfield
Chester A. Arthur

■Barton
Leland Kinsey

■Hardwick
Vrest Orton

■Burlington ■Jericho Center
Ethan Allen Marguerite H. Wolf
Ira Allen
Ralph N. Hill
The University of Vermont

■St. Johnsbury
The St. Johnsbury Athenaeum

■Waterbury
Robert L. Duffus

■Montpelier
Mari Tomasi
James Hayford
The State Museum of the
Vermont Historical Society
State Capitol

■Shelburne
Shelburne Museum

■Berlin
Daniel P. Thompson

■Barre
Wendell P. Stafford

■Ferrisburg
Rowland E. Robinson
Rokeby

■Northfield
Norwich University

Vergennes■
Ella W. Fisher

■Middlebury ■Ripton
Murray Hoyt Robert Frost
Middlebury College
The Sheldon Museum ■Breadloaf
William Hazlett Upson
Breadloaf School of English

Thetford Center
Noel Perrin

Ticonderoga N. Y.
Fort Ticonderoga

Norwich ■
Dilys Bennett Laing

Barnard ■
Charles G. Eastman

■Hubbardton
Hubbardton Battlefield

Bridgewater ■
Zadock Thompson

■
Rutland
Julia C. R. Dorr
Tuttle Publishing Company

Woodstock
George Perkins Marsh

Plymouth
Calvin Coolidge ■ ■West Windsor
Daniel L. Cady

Windsor
Ann Batchelder
The Constitution House

■ Danby
Thomas Rowley

Pawlet
Arthur W. Peach

Springfield ■
Helen Hartness Flanders
The Miller Art Center

■ Dorset
Zephine Humphrey Fahnestock

■
Manchester
Sarah N. Cleghorn
Walter Hard

■ Jamaica
Genevieve Taggard

■ Arlington
Dorothy Canfield Fisher

■ Bennington
Bennington College
Historical Museum
and Art Gallery

West Brattleboro ■
Arthur Goodenough

■ Guilford
Royall Tyler

Literary Vermont

Credits

Part I:
Settlement, Revolution, and Early Statehood

Ira Allen. "Coming to the Grants," from "Autobiography," in James B. Wilbur, *Ira Allen, Founder of Vermont, 1751–1814* (Boston: Houghton Mifflin, 1928), I, 15–20.

Thomas Rowley. "Addressed to a Clergyman," from *The Rural Magazine*, June 1795. "When Caesar Reigned King at Rome," from *History of the Town of Shoreham* (Middlebury, Vt.: A. H. Copeland, 1861), p. 165. "The Rutland Song," from the same book, pp. 165–168.

Ethan Allen. "The Capture of Fort Ticonderoga," from *A Narrative of Col. Ethan Allen's Captivity* (Walpole, N. H.: Thomas and Thomas, 1807), pp. 13–21.

Royall Tyler. "The Death Song of Alknomook," from Marius B. Péladeau, ed., *The Verse of Royall Tyler* (Charlottesville, Va.: The University Press of Virginia, 1968), p. 10. From the same book: "Anacreontic to Flip," pp. 27–28; "Ode Composed for the Fourth of July," pp. 47–48; "Lines on Brattleboro," pp. 116 f.; "Old Simon," p. 124; "Ode to the Hummingbird," p. 126; "November," pp. 178–179; "Stanzas to ****," p. 187. Reprinted by permission of the Colonial Society of Massachusetts. *The Contrast*, Act II, scene ii, from James B. Wilbur, ed., *The Contrast: A Comedy in Five Acts* (Boston: Houghton Mifflin, 1920), pp. 53–63.

Thomas Green Fessenden. "A New England Country Dance," from *Original Poems* (Philadelphia: Lorenzo Press, 1806), pp. 24–27. "Eulogy on the Times," from *Terrible Tractoration and Other Poems* (Boston: Russell, Shattuck, 1836), pp. 250–254. "Tabitha Towzer," from the same book, pp. 212–215.

Part II:
Potash, Morgan Horses, and Merino Sheep

Zadock Thompson. "The Character of the Settlers and Their Modes of Punishment," from *History of Vermont, Natural, Civil, and Statistical* (Burlington, Vt.: Chauncey Goodrich, 1842), Part II, pp. 30–32.

Anonymous. "Election Ode: 1801," from Jeremiah Ingalls, ed., *The Christian Harmony* (Exeter, N.H.: Henry Ranlet, 1805).

Charles G. Eastman. "The Reaper," from *Poems* (Montpelier, Vt.: T. C. Phinney, 1880), pp. 76–77. From the same book: "Song," pp. 95–96; "The First Settler," pp. 171–173; "The Old Pine Tree," pp. 185–189.

John G. Saxe. "A Connubial Eclogue," from *Poetical Works* (Boston: Houghton Mifflin, 1892), pp. 24–25. From the same book: "The Great Magician," pp. 64–65; "To Spring," p. 245; "Somewhere," p. 246; "The Explanation," p. 250; "On an Ugly Person Sitting for a Daguerreotype," p. 252.

Daniel Pierce Thompson. "A Vermonter in a Fix, or A New Way to Collect an Old Debt," from *The Shaker Lovers, and Other Tales* (Burlington, Vt.: C. Goodrich and S. B. Nichols, 1848), pp. 67–73.

Cornelius A. Logan. *The Vermont*

Wool Dealer (New York: Samuel French, 1854).

George Perkins Marsh. "The Destructiveness of Man," from *Man and Nature; or Physical Geography as Modified by Human Action* (New York: Charles Scribner, 1867), pp. 35–41. "The Instability of American Life," from the same book, pp. 328–329.

Part III:
A Time for Reflection

REFLECTION

Folk Songs. "Stratton Mountain Tragedy," from Helen Hartness Flanders and George Brown, eds., *Vermont Folk Songs and Ballads* (Brattleboro, Vt.: Stephen Daye Press, 1931), pp. 27–28. "John Grumlie," from the same book, pp. 104–105. "The Wisconsin Emigrant's Song," from Helen Hartness Flanders et al., eds., *The New Green Mountain Songster* (New Haven, Ct.: Yale University Press, 1939), pp. 106–107. "The Song of the Vermonters, 1779," from the same book, pp. 269–272. Reprinted by permission of Mrs. Elizabeth Flanders Ballard.

Julia C. Dorr. "To a Late Comer," from *Beyond the Sunset* (New York: Charles Scribner's Sons, 1909), p. 15. From the same book: "The Joy," pp. 30–31; "Moon-Pictures," pp. 78–79. "What She Thought," from *Poems* (New York: Charles Scribner's Sons, 1913), pp. 168–169. "The Armorer's Errand: A Ballad of 1775," from the same book, pp. 417–422.

Ella Warner Fisher. "Nothing More," from *Homeland in the North* (North Montpelier, Vt.: Driftwind Press, 1936), p. 87. "My Neighbor's Barn," from the same book, p. 93. "My Prayer," from *Green Mountain Echoes* (Rutland, Vt.: Tuttle, 1927), p. 51. "The Cedars," from the same book, p. 53. Reprinted by permission of Charles E. Tuttle Company.

Daniel L. Cady. "A Vermont Pasture," from *Rhymes of Vermont Rural Life,* Second Series (Rutland, Vt.: Tuttle, 1922), pp. 15–17. "An Old Vermont Cellar Hole," from the same book, pp. 20–21. Reprinted by permission of Charles E. Tuttle Company. "Adam and Wife," from *Miscellaneous Poems* (North Montpelier, Vt.: Driftwind Press, 1947), pp. 59–60. "Carcassonne," from the same book, pp. 116–117.

Rowland E. Robinson. "The Fox and His Guests," from *Sam Lovel's Boy and Forest and Stream Fables* (Rutland, Vt.: Tuttle, 1936), pp. 249–250. "Gran'ther Hill's Pa'tridge," from *Danvis Folks and A Hero of Ticonderoga* (Rutland, Vt.: Tuttle, 1934), pp. 17–35.

Dorothy Canfield Fisher. "The Bedquilt," first appeared in *Harper's Magazine,* Copyright 1906, 1934 by Harper & Row. From *Hillsboro People,* pp. 67–78, by Dorothy Canfield. Copyright 1943 by Dorothy Canfield Fisher. Reprinted by permission of Holt, Rinehart and Winston, Inc.

Zephine Humphrey Fahnestock. "Is This All?" from the book *The Beloved Community,* by Zephine Humphrey, pp. 62–76. Copyright, 1930, by Zephine Humphrey. Renewal, ©, by Wallace W. Fahnestock. Published by E. P. Dutton & Company, Inc., and used with their permission.

Arthur Goodenough. "The Fir Wood," from *Maine and Vermont Poets* (New York: Henry Harrison, 1935), p. 147.

Wendell Phillips Stafford. "Song of Vermont," from *The Land We Love* (St. Johnsbury, Vt.: Arthur F. Stone, 1916), p. 58.

Part IV:
Vistas Old and New

Robert L. Duffus. "The Stingiest Man," from *Williamstown Branch: Impersonal Memories of a Vermont Boyhood* (New York: W. W. Norton,

1958), pp. 40–57. Copyright 1958 by Robert L. Duffus. Reprinted by permission of Brandt & Brandt.

Alton Hall Blackington. "Human Hibernation," from *Yankee Yarns* (New York: Dodd, Mead, 1954), pp. 134–149. Reprinted by permission of Dodd, Mead & Company, Inc. from *Yankee Yarns* by Alton H. Blackington. Copyright © 1954 by Alton H. Blackington.

Walter Hard. "Always Hollerin'," from *Some Vermonters* (Boston: Richard G. Badger, 1928), pp. 116–117. "Youth of the Mountain," from *Salt of Vermont* (Brattleboro, Vt.: Stephen Daye Press, 1931), pp. 22–23. From the same book: "A Monument," p. 24; "The Deserted House," pp. 25–26. Reprinted by permission of Walter Hard, Jr.

Arthur Wallace Peach. "Weasel in the Wall," from *First Harvest* (Montpelier, Vt.: Poetry Society of Vermont, 1954), n.p. Reprinted by permission of Mrs. Roberta Goldstein.

Robert Frost. "The Runaway," from Edward Connery Lathem, ed., *The Poetry of Robert Frost* (New York: Holt, Rinehart and Winston, 1969), p. 223. Also from the same book: "The Onset," p. 226; "Good-by and Keep Cold," p. 228; "A Drumlin Woodchuck," pp. 281–282; "On Being Chosen Poet of Vermont," p. 469. Copyright 1923, © 1969 by Holt, Rinehart and Winston, Inc. Copyright 1936, 1951, © 1962 by Robert Frost. Copyright © 1964 by Leslie Frost Ballentine. Reprinted by permission of Holt, Rinehart and Winston, Inc.

Vrest Orton. "What Else Had Failed," from *Vermont Afternoons with Robert Frost* (Rutland, Vt.: Tuttle, 1971), p. 35. Reprinted by permission of Charles E. Tuttle Co.

Dorothy Canfield Fisher. "Scene ii," from *Tourists Accommodated: A Play in Six Scenes and One Setting* (New York: Harcourt, Brace and Company, 1934), pp. 11, 27–38. Reprinted by permission of Mrs. J. P. Scott.

William Hazlett Upson. "Botts Runs for His Life," from *The Best of Botts* (New York: David McKay Company, 1961), pp. 134–152. Copyright 1961 by William H. Upson. Reprinted by permission of Brandt & Brandt.

Murray Hoyt. "Trout Fishing in Vermont," from *The Fish in My Life* (New York: Crown Publishers, 1964), pp. 47–56. Copyright © 1964 by Murray Hoyt. Reprinted by permission of Collins-Knowlton-Wing, Inc.

Ralph Nading Hill. "Steamboating to New York with Brian Seaworthy," from *The Voyages of Brian Seaworthy* (Montpelier, Vt.: Vermont Life Magazine and the Vermont Historical Society, 1971), pp. 67–87. Reprinted by permission of Ralph Nading Hill. Copyright © 1971 by Ralph Nading Hill.

Sarah Cleghorn. "The Golf Links," from *Portraits and Protests* (New York: Henry Holt, 1917), p. 75. "Comrade Jesus," from the same book, pp. 81–82. All rights reserved. Reprinted by permission of Holt, Rinehart and Winston, Inc. "Nightfallen Snow," from *Green Mountain Verse*, Enid Crawford Pierce and Helen Hartness Flanders, eds. (New York: Farrar and Rinehart, 1943), p. 43. Reprinted from *The Atlantic Monthly*, 1921 by permission.

Ann Batchelder. "Warum?" from Walter J. Coates, ed., *Favorite Vermont Poems*, Series III (North Montpelier, Vt.: Driftwind Press, 1930), p. 51. "East of Bridgewater," from Enid Crawford Pierce and Helen Hartness Flanders, eds., *Green Mountain Verse* (New York: Farrar and Rinehart, 1943), pp. 33–34.

Genevieve Taggard. "To Ethan Allen," from *A Part of Vermont* (East Jamaica, Vt.: The River Press, 1945), pp. 3–4. Also from the same book: "The Nursery Rhyme and the Summer Visitor," p. 5; "On the Trout Streams," p. 9; "In Flame over Vermont," p. 19. Copyright © by Genevieve Taggard, 1945; renewed 1973 by Marcia Durant Liles. Reprinted by permission of Marcia Durant Liles.

Mari Tomasi. "Stone," from *Common Ground* (Spring 1942), pp. 44–49. Reprinted by permission of Marguerite Tomasi.

Marguerite Hurrey Wolf. "Pig in a Bucket," from *Anything Can Happen in Vermont* (Coral Gables, Fla.: Wake Brook House, 1965), pp. 69–73. Copyright © 1965 by Marguerite Hurrey Wolf and reprinted by her permission.

Noel Perrin. "Steam Coming Out the Vent," from *Amateur Sugar Maker* (Hanover, N.H.: University Press of New England, 1972), pp. 71–97. Copyright © 1972 by Noel Perrin and reprinted by his permission.

Frances Frost. "The Children," from Enid Crawford Pierce and Helen Hartness Flanders, eds., *Green Mountain Verse* (New York: Farrar and Rinehart, 1943), pp. 79–80. Reprinted by permission of Mrs. Joan Blackburn. "The Inarticulate," from *Hemlock Wall* (New Haven, Ct.: Yale University Press, 1929), p. 10. "Advice to a Trespasser," from the same book, p. 32.

Reprinted by permission of Yale University Press. "Language," from *This Rowdy Heart* (Francestown, N.H.: Golden Quill Press, 1954), p. 17. "Tide of Lilac," from the same 109. Reprinted by permission of Mrs. Joan Blackburn. "Footnote," from *Blue Harvest* (Boston: Houghton Mifflin, 1931), pp. 38–39. "Little Poem for Evening," from the same book, p. book, p. 35. Reprinted by permission of Golden Quill Press.

James Hayford. "Processional with Wheelbarrow," from *Processional with Wheelbarrow* (Amherst, Mass.: Oriole Books, 1970), p. 30. "On the Opening of a Superhighway," from the same book, p. 15. Reprinted by permission of James Hayford.

Leland Kinsey. "Deep in the Sleep Gorged Side," previously unpublished. Printed by permission.

Howard Frank Mosher. "Alabama Jones," from *Cimarron Review*, No. 16 (July 1971), 35–45. Reprinted by permission of the Board of Regents for Oklahoma State University.